THE SCOURGE OF CAPTAIN SEAVEY

BY
Karl Manke

Author of:
Unintended Consequences
The Prodigal Father
Secrets, Lies and Dreams
Age Of Shame
Gone to Pot
The Adventures of Railcar Rogues
Harsens Island's Revenge
Rewired
Hope from Heaven

All of Karl's books are available at karlmanke.com

Publisher: Curwood Publishing

Cover Layout: Ralph Roberts
Cover Art: Jeffery Gulick
Editor: Pat Roberts

Copyright ©2020 Karl Manke/ Curwood Publishing
Third Printing 2020
All rights reserved.

Reproduction and translation of any part of this work beyond that permitted by Sections 107 and 108 of the United States Copyright Act without the permission of the copyright owners is unlawful.

ISBN: 978-1-7338029-2-5

The author and publisher have made every effort in the preparation of this book to ensure the accuracy of the information. However, the information in this book is sold without warranty, either express or implied. Neither of the author nor Curwood Publishing will be liable for any damages caused or alleged to be caused directly, indirectly, incidentally, or consequentially by the author in this book.

The opinions expressed in this book are solely those of the author and are not necessarily those of Curwood Publishing.

Trademarks: Names of products mentioned in this book known to be or suspected of being trademarks or service marks are capitalized. The usage of a trademark or service mark in this book should not be regarded as affecting the validity of any trademark or service mark.
Curwood Publishing

All of Karl's books are available at karlmanke.com

To my beautiful wife Carolyn for her immitigable patience and...

*To my parents:
Richard and Aristine*

1 CHICAGO

The night is black as coal. The watch has changed. The first mate is retiring as the second mate takes the wheel. The *Ahab's* deck is fully loaded with a cargo of lumber headed for the port of Arcadia on the Michigan side of the Great Lake Michigan. The lake is quiet with only the sound of the bow cutting through the almost resistless water. His eye is fixed on the light attached to the small buoy marking the entrance to the harbor. With a sudden THUD the ship comes to a sudden stop throwing the second mate along with the rest of the crew to the ship's decking. Down below the ship's master finds himself thrown to the floor. Picking himself up with his bedding still wrapped around him, the half awake captain knows exactly what has just taken place. THEY'VE RUN AGROUND!

"ALL HANDS ON DECK!" he shouts as he untangles a blanket from around his ankles.

This command is quickly obeyed without a blink as the water pours into the crew quarters. A gaping hole ripped open by a submerged rock is the culprit. Panicked men are scurrying in every direction as a fuller impact of the direness of their situation makes its way into their consciousness. Without a moment to waste the first mate is already preparing the life boat to abandon ship.

Quickly assessing his situation, the captain shouts a final order, "PREPARE TO ABANDON SHIP!"

Within minutes the crew of six, along with their captain, is making their way safely to shore as they hear the not so distant agonizing groans of their scuttled ship. The first mate is the first to speak.

"Captain look over there." He's pointing in the direction of a buoy-like object bobbing innocently off to their port side. It's an anchored wooden beer barrel with a lantern attached to its lid. The captain's silent look of surprise is followed with an outburst of anger that comes with the awareness that he has been "moon cussed." (Moon cussing is the term used when a buoy light has been purposely moved to cause a ship to flounder in treacherous waters.)

"The dirty sons-a-bitches did this on purpose!" shouts the angry captain hardly able to believe his eyes. "The bastards wrecked my ship deliberately. If I get my hands on these Jack Nasties, I'll give 'em a good Irish coat of arms." (two black eyes and a broken nose)

Meanwhile, less than a hundred yards away another ship lies anchored in the darkness. It remains silent as its crew listens to the havoc among the neighboring crew desperately trying to escape the inevitable. The voices grow weaker as the fleeing lifeboat makes its way safely to shore.

The foundered ship finally settles with its hull resting on the lake bottom leaving its lumber laden deck fifteen feet above at the water's surface. Slowly, like a creeping cat of prey, the hidden ship begins a slow, deliberate course toward its grounded quarry. With the deftness of those who have this maneuver well rehearsed, and with a few strategically placed lanterns, they begin to operate a pulley system designed with one purpose—moving lumber from one ship to another. Within less than an hour, they have successfully transferred several thousand board feet of lumber and are well on their way to a market in Chicago without firing a single shot.

The leader of this clandestine pirate gang is none other than the infamous Captain Dan Seavey. It's reported that he was born in Portland,

Maine in 1867. Like many young men in this period, he left home at an early age, joined the navy for a short time and finally made his way to Wisconsin in the late 1880s. He became an agent for the bureau of Indian affairs ferreting out smugglers and bootleggers on Indian reservations. He married a young girl and within a few years had fathered a daughter. He became the owner of several properties, including several successful taverns along Milwaukee's waterfront. Possessed with gold fever, he abandoned his family for a fruitless expedition to the Klondike gold fields from which he returned penniless. His father had been a seaman and whether or not that influenced him, he soon found himself once again abandoning his family much as his father had done before him in favor of a life on the water. He soon, by some questionable means, became the possessor of a schooner named the *Wanderer*. This began his early career as a legitimate freight hauler on the Great Lakes. Being the opportunist that he's reported to be, it isn't long before he is entrenched in smuggling, poaching, bootlegging, and last but not least, pimping.

The present-day is early April sometime around 1907. It's a Wednesday morning. The ice has just broken up and the shipping season is getting back in gear. The ice has kept the ships in port for the past few hard winter months. Consequently, for commercial shipping paydays have been far and few between, not to mention the hardship it's put on pirates, the likes of Captain Dan Seavey.

A hanging lantern swinging from a roost on the port side casts a strobe like beam across a massive lumbering man wearing a rain cape.

"Lash her down good boys," barks this oversized inland sea captain ordering his crew to secure their ill-gotten booty to the deck. Captain Seavey is not an ordinary appearing sailor. At six foot six and 300lbs, he is not only known for his size and chosen occupation, but also for his desire to dress like a Wall Street banker. It's not at all unusual to see him wearing a suit and vest while at sea. Partially concealed under a suit coat is a pair of holstered pistols. He also has a constant canine companion named Duke. He's a mixed breed of questionable ancestry. Captain Seavey found him as a wandering pup with dirt on his face. Immediately capturing his heart, he took him aboard. Even to this day when it comes to his food, he has no manners at all.

Before daylight, they have set a good distance between themselves and their unfortunate victims. The crew has spent the winter in the Michigan coastal city of Frankfort and is more than primed to get their pirate season underway. So far they're satisfied that this is starting out as they have hoped. All the crew are experienced sailors as well as undaunted thieves.

For the present time, Seavey is manning the wheel while Archie Kerby, the first mate, oversees setting the sails to carry them as quickly as possible to the south. The second mate is Willis Wells. The riggers and deck hands are Doe Pierce, Jack Perry, and Ob Nelson.

These men would be incensed if anyone suspected them of stealing from a neighbor, but all bets are off as soon as they hit the open water. Opportunity knocks with every passing ship. The only question considered by this band of buccaneers is how they're going to compromise the ship and get the cargo off. Of course a well executed get-a-way is also a big concern. At least for the present time, all attention is set on getting this booty down to the bustling Chicago river front where obscurity cloaks many an underground business transaction.

The *Wanderer*, rigged for full speed, plows its way toward its predetermined destination. As they sail south, the majestic high sand dunes marking the eastern shore line of this Great Lake gradually give way to a much flatter environment announcing the upcoming Chicago basin.

This is a well worn path for this crew as they have found ready buyers for anything they can get past the Harbor Master.

For this very reason, Doe Pierce, an accomplished forger and counterfeiter, is busy in the cabin below making up a phony invoice for the lumber gracing their deck. Seavey has furnished him with a small printing press and all the various inks he asks for. He also has an assortment of official looking seals that have been gathered from other forgers. These include some he's crafted himself out of various materials from metal to wood. It's always been more than just hobby for Doe. It began when he was a kid in school forging his parents' names on slips giving him permission to leave class.

Doe first caught the attention of Seavey a few years back when he offered him information on a cargo schooner that was leaving Frankfort with a load of cedar shakes. Doe had been in charge of loading this cargo when that captain objected to the way he positioned the bundles. In a rage, he tossed poor Doe, clothes and all, into the harbor. By the next morning with the assistance of Seavey, Doe had the opportunity to return the favor. Five miles off the coast Captain Seavey shot a cannon ball across the bow of their ship, boarded her and set her terrified crew adrift with nothing but a set of oars. They then relieved this obnoxious captain of his cargo. The next piece on the agenda was giving Doe the opportunity to set a sentence. Being a traditionalist of sorts, he ordered this captain to walk a make-shift plank. By all accounts, the captain couldn't swim, especially with a chain wrapped around him. After what must have seemed like a lifetime to this wretched man, they pulled him out short of drowning. If that weren't enough, they then hung him by the ankles from his ship's yard arm allowing him to dry, and then, while yet unmanned, set his ship adrift.

But back to this present voyage. It is a standard twenty hour trip with all hands taking a watch and manning the wheel. For the most part—weather permitting—this is a routine trip. Presently, all the crew is topside finding things to do. The closer they come to their destination, the more this adventure begins to put on a new face. As many times as they've made this trip, it still holds the same allure. After all, it is Chicago, and all in Seavey's crew are young single men. None of them have found a compelling reason to venture beyond the businesses located on the wharf, but that's only because they have the distinct impression that anything deeper into the city would only be more civilized and certainly not to their liking. Each of these men have in their own way immortalized their private memories of the last time they were here with each seeming eager to replay them once again.

Ob is the first to share a concern with a recollection of the previous season.

"Hey Jack, you think ole' Chick is still in business?"

Without any further discussion Jack's simple speculation consists of a simple reply.

"I sure as hell hope so."

Chick is an hotelier of sorts. He has a restaurant/tavern/boarding house/bordello, and hot baths for those who can manage to pay the fare. It consists of a few clapboard buildings whose origins began as leftovers from the Great Chicago fire years earlier. Even though the bloom of youth is off Chick's "fallen angels" for these young lads from Frankfort, they may as well be the latest beauty queens. He makes sure these "beauty queens" make a "king" of every sailor who walks through their doors.

Now that they have entered the mouth of the river it's all business. The river water appears dark and cloudy carrying all kinds of floating debris. Seavey has retaken the wheel. He skillfully maneuvers his forty-six-foot schooner between steam-powered propeller-driven vessels, large and small sailing ships of every type, all positioned according to written and some unwritten protocol. If the wind continues to be right, it's a matter of pride for him not to depend on a tug boat to pull him in. Today it's overcast. The air is heavy with the smell of coal smoke belching from freighters lining the wharfs. They're all in various stages of loading and unloading. Captain Seavey continues to skillfully navigate his way as a weaver would through this orderly mayhem of navigational etiquette. There has never been any question regarding his talents in maneuvering any kind of ship.

The jibs are down. The current is slowly carrying the ship to a slip some hundred feet ahead marked as Boyley Lumber Company. Seavey orders the anchor dropped just below the water line. The extra drag allows him to gracefully dock with nothing more than a slight bump. With the bow and stern both tied off, this challenge has been successfully met once again.

The crew is ordered to stay with the ship and cargo while Captain Seavey makes his way into the havoc of shouting men and equipment moving freight. Within a short distance, he enters a warehouse. He's met by a much shorter man chomping on the stub end of an unlit cigar.

"Holy jumpin' catuttors Seavey, you survived another winter. Hell I figured you'd been hung by now."

"Ya can't hang what ain't got a rope around it," says Seavey with his mild-mannered, almost professional, smirk.

Harold Boyley survived the Chicago fire thirty-five years earlier and has been doing his part to supply the city with needed lumber for reconstruction. Because of the urgent need for materials, their origins are mostly overlooked. With no questions asked except how much is on board and available, a price is quickly agreed to and the unloading begins.

2 MORE BOOTY

By late in the afternoon, Seavey's ship is empty and his crew's pockets are full of their cut of the plunder. It's time to make their way to Chick's place. On a back street littered with trash, aligned with a dirty canal hangs a sign secured to a rusting metal protrusion announcing *Chick's Hotel*. Even though its siding is weathered and the poor building has never had a coat of paint, it may as well be the Taj Mahal to these young buccaneers. They can hear the dance music drifting out from the inner sanctum even before they have rounded the corner. The familiar barroom's pungent smells reach out to greet them. With wide grins of excitement, they nearly trip over one another to be the first to make it through the entrance.

Not only does this place serve as a spot to get a drink, but also the lobby for the hotel. The sound of the mechanical player piano along with a half dozen of Chick's gals sitting about looking as sexy as is permissible without payment, has their complete attention. From the amenable looks on the faces of these northern Michigan boys, they appear to be entering heaven—at least it's the way they wish it to materialize. With a stupefied gaze and not a word spoken among them, like automatons in unison, they step up to the bar.

Chick is a mustached man with a sophomoric attempt to portray a city slicker appearance. His hair is greased back with a distinct smell of Southern Rose Oil. He's wearing garters around his biceps, keeping his sleeves well above his wrists, and speaks with a clearly pronounced Chicago accent. Butting a cigarette in one of the nearby ashtrays, he flattens both his palms on the bar top.

"Whadda you boys gonna have?"

Trying his best to set aside his backwoods demeanor Doe is the first to speak up.

"Whiskey and water will do me just fine."

The others follow suit careful to order only drinks that men drink. They make their way to a vacant table with a keen eye on the ladies whose attention they have caught. These boys are convinced that it's their overwhelming good looks that's bringing this bevy of bosomed babes from across the room to sit with them. On the other hand, these ladies know a payday when they see one and will sit with anyone who has a pocket full of cash. In well-rehearsed moves, they begin to shove chairs around the table all the time smiling at no one in particular. They are truly professional in their attempt to remain spontaneous as these boys are jumping up to offer the ladies their own chairs. Soon they are all sitting in a cozy group with these impetuous young bucks nearly stumbling over one another to offer a light to any waiting cigarette held in the delicate hand of one of these "soiled doves."

Millie is the first to speak.

"You boys are kind of cute, why haven't we met before?"

Looking around at each other, Ob takes the cue. "We was here last fall but you ladies wasn't."

Realizing that these are actually return customers, Millie quickly changes tactics.

"Oh, those girls all quit. We came on last month. You must be those guys from Michigan they were saying liked to have a good time. They sure did brag you boys up."

Aware of their whole new status causes Jack to suddenly decide to sit up a little straighter, hailing the bartender to bring the ladies a round of drinks.

As the evening wanes, Chick catches Millie's attention. With a slight head motion, he indicates that he wants the girls take this to the next level.

Chick has a whole other floor above with hotel rooms. Millie, in turn, makes a quick eye signal with each of the other ladies. By this time, the boys believe they have managed to move the ladies from their chairs to sitting on their laps. After another round of drinks, Millie bends towards Ob's ear and whispers.

"What do ya say you and me take this upstairs?"

Ob knows the routine. Walking over to the bar, he pays for a room that comes with a woman and a hot bath. Soon he is behind closed doors with a hot female and a tub full of hot water. Without a lot of unnecessary fan fare, both have stripped and climbed into the tub. A bit of splashing and teasing foreplay continues until Ob is pulling her dripping wet onto the waiting bed. The rest is history as Ob's alcohol consumption has caught up with him causing him to promptly pass out. It's hardly a monumental romantic night that will last in Millie's mind, but for Ob it will provide enough bragging rights to last until another trip is made.

One by one, the motley crew makes their way back to the ship. Each has had a memorable encounter with a lady of the night and will brag *ad nauseum* as though it were an unrepeatable conquest. Making sure that their listener realizes a lesser man than themselves could hardly make the cut. Ob is the last to arrive. He's hardly in any shape to begin any bragging.

"Holy shit Ob, you look like you had your timber sawed," declares an equally gruesome looking Jack.

"Well I damn near did—all my blood rushed to that big pecker of mine and I passed out," declares Ob trying to hold a straight face, adding, "and that woman took awful advantage of me."

Jack and the rest of the crew just sit and stare at Ob after this announcement. Jack finally breaks the hush.

"If bullshit were concrete, you'd sink this ship."

Before long everyone is back on board and in their bunks with the exception of the captain. It's not until the next morning that he shows up. He's looking refreshed as usual. It's not at all unique for Captain Seavey to be missing for periods like this. He's a devout Catholic as well as an earnest sinner. It's not unusual for him to spend a night in the throes of debauchery and just about the time the devil thinks he's got him, he finds a confessional. It's obvious from the length of time he's been missing that he's accomplished both missions.

"All right you reprobates, I want this ship scrubbed from top to bottom and ready to sail by noon," expressing this decree in very definite terms, "that means every inch of her."

This ship hasn't had a scrubbing like that in its life. First mate Archie Kerby finds it somewhat amusing, but also knows better than to shirk the order. He immediately starts digging out deck mops that have never been used and still have the price tags on them. With each man assigned to a section, the work is soon underway with a good degree of cussing and carping about the insanity of such an order.

"What in the name of all that's holy has come across this captain of ours. I thought we was pirates, not scrub women," complains Jack as he refills his mop bucket for the, seeming, hundredth time.

Looking up from his undertaking, Jack spots a couple of familiar forms making their way down the wharf. One wears a suit, tie, and captain's cap and walks with a little swagger. The other, established as the Captain's pet dog, Duke, has been scrubbed, combed and is sporting a new fancy glass studded collar.

Captain Seavey appears to be leading two rows of three parasol carrying belles. Not quite sure that it's not the altar guild ladies from St Mary's, a closer look rules that thought out. It's the same set up one would see for a funeral procession of six mourners. The six ladies are lined up as though each were a pallbearer, with three on each side. The head pallbearer being

Captain Seavey out front, but in this case, the coffin being carried is their own personal reputation and character.

"Well I'll be damned," is all Jack can think of to say as it becomes apparent that this is the same bevy of "belles of the night" he and his brother revelers had just left the evening before. By this time the rest of the crew have stopped dead in their tracks with mouths agape as Captain Dan orders all available men to stop what they are doing and assist the ladies aboard.

Second mate Willis Wells is the first to draw the captain aside with a very pertinent question.

"What in the hell are you doin'?"

Seavey leaves his second mate without an answer as he very attentively makes sure all the ladies' baggage is brought on board. Willis is not to be put off that easily, raising his voice to indicate the captain may not have heard his question the first time.

"What in the hell are you doin' Capn'?" becomes his mantra for the second time.

"Don't worry yourself Willis, everything is under control. Ole Chick claims the 'shine' has worn off his ladies and wants to trade 'em out for a younger bunch. Before we left Frankfort, Squeaky Schwartz was complainin' of the same thing with his ladies. I sent him a telegram, he replied that he'd welcome a new supply of 'fresh faces'. He says he can pack up his present ladies and send them on up to the Soo (Soo St. Marie). He's sure those boys up there will welcome anything they don't have to chase down in the woods."

This is hardly the consolation Willis is waiting to hear. His mantra changes slightly, but still has a whiny tone connected.

"Where the hell you expect we gonna put them with all their trappins?"

"I'm sure you and the boys won't mind moving out of your quarters down to the cargo hold and let these ladies—whose fares been paid in full—move in and enjoy the trip," says Seavey with a grin that says one thing, but there's a dead set to his gaze that means only one thing—*"You better get this done"*!

Willis knows his captain too well to argue any further. With a resigned sigh, he sets about to organize the changes. There's a lot of carping connected with this new development, especially with not knowing how long this new set up could last. Within the hour, the crew has reluctantly surrendered their bunks for the downright Spartan conditions the cargo hold offers. With a bit of ingenuity, they manage to rig up a network of hammocks. Finally able to take turns napping, they begrudgingly settle into the alterations. The ship itself ignores all the quibbling. It could care less how its interior arranged as it cuts through the near perfect placid water.

3 A NEW SCHEME

Captain Seavey discusses another strategy with first mate Archie as they take advantage of the break they're enjoying from an offshore southwest breeze.

"Wadda ya think of this scheme Archie? We got these ladies on board for a few days. Why don't we see if we can make some money? We can pull into every port between here and Frankfort, anchor offshore away from the law and let these ladies do what they know how to do best. They can make some money and we can too."

What keeps Archie on board is action like this that only his captain can dream up. Archie breaks out in a broad grin.

"Ya know Cap'n I've heard tell that some calls us low down sons-a-bitches, but I think that we're just old bastards." Both let out a roar of laughter that nearly shakes the ship. They then remind each other how "damn lucky" they are to be living such a life.

"Okay, Cap'n count me in. Ya want me ta 'splain this enterprisin' venture to the rest of the crew?" asks Archie still grinning like a schoolboy getting away with stealing a kiss.

"Yeah, tell 'em we're renting their bunks out for a buck—that oughta make em happy."

Looking out over the lake to the east, the shoreline is beginning to rise a bit indicating they are in the vicinity of Benton Harbor. This small agricultural community has just the right kind of harbor to experiment with the *Wanderer's* unique new enterprise. Captain Seavey gives the order to anchor off shore. He next orders the crew to assemble on deck along with the ladies. The sun has come out promising a decent day and it is Saturday.

"Listen up!" he shouts. The ladies are in various stages of not paying close attention and continue to chatter among themselves.

"Maybe you ladies don't understand clear English. Do I need to learn to stutter?"

This time his voice has gone from a shout to a roar.

"I want you to pay attention!!"

With that said, he goes on to bring the ladies up to speed with this new venture. Once finalized and sure that everyone on board is on board with his plan, he brings his briefing to a close.

"If we all work together on this, we can make a few bucks before we have any trouble from the local constabulary."

"Some of them local lawmen have been our best customers," says Millie with a knowing little laugh.

Ob has had his eye on Millie ever since she came aboard. He's been very quiet. This whole deal is bothering him. He's still savoring the personal attention Millie gave him the night before and he's not quite sure he's ready to have Millie share that same attention with other men. For Millie, he's just another "John", but for men like Ob, whose female encounters are far and few between, it's as though she should be held accountable for cheating.

Captain Seavey's face has taken on a no nonsense, all business demeanor. He continues.

"Archie, we will take the jon boat ashore. We need to drum up a bit of interest in our ladies. Willis, you stay here with the crew. When our guests begin to arrive, be prepared to break out a jug of whiskey, delegate the rest of the crew as bartenders and bouncers in case we need 'em, manage the money, and you ladies get yourselves gussied up for a brand new dog and pony show."

Seavey and Archie do not waste any time getting ashore. The first place they head for is the local billiard hall. Since today is a Saturday, it should be jammed with young bucks. The plan is to get a couple of these young, horny cavaliers out to the boat, treat them right and let them do the advertising. Within minutes, they have spotted a young man of about twenty years. They hear him referred to as "Cooch." He's a slightly built lad with a hat cocked off to one side. His britches are held up with one suspender, leaving the other draped down around his thigh. His pant legs are shortened in an impudent way, showing all but the top two inches of his brogan boots. Presently, he's demonstrating his deft ability to roll a cigarette with one quick movement of the fingers. Watching him shoot billiards gives the impression that most of his movements are designed to draw attention to his virility. His speech is besprent with cuss words in a bold presentation of what he hopes is his uniqueness.

"Listen to me Archie, you play this 'sonny boy' a game of billiards for a dime a game. I know you can beat him hands down. When you get a buck out of him, let him know how bad you feel about taking his money.

Tell him you'd like to make it up to him with one of our girls, and we'll get him out to the boat. He'll be the best damned promotional do-jigger we could hope to come up with," says Seavey with a wry smirk.

Within an hour, Archie has methodically cut this young scallywag's billiard prowess to ribbons. Now careful not to leave his bruised ego out to dry, he carefully measures his next move.

"I gotta tell ya Cooch, I thought you had me pinned in there pretty tight more than once. I think you're a damned good opponent and I'd like to make it up to ya," says Archie striking a match to light Cooch's newly rolled cigarette. Measuring his words, he continues, "We got a boat out in the harbor with a cargo load of Chicago whores we's taken up north. I'll give ya a pick of the whole kit and caboodle fer bein' such a damn good sport. How's that sound to ya?"

Cooch is dumbfounded for a second. Instantly, he looks around to see how many of his friends may be observing. Satisfied he's got their attention, he re-cocks his hat, snaps his single suspender, and sticks his thumbs in his waist band.

"Hell yes. That's pretty damn white of ya. Lets have a look at what ya got."

Making their way back to the jon boat, they place Cooch on the aft seat as if to be chauffeured. A group of about ten of his pool hall cronies have followed to watch as their cohort is being delivered to the waiting bevy of babes lining the deck only a hundred yards off shore. He's eating the attention up: leaning back with his elbows resting on the stern behind him, with his cocky hat in place, one leg crossed over the other, and a cigarette between his lips.

"Take a piece for me," bellows one of the onlookers as he slaps another on the back. Watching in almost disbelief at Cooch's seeming good fortune, they all break out in an unfettered laughter. It's as though they are being left behind only to watch their friend float on to the promised land. With every turn of the oar, Cooch's anticipation heightens. His eyes are fixed on the twirling parasols lying ahead. There're only six girls, but to this hormone with clothing, it may as well been a thousand.

These girls know the male psyche better than most psychologists. They are more skilled in their perceptions than nearly all of these college boys with all their highfalutin' degrees. They've lined the deck around the boarding ladder waiting for this first client. They've formed a welcoming committee that would rival that of royalty. Cooch has never been fawned over like this—not even from his elderly aunts. His hands are sweating along with every other gland engendered region across his body.

Millie is the first to engage this young roe.

"Captain, I gotta hand it to you. You told us you'd bring us back a good looker, and you did just that," says Millie. She has not taken her eyes off this young buck.

"What's your name so I can properly introduce you?" she asks.

"C-Cooch, Ma'am" he manages to stammer.

"I've got just the lady for a man like you," she says grabbing him by the hand and pulling him over to a big-busted, ivory-skinned, parasol-twirlin' belle with a pair of hips that would rival a broad ax handle. Cooch has never in his young life seen a lady of this caliber much less been introduced in order to spend intimate time with her.

"Lillie, I'd like you to make Cooch feel at home. He's in need of some lovin' care."

A huge smile, exposing one bad tooth, comes across Lillie's face. With all her other attributes in place, Cooch feels that one bad tooth can quickly be forgiven. After all anyone who smells like lilacs can't be too blemished.

For Cooch to imagine he has entered Paradise only lasts from start to finish about three minutes. But it was the most thrilling three minutes he has ever experienced. For a nineteen year old male from Benton Harbor to have had a sexual acquaintance anywhere beyond "Madam Palm and her five daughters" is more of an exception than a rule. He couldn't wait to brag about this exploit to all those buddies waiting on shore more than eager to hear about it. To insure that Cooch will have the evangelical zeal to spread the good word, Captain Dan decides to sweeten the pot.

"I'll tell you what I can do for you, Cooch. If you want to make your buck back and maybe a few more, you go and tell your mates what you just been schooled in. What's more, if you dingy them out to the ship, I'll give you an extra ten cents a head."

Armed with this new worldliness and also asked to be a business associate, Cooch believes his ship has just come in. Eager to get started, he shakes Seavey's already extended hand.

"You got yourself a deal!"

Once on shore, his cronies gather around with the same curiosity Eve had with the forbidden apple. Cooch, like ole Clooty, is more than ready to deflower as many of his friends as can scrape up a dollar.

Taking a deep drag on his cigarette, Cooch begins his braggadocio.

"I'm here to tell you that babe is a real ball-buster. She gave me such a hard-on I didn't have enough skin left to close my eyes."

This raucous, irreverent testimony is leaving eyes wide open, mouths agape, and imaginations running amok. Within the afternoon, he has ferried enough of the town's young men to make back his dollar and then some. Happy with his newly acquired status among these venal swashbucklers, he shakes hands once again with the good Captain Seavey who is more than happy with the day's business. Bidding them all a bon voyage, feeling older, tougher and certainly more worldly, he happily rows back to shore.

One matter Seavey has triumphantly put the lid on is the reason behind the success of many of his exploits. It's because he doesn't over stay his welcome. He seems to have an extra sense telling him when enough is enough—including the time limits on this fiasco. By the time the city fathers figure out what has just happened, he'll have left them muttering between themselves and be well on his way to the next port.

As the day wanes and the light fades, evening advances and a magnificent breeze out of the southwest promises some easy sailing. This allows the *Wanderer* to continue a course within sight of shore making for a very comfortable journey. For the next six hours of darkness the sailing routine remains the same. When sailing in ideal conditions, the waves and the wind are assets, not adversaries and this is such a marvelous night. They've made astonishing speed, at times reaching fifteen knots. By daylight the ship has covered an astonishing fifty-five miles.

Normally Doe takes care of the galley. Making sure the crew is well fed is not a chore to be taken lightly. But things have changed this morning. Millie is not going to have some "nose-pickin" seaman handling her breakfast and she has taken over Doe's galley. The *Wanderer* is well equipped with a coal burning cooker and plenty of fresh eggs, side pork, and coffee. In no time at all, she and a couple of the ladies have whipped up a breakfast.

"Now this is what I call livin'," says Doe taking a big slurp of hot black coffee given to him by the kind hand of a lady named Ginny. He's more than happy to get a little relief from his galley duty. Of course the rest of the crew is undeniably grateful for the change in cooking style. They also realize this is only temporary and are careful not to let Doe see them excessively enjoying the switch.

4 ESCANABA

The night is not going as well for Seavey. A demonic apparition that has been the bane of Seavey's life for years is a Chippewa Indian woman who has given her name as "Abequa." Unfortunately, she has become a routine, but extremely unwelcome visitor. She spends a good portion of the captain's sleeping time sitting on the end of his bunk accusing him of his sins.

He was born Daniel Seavey in Portland, Maine in the year 1867. His parents were devout Catholics, especially his mother. She planned for him to have a life in the clergy and prepared to have thirteen year old Daniel placed in a school to begin his training for the priesthood. By this time, they had already been abandoned by her husband for a life on the sea. When young Dan overheard his mother's conversation with the bishop, he ran away from home and joined the navy.

Several years pass and he finds himself in Wisconsin, married and the father of a daughter. Like his father before him, he soon abandons his family for a life on the water.

Abequa's entire reason for making herself known is to castigate Captain Seavey, pointing the finger of scorn at his many shortcomings as a husband and father.

"Listen! What's it going to take to get your attention? What kind of Catholic do you call yourself? You've abandoned your family for a life of serving your own perverted wants. You've nearly made a destitute orphan of your daughter. Your faithful wife, who loved you, has been deserted to fend for herself in order for you to satisfy your own selfish ends. You'll never change and you'll spend eternity in hell because that's what you deserve."

Hearing these words always brings with it a strong reaction on Seavey's part.

"Oh please don't send me to hell. I'll change, I know I can. Please give me another chance," he begs. The truth within this chastisement always brings with it a sense of hopelessness.

Abequa listens without sympathy adding even more accusations.

"How can you change—a man as sinful as you! Your penance will forever remain that you will continue to be trapped in your own lostness." Seavey listens as a helpless captive, held prisoner by the accusing voice of own defects.

As quickly as the apparition appears, it disappears leaving him to awaken soaking wet and in a frightening depression. On this particular morning, rather than join the crew for breakfast, he stays in his quarters on his knees, lighting candles and begging Jesus' Mother to pray for him to her Son.

This behavior has become fairly routine as his guilt continues to plague him. He has not faced his ex-wife in ten years and has lost track of her and his daughter. What's worse is that he has done nothing to find them, thus leaving him alone with his remorse and no hope of reconciliation. He has confessed his sins over and over before every priest in every confessional that his path has crossed. He has received the promise of absolution each time providing he fulfill the penance to rejoin them as a husband and father. What's more, he finds himself unable to forgive himself and therefore makes no attempt to locate them—thus, he remains in a perpetual state of guilt and remorse. With no relief, he finally follows the same path he always has in the past—he arises from his prostration fatigued, weary, and defeated. This kind of defeat always leads him into a "To hell with everything" attitude.

"I'm going to burn in hell anyway, so let's be at it," are his final words as he opens his cabin door. He goes up on deck to meet the day and prepares to kiss the devil good morning once again.

On a more positive note, the wind direction has remained constant allowing them to sail faster and straighter without a lot of tacking. Getting these women to Frankfort is becoming a pleasant diversion for the rest of the crew. Millie has set a breakfast aside for Seavey as he pokes his head into her galley.

"Well look what just rose up from the dead," says Millie handing Seavey a plate of scrambled eggs and side pork.

"I kept these warm for you," she adds.

Without a word, looking like death warmed over, he nods approvingly. Taking his plate, he retires to a spot on deck where he can continue to be alone in his slump. His countenance is tanned from the sun and sea, giving a first impression of health and vigor, but a closer look reflects a strain. It's the kind of strain that a man with a lack of contentment reflects. The creases crossing his face are deep this morning, giving him the appearance of a man much older.

Finally finishing his breakfast, he diverts his attention by beginning a survey of his ship. What he is particularly preoccupied with this morning is his cannon along with the condition of the primer and gun powder. This ordnance is his pride and joy. He has it on a swivel mount secured in the bow. From here, it can easily be swung to either the port or starboard side of the boat.

Like all predators, he keeps a wary eye out for easy prey. With this weapon, he simply fires across the bow of a ship intent on ignoring his intention of overtaking them. This has the double effect of not only leaving his victims willing, but, at the same time, begrudgingly compliant to being robbed.

Having these women on board is forestalling him from taking advantage of some of these available opportunities. Consequently, the next line of business is to get these women delivered to Squeaky up in Frankfort as quickly as possible.

Not so willing to merely bide his time, he turns to Doe.

"While we got some smooth sailing, why don't you see if you can doctor up a few of these bills," says Seavey, handing Doe a fist full of currencies. Doe is not only a forger of documents, he can successfully alter currencies enough to pass a one dollar bill off as a five. It can never be said of these pirates that their lives are of wasted leisure. Being a successful pirate in these times demands remaining one step ahead of the law at all times and the plans of this crew of "Jack-tars" are to do just that.

They're soon approaching the harbor mouth at the port of Arcadia. This is where they had "moon cussed" the Ahab. It is still laying offshore waiting for a tug boat to come and repair it. Quite sure they're not able to identify the *Wanderer* as the culprit, they boldly sail by.

Never tiring of gazing at the 300-500 foot high sand dunes bathed in the late afternoon sun, Seavey pays closer than usual attention to the crop of mature trees that spring out of their top ridges.

"If it weren't so damned hard to get to those trees, I'd have a boat load settin' on the pier in Chicago tomorrow," he thinks to himself. But this also reminds him that there are forests along the shore in the upper peninsula that are "easy pickin's" compared to these.

"As soon as I can get these sporting ladies delivered, we're on our way to the upper peninsula," he further muses to himself.

The afternoon has dwindled into evening when the *Wanderer* enters the Frankfort harbor. Frankfort is still a wild and rough port town, free of a lot of excessive law enforcement. It's situated on the eastern shore of Lake Michigan. It's also isolated in such a way that it's not on the way to anywhere other than a trip out in the lake. Accordingly, people here tend to handle disputes in their own way. Strangers are given a wary eye. This causes them to either move on, or succumb to the particular norms of the community.

The ladies on board are physically rested, but travel weary. Now that they're getting a close look at their new address, they're a bit more apprehensive about being farmed out to such a remote hick town. The saving attribute they all have in common is that in spite of being dubbed as "shady ladies," they have quickly learned that in order to survive in this business, they have to be as tough or tougher than their circumstances.

Squeaky Schwartz has gotten the word that his new ladies have arrived. He's a diminutive man who makes up for his small size by smoking huge cigars. Eager to see if he's gotten his money's worth finds him peering through a telescope from his upstairs window in his bordello that overlooks the harbor. He's already lost half his old stable as those ladies have run off to Traverse City looking for a more lucrative clientele. It's even rumored that one of these girls married a wealthy Traverse City man in the fruit business. Either way, only three of his original six girls are still willing to make the trip to the upper peninsula. They're older women and as Squeaky puts it have "lost their blossom." They are also much less willing to put up with what they've in turn dubbed as, "Squeaky's bull-shit."

Squeaky's been heard from time to time to whine excessively about those women who are no longer willing to put up with him. "That's what happens when ya try and give these girls a break, they get uppity and independent. Next thing ya know, they think they're runnin' the joint. Then it comes time to move 'em out."

Doe is glad to be getting back to port. He's got a girlfriend over across the bay in South Frankfort, named Daisy. She was born here soon after her father and mother arrived from back east. They had followed the timber cutting from New York to Michigan, working their way throughout the mid-east states to finally settle in South Frankfort.

While talking with her friends, Daisy has been heard more than once to say, "I sure as heck ain't crazy about Doe working on ole Seavey's boat, but then work is hard to come by this far north. To work a timber job would mean he'd be gone for the whole season starting in April til the snow flies. At least this way, he shows up every few weeks and sometimes more often."

She says this with the determination of a woman who's hell bent on finding a way to get things done her way. She's set on getting him off that boat and into an onshore job.

Most of the town has a pretty good idea what the *Wanderer*, along with her crew is up to, but much of what they hear is a lot of speculation. Nonetheless, there is no denying that their speculations have more than an element of truth. Regardless of the veracity regarding the authenticity of these events, whenever they are in port Captain Seavey and his crew are treated as celebrities. Daisy is one of those who reckon the entire lot as not much more than a bunch of immature boys, who have never wanted the responsibilities of being husbands and fathers. Most of the crew will agree with this assessment, considering it more as a badge of honor—and to be worn proudly. After all, it's their belief that half of those so-called "responsible town men" would trade places with them in a heartbeat.

Captain Seavey chooses to stay on board for the time being. As usual, after his encounters with Abequa, he's in no mood to socialize. The rest of the crew has left for shore intent on getting their land legs back in action. For the present, he's content to stand in the ship's bow observing a ritual scene he has never grown tired of viewing. It's the setting of the sun. Some sunsets are similar, but like many other things in nature no two are alike. This evening's presentation is a red and purple display giving a beautiful murky gloom to the sky. Like the thousands of other sunsets he's watched, there is that moment of lonely finality watching the death of yet one more day as that last bit of light sinks below the water line.

While there is still enough light to read, Seavey unfolds a paper he had slipped into his pocket years before. He reads it again for the thousandth time. *"Decree of divorce granted on grounds of desertion."* He wonders about his daughter. *How old would she be now?* Trying hard to recall, he remembers she was losing baby teeth at the time. The mental anguish that accompanies thoughts like these must be quelled immediately and never allowed a platform, lest they overtake him. A jug of moonshine whiskey rests at his feet. Without a second thought, he reaches for this singular solution. It's the only one he has ever afforded himself. Purposely, he loosens the cork from the jug and tips its contents up and pours it down his throat. The warm burn is a familiar friend that keeps him going when nothing else seems to help. He spends this moment staring into nothingness as he waits for the magic to kick in. It instantly provides the relief he's come to expect. He welcomes the rapid change its effects have on his thoughts. The anguish is quickly replaced with a lightheartedness he couldn't possibly produce without it.

"Thank you old friend, you've saved me once again," he says kissing the side of the jug as he lifts its contents once more to his waiting lips. For the next two days Captain Seavey remains aboard his docked schooner killing the avenging angels that haunt his consciousness. Recovery from the physical sickness that accompanies this kind of self-medication soon trumps the mental state that preceded it, with the illusion that the demon's been squelched once again, and it's time to put the plug back in the jug.

After three days in Frankfort, it's determined the *Wanderer* should be on its way again. Escanaba, Michigan is their destination. Seavey has agreed to take on as fare, Squeaky's three ladies that are attuned to a change of scenery to the Upper Peninsula. The crew, as yet, has not moved back into their bunks. They are still expected to make them available for their new female counterparts.

These ladies are originally from the Chicago area and came up north some three years ago to work in Squeaky's Frankfort bordello. As things go in this business, they have become old hat. They're now going to make their own way further north to the copper country, specifically Houghton-Hancock. Mining is a huge endeavor in this part of the world, promising a more appreciative clientele. It's been said many times that as long as these men don't have to resort to going out in the woods to chase down some four-legged object of their affection, the fact that these soiled doves have lost their bloom, is quickly over-looked.

This is not the only purpose for this trip. Seavey has much bigger fish to catch than the fare from these three ladies. His plans are to return to a well worked scheme that guarantees to bring him a lot of money. He's settled his eye on a stand of timber that appears to be easy picking. The area is remote, generally outside the scope of its overseers. It just happens to be on government land, making it even more enticing.

Doe has said his good-byes to Daisy with the promise that he'll be back soon. More often than not, she is presenting her protests to a hardened ear. The rest of the crew, at the behest of their captain, has picked up enough logging equipment to begin their project. With a strong southerly breeze billowing into their sails, they begin their next adventure.

"Doe I need you to make up some documents that are going to give us permission to cut timber on government land—at least good enough to keep the locals out of our hair," says Seavey, "can you do that?"

Doe gives it a minute's thought.

"I think I can come up with something passable."

Being an excellent counterfeiter and now working for Captain Seavey, he's called on for various undertakings. So far, he's more than met expectations. The last time they were in Escanaba, Doe had managed to liberate some paperwork from the government assay office. It's now giving him guidance on documents that are sure to impress them. Whenever he is working on a project, he is given whatever he needs with no argument, along with no undue interruptions.

"Doe, if I could pay you in gold, you'd be worth every ounce. But since I can't, just be reminded every successful caper we can pull off out here on the water is one more day you don't have to have a land job," says Seavey with a big broad smile. Even this is not the highest motivation for men like Doe. He does what he does for the thrill of pulling the wool over the eyes of somebody who believes they are too smart to be fooled.

Before the afternoon is complete, Doe has organized a group of papers with stationary indicating it's from governmental top dogs that people in this region have heard of, but have never met. These papers give the Chicago Milling Company exclusive rights to deforest a particular section of government-owned woodlands detailed in the script. They are crested with very official looking government letterheads. If this were not enough, they are elaborated with official looking seals to give them further authentication. In this case, Doe has named Captain Daniel Seavey as its representative.

By the following morning, the Escanaba port is in sight. The ladies are quiet. They have taken on a pensive demeanor. This is not to say these women are lacking in their abilities to make their way along their chosen path. Compared to the average women being taken care of by men, these women are head and shoulders above them in determination. They have proven to be much more capable of meeting their daily needs by their own initiatives than their housewifely counterparts.

Captain Seavey and the rest of the crew say a bon voyage to them as they watch them head for the train station that will take them on the next leg of their lives' adventure.

The women are barely out of sight before the displaced crew is recovering their vacated bunks.

"Damn Ob, I'm sure glad to get out of that stinkin' bilge water cargo hold," declares Jack.

"Ya, me too. I was beginnin' to believe I was conceived, born, and raised down there!" says Ob, tossing the rest of his possessions on his freshly reclaimed bunk.

Captain Seavey, oblivious to the crew's actions, also has his own agenda. His mind wanders over vast areas of opportunity that most men are seldom aware even exist. He pulls first mate Archie aside along with Doe. To Seavey, the door is commencing to open for them to begin helping themselves to that government owned timber down the coast a ways.

"Boys if we work this right, we have a chance to clean up good. Thanks to Doe, we got some good lookin' paperwork that's gonna get us into the timber for sure. All we gotta do now is see what we can do to get that lumber cut."

Ready to meet this challenge, he turns to Archie. Archie has seen this look of anticipated excitement more than once in his captain's eyes. It's a look of self-assurance that all the stars, earth, and sky are his for the taking.

"Archie, I want you to go into town while Doe and I get some other details out of the way. In particular, scout around for a crew that can bring a portable saw mill and some mules out to our site. Tell 'em we'll pay 'em in banknotes," says Seavey handing him a hand full of Doe's handy work.

The rest of the afternoon goes by without a hitch. Doe's forgeries seem to satisfy the county assayer considering, of course, it isn't everyday they have these important appearing documents presented to them by such a colorful and convincing personality as Captain Seavey. The only other relic of ostentatious flamboyance he has is an impressive gold nugget he had melted down and mounted into a pinky ring. It's the only artifact he has left to show from an unremarkable trip to the Klondike gold fields a number of years before. Nevertheless, he loves to display it as an augury of his success. Even at that, it came from a card shark he caught cheating in a game of stud poker. It turns out it's the spoils from several gold teeth he knocked out of the front of the cheater's mouth.

Archie has begun his leg of this new escapade, making his way down a dark street toward the only light that can be detected. The Buck Horn Inn is a local watering hole. It's a saloon that by its very deportment lends itself to an underclass where some of the less sophisticated drinkers do their drinking. There among the whiskey drinkers, smoke, and smell of sweaty men, Archie has come across a family of Irish descent that have a gasoline powered portable mill, a crew of clan members, and a stable of donkeys ready to go to work. They know the area and are willing to negotiate the terms.

"You come up with fifty dollars cash money and we may be able to make a deal," says a young spokesman by the name of Newt McClain taking a drag off his cigarette and a gulp from a large glass of beer.

Archie tries to remain as businesslike as he can.

"That's not going to be a problem Mr. McClain," says Archie handing him several of Doe's counterfeit five dollar bills, "this should be enough to get you started."

Before they can finish shaking hands on the deal, Captain Seavey and Doe walk through the saloon door interrupting their transaction. Newt and Doe spot each other at the same time. Newt's attention suddenly changes from Archie to these new arrivals. He quickly withdraws his hand leaving Archie questioning. The next moment, he lets out a bellow loud enough to wake the dead.

"Doe, you old bastard. How the hell you doin'?"

Before Doe can react, Newt has him by the hand pumping it like it was going to produce water, finally slowing down just enough to let Doe get a word in.

"Newt, you're livin' proof the devil ain't never in a hurry of them he's sure of, and you still just as ugly as you was five years ago," says Doe returning the salutation.

Turning to Seavey, he says, "Cap'n Seavey, I'd like you to meet my ugly cousin Newt McClain." As the two shake hands, a lone drinker's head at a near by table snaps in their direction unnoticed by the Seavey crew. It's apparently in reaction to something he has overheard.

Meanwhile, Archie stands by. For the moment, he's swept up with all that's happening, leaving him questioning if, and how, this new development can be turned to their advantage. Finally, after all the hoopla, the opportunity to explain the arrangements he and Newt have worked out presents itself. Seavey is happy with the agreements and demonstrates his approval by buying a round of drinks—of course paying for them with one of Doe's creations. (The chance of having one of these bills questioned in this backwater saloon is next to nothing.) With only a twinge of guilt, Doe remains a little apprehensive about giving his cousin counterfeit bills, but certainly not enough to change the prearranged deal.

"He'll get 'em passed okay," is his thought. It's certainly not a good thought, but it's his best one for the immediate situation. With all in agreement, they say their good-byes until the time they meet the next day at the site.

Without being noticed, the stranger from the nearby table continues to eavesdrop on this new alliance. He waits until they leave, quickly crosses the room, then follows them out. The group continues to talk at the tavern entrance. Seemingly inadvertently, the stranger brushes against the captain in his haste to get by. Seavey barely notices. After all, this is not a man of definable characteristics other than one could easily describe him as sullen, rather short, and maybe in his fifties, certainly not a man that will be remembered for anything other than being nondescript.

With the day having spent itself, Captain Seavey, along with the crew, returns to the ship. The prospect of having successfully pulled the wool over so many eyes thrills Doe as well as the captain.

"Boys in a few days we'll have a pile of lumber and a pile of Chicago money chasing after it. Get some sleep, we've only got a couple of bone-crushin' days to get this done."

Seavey is well aware from his many past experiences with duping people that if not careful, the wool pulled over someone's eyes has a way of quickly sliding back up again. To be content to merely remain one step ahead of the law could prove to be fatal. Expedience is the key to his success. With a little luck, by the time his victims realized they've been gulled, he and his cargo are long gone. There is no sense in pushing his luck by hanging around one minute longer than needs be. "Plan the work and work the plan" has been the continuing mantra of his success.

Morning arrives bright and sunny with a squadron of wood ducks in the surrounding waters waiting for a handout. With the distinct aroma of pancakes invading his quarters, Seavey pushes his body out of his bed-chamber.

A bowl of steaming hot fresh water along with soap and a razor adorns a table near by. Assuring this task is completed, is one of the many duties falling upon Doe. Seavey has joked that he may be the only pirate in history that's clean shaven.

Quickly eating breakfast, the crew set sail down the coast to their rendezvous with the McClain clan. It's only a mile down the coast and could be easily reached by carriage, but Seavey likes to keep his edge and have his ship close by in the event of having to make a run for it.

The lake has provided a breath of fresh air this morning. It's quickly filling the small jib with enough sail to push the schooner to their new location. Looking ashore tells them that the McClains have already set up their mill and are ready to go to work. After setting the jon boat afloat, they load enough supplies to get them through the day. First mate Archie Kerby is left on board to ready the ship to respond to any crises that may arise.

In a matter of minutes, the rest of the crew find themselves on shore. Captain Seavey promptly sets everyone to work with an assigned task. In good order, he begins to scout the area as a precautionary measure.

"It's always good to know what may be lurkin' about blockin' my road," he speculates.

The area is fairly flat with a small rise at the far end. It's a curious mound, totally out of place with the terrain. Some motion catches Seavey's eye. It disappears as quickly as it appeared. It definitely had the shape of a human. It seems to have darted around to the back side of the mound. Reflexively grasping the butt of his pistols, staring in that direction for a moment, waiting for the possibility of more movement, he ultimately opts to investigate. Moving slowly, with pistols in hand, Seavey rounds the back side of the mound. To his amazement there is fresh digging gouged into the side of this outgrowth. With the curiosity of a cat, while keeping a keen eye open for the unknown, he kicks a clod of upturned earth. What it reveals shocks him to his very core. It's a SKULL!

"WHAT THE HELL!" he gasps. For a few years in his younger days, he worked as an agent for the Bureau of Indian Affairs. It's readily obvious what is happening here. The culprit is digging in an Indian burial mound attempting to recover Indian artifacts—more than likely for resale. In spite of Seavey's own pronounced trespasses, this illegal action hits a chord of outrage. Recalling his days of law enforcement, this was the very activity that riled the Indian community more than anything. The last thing he needs at this time is for the local tribes to cause him trouble. With this warning of trouble lurking, his eyes dart around searching for that shadowy figure he had previously spotted scurrying through the brush. Seeing nothing, he returns to further inspect the ruins. A short distance away is a hurriedly discarded gunnysack, along with a shovel. A closer look reveals the bag is full skulls. Fortunately for the culprit, he or she has successfully escaped, but at the cost of abandoning their booty. Throwing the bag of these ill-gotten gains over his shoulder, Seavey has the distinct feeling of being watched. By whom, he doesn't know, but he has an uncanny sensitivity to whatever power lays behind these prying eyes.

Not wanting to alarm the crew, Seavey sets the bag of skulls out of sight in the jon boat. His idea is to hold them as evidence, then at some point in this venture to return them to their ancient resting crypt, but not until he's dealt with the grave robber.

Meanwhile the McClains are making good progress. With the *Wanderer* crew doing the cutting, and the McClain clan, along with their donkeys dragging timber to the mill, they find they are making fast work of this undertaking. By the end of the day, the two crews working together have managed to mill a half a boat load of lumber.

"The Good Lord willin' and the creek don't rise, one more day and we'll be out of here, and—hopefully—on our way to Chicago with a load of timber," muses Seavey knocking his knuckles on wood for good luck.

With the day ending, the McClain clan retires to town leaving their equipment and a healthy sized pile of sawed planks. Meanwhile, Captain Seavey and his crew rejoin Ob on the *Wanderer* for an evening meal of cold venison jerky and hardtack biscuits. The whole crew is exhausted and ready for their bunks when Willis sounds an unwelcome alarm.

"FIRE, FIRE, FIRE!" Willis is frantically pointing toward the mainland. All heads turn in that direction to see their day's work going up in flames, along with what appears to be, the McClain's gas powered sawmill.

"All hands on deck," blasts Seavey at the top of his lungs, "break out the fire pails and get that jon boat afloat now!"

All hands are racing to get to the mainland as fast as they can row. Seavey is the first man out before they even touch shore. Scooping up a pail of water, he races toward the flaming pile of timber. In his haste, he trips over a log and falls into the torrent of burning wood. Immediately his clothing is on fire. His first thought is to run, but his second thought has him rolling in the dirt followed by pails of cold lake water thrown by his anxious crew. All attention is on the captain as the pile of lumber continues to disintegrate into smoke and ash. Helping their fallen leader to his feet, they quickly assess his condition. He's truly shaken up more with this experience than any other he's endured of late.

He's soon feeling the effects of his injuries. What's apparent is that his injuries are confined to suffering some burns on his arms. Reflexively, he heads for the lake and submerges himself. The cold water soon relieves the pain of his burnt flesh. What is reducing the pain as much as the cold water is his increasing anger. With his arms still submerged, the bellows of his distraught voice tear unimpeded across the still lake water.

"The son-of-bitch guilty of this will pay for this with his life!"

Immediately Ob and Archie and the rest of the crew have entered the water trying as best they can to aid their fallen chief.

Doe is the first to check the extent of his wounds.

"We've got some coon fat on board. We need to get it on those burns right away." Captain Seavey ignores the recommendation. He's more concerned with the condition of his wet pistols.

"Get my wet ass back to shore and get back to the ship and bring me some dry ammo," he continues to roar. The crew knows better than to try and dissuade him from any judgments he's making at this point. Without a word, Doe, along with Jack, are in the launch boat double timing their way back to the ship.

Captain Seavey slips back into the mind set of his previous life as an

Indian agent investigator. In analyzing the area, the first thing he discovers is the strong smell of gasoline around a hastily discarded empty pail indicating its clandestine use very recently. On further inspection, the gas tank the McClain's had brought with them is empty. It's obvious the culprit soaked the green wood with the incendiary in order to cause it to burn so thoroughly. Ignoring his wounds, thoughts are bouncing off the walls of Seavey's mind. He knows that time is going to be of the essence if this perpetrator is to be caught. After the fire finally dies down, it leaves them with a darkness this time of day forever brings with it.

Shortly, Doe and Jack are back with the dry ammo, along with coon fat, clean dressings, and dry clothing. Seavey slows down long enough to address all four of these resources. Satisfied with Doe's diligence, he puts them to use, then quickly moves on.

He stands for a moment with a torch in hand staring down at some of the boot prints. After checking the trail back towards town, his thoughts are beginning to come together. In a flash, his huge six foot six inch frame is down on all fours smelling the remnants of these prints. Then another, and another. All that can be heard is a sound like, "Hum." He's making the same sound over and over. It's plainly not much more than rough breathing with vocal noise. Nonetheless, making these sounds seems to satisfy his hunch about these footprints. Within a minute of all this scrutiny, he begins to bark orders.

"Boys, I want all of you to go back and ready the ship to sail. I'm taking Willis with me. We're heading into town to the Buck Horn."

Looking off in that direction, it's apparent he's chewing over in his mind what could be an end to this mystery.

"I have a suspicion we may hit pay dirt."

The mile is eaten up quickly by their singleness of purpose. Careful not to be seen, Seavey stands slightly outside the door of the Buck Horn, cracking it only enough to stick his nose into the odors emanating from the inside. He smells the very thing to bring an end to his suspicions.

Now more than satisfied that they're on the right trail, he turns to Willis. "I was in here last evening. I don't want the guy we're looking for to be spooked by me showin' back up. What I want you to do is walk through the crowd until you come upon a person smelling like gasoline. Don't do anything to make him suspicious, just come back and let me know."

Without question, Willis fearlessly begins his assignment. He's a rather short man with a freckled complexion and reddish hair. His size has never been to his detriment. He's a fearless brawler and has been known on more than one occasion to fight men much larger, only to have them wonder what had made that such a good idea.

Proud to have been given such an important assignment, he dauntlessly strolls through the tables and chairs. The stench of gasoline suddenly fills his nostrils. Looking for its origin doesn't take more than a glance at a pair of shoes poking out from under a table. Their owner, oblivious to any pursuers, remains hunched over a glass of beer without as much as a glance in Willis' direction. With this significant information, Willis unobtrusively makes his way back out the door reporting to Seavey what he encountered. Seavey remains pensive. He's listening while babying his burns. Each throb of angry exposed raw nerves lessens his desire to do anything other than, *Dose this bastard with gasoline and burn him alive.*

He has Willis return and buy a bottle of whiskey. Taking a long draw, he begins to feel the pain lessen enough to think how he's going to handle this situation. Hidden in the shadows they wait. Within the hour a hunched over person with his hands jammed in his pockets makes his way out the door.

Bolting up straight like a predatory animal, Willis whispers in his loudest whisper, "That's him! That's him!

Seavey recognizes him immediately as the same nondescript drunk that stumbled into him the night before.

"Okay, Willis good work. Let's just stay back a bit, but keep him in sight. We're going to follow and watch where he goes."

Staying back and out of sight in the darkness, the two of them manage to stay on his trail without being detected. It leads down a two track out of town. Soon, he disappears off to the left down a narrow foot path. Picking up the pace a bit they realize it leads to a cabin some fifty yards off the road. Waiting until they see a light in the window, they draw in for a closer look. Peering through a curtain-less window, they see no one other than their intended target. Getting a better look at him with the lantern reflecting against his face, abruptly brings a sense of familiarity—a veiled recollection, some awareness of a past relationship. Seeing no one else in the cabin and satisfied he's alone, Seavey, with pistol drawn, cocks back his huge leg and with a single crushing blow kicks the cabin door completely off its hinges. The man is wide-eyed and for the moment paralyzed with shock as this huge man he was hoping to avoid has hunted him down once again. Before he can recover, Seavey has his huge hand around his pathetic scrawny neck.

"Don't hurt me Seavey, I'll pay you, I'll pay you!"

"Your damn tootin' your gonna pay me," replies Seavey. "And how in hell do you know my name?"

"You was the Indian agent that sent me to prison years back fer scabbin' up relics and sellin' em ta out east traders."

"So you ain't only an arsonist—you're the pecker-wood that's diggin' up them Indian bones too?" demands Seavey.

The look in Seavey's eyes, along with his tightening grip, lets this grave robbing arsonist know that with one wrong word he'll be conjoining the same fate as his stolen relics.

"Yes sir I did, I did it all. I'm guilty, I did it, I did it sir, and I'm sorry." says Otis sounding pathetic and still looking like a man with the devil in his eyes.

"I remember you now, you weaselin' turd. Your name is Otis Redman. You was a weasel then and you is the same weasel today."

Otis, seeing his chances of surviving this ordeal beginning to slip through his fingers, makes a quick decision to barter for his life with one last effort.

"I gots cash Cap'n, honest I do. You let me go and I'll tell you where it is," Otis pleads.

Captain Seavey remembers this whining sniveler as an opportunist who would do anything to save his own skin. He rolled over on his own brother to plea bargain a lighter sentence. Careful to keep total control, he keeps a firm grip with one hand on Otis's scrawny neck, motioning with the other for Willis to bring a rope that's lying in a box with Otis's grave robbing tools.

"Make a proper noose on the end of that Willis and bring it to me," says Seavey. Quickly forcing the rope into a coiled configuration, Willis presents it to Seavey. Seavey motions him to place the looped end around Otis' neck and tighten it snug. With the rope in place, Seavey then moves his grip from Otis' throat to a point on the rope.

"Tell me one lie, or piss me off in any way, and I promise you the end of this rope goes over one of those rafters up there. Ya understand that Otis?" roars Seavey in an absolutely no nonsense tone. Seavey throws the rope over his shoulder, placing just enough tension on Otis' scrawny neck for him to get the message.

"Okay Cap'n I got ya," says Otis, feeling his neck stretch. With their height difference the tension in the rope leaves Otis on his tiptoes.

"So now that we understand one another, tell me about this cash that's going to help fix your situation," pronounces Captain Seavey with the boldness of one that clearly understands who has the upper hand.

With his neck taut from the rope, Otis manages to lift a shaking finger and point to a large trunk hidden under a pile of coats, pants and blankets.

"In there, right in there you'll find the money," expresses Otis, his voice raspy from a slow, purposeful strangulation.

Still maintaining the tension on Otis' neck, Seavey motions to Willis to open the trunk. Quick to follow orders, Willis throws the debris aside. The screeching sound of metal on the wood floor fills the room as he drags the trunk across the planks, leaving scrape marks trailing behind. Willis lifts the lid exposing its contents. It's not at all surprising to Seavey to see a black-market assortment of beaded Indian burial jewelry, flint stone spear heads and other relics—all stolen. Still on his tiptoes, Otis continues to point to a small canvas bag in the corner of the trunk.

"Right there in that bag," he insists with a tone of voice that is clearly being strained by the noose.

With another nod of the head from Seavey, Willis empties the contents from the small canvas bag on the floor. The clanking sound of silver dollars bouncing on the wooden planks resounds through the room. In less than a minute Willis reports the tally.

"Thirty two dollars Cap'n."

"THIRTY -TWO DOLLARS! THAT'S IT? THIRTY- TWO DOLLARS." Seavey flies into a rage, driven by the discomfort of his burned arms and being in the presence of a lying sniveling coward named Otis Redman.

"You burn up five hundred dollars of my lumber and you dare present me thirty- two dollars as payment."

In one motion, Seavey tosses his end of the rope over a ceiling rafter and begins to lift Otis off the floor. Otis realizing the absolute peril he's put his life in with this last stupid gesture makes a final attempt to save himself. With his toes barely touching the floor, he can barely manage a gasp.

"Okay, okay there's more, there's more."

"Your a lyin' scrawny bastard and I'm going to hang you and watch you shit your pants," says this truly upset and insulted adversary.

With the tension reaching the limits of Otis' ability to speak and his eyes beginning to bulge, he nevertheless, manages to make a gasping blurt out, still using the same finger pointing to an old worn out rug covering a corner of the floor.

"Under there!"

With another nod of the head, Seavey motions Willis to check it out. Once the rug is removed, they find that it had concealed a trap door. Willis lifts it to reveal a ladder leading to an underground cellar. Grabbing a lantern from its perch on a nearby table, he lights the wick and carries it down the ladder.

"Holy crap Cap'n, come 'ere and look at this!"

Taken back by the uncharacteristic tone of Willis' voice, Seavey loosens the tension on Otis' neck (much to Otis' relief) in order to take a peek.

"He's got a 'stillery down here."

There, lining the walls, are at least fifty gallons of distilled moonshine whiskey. Continuing to hang on to his end of the rope with enough tension to keep Otis a believer, Seavey takes enough steps down the ladder to see for himself. All the while Willis is making his own investigation.

Suddenly, he comes across a part of the dirt floor that has a more solid feel to it. Kicking around with the toe of his boot, it becomes apparent that he's standing on a buried metal box.

"Get me a shovel Cap'n and we'll see what we got here," says an excited Willis.

Within minutes he is digging the mysterious box out of its resting place and soon has it out. Not bothering to request a key to the padlock securing it, Willis, with one well-directed shovel blow, knocks the lock apart. In his next move, he tosses the shovel aside, brushes the dirt from the top of the box and lifts the lid. Just as Otis had promised, it's filled with cash. Handing the box up the ladder to Seavey, the look on Otis' face is one of utter dejection. As has happened so many times in this reprobate's existence, his whole life has flown completely out of his control. In contrast to this, Captain Seavey has the grin of a Cheshire cat.

"Congratulations Otis ole buddy, you just bought yourself another day of life."

Otis remains expressionless. He looks pathetic with the noose around his pencil thin neck. To add to his misery, he is standing in wet pants. It seems that in his extreme anxiety, he has pissed himself.

Willis soon finishes his tally—$780.00 plus the $32.00 in silver plus the fifty gallons of moonshine.

"We want to thank you for your contribution, Otis," says a still smiling Seavey.

"Yes sir, Otis, this here sure beats wearin' my ass off cuttin' timber," adds Willis.

Seavey contemplates their situation for a moment before addressing Otis once again.

"There is yet one more thing you're going to do for us Otis."

Otis' dejected expression tells his whole reaction. *What more can they do to me?"* is his only thought.

"You're going to load that fifty gallons of 'shine into your wagon and then you and your mule are gonna pull it to my ship. You can start now."

"Can I take this noose off my neck first?" asks Otis in a hapless voice. He's nearly in tears.

"No, I think we're going to leave that in place in case the McClains want to make use of it for you destroying their mill." Seavey is roaring with laughter over this yet unresolved bit of business.

Instead of Otis's anxiety ending, Seavey keeps it coming his way. Otis has now reached a point where he feels it would have been easier to have let them hang him rather than to suffer through his present anguish.

With all the commotion coming to a halt, Seavey's pain in his arms is reminding him, yet again, just how seriously he's been violated. A few more pulls from Otis' moonshine relieves some of the discomfort.

It's not long before they reach the ship. The still smoldering lumber pile is a reminder to Otis of the cause of his present circumstance.

Ob is waiting with the launch boat. He's more than happy to help load the alcohol into the boat even though it takes a couple of trips. When all is finished, Captain Seavey has one unfinished task. He ties Otis to a tree with a note pinned to his shirt explaining to the McClain clan what happened to their mill. The sound of Otis' hapless protestations can be heard drifting across the water. Glad to have recouped his losses, Seavey is happy to be back out to sea. He finds it freeing. To distance himself from these land dwellers' problems is a bonus most men don't have.

5 A SOLO VOYAGE

Meanwhile, Doe is doing all he can to minister to his captain's wounds, but unfortunately merely changing the bandages is not doing much for the pain. With his raw burned arms raging, Seavey has put away enough whiskey to kill not only his pain, but also himself.

The wind is variable out of the east-northeast and growing in intensity. It's unmistakable that these easterly seas are beginning to change from a relatively calm state to rough. Easterly winds often precede trouble on the Great Lakes. Archie has taken over command in Seavey's absence and as the fierceness of the winds begins to pick up, he is giving serious consideration to heading for Green Bay, Wisconsin. His hope is to get to Menominee without incident and wait for calmer seas. Another factor in favor of this option is that he is aware of an opium dealer doing business there. More than sure this drug will help Captain Seavey's pain, he's also sure the trafficker won't be difficult to persuade to dispense him a supply of the drug for a price. With all this on his mind, he prepares for the trip.

With a snoot full of whiskey, Captain Seavey gives all of the outward indications of one who has passed out, oblivious to everything. Inwardly, this is a long way from what is happening. In another world that only he has access to, Seavey has reopened a door that he would do nearly anything to keep closed. It's the passage way to Abequa. He's never sure whether she finds him or because of his behavior he is led to her. Either way, they are now in each other's presence. He finds it alarming that she is wearing a gourd Booger mask. It's oftentimes associated with death among the Cherokee. He also becomes conscious of a strong scent of lavender, which is also associated with a cleansing ritual of the dead. All in all, these are indicators pointing to a ritual for the soul of the departed. What is forcing itself into his thoughts is the very real fear that it may be his death that has brought up this apparition. He can't help but feel a sense of panic as he calls upon the Virgin Mother for consolation.

"Holy Mary, mother of Mercy, what is happening to me? I know my sins are great. Please, I beg of you ask your Son, Jesus, to take this tormenter out of my sight."

Even though this is a heartfelt prayer, he is fully aware that in his case, he doesn't deserve anything more than what he is getting. Besides, he is used to God apparently ignoring him, cheating him, and letting him down.

Abequa is reciting names that are clearly names outside of the Caucasian understanding. It's becoming unmistakably clear to him that these are Indian names. She is reciting them in an orderly chant that is much more prescribed than impromptu. Seavey finds himself held in the grip of a dreadful terror as Abequa continues to recite name after name.

"What do you want of me, you demon of Satan?" he screams in horror. "Are you here to call my name?"

Guilt, shame, every failing and fault is revisiting him. The faces of his abandoned wife and daughter stare pale and unloved. Next, he views an adolescent boy whom he recognizes as himself. Then his departed mother appears. She has a forlorn look as he is refusing her request to go into the priesthood. One by one his sins march past him, stopping only long enough to accuse him and move on as another attacks from an unseen direction. This type of emptiness and hopeless loneliness can only be in a place where God is not to be found, where God has been dismissed.

Not to make less of the differing kinds of terror as though a contrasting variety can be less horrific, for at this very moment above deck in the physical world, the *Wanderer's* crew is involved in a nor'easter that has switched to a sou'wester. The turbulence is reaching proportions where the ship is no longer navigable. It is completely at the mercy of the storm. Waves are breaking broadside over her sides in a manner that threatens to capsize her.

Archie's struggle against this storm has put him at the end of his rope. His arms are growing weary in trying to keep the wheel positioned to force the rudder to channel the ship through the waves. The raging furor seems to be attacking from all directions, pushing, slamming, and crashing over the deck. All sails have been lowered before they're ripped to shreds. With the unrelenting force of this tempest, Archie has no choice but to rouse the captain out of his alcoholic stupor, all in the hopes of saving the ship. Tying the wheel to a mast pole, he fiercely fights his way to

Seavey's quarters below the quarterdeck. Entering this bastion of chaos, he encounters Captain Seavey bunked in a tangled disarray.

Shaking him and slapping his cheeks only results in an indistinguishable mumbling. After repeated attempts, he is finally able to partially rouse the captain. Seavey's eyes dart open, visibly startled. His first sense is that it's dark and cold. His mind struggles to inform him what this new phenomenon may be. His first thoughts are that it's still Abequa, ostensibly and relentlessly, continuing to come at him from her demonic depths.

"Cap'n, Cap'n, wake up sir, we have a storm tearin' at us," shouts Archie endeavoring to remain on his feet against the rocking ship.

He's trying to scream over the sounds of the storm while Seavey is, however, still struggling to leave the world of Abequa and enter this sudden, imminent, differing reality. The two worlds are somehow trying to blend as one, resisting a separation. Duke also seems to have a perception of the spirit world, and is reacting in a nervous panting, sensing it has been disturbed. He's whining and obviously agitated. Between Duke licking his face and Archie's efforts, the two worlds suddenly become disconnected.

Fully back, Captain Seavey takes stock of the conditions. He has seen this phenomenon before, back when he served as an Indian agent. Seavey has never been one to duck from trouble—at least not in the physical world. But hell's fury reigning down from Abequa's underworld is another matter. Seavey's mind is racing for a solution. Suddenly everything becomes clear. Captain Seavey knows, without a shadow of a doubt, what is going on. Abequa was reciting the names of Indians whose souls have been troubled. The sacred burial ground of those long dead Indians has been disturbed in such a way that hell's fury has been released on those daring to disorder their eternal sleep. In an instantaneous flash of memory, Seavey pulls himself out of his bunk.

"Oh my God, I have that bag of skulls!" he shouts out loud remembering that he placed them in a bag and left them in the launch boat. He is fully acquainted with the kinds of rage this demonic world is capable of bringing to bear. A wave of terror envelops him as he grapples for a solution. Battling his way up the steps to the quarterdeck, he struggles against the fury of the storm to reach the wheel. These rantings of Seavey are as foreign as Greek to Archie, but, nonetheless, he is right on his heels. Quickly reviewing their circumstances, Seavey bellows out an order to whomever is in earshot.

"Lower the anchor till you feel her drag."

Without a moment's hesitation the anchor is quickly dropped from its position off the bow. By attempting this maneuver, he hopes to stabilize the ship in a straighter line allowing it to ride the winds, pushing the ship back in the direction of Escanaba. It's a tricky operation that only the most experienced sailors would ever attempt. Since the rudder is nearly useless the ship gets turned around and rides with the storm backwards dragging the anchor from the bow.

"Keep yer eyes peeled for any harbor lights. The last thing we want to do is run her aground," roars Captain Seavey above the fury of the storm.

Their maneuvering over the next hour proves successful. This is all done in the black of this nighttime storm. It's a welcome relief to have the harbor lights come into sight. They're struggling to keep the ship positioned in hopes of anchoring just above their old logging site. The sea continues to be unforgiving. Nonetheless, Seavey remains privately adamant about getting these bones back in their resting place. So far, he has not had any dialog with any member of the crew concerning his participation in this disaster, nor the purpose of this mission. The rain is pelting them hard, along with breaking waves hammering the deck. It is every man for himself, gripping whatever provides a handhold. It's a miracle that no one has been washed overboard. They all are feeling more and more helpless. With each flash of lightning, Seavey continues to search the shoreline. Suddenly something catches his eye. It's the ruins of the McClain's sawmill.

"Lower the anchor till she grabs bottom," he bellows still keeping a steel eye on the shoreline. With that done, he orders the launch boat lowered.

Archie, along with the rest of the crew look at him as though he is still drunk out of his mind.

"Sir that's suicide, she'll swamp before we get ten feet."

"Do as I tell you, that's an order!" bellows Seavey once again. At the same moment, he boards it alone. Jack and Ob, together, release the jon boat. Both hope they are not going to be asked to join him. Surprising everyone, Captain Seavey is making this voyage solo. Finding the bag of skulls still safely lodged in the bow of the boat, he positions himself with the oars in hand to attempt this perilous voyage.

He promptly finds himself in an open body of water with no place to hide. He's solely at the mercy of the unrelenting turbulent weather conditions crashing around him. Rowing with brute force, the storm drives the small craft on top of a wave, than another, and another until he slams onto the beach. Grabbing the boat with all his strength, he manages to pull it out of the water, wrestling its awkwardness alone onto the sandy shore. Driven solely by some mysterious force deep within himself, he secures it to a cedar tree along the water's edge. With rain driving into his eyes, he nonetheless, waits for the next lighting flash to get his bearings. He's able to make out the land marks as the sky continues its sporadic incandescence. Wasting not a moment, he grabs the bag of skulls, tossing them over a shoulder, and begins his trek up to the burial mound.

Off to his right something catches Seavey's eye. It's poor ole Otis, half-drowned, tied to the tree with the noose still adorning his neck. Staring at him for an instant, he witnesses the terror of another human helplessly staring back. In a weak moment of unwarranted compassion, he lowers his bag and cuts Otis' bindings. Otis stares back, but only long enough to realize that he has just received a reprieve that not even heaven's angels would have granted him. Not one to push his luck, without a word, he quickly disappears into the darkness.

Seavey returns to his quest, struggling to the backside of the burial site, clambering through slippery mud and rotting logs, intent on not giving up until his mission is accomplished. For the moment, he senses a feeling rising up from some part of his person that has not had much exercising. Truly it's a feeling he hasn't experienced since he was a very young man—that of doing the right thing! With this overwhelming intuition there remains only one thing left to do. He carefully empties the bag. The spirit of each of the bones seems to recognize their resting place. Their sigh of relief is reflected in the sudden quelling of the storm.

6 CUBAN GREEN

By the time Captain Seavey finds his way back to his ship, the world has recovered. The storm has ceased. A bright window shines in the north. Miraculously, the pain from his burns is also quenched. The crew is preparing the ship for sailing. With a cargo hold full of moonshine liquor and a pocket full of cash, Seavey takes stock of his options.

"Traverse City boys! Set our course for Traverse City. We need a bit of recreation," roars Captain Seavey with a renewed vigor.

Along with that command comes a much relieved crew. It's as though they have just inhaled a breath of new life.

The course is set and the rotation of the ship's watch is in place. Captain "Roaring Dan" Seavey retires to his quarters feeling assured that the worst is over. His feeling by morning has proven to be true. Abequa has released him for the moment. He arises well-rested.

Sailing all night has brought them within sight of their destination. The first order of business is to find a suitable spot to anchor. The Grand Traverse Bay soon presents itself. It is an eighteen mile long peninsula divided by an east and west bay. The West Bay, as it is referred to, looks to him to be the better of the two choices since this side of the peninsula is more likely to provide a stronger prevailing wind. Always in the back of Seavey's mind is a fear of an unknown. By keeping this thought as an edge, he keeps his options open for a quick escape.

The crew always feels at home in any number of saloons arranged along the water front. Captain Seavey, on the other hand, prefers the watering holes in the upscale hotels in the downtown region. After a bath, a shave, and a haircut, provided as a convenience in the Park Place Hotel, he avails himself of the hotel's barroom.

While sipping a glass of Bourbon and water, he can't help but overhear a nearby conversation concerning the purchase of hay. It seems one of the men is a gentleman from Chicago representing a stable of race horses. The representative is convinced that a special grade of meadow grass, grown only in the Upper Peninsula is what makes their horses run faster. He gives his listener the impression that he is an expert on this subject and is willing to pay a premium for the extra purported nutritional value. This buyer is currently on his way to this U.P. outpost to broker a deal. He has traveled by train thus far and is now subject to a delay due to a track washout north of Traverse City.

Captain Seavey remains on his barstool quietly nursing his drink waiting for an opportune time to enter the conversation. The discussion is suddenly brought to a halt as the confidant is called out by a page, leaving the hay buyer to look around for another confederate to impress with his Brobdingnagian wisdom. Being the opportunist that he is, Captain Seavey is more than ready to fill that vacancy.

"My dear fellow," Seavey, pausing only long enough to seize the man's attention, begins, "I couldn't help but overhear your conversation pertaining to the nutritional value of certain strains of grasses. It so happens I have some experience in that area. Let me introduce myself to you, my name is Seavey, Captain Daniel Seavey, skipper of the schooner *Wanderer*." With his biggest, broadest salesman's smile, he extends his hand in friendship.

The stranger obviously has had a few drinks and is more than ready to engage in conversation with anyone who is willing to listen. Extending his own hand in response, "Nice to make your acquaintance, Captain. My name is McGregger, Micheal McGregger. You can just call me Mike. What kind of familiarity do you have in the hay business?"

Seavey politely listens to his question as if he is giving it his entire attention. He is also very aware of the superstitions of horse racers.

"I'm very well-acquainted with the type grass you're seeking. I've dealt with owners and trainers for years involved in this same quest for high nutritional grasses. I happen to have a contact in the same general area that you mentioned. I know them personally, and can arrange a pow-wow for you to make an inquiry."

Aware of McGregger's problem with the railroad delay, Seavey arranges his words to circumvent the dilemma. Noticing that he has this city slicker's full attention, he quickly assesses the situation.

"I can get you there in a day, weather permitting, and can load as much as my ship will carry back to this port ready to load on a rail car in less than three days."

The last sentence is the only part of these statements that's true, and then that is only partly true. Nevertheless, it's caught the attention of this Chicago buyer, who is sure that these northern Michigan greenhorns are incapable of hoodwinking a big city buyer such as himself. Seavey also prides himself on allowing these city folks to believe that he's their humble servant and incapable of making the sophisticated kinds of transactions they're used to.

McGregger is all ears as this could be the answer to his dilemma. With the drinks he's downed, combined with his own arrogance, he's sure that he's hit the jackpot.

His only reply for the moment is, "What's this deal going to cost me?"

"I'll cut your railroad costs in half and give you a bunk and meals to boot," says a still smiling Seavey.

McGregger is already calculating how he can pad his expenses.

"Captain, I believe we may work out a deal," says McGregger with the thought still lingering in his head that there may still be more to be gleaned in this deal.

"When can we get started?" says McGregger extending his hand, ready to shake on the deal. This is the question that Seavey has been waiting to hear.

"I'll send a carriage to pick you up along with your luggage tomorrow morning at 7:00 am."

The two of them part after several drinks and small talk. Seavey wastes no time seeking out his crew, who he knows will be well into a much deserved gala of drinking and womanizing. Between himself and Archie, he manages to roust them out of their partying with only minor threats to break their skulls. He spends a bit of time with all of them, explaining the hustle that will be going down with this city slicker.

"This guy has money to spend on hay, and we want to help him buy."

Being old hands at this kind of chicanery, the crew knows how to play along with their captain without getting in the way.

"Archie, I want you to head out to Tom Murphy's farm on the peninsula. By now, he'll probably have a good share of his first cut in bindings and ready to sell. I know that more than likely, he'll have more available than we can handle. You make a deal with him and get that hay out to Holder's landing. I want you to tag each bound sheave with the label 'SUPREME CUBAN GREEN.' We'll meet you there along with our new friend tomorrow before dark. Remember as far as McGregger's concerned, we are in Garden City in the Upper Peninsula at the Green Meadows Farms, the home of "Cuban Green."

Exactly on schedule, a carriage arrives to greet McGregger. He's waiting with a porter to load his only piece of luggage, which he is perfectly capable of taking care of himself, but then men like him like to be big shots with other people's money. After tipping the porter, he arranges himself to be chauffeured. It disappoints him that this early in the morning, he has such a small audience to view his importance. The journey is short, no more than five minutes. Second Mate Willis Wells is there to meet him, along with Ob. Ob's strong back on the oars guarantees them arriving at the anchored schooner in a matter of minutes.

"Welcome aboard the *Wanderer*, Mr. McGregger. I hope you slept well," says a deliberately fawning Seavey. Not waiting for an answer, he continues, "Let me show you to your quarters."

With a motion from Seavey's hand, Jack picks up McGregger's suit case and trots along behind as a willing sycophant. Seavey has already had Doe print out a bill of sale from "Green Meadow Farms, Garden City, Michigan." Second Mate Willis is on the wheel. Ob is making the final adjustments on the rigging, they have a willing "mark" to be dealt with, the anchor is up and they are ready to sail.

Willis's orders are to chart a course that will take them in a large circle in such a way that they'll arrive back on the Old Mission peninsula only ten miles from their starting point this evening. This ploy is designed to make McGregger believe he has arrived in the Michigan Upper Peninsula area of Garden City.

It's a perfect day for sailing with a westerly breeze and fairly gentle seas. In another gesture of feigned attentiveness, McGregger has been supplied with a deck chair high up on the quarterdeck. He has a way of positioning his sitting as though he were occupying a throne. By mid-morning, he has smoked several pipes and is beginning to give the appearance of one who is no longer enjoying himself. In a flash, he is bending over the rail. His stomach is convulsing, resulting in a projectile of his earlier breakfast hurling itself toward the water. It seems seasickness has gripped him. This had been predicted already in the mind of Captain Seavey. His hopes are that this will confine their guest to his bunk for the remainder of the journey. Another concern had been, up until now, whether their city slicker friend would notice the position of the sun in relation to the circle they are traveling. They doubt him being that perceptive, but now with him confined to his quarters, this concern has been eliminated.

The day is one of little concern for anything other than an occasional adjustment to the rigging. By early twilight, Willis has managed to complete his circle undetected. Their poor guest is not feeling much better as they tie up at Holder's landing. Archie has completed his task and has a very impressive display set up in a large barn adjacent to the landing. The building is used to house perishables grown on the peninsula ready for shipping to markets all over the country. It has a wonderful smell associated with it blending all the differing commodities that come together here. Archie has secured a space capable of handling several tons of hay. He has made his deal with Tom Murphy and is ready to sink his hook into McGregger for a healthy 100% markup.

After being brought ashore, McGregger is more than happy to find his feet on flooring that has no movement. His recovery is quite swift with Captain Seavey making an introduction to Archie. Archie has been through similar transactions with other city folk and knows they like to envisage how they have the upper hand.

"Very nice to meet you Mr. McGregger. I've done business with some of the other stables in your region, competitors of yours I suppose. Many of them have a standing order with us, but we have some new fields this year and are able to expand into some new markets."

McGregger is all but ignoring Archie as he goes through an elaborate examination of rubbing, sniffing, tasting the grasses, giving one the impression that he is one who knows what the grass business is about. Both Seavey and Archie give each other a knowing wink as McGregger continues with his nonsense.

"What did you say that you want for this per ton?" asks McGregger not looking up, but rather continuing his scrutiny.

"Well, with this being the first cutting and all, we are expecting the quality to surpass anything grown from here on, so we are requiring $25 a ton," says Archie with a very clear air of authority.

For the first time, McGregger looks up squarely in the eyes of Archie. He has a look of one who has just discovered that he's being taken advantage of. With a look of utter disgust, his whole demeanor takes on a drastic change.

"Do you think I was born yesterday? Do you think I just fell off the turnip truck? You may get that kind of price from some greenhorn, but you can be sure as hell, it won't be from me. I'll offer you $18 per ton and not a penny more."

Archie breaks out in a grin from ear to ear.

"Well Mr. McGregger, it's been a pleasure meeting you, but I have other stables that have already contracted with me at that price and are happy to receive it. I'm sorry we can't do business."

With that he turns his back on McGregger and begins to walk away leaving him with his jaw hanging in mid-air.

Recovering quickly McGregger shouts after him, "Make it $22 and you got a deal."

Archie continues walking with his back to McGregger, raising five fingers and busies himself with some adjustment to some fallen bundles.

Seeing this opportunity may be slipping through his fingers, McGregger succumbs. "Okay, Okay. I'll pay the $25. You drive a hard bargain Mr. Kerby," says this obviously dejected grass buyer.

"Nothing personal Mr. McGregger, it's just business," says Archie with a wry little grin. "How much would you like?"

"I'll take all you got right here today," says McGregger almost defensively.

"Okay Mr. McGregger we'll write that up for four tons and load er on board for ya," says Archie. In the commotion of all the loading, Seavey slips Archie the bogus sales slip. Before presenting it to McGregger, Archie takes it to a small office off to the side and fills in the details. They shake hands with Archie promising to give him a better deal on the second cutting. Still smarting from his inability to hornswaggle these hayseeds, McGregger doesn't make any promises. The only thing on his mind is having to get back on the ship for a voyage he believes will take the rest of the night. This is not to mention having to deal with whatever stomach he may have left.

Once again hoping to incapacitate their guest, Captain Seavey has a plan. Remembering how well McGregger likes drink, he makes a proposal.

"Micheal, it's a custom aboard this ship to celebrate most nearly everything. Before we set sail, I would like to celebrate the good fortune you've had in securing a load of the best damned grass Michigan has to offer, and I might add, at a good price. I've seen that strain up as high as $30 for a first cutting, so let's have a drink and settle your stomach and your nerves."

This is just the elixir McGregger has in mind himself.

"Captain, I believe you read my mind," says McGregger with a bit of a sigh. He's clearly relieved to have the hay and be on his way.

Continuing to assure him that his glass will never be empty and with darkness arriving, he soon retires. The night is calm other than the heavy snoring from McGregger's bunk. Willis opts to tack the ship out to an area where he is sure they can anchor and wait out the night. Morning arrives with Willis already having pulled the anchor and setting sail for the short voyage to Traverse City. McGregger soon awakes none the wiser and still under the impression they had sailed all night.

With the deft hands of a surgeon, Willis brings the sailing ship into port, securing it near a rail spur designed for just such occasions. McGregger gladly pays Captain Seavey his agreed fee and is left on the dock with a crew of rail workers loading his four tons of Captain Seavey's special "Cuban Green" with the assurance this blend will produce the fastest horses on the circuit.

7 FISH CAMP

Once more, the crew reminds Seavey of his promise for a break. Seavey couldn't be more pleased with their superb performance and more than happy to comply.

"You boys have done a great job once again. We couldn't have pulled this last deal off if it weren't for your support and I promise you, we'll put in for a few days—just not here. With McGregger hanging around Traverse City for a few more days, I'd just as soon be elsewhere. We'll sail around the Leelanau peninsula and head for Frankfort for a while. You boys can visit a few of your old Frankfort girlfriends." With that, Seavey roars with laughter.

Within the hour, Archie arrives back on board from his little jaunt on the peninsula. He hands Captain Seavey the wad of cash he received from McGregger. Seavey has a loyal crew. They realize they will all share in whatever successful endeavors he leads them into. His usual way is in the form of extra bonuses. Leaving Traverse City behind, they set sail. They enter the old familiar harbor in Frankfort in the middle of the afternoon.

He chooses to anchor on the opposite side of the bay from the 200 foot rail car ferry named the *Ann Arbor#1*. Since it's docked directly in front of the life saving station, it blocks their view, providing him the anonymity he wishes to keep. The official in the life saving station is paid by the federal government and is expected to keep an eye on Seavey's ship for any infractions. On the other hand, the crew stationed here are more inclined to be on the lookout for his ship for other reasons. They are more concerned with his willingness to share his supply of bootlegged whiskey, along with the fresh supply of soiled doves than they are supplying the revenuers with information.

Seavey, out of appreciation, makes it a practice to gift these non-commissioned sailors with a jug of his John Barleycorn. With this exchange, they are more apt to turn the tables and share with him the recent comings and goings of revenue officers, especially those in search of illegal bootleggers.

After drawing straws to determine the first watch, Jack Perry is left with the ship while the rest of the crew dingy their way to shore. The men immediately head for the Blue Slipper saloon. Seavey on the other hand, heads for St. Ann's Catholic Church. Barely has he crossed the church threshold before he spots Father Daniel. Without hesitation, the father knows exactly why Seavey is there and heads directly toward the confessional. He has a mixture of dismay and curiosity at these confessed misadventures. As his confessor, he has, confessedly, a hint of envy for the cavalier antics of this swashbuckler. Nevertheless, he is only allowing himself a brief moment to vicariously relish the injudicious reminiscences of this confession.

By all accounts, Captain Seavey has a likable character and is just as capable of performing a righteous deed as an unrighteous. Father Daniel is well aware of this sinner's transgressions and equally aware of his good heart that can also perform a very compassionate deed. After giving him his promise of absolution along with a penance providing he rejoin his abandoned family, Father Daniel's prayer is that Seavey will begin to take delight in his penance and make it a new course in life—but he admittedly is not holding his breath.

Considering himself amply forgiven because of his good intentions, Seavey heads for the Blue Slipper to join his compatriots. He considers Frankfort his home port and has developed many friendships among the local people. Once there, he runs into an old poaching buddy named Dee McDonnell. Between the two of them, they have broken every game law that's ever been put in place. Fortunately for both, neither have at any point been held accountable for their rues.

"Dee, you old bastard, I see they haven't yet found a rope strong enough to hang ya," roars Seavey over the wordless din of the bar.

Dee in turn slams his drink on the table and returns the acclamation with one of his own.

"Well lookee here what shows up when I ain't got a gun."

They are both on their feet giving the other a hearty handshake. Dee has been in this area since birth. He actually comes from south Frankfort across the Betsie Bay, but spends his money in the Frankfort bars. Dee is a man of about thirty-five years. His wife died of pneumonia a year ago. For reasons unknown to either of them, they never had children. He spent most of this year drunk. It's only been the last few months that he has come back into the land of the living. After a few more drinks, they begin to discuss the spring fish runs.

"They're paying damn good money for lake trout this year," says Dee. "The game warden's a new guy and doesn't know the area that well. He's more inclined to be payin' attention to the mouth of the harbor than he is to places down the Betsie (the local river that exits into Lake Michigan)."

Dee is a known poacher and regarded as active. He has outlasted several game wardens and has no plans to allow this one to disrupt his way of life. This new fellow, named Burt Morse, has vowed not to rest until he has Dee behind bars. It gives a thinking person the idea that Morse is driven more by his ego than a love for the law.

Seavey listens with an attentive ear. He plans to hang around in Frankfort for a while and he may as well make it pay a dividend.

"I think you're on to somethin' Dee. I know damn well there's a big market for fresh fish. Then again, if we smoke 'em, they'll keep long enough to get 'em to Chicago. Those immigrant hunyuks snatch those things up like they was candy. Besides, I still got a load of shine I gotta get down there."

Dee is listening with greater interest now that both he and Seavey appear to be on the same page. Dee would never say he was a man who hunts trouble, he only admits to flirting with it.

"Take a little ride with me, an I'll show you a place where we can throw a net and set up smoke barrels out of sight of everybody," elicits Dee.

Seavey has no other pressing obligations and readily takes Dee up on the offer. With a sturdy buckboard stationed outside, the two of them climb aboard and head south out of town, and up river. Within a half hour, they run out of road. A clump of cottonwoods greets them. After tying the horse to a tree, Dee motions for Seavey to follow him. An improvised trail leads them through the brush and twisted undergrowth of wild grape to a natural clearing created by a canopied growth of cedars along the river. Suddenly they come upon a makeshift fishing cabin with a number of smoke barrels, an assortment of nets, a flat-bottom wood-plank fishing boat turned upside down, and a rickety old dock made out of cedar poles. All this is arranged in an attempt to give it a civilized appearance.

"I ain't cared much about nothin' for a while, but I'm a getting past the worst of it. I think you and me could get this place cookin' again. I ain't been out here since Aggie died," concedes Dee apologetically.

Seavey is quietly surveying the location. Fulfilling his concern to always have an escape route, he scrutinizes the tangle of brush on the opposite side of the river. Measuring it for a minute provides a moment to listen to the babbling of the water pushing its way around a rocky drop in the river's elevation. It's moments like this that give him peace.

"Yeah Dee, you're on to somthin' fer sure. We can run a seine net across the river and be out of here with a boat load in just a couple days," says Seavey after a quick inspection. They spend the next few hours taking stock of what's going to be needed for a few day's supplies.

Meantime back in town, Doe has opted to forgo hitting the bar with the rest of the crew. Instead, he has gotten together with Daisy. He has to confess she has truly practiced her witchcraft on him. Lately it's to the point that he has nothing else on his mind other than thoughts of her.

It's also obvious that Daisy has set her eye on the likes of Doe Pierce. She has prepared herself for their meeting with a well-fitted bustled dress designed for the purpose of magnifying her small waist, well-formed derriere, and ample breasts. Just the sight of her makes his heart jump to a marathoner's beat. Her head is angled in such a way that her dark hair seems to glisten as an accessory to the sun. Doe stands as close as he can to her as the smell of a fine rose water seemingly emanates from her every pore.

Her countenance is of a darker hue than that of the many Swedes that dominate the region. Its origins seem to be held tight within a family secret. It's been rumored that her lineage lies in a Hebrew heritage. Aware of anti-Semitic feelings, no one in the family is sure how well this information would be received, no one has readily admitted to it. Regardless of her linage, he finds himself with a kind of involuntary grin dominating his face that is only formulated when a young man's heart is full of another.

There is a baseball game at the ball field this afternoon. Doe is hell bent on getting Daisy out where he can show her off. She in turn, is more than ready to demonstrate to the other ladies what her female wiles are capable of capturing. All in all, they are finding that each has beguiled the other. Their hearts burn with a fire as if stirred by strong drink. For them the day is young.

The day has also begun for Deputy Burt Morse. He has been assigned by the State of Michigan to this region as game warden. He's taken an oath to uphold the game laws of the state. Since this is his first assignment, he approaches this undertaking with the zeal of a tent preacher. He has been briefed by the previous warden and has been given the low down on the troublemakers in the region. Dee McDonnell is at the head of his list. Morse has vowed to bring him in one way or another. Now that he's arrived, he's hoping to develop a working relationship with the chief harbor master, named Bill Wilson, stationed at the life saving station. Wilson always becomes overly nervous when a law man calls on him. He's been siphoning monies out of the budget relegated to repairs into his own pocket since he's been posted at the Frankfort facility. On this particular morning, at Morse's request Wilson has agreed to meet with him.

Setting aside the McDonnell question for the time being, Morse opens another can of worms.

"Bill, tell me, who's this guy Captain Seavey everyone seems to be talking about?" asks Morse with an official tone to his voice.

Happy once again that the heat is not directed toward himself, Wilson lets loose with a guffaw that Morse hardly expects.

"Oh he's the closest damn thing to Captain Long John Silver that you'll ever encounter."

Morse steps back with his hands on his hips, his face slightly twisted with a puzzled look. "What the hell is that supposed to mean?"

"It means that unless you know what you're doing, it's best to stay clear of him," says Wilson.

Morse is visibly surprised at Wilson's response. He senses that in this case, Wilson doubts his abilities as a lawman.

"It sounds like you may be ah scared of this guy," shoots back Morse sarcastically.

"Let's not use the word 'scared.' I'd rather think the word 'prudent' may be a better fit," says Wilson, hesitating ever so briefly. In his world, one is careful how things are said and done, especially if one personally expects a good result.

Morse gives no thought to his next statement.

"Well on my watch, he better be watchin' himself cuz I sure as hell ain't puttin' up with none of his damned shenanigans." With that said, he nods his head in agreement with himself, turns on his heel and leaves.

Wilson shakes his head with that little shake that says, *Boy does this young buck have some things to learn,*" and returns to his paper work.

After this friction, Morse is more determined than ever to get to the bottom of this "legendary" Captain Seavey. In days to come, it's not unusual to see Morse sitting on a bluff in South Frankfort overlooking the bay with a telescope spying on the *Wanderer*. On this particular day, he spots Dee McDonnell bringing his flat bottom fishing boat alongside Seavey's ship. Two of the *Wanderer's* crew lower what appears to be a hoist made from rope netting. They are loading something, concealed by a large canvas cover, onto the boat. It's impossible to detect what this could be since it's covered so well. Nonetheless, he has his suspicions.

Heedful that the change of seasons generates the trout runs, he is very mindful of the illegal use of seine nets. He's sure, with Dee's strange activity that he's probably up to no good and is not about to be put off by the lack of visible corroborative evidence. He makes it a point to observe where Dee beaches his boat. Making his way across the bay, he rows past the *Wanderer*. The air surrounding the boat has the unmistakable pungent smell of smoked fish. As far as he's concerned, his suspicions have been confirmed.

The lack of evidence, other than what he smells, but can't see, gives him no other choice than to row on by. Nevertheless, he's hardly finished with this investigation. Making his way to Dee's beached row boat, he discovers the folded canvas used to cover the cargo also has the distinct pungent odor of smoked fish. The size of the haul he spotted earlier going aboard the *Wanderer* indicates this is scarcely an afternoon of family fishing. There isn't enough evidence to make an arrest, but in his mind, all this surely raises a red flag.

Meanwhile in town, Dee has found himself in the company of one Virginia "Ginny" VanStattler. She is one of Squeaky Schwartz's latest soiled doves. Ginny is the product of an absent alcoholic father and a sickly mother. After her mother discovered she could no longer care for her daughter, she gave her up to an orphanage at the age of ten. Ginny ran away from there at the age of sixteen, and, out of desperation to merely survive, began her career as a prostitute.

She and Dee have struck up a relationship outside the walls of Squeaky's bordello. It all began when he came across this attractive young lady in distress over losing her cat. Taking pity on the poor woman, and having nothing better to do, he agreed to help her find the missing feline. They spent the better part of an hour together, peeking into nooks and crannies where one would spend time if one were a cat. They soon found Buster counseling a cute little female on the edge of town. This event began a burgeoning relationship that has survived to this day.

Ginny is a pretty woman in many ways, but definitely has a hardness that commonly makes its way into the lives of those who choose her profession. Men, as a species, have become a source of money for women like Ginny. She has a fake persona she uses for business to lure men into a "sex for money" performance. She, nonetheless, has many qualities that Dee finds attractive. It seems she has found a father figure in him, since he is much older than herself. She has been longing for a stable man and believes that she has found it in Dee—at least what she considers to be stable enough.

The years behind Dee are peppered with about everything dishonest a man could do, but all the same, he possesses a rare kindness for the underdog. This attribute, in turn, has become a power of attraction to her. Even though his life is far from being what can be described as impeccable, compared to hers, his looks much less bumpy, or maybe it may have something to do with him never misusing her. Trustingly, she in turn uses him as a sounding board for her troubles. Understandably, he seems flattered that a woman as young and as attractive as she is, is paying attention to him. Neither of them is certain where this relationship should will take them, so at least for the moment, they let time and events shape the day.

Today he has brought her a bouquet of wild flowers he went out of his way to pick. This has elicited a girlish response from Ginny. "Oh they're lovely Dee, you're so thoughtful," she says giving him a lighthearted kiss on the cheek.

He is not sure whether this reaction is from a daughter figure, or if it's a romantic response. Either way, for the moment, he basks in its intimacy.

Both of these social castoffs long for a human closeness that they sense the other can somehow provide. However, at this point, neither is sure what kind of pairing they're developing. But the one thing that is obvious to them both is how quickly they are growing attached to the other.

"How'd you like to take a buggy ride this afternoon? I've got a place I'd like to show you," says Dee anticipating she will agree.

A smile begins to appear across her face. It's the kind that starts from the heart and makes its way to the face. "I will if you let me take a picnic. I haven't been on a picnic since I was at the orphanage."

"I can't think of anyone I'd rather eat a picnic lunch with. I've one more thing to do and I'll be back and pick you up," says Dee with his heart about to explode with an inexpressible joy.

With this date decided, he heads directly to the boat landing to retrieve his rowboat. It's much easier to load it on his wagon than to row back to camp against the current. Having secured the boat to the bed of his transport, he returns to pick up his date. This carefree attitude has induced a careless lapse in his attention. What he hasn't noticed is who is shadowing him from behind—it's none other than Warden Morse.

"You didn't tell me we were going for a boat trip," Ginny exclaims with a puzzled look.

"It's all part of the 'mysteree' when you agree to a ride with Mr. Dee," sings Dee trying to sound pawky. It elicits a small smirk from Ginny, but not much more. Wit and artfulness are not Dee's forte.

They're soon on the two track road that leads south and up river from town. The road is used primarily by fishermen, along with a few homesteaders. Careful not to be detected, officer Morse stays far enough back to keep his own rig unobserved.

"This is absolutely delightful," notes Ginny, "you couldn't have picked a more beautiful day."

Dee is about as proud as he could be for picking an event that pleases her so much. Even though the road is bumpy, the two of them couldn't be more content simply enjoying the other's company and the pleasantness of the spring day.

All the while back in town, having completed some business, Captain Seavey is making his way back to his ship when he is overtaken by one of the young crew members from the Life Saving Station.

"Captain, may I have a word with you for a moment?"

"Certainly young man, what can I do for ya?" replies Seavey.

"You've always been more than generous with us men over at the Station and we're all appreciative, so I just want to return the favor. That new game warden was in asking questions about you and Dee this morning. Then later on we observed him sitting across the bay watching your ship. He was taking account, with a lot of interest, what Dee might be bringing on board. Then we seen him doggin' Dee leavin' town," reports the young sailor.

Seavey listens with an appreciative interest.

"Young man, I want to thank you. You are, indeed, a gentleman and a scholar. I will certainly take this information seriously," says Seavey shaking the young man's hand and deciding to return as quickly as possible to the fish camp. Stopping off at Barney Yunk's livery, he rents a horse for the day and begins the twenty minute trek out to the camp.

Dee and Ginny have already arrived at the end of the road. They take care to tether the horse in the shade and are making their way down the path to the camp. Dee made an effort to tidy things up around the site, hoping Ginny won't regard him as a total slob. Picking one of the cleaner benches, he directs Ginny to sit down and draws up a table to share their picnic. She has provided a nice luncheon of pickled herring, boiled potatoes, and a pot of herbal tea. As they sit across from one another, their voiceless eyes say more of their feelings than do the words both are finding hard to communicate. She is the first to speak.

"Dee, what do you think of the work I do?" She has chosen a perfect time to ask this question. They have certainly gotten to know one another well enough to bring this question into their circle of conversation. So far they have made no demands on one another, and are not in any way obligated to behave in a prescribed norm.

"I was hoping we could avoid that question for a while, but I suppose it depends on why you ask," says Dee looking over the top of his tea cup waiting for her response.

Without overreaching the parameters of their fledgling relationship, she tries to give reasons as to why this has suddenly concerned her.

"I'm asking because I'm concerned what your thoughts are about me." She's stumbling around trying to uncover Dee's feelings for her. "I mean what do you think of me being a prostitute and all?" she continues.

"Let me ask you the same question before I answer. What do you think of yourself as a prostitute?" asks Dee.

Ginny is perceptibly worked up over this discussion.

"Damn it Dee! Can't you just answer my question?"

"Ginny I'd love ta be able to answer your question, but I ain't sure what hat I'm wearing with you when I do. Am I answering you as a friend, a Dutch uncle, a boyfriend—which?"

Their eyes meet. There is an uncomfortable pause as they continue to gaze.

"I have never had anyone as kind in my life as you Dee. Whichever of those you want to be with me is more than I've ever had. I'll take as much as you're willing to give me," says Ginny as her eyes begin to well up with tears, "I just don't want to be without you."

Without a conscious thought, lead only by a driven instinct, Dee finds himself rising from his bench and embracing this fallen angel with arms containing more care and concern than he's had with anyone since his Aggie died.

"Oh Ginny, I don't want you ta do anything that's gonna hurt you. I love you too much to see you degraded night after night by a bunch of drunken men," says Dee while taking one of his hands to wipe away her tears. They continue to hold on to one another interrupting their grasp only long enough to kiss, and kiss, and kiss.

Back at the trail-head, Captain Seavey has arrived to find both Dee's wagon containing the boat and another buggy behind it with both horses tied to a tree. There is no mistaking the other transport. It's clearly marked as that of a game warden. He slowly and methodically takes stock of his surroundings.

Assuring himself that his pistols are loaded, he takes a particular pleasure in their feel. Quietly slipping from his horse, he steals his way toward the path. Each step is measured. Not sure what to expect, he stops to look and listen for any unusual disturbance. Soon he hears what he was hoping not to hear. Even through the underbrush and brambles, he immediately recognizes Dee's voice, which is interrupted by the brashness of another male voice and a female voice that he doesn't recall hearing before. Still too far away to distinguish the conversation, he picks up his pace. In less than a minute, he covers a hundred yards down the path. Not eager to show his hand at this juncture, he remains hidden, but is able to see everything that's transpiring.

What becomes immediately clear is Warden Morse is holding a pistol on Dee and a woman he remembers bringing up from Chicago for Squeaky. From the conversation, it's evident that Morse has discovered the illegal seine net stretched across the twenty-five foot span of the river and he's taking exception to it.

"You goddam poachers are all alike. You all think you're smarter than the law, but I'm here to let you know yer dealin' with a new breed ah lawmen. I don't put up with the likes of yer kind for a minute. I'm placin' you and yer whore under arrest."

Seavey can feel his mouth go dry as he struggles with a plan. His heart is pounding along with the thought that he can't just remain where he is and wait for Morse to make the next move. While he's still struggling with the thought of what to do, someone else makes the first strike—and it's not Morse.

With cat like reflexes, Ginny has drawn a knife concealed in her garter and lunges at Morse. He is able to knock the weapon from her hand without it doing any damage. His next move is to begin to pistol whip her, knocking her to the ground. His next move shocks Dee to his very core.

"You dirty whore. Nobody pulls a knife on me and lives to tell about it," with that said, he cocks his pistol preparing to shoot the helpless unarmed woman laying defenseless on the ground.

In less than a second, Dee springs between Ginny and the pistol and takes a shot to the arm. With both of them now writhing on the ground and Morse standing over the two of them with his pistol re-cocked, it becomes apparent to Seavey that the time for thinking is over. He needs to step in quickly. He fires a shot in the air, rather than risk hitting Dee or Ginny as they are all clustered together. Morse swings around to face the direction of the shot and sees nothing but brush. Still concealed, Seavey roars out in his loudest voice, "Drop the pistol or take the next one between the eyes!"

Clearly in a panic mode, Morse's eyes dart across the whole landscape, seeing nothing but trees and undergrowth, he nonetheless places a shot in the general direction. Another shot bursts across the yard ripping Morse's hat from his head. Realizing his total disadvantage throws him into a dither.

Without being asked again, he drops his pistol from a clearly weakened hand and throws his arms in the air. He's clearly terrified.

"Please don't shoot me, please don't shoot me," he pleads out to his phantom shooter.

Stepping out from his cover with both his pistols pointed directly at Morse's head and the look of a perturbed beast, Seavey only stops when his pistol barrels are resting firmly against Morse's forehead. In the same moment, surely expecting to be executed, Morse closes his eyes and promptly begins to utter an almost sobbing sound. Instead, Seavey holsters his pistols and with all the power behind his 6ft. 6in. 300 pound body knocks Morse flat out leaving him laying unconscious on the ground.

His attention quickly turns to his wounded comrade. Ginny is also trying to comfort him. Dee has taken a bullet in the shoulder that was clearly intended for her. She is very aware of this unsolicited sacrifice to save her. She immediately begins to have guilty feelings, as though she is responsible for Dee's demise.

"Oh Dee don't die now, I need you. It's all my fault. I never should have pulled the knife."

Trying to make the best use of the time for everything that needs to be done, Seavey attempts to make sense out of what's going on. The one thing he is very aware of is Dee's need for medical attention. The next thought is to neutralize Morse's capacity to do any more damage. At once he removes Morse's manacles from his belt. He drags the unconscious man to a nearby tree, wraps his arms around its trunk, and slips his wrists into the trammels. Then he quickly turns his attention back to his fallen friend. His intention is to get Dee medical attention and then return and deal with Morse.

"Ma'am how're ya doin'? I saw him knock ya to the ground," asks Seavey with a definite look of concern.

"I'm fine, but please, we have to get Dee to a doctor. I just can't let him die now," cries Ginny, desperately trying to lift Dee. How many times has she experienced men entering her life, only to have them leave? It's a routine that's happened all too many times for her.

Examining Dee's wound a little closer, Seavey realizes that it's not life threatening. Fortunately, the bullet didn't strike any major arteries. Dee is desperately struggling to get to his feet.

"I'm fine, I'm fine," he mutters as unconsciousness overtakes him and his knees buckle beneath him. Seavey reacts quickly, catching him before he hits the ground.

"Okay Mr. Tough Guy, let's get you to town before you do any more damage to yourself," barks Seavey, carrying him back up the path to where the wagons are parked. Ginny is running along beside, thanking him for his help. It's obvious to each that they are remembering how they met. Without going into those details, together they pull the boat off Dee's wagon and arrange him in its place as comfortably as the hard planks will permit. Seavey's next step is to give Morse's horse a good swat on the back end and watch the startled critter tear across country dragging its riderless buggy behind.

By the time they reach town, Dee has regained consciousness. Doc Jamison is just coming into his office from delivering a baby. He's quite an engaging man, always ready with something humorous, especially when conditions appear fearful. His reasoning is that it's done to put the patient's mind at ease in the midst of a seeming crisis. After taking a quick glance at Dee's wound, he concurs with Seavey's earlier assessment that the wound is not in itself life threatening.

"Infection's the killer here," he says as he begins to clean the wound, talking all the time he's working. "I had an interesting case this morning," he begins, pausing long enough to catch their attention, "I had a baby born without a penis."

Ginny and Seavey give each other a glancing look—even as much pain as Dee is in, with the same awestruck expression, they all look back at Doc who is maintaining a very serious composure. Taking note of their concerned faces, he's aware that he has the attention of all three. With a wry little smirk and a bit of twinkle in his eye, Doc pauses from his wound cleaning for only a moment then adds, "But she'll have a nice place to put one in about eighteen years." Both Seavey and Ginny shake their heads at Doc's success at comic relief. Dee is trying hard not to laugh as it hurts too much.

Dee along with the other two has left the doctor with the impression that this was an accidental shooting while cleaning his gun. Doc learned a long time ago that unless you want to involve yourself in an area that you can't manage, it's best to let sleeping dogs lie. With Ginny agreeing to look after Dee until he heals enough to care for himself, Doc has a better feeling about his recovery.

"Make sure you clean that wound every day with alcohol and repack it with boiled gauze," he instructs her.

As for Seavey, he has some unfinished business with a certain game warden that has truly stepped into a pile of horse pucky. Having been on the side of the law and a lawman himself, Captain Seavey knows how this kind of case will go. It will be the word of an "honest" lawman trying to do his job against the word of a known poacher, a whore, and a suspected pirate. There is no question in his mind which way a jury of "decent" people will adjudicate.

With this clear in his mind, Seavey returns to his ship long enough to pick up first mate Archie Kerby.

"Archie that damn game warden has caused us some serious problems. He shot Dee, damn near killin' him. Right now I got him pinned to a tree out at the camp. We need to get out there and take care of him before he turns into the kind of trouble we don't want."

Archie listens as one would who believes his captain's major concern is for the welfare of his crew. Archie agrees and picks Ob, and Jack to accompany them. Taking Dee's wagon, they make the twenty minute trek back out to the camp. On the way out, Captain Seavey and the crew debate on how they are going to handle this kettle of fish.

"We're in this debacle up to our armpits," says Seavey.

They all conclude that they are going to have to "Shanghai" Morse and get him out of commission. That basically means they will have to keep him prisoner on board ship, giving him the option of becoming a compliant deck hand, or face drowning. It also means that once his hands are stained with pirate activities, he'll never be allowed to return to a law enforcement career.

Warden Morse has recovered his consciousness along with his bravado. Still well secured to the tree and hardly in any bargaining position, he begins to run his mouth.

"You sons-a-bitches are gonna pay for this you know. Cut me loose now and things'll go easier on ya."

Paying no heed to his pattering, Seavey unlocks his manacles releasing the tree from having to endure the abuse. In the meantime, the others are dragging Dee's rowboat back to the camp's shore. Seavey remanacles the still cursing game warden's hands behind his back and marches him down to the waiting row boat. A rag is stuffed in his nonstop mouth and he's placed in the bottom of the boat. Knowing the fear he had placed in this man previously, Seavey bends toward him. Within an inch of his face and looking him directly in the eyes, he gives what he hopes will be a well-taken imperative.

"If you so much as wiggle, I'll throw your sorry ass overboard and you'll be fish food. Do you understand me?"

Morse doesn't respond, remaining defiant. With a canvas tarp placed over him, Archie and Seavey plan to row him out as inconspicuously as possible and load him onto the ship without being seen. Ob and Jack are remaining in camp to handle the nets and get the remaining fish smoked and ready for shipping.

The trip down river begins without a hitch—that is until Morse decides to get frisky. He's under the tarp in the bow. Archie is in the middle manning the oars. Seavey is sitting in the stern smoking his pipe. Suddenly from under the tarp, the manacled, and still gagged, Burt Morse pops to his feet with fire in his eyes. He doesn't appear to have either a clear or unclear plan in mind. The boat begins to rock as this shifting cargo is at full height standing precariously in the bow of the boat. In a split second, he loses his balance toppling overboard. Captain Seavey is on his feet with even less of a plan. The gap between the thrashing form of Morse and the boat is quickly widening. Archie struggles with the swiftness of the current, making every effort to get the boat swung around. With all the skills Archie has in maneuvering a water craft, he's finding it nearly impossible to get this done quickly. Meantime, Morse is being carried, face down, by the current to an impossible distance for any hopes to retrieve him alive. By the time they reach him, the deed is done. He's no longer floundering and is nothing more than a piece of compliant drift material being carried along at the mercy of the river. They manage to hoist his lifeless body into the boat, silently rowing on. Upon reaching the ship, they wrap the body in the canvas tarp, storing it out of sight in the hold until a plan on how to dispose of it can be reached.

Doe, who has been absent for several days, suddenly appears with some unsettling news for Seavey. "Capn' I'm here to give ya notice that I won't be sailin' out with ya. I'm gettin' married and Daisy says she won't put up with worrin' about me bein' gone all the time. So at least for the time bein', I'll have ta be a landlubber."

In spite of Seavey's disappointment, he wishes Doe a good life. "If you ever decide you want your job back, it's yours."

With that, Doe says his good-byes to the rest of the crew, cleans out his bunk and leaves. Seavey can't help but think that now with Doe gone how handy Burt Morse could have become.

The day has come to a close. No one could ever say it has been uneventful. Pouring himself a large glass of moonshine from his ample supply, Captain Seavey is already speculating on his next venture. With sleep overtaking him, he soon retires for the night.

8 MANITOU ISLAND

The night passes by uneventfully and Seavey is up at 5:00 a.m., just in time to make 6:00 a.m. mass at St. Ann's. It's difficult to tell if his devotion is out of love for Christ and His Church or if he hopes it will serve as an insurance policy for his wayward life. Most would be inclined to believe the latter. Nonetheless, after mass he stops by to see how Dee is getting on.

Ginny is busy fussing over a breakfast of ham and eggs. Seavey stands looking through the open kitchen door. The domestic scene stops him for a moment as he recalls how his Mary looked the most appealing when she was in charge of her kitchen. It's bringing with it a sad picture, but nonetheless, also an image to be envied. Looking up, Ginny sees Seavey standing at the opening with his hat in his hand, hardly the "in charge" character she last remembered in his dealings with the warden.

"I just happened to be in the neighborhood and thought I'd stop by and see how Dee is doing," says Seavey with the hint of humility that accompanies one's speaking when they believe they may be intruding into the privacy of others.

"I'd be doin' a hell of a lot better if that damn revenuer hadn't put lead in me," says a voice from another room.

Ginny says, "Go on in. He's gettin' babied and suckin' up all he can get away with. By the way, I'm settin' a plate at the table for you."

Following Ginny's pointed finger, he finds Dee propped up in a chair with his arm in a sling.

"Damned if you ain't a sight. One thing's for sure—the devil ain't never in a hurry for them he's sure of," roars captain Seavey as he looks at the pitiful picture confronting him.

"Well you ain't the one with the bullet through ya," says Dee with the whiny little helpless voice that's worked well with Ginny. She is putting up with it for a myriad of reasons. She was falling in love with Dee, even before he took a bullet for her. *"After all he did save my life."* is her thought.

During breakfast, Seavey catches the two of them up on the demise of Warden Morse. This comes with the bidding that they keep what he is telling them a secret for as long as they wish to stay out of jail.

Changing the subject, Seavey says, "Jack and Ob are finishin' up the smokin' of the last of them fish Morse caught you with. I want you and Ginny to come on board tomorrow morning. We're going to take poor ole Warden Morse's carcass out to sea and give him a proper buryin'," says Seavey with a feigned reverence. Ginny is not sure she wants to be that deeply involved with all this, but because Dee may need her she agrees.

The next morning the two of them arrive in time to see and smell the last haul of smoked trout being loaded in the hold. The pungent smell is the smell of cash.

Captain Seavey has arranged for Ginny and Dee to remain in his quarters until they pass through the breakwater walls. "No sense in drawing unnecessary attention to the extra passengers on board."

As soon as this is accomplished, Archie brings up some folding deck chairs from below and arranges them so Dee and Ginny can view the trip as somewhat of a pleasure excursion. After about a half hour of sailing straight west into the lake, Captain Seavey orders Jack and Ob to bring the canvas-wrapped Morse up from the hold. The ship is silent other than the soft sound of the bow making light ripples. The only visible portions of Morse are his legs. A chain has been wrapped around them. The ship's hoist is hooked to the chain with a release mechanism. On Captain Seavey's order, Willis, operating the ship's hoist, lifts the body out of it's canvas crypt and swings the arm out over the port side. As the body sways in rhythm with the ship, it leaves the impression that he may be flying. For a moment Captain Seavey seems to be saying something under his breath. He then makes the sign of the cross on his chest and motions for Willis to release the body. The weight of the chain flips the body around and ole Morse hits the water feet first and sinks out of sight.

Everyone is quiet. Dee traces his fingers lightly over his wound with the thought that had circumstances been even a little bit different, that body could just as well have been his. Ginny is crying—not for Morse, but for the whole state of affairs. Despite her worldliness, this experience leaves her shaken. The whole situation is so far removed from her comfort level that she finds herself grabbing on to Dee with a grip that is also an alien response to anything she has thus far experienced in her life.

The trip back to port begins with a somberness, but it soon turns to life as usual for those on board. Ginny is fussing over Dee's wound. The crew is busy checking how the sails are performing. Captain Seavey is giving some thought to his next venture. For the moment, he's looking at the two of these love birds and wondering how he can best use what both have to offer. Since Doe quit, the ship has lost its cook. For what he has planned next, he's going to need Dee. With the ship coming back to

Frankfort, Seavey motions for Ginny and Dee to go below to his quarters. He follows them down with a look that suggests he has something on his mind. As soon as they are settled, he poses a question.

"How'd the two of you like to come and work for me? I need cook and a deck hand. The two of you could easily fit the bill if you choose to say yes."

The two of them are taken by surprise with this offer. They look at each other in a puzzled way. Ginny is the first to speak.

"If you think I'm going to bunk in with all these guys, you must be out of your mind."

"I've already given that some thought. There's a small storage room off the galley that can be cleared out with just enough room for a bunk," says Seavey. "As for you Dee, you can take Doe's bunk.

Both Ginny and Dee look at one another as though someone had just breathed new life into them. Ginny is ready for anything that will get her out of Squeaky's bordello, especially if it allows her to be with Dee. As for Dee, he has at last accepted his wife's death and is ready to move on. Without words, Dee can see on Ginny's face how ready she is to make this change.

It also raises another concern.

"How you gonna deal with a one armed gimp like me? There ain't a whole hell of a lot I can do," says Dee protectively.

Captain Seavey strokes his stubbled face as if in thought.

"I've already thought of that, too. I've got just the job fer ya Dee. Our next project is a bit more detailed. I want ya to do some barterin' with these outlaws around here and see if ya can't trade some whiskey for guns. Down in the hold are enough jugs of moonshine whiskey to keep this county drunk for a month. I'm going to need a few more rifles," pausing for a moment, he thoughtfully adds, "more than we already have, along with enough cartridges to last us awhile."

Seavey couldn't have picked a better man for the job. Dee knows every poacher, gun runner, and bootlegger in these parts.

"Sounds like you're plannin' a war Cap'n," says Dee with a small knowing smirk.

"And you probably got an idea what we're gonna be battlin'," replies Seavey with the same knowing grin. "Meantime, I'm going down state to a dealer in Grand Rapids that I'm sure will be ready to take these fish."

Dee agrees to do what he can and after dark the crew carries enough moonshine ashore to get the job done. Pudd Hesster is a local roust-a-about and the first person Dee contacts to give him a hand.

"Pudd, I'll give you a gallon of whiskey if you can help me get a half dozen good aught 3 Springfields." Pudd's eyes light up like it is Christmas. He knows the area very well and the "no questions asked" routine that it will take to get the rifles. He also enjoys the chance to be an important link to the local underworld where poachers and bootleggers find a common undertaking. In this instance it's whiskey for guns. Captain Seavey is confident that on his return, Dee will have this project ready to roll.

The more difficult task has landed in the lap of Ginny. She has approached Squeaky with the news that she will be quitting. Squeaky, like all pimps, regards his stable of whores as his property.

"What the hell you mean your leavin' me. You owe me, you little wench. I paid to get you up here from Chicago when you had no place else to go. I've given you a place to live and taken damn good care of you. And now you think you're going to walk out of here? You better think again." With that as a final statement, he gives her a good back-hand across the face, splitting her lip. It's a hard enough blow that it knocks her to the floor. The blood begins to flow, staining her teeth and mouth. This is nothing new to her, as her relationship with men has been a mess her entire life.

"Now look what the hell you made me do," bellows Squeaky. "You ain't gonna be worth a tinker's dam till your mouth heals up. For the next week you're gonna be my goddam housekeeper, so get your ass in there and start some cleanin'."

Ginny can feel the rage within her starting to build. Nonetheless, for the present she is willing to bide her time. Dee is out with Pudd someplace in the county and won't be back for a couple of days. It's just as well because Ginny has her own plan to handle Squeaky. What she has planned is something women think about but rarely put into action. Closing the door on even a small indefinite bit of safety is dangerous for these women, unless they already have their feet securely planted in the door of someplace even more safe. Having found this security with Dee, she is emboldened to make her plan become reality.

As is Squeaky's normal habit, he starts his drinking about mid-evening and continues until he closes the bordello at midnight. It's a week day with business on the slow side. Consequently, his drinking has taken hold of him early. By midnight the bordello has been closed for an hour and Squeaky is already passed out. Slowly and purposely, Ginny creeps up the stairs to his room with a broom in hand. Putting her ear near the door, she can hear him snorting in his usual drunken state. She quietly tests the door knob, it twists open. Pushing the door open a bit more, she can just make him out in the dim moonlight that's trying to pierce the grimy window.

He's laying face down on an unmade bed, buck-naked, in a spread-eagle position. Her thoughts could cut rags. Setting the broom aside for the moment, she removes four pieces of cord from her apron pocket. Careful not to wake him, she begins her task by slowly and carefully tying one cord around each of his wrists and ankles. The other ends are fastened tightly to each of the bed posts. Her next step is to pick up her broom from its resting place, flipping it around and fitting it in her hand as one would a club. Walking over to the puny naked body of Squeaky Schwartz, she lifts the broom handle high over her head and brings it down on his skinny naked ass with the force of an angry banshee. WHAP!!! WHAP!!! WHAP!!! Squeaky comes out of his stupor gasping for a breath. He has just sucked enough drool into his windpipe to cause him to go into a convulsed struggle to catch some air and cough at the same time. It stings like an east wind. With his hands and feet tied and his face buried in his pillow, he cannot see his attacker. WHAP!!WHAP!!WHAP!! Ginny continues her revenge.

Squeaky's painful howls resound through the entire bordello bringing the rest of girls to investigate its origin. One by one, they stand outside his room watching Ginny continue her pay back. Not one of them so much as lifts a finger to aid their hapless panderer. Powerless to stop her, Squeaky is caught between sobbing, gasping, and begging his unseen assailant for mercy. Ignoring his pitiful pleas, she continues to beat the poor helpless lout until she breaks the broom stick. By now she is too exhausted to get another. Without a word, Ginny gathers up her few belongings and departs. She leaves her miserable victim still rendered powerless and tied to his bed.

While all of this is taking place, Dee is busy with Pudd twelve miles inland in the small village of Honor. They're meeting with two brothers who are willing to make an exchange of whiskey for guns providing the deal is heavily favored to their advantage. Since Captain Seavey has no cost in the hooch, Dee is comfortable giving them a break. A good rifle along with an ample supply of ammunition can sell for upwards of $10. The agreement is made for three gallons of whiskey for each of the six units of guns and ammo. The deal is finished except for the four of them sharing a drink to consummate the deal. Since there isn't a limit to the size of their drink, they spend the rest of the night in the wagon somewhere along the way back to Frankfort sleeping off their excesses.

Late the following morning, they arrive with six new Springfield rifles. Unencumbered by any time restraints, they stop at Favrow's diner to grab breakfast. The topic of the day is how Warden Morse was stupid enough to have his horse and cart run off leaving him, only God knows where. The beast arrived alone at the livery some time during the night.

With Captain Seavey returning, having left his load of smoked fish in Grand Rapids, Dee with the rifles and cartridges, and Ginny's success at leaving Squeaky's, everything is set to begin the next project. The ship is restocked with all they are going to need for several weeks. One more trip to Doc Jamison is required only to be told that Dee's shoulder is doing well, he has no infection and the wound is healing in fine shape. Within the day they have closed the books on Frankfort for awhile, happy to let sleeping dogs lay for a spell.

For Ginny it's as though a whole new world is opening up before her. For most people the constraints of a ship this size, surrounded only by water, gives them a feeling of confinement. For her, it's the ticket to a freedom that she has never experienced before in her life. Other than a bit of raw tissue inside her mouth to remind her of what she no longer has to endure, she feels exhilarated. Standing in the bow, the breeze licks against her cotton dress forcing it to cling to her body, exaggerating her young figure. With the sun stroking her long, wind-whipped, amber-colored hair, she strikes an almost regal pose. Dee has fallen hard for this fallen angel. She may as well be the Madonna in his eyes. There are only few men in the world that could accept a seamy past such as hers and Dee is one of them. She is most fortunate that he has always seen beyond appearances and cares for her as a person despite her association with the bordello.

For reasons of her own, she has not disclosed her falling out with

Squeaky. Maybe it's because no one has romanticized her person as Dee has and she doesn't want to burst his bubble just yet. She can't help but wonder what he would have thought of her had he witnessed the ballyhoo. So far living up to the vision he has of her hasn't been so hard, but their relationship is still in the budding stage. At this stage, she is willing to sit at his feet blinking her eyes at his every word. Up to now this stratagem hasn't cost her anything. Without a doubt, further testing certainly could still be down the road.

As soon as the ship is stabilized, Captain Seavey calls the crew on deck for a meeting.

"You boys," for a moment he catches himself, while looking straight at Ginny, quickly adding, "and girls are probably wondering what I've been planning for the past week with these new Springfields. Today is the day to tell you we are on our way to the Manitou Islands. We are all going on a private hunt. Those islands are blessed by our Creator to be teeming with venison and I have a buyer in Chicago ready to take all the venison we can supply."

A hoot goes up from every man on the ship.

"Captain, you sure know how to give a man a good getaway vacation. It's not even deer season and you've already found a hunting reserve for us," says Archie with tongue in cheek.

Once on the high seas, as a precautionary measure, Seavey orders the swivel cannon be brought on deck and placed back on its mountings in the bow. Its two pound ball is capable of puncturing the hull of any wooden ship. When in port, it is placed below deck so as not to draw unnecessary questions. Seeing it mounted on deck one time by a curious spectator, Seavey was asked what he was so afraid of. He answered succinctly, "Not a damn thing sir, not a damn thing."

The Manitou Islands lay off the coast of Leland on the northern part of Michigan's lower peninsula. Dee has worked these islands in the past and is ready to act as both a scout and guide. Along with Captain Seavey, Dee is a crack shot. Both are reported to be able to shoot the eyes out of a fly at fifty yards. They're all hopeful of a good hunt. Once the mainland is left behind, so are the lawmen. There is very little, if anything, to act as a deterrent or to thwart their efforts.

"What I want to do is take some time and let Dee here show us the ropes. He knows these islands like the back of his hand," says Captain Seavey turning the meeting over to Dee.

As well as Dee knows these men, having this kind of attention on himself makes him feel uneasy. Nevertheless, he manages to pull himself together to carry on.

"I built a huntin' shack up here a few years ago when me and Cap'n were poachin' for a couple weeks. It's probably gonna need some renovatin', so we're gonna take a few days to get 'er back in shape. With the good Lord willin' and the creek not risin', we should be out of here and in Chicago in a week."

Meantime Captain Seavey is maneuvering the *Wanderer* into a deep water hole on the east side of the island. It's a spot that allows him to bring his ship in closer to shore insuring only a few limited yards to ferry their supplies. Being this close is a great time saver and with a little luck will prove to be beneficial in loading 150 pound deer carcasses from shore to ship.

Within the day, the crew has arranged the hunting cabin to allow Ginny to provide meals without having to return to the schooner. The following day Captain Seavey and first mate Archie make the short trek into Leland to procure enough ice from the city ice house to cool the hold down to about 40 degrees Fahrenheit. It's the ideal temperature to cool a hanging deer.

Simultaneously, for the men on the island the hunt begins. Dee has placed each man on a ridge that surrounds a small inland watering hole. Each hunter is in possession of a 1903 Springfield. These rifles pack enough power to bring down any of the largest deer these men are likely to encounter. Being strictly meat hunters, they aren't particular what size or sex the deer happens to be. If it wanders into their peep sights, it will be just another dead deer ready to provide an expensive meal for a Chicago diner. The terrain is tough when it comes to dragging these beasts to the shore, so some considerations are given to the size they are willing to contend with. Dee's final words are crucial to the success of this project, "Don't shoot anybody."

After Dee has placed the crew around the ridge, he returns to his own favorite spot. It's only a stone's throw from the lake's edge making it easy to drag the kill to the jon boat. His arm is healing well. He's particularly grateful that his wound is not in his right shoulder which would make taking the recoil from a rifle impossible.

He has a special deer hunting tactic that he's not ready to share with the rest of his compatriots. After bringing out a windup alarm clock and a galvanized water pail, he searches out a familiar game trail. When he determines where the most vulnerable spot is for him to get a clear shot, he sets the ticking clock inside the pail and retreats to a brushy deer blind providing him a good view. Deer are elusive, but they are also curious. The ticking clock reverberating from the metal pail across the forest is bound to attract the attention of one of these inquisitive creatures. It's not long before he makes out the familiar movement of a tan colored roe. He can barely see it through the foliage. Not able to get a clear shot, Dee's experience tells him to be patient until he is in a better position. His intention is to drop the critter with no more than one shot. Soon his patience pays off. Unable to resist the temptation of investigating the ticking sound, a large buck steps into firing range. BAMM! The buck drops without a whimper.

At this time of the year, these animals lose their horns and don't grow new ones for a couple of months. This buck has a rack that is about to fall off, as the buds of the next rack begin to force their way through his skull. In spite of Dee's overwhelming propensity to poach, he still enjoys the thrill of bagging a large deer with or without horns.

All morning, the sound of shooting resonates through the forest as deer after deer is dropped by the rest of the crew. By evening, Captain Seavey returns to find sixteen deer carcasses waiting to be loaded. It's about all the ship's cargo hold is capable of transporting.

"Good job boys!" roars Seavey when he sees the carcasses. "I wish I could have been here with you. From the looks of it, this must have been like shootin' fish in a barrel."

"Pretty damn close," says second mate Willis sporting a big grin. "We was done shootin' by noon."

The hold is soon arranged to accommodate sixteen hanging deer. The bottom is lined with blocks of ice packed in sawdust to act as an insulator extending the life of the ice. All of the ice that's being used was harvested from last winter's frozen lake, carefully packed in sawdust in well-insulated ice houses and is sold throughout the year.

Ginny is preparing a feast from a back strap of one of the small deer they held back to feed the crew. Dee has been particularly attentive to her as he fusses in the small galley, only managing to get in her way.

"For Pete's sake, Dee will you get out of my way till I'm done getting this grub put together?"

He can't help himself. He is still floating around on the pink cloud created by her attentiveness. Coming up behind her standing over a pan of frying venison steaks, he wraps his arms around her small waist enough for her ample breasts to rest on his folded arms.

"Ginny will you marry me?"

It's a question he has never rehearsed. The fact that he said these words is as much of a surprise to him as it is to Ginny. All the same, by putting her past to rest, Dee feels this relationship has matured enough to present her with this question. It's the natural result of a trust that's developed through the different phases enveloping their growing relationship. He feels the impact of his question on her as she hesitates for a moment before swinging her whole body around. With tears welling up in her eyes and her heart about to leap from her breast, she grabs his leathery face in both her hands and draws him down until their lips meet. These are words she never expected to hear from anyone other than an intoxicated client. She is left speechless as her fingers touch her gasping, still quivering lips. It's as though this will help to calm her enough to begin to form words.

"Yes Dee, yes, yes yes!" These words are the most pleasing words Dee can ever remember hearing. His heart is lifted higher than the crow's nest. Not willing to waste a moment of this excitement, he pulls Captain Seavey aside long enough to tell him the news and ask him if he will be so kind as to marry them. Seavey receives this news with a blank stare for a moment as feelings from his past overcome him on his blind side. He had selfishly left the love of his life for the sea until she grew tired of the abandonment and divorced him on grounds of desertion. Catching himself in this momentary lapse, a wide grin gradually makes its way across his face, roaring with laughter as only he can.

"Hell yes, old friend. I'd be honored to tie the old ball and chain around the leg of as good a friend as you."

With that agreement made, and while still roaring with laughter, he grabs Dee up off his feet and swings him around in a circle.

Arrangements are made the next morning interrupting their departure. Ginny appears on deck with a signature bouquet of wild island flowers picked by Dee just for this occasion. She looks stunningly radiant in the brilliance of the morning sun. Since her break with Squeaky, the stress lines webbing her face have disappeared. Dee, in his own way, has prepared himself for this very special occasion. He has dipped himself in the lake long enough to refer to it as a bath, his hair is wet and slicked back, and he is wearing his cleanest dirty shirt. With what they both have to work with, Ginny looks very feminine and Dee looks very masculine. Both are adequately nervous, but happy.

Captain Seavey has put on a different captain's cap. This one is a newer style that reads "CAPTAIN" across the front. He looks quite the professional. Standing on deck smiling, wearing his vest and seaman's coat, and holding his little book containing the marriage protocol, he motions them both forward. Looking very demure, Ginny makes her way in front. Watching Dee slowly following behind, one could think he may be having a change of heart and contemplating jumping overboard. On the other hand, he is out of his everyday element and somewhat hesitant with all the unfamiliar officialness this ceremony is taking.

The crew is standing around with goofy grins that make them look like Cheshire cats. Within five minutes they are declared man and wife. Captain Seavey tells Dee he may kiss the bride and with another nod he motions to Jack. At this subtle signal, still grinning from ear to ear, Jack begins to crank the fog horn to honor the occasion. Ginny unceremoniously throws her bouquet at Jack's stupid attempt to celebrate. He manages to duck and uproariously continues his cranking.

The bride and groom are allowed to retire to Ginny's pantry bedroom for the rest of the morning, but not without the crew interrupting with a shivaree of banging pans, and the fog horn accompanying their hilarious laughter. By afternoon, the ship is taking on a more sober note as they begin to get serious-minded again about getting this load of venison to a Chicago market.

Because of the unfavorable winds, sailing requires a tacking method of zigzagging the schooner in and out of the wind. This guarantees at least a three day trip before they can unload. Not one to waste time, they keep their sails full night and day, arriving on schedule.

The taste for venison year around is unrelenting in the high end restaurants in the big cities. With this in mind, Seavey understands he can get a good price if he plays his cards right. Most of the beef that passes through the cattle yards in Chicago ends up in various slaughter houses owned by what can be best described as gangsters. There is a large fishery, named Booth Fisheries, which is also rumored to have underground connections. They are considered to be attempting to establish themselves on the forefront of the venison black market.

The man said to be on the vanguard of this operation is a Booth contractor named is Zig Traub. He considers himself a man who gets things done and by that he means—done his way. Like many big city companies during this period, they don't necessarily have an aversion to poaching any sellable game. The success of this activity is to not get caught. Having a lot of important contacts high up in government positions also decreases the chances of anything sticking to them for long. Zig has heard of Seavey and his exploits and is prepared to make him a deal that will give Booth Industries a slice of the venison trade. Considering the price he has given Seavey, Zig believes he has a proposition Seavey can't turn down. Pumping his hand with a wide grin, Zig lays out his proposal.

"Captain Seavey, you're a damn good supplier for us. I know you're capable of a lot more if you had a bigger operation. What we at Booth would like to do is to supply you with a ship twice the size of what you have now along with a crew. All that would be required of you is to supply us with venison year round. We would be willing to put you on the payroll and give you a percentage of the profits."

Seavey at his full six foot six inches, towers over this pipsqueak of a gangster and returns his condescending grin with one of his own, at the same time releasing his hand.

"So if I take all the risk, out of the graciousness of your hearts, you folks will give me some small pittance for the chances I'm taking, and you keep the lion's share for yourselves." he roars with laughter. It's a typical response he always has when someone is trying to boondoggle him with their flimflam. It's his way of letting them know that despite him being a country boy, he's not about to be bamboozled by their city ways. Instead he folds up his payment, sticks it in his pocket, and walks away still shaking his head at Zig's attempt to play him for a sucker.

For the moment Zig is left speechless—not his typical response and certainly not one he's comfortable with. He's certainly not about to go down without an aggressive show. Trying his best to regain the upper hand, he shouts after Seavey hoping to get the last word. "You're making one damn big mistake you know. You have no idea what we are capable of doing. We can destroy you in a minute."

Captain Seavey can feel the beginning of an effect at these words. It starts at his heels, shoots from there up his legs, jumps to his spine, and immediately dashes unimpeded up to the hair on the back of his neck leaving it bristling. Without turning around, he gives his only reaction as an extra loud roaring laugh. This only infuriates Zig all the more. Those that know Seavey would know that this reaction suggests they should tread very carefully from here on.

9 BOOTH FISHERIES

By the next morning, Archie has rigged the sails for a nice south-east breeze guaranteeing it to be an easy navigation back up north. All the crew, including Ginny, had a night out in Chicago so it's business as usual for the *Wanderer*. As is common, the traffic is heavy at the mouth of the Chicago River, but then very quickly thins and spreads out as each ship has a different destination.

The weather is clear and sunny. The crew is busy cleaning out the water and sawdust from the hold. There is nothing that makes Captain Seavey happier than a clean and orderly ship.

The cannon had been hidden away during their time spent in the Chicago port. "Bring her back out and mount her up, I like to see her sittin' proud on the bow," orders the captain. The rest of the crew appears to be just as anxious to have it back in its proper place. In short order, they have it remounted.

Meanwhile, Willis is at the top of one of the mast poles repairing a frayed tie down. He likes to spend much of his time up there.

"I get a good overall feel of the ship when I'm up there alone, like it's spiritual or somthin'," he says. At the moment, he's paying particular attention to another ship that's about a mile off their stern. It's been tracking them all morning. Using a telescope, he discovers the words "BOOTH FISHERIES" on a banner flying off a mast pole. Willis climbs down and reports this discovery.

"Cap'n, just to let you know, we got us a Booth boat trackin' us."

Seavey's head snaps in the direction Willis is pointing. Grabbing the telescope, he focuses in on the probable intruder. Holding the glass to his eye, he watches the trailing ship for a few minutes.

"Well, well, what have we got here?" he mutters nearly inaudibly. Handing the glass back to Willis, he's satisfied that he's seen enough for the present.

"Keep a good eye on 'em," says Seavey.

The afternoon turns into evening with no change in course from their retinue. Seavey's plan is to sail all night with two hour watches. At dusk, he gives the order to tack off 90 degrees to the port side. Now closely watching the Booth boat, they are not surprised when it follows suit. Running with no lights, the *Wanderer* waits until after dark and then makes a move. Captain Seavey has given the order to turn 180 degrees to the starboard side. Predictably this maneuver will leave the Booth boat wandering about without them. Soon they're back on course heading toward the Manitou Islands, hopefully alone.

As morning arrives, there is no lack of seafaring traffic, and as hoped, no sign of the Booth boat. They still have another twenty-four hours before they arrive at North Manitou. Quite confident that he has managed to shake this likely nemesis, Captain Seavey relaxes his guard, allowing the crew time to nap, relax, and clean the rifles for the upcoming hunt.

This down time shortly turns to challenging one another to arm wrestling competitions. Ob is usually the instigator of that—and the usual winner until Captain Seavey lays his elbow on the table—then all bets are off. Story telling is also a favorite past time. This past winter Dee had heard from a guy up in Escanaba about a guy who had gotten in a barroom brawl with Seavey and didn't survive the clash. He hadn't had the opportunity to question Seavey about it and is taking advantage of this lull to bring the incident up in the hopes he'll tell the story.

"What happened to that guy anyway Cap'n?"

Seavey ponders the question for a moment before giving an answer.

"Oh hell, that guy got what he deserved. That all happened back when I was working as an Indian agent for the government. He was keepin' the Indians drunk all the time, tradin' 'em whiskey for their furs. When I tracked him down, he was crazy drunk in Ed Higgins' saloon and not about to be arrested. When I ordered him out, he told me I wasn't man enough to take him out. To impress on him how untrue that was, I was goin' ta have to fight him. He proved to be pretty tough. Right away he started swingin' tables and chairs and wreckin' poor ole Ed's bar. We probably fought for the better part of two hours. He had thrown about every bottle of Ed's whiskey at me till he'd smashed nearly all of 'em. That's when it came ta me ta end this fiasco quick or there wasn't gonna be enough liquor left ta pour myself a drink."

They're all sitting around waiting for the end of this debacle when Dee finally asks, "Well, what the hell did you do to this guy to end the fight?"

It's as though Seavey is reliving the next circumstance involving this victim. "I could see the look on Higgins' face every time that bastard would smash another bottle, so soon's I got him on the floor, I ordered Higgins to bring me a hammer and some nails. While I was sittin' on him, I commenced to nail his clothes with him in 'em to the plankin'. I left him there while I got a drink from what whiskey wasn't broken. When I come back, he was passed out. I told Higgins to leave him there till I could pick him up the next morning."

The whole crew is all ears as he spins this piece of lore that has made him a legend in his own time. "What happened then?" Dee continues to ask.

"Nothin' really. I wrote my report up sayin' he was resistin' arrest but I had the problem nailed down," says Seavey with a grin and a wink.

The entire crew is aware that many of the actions ordered by their charismatic captain are mostly illegal, immoral, and often life threatening, but nonetheless, they find themselves drawn to the excitement of this life and are willing to set aside any notions to the contrary.

For the moment, all is well on board. They have plenty of food, fresh water, good winds, camaraderie, and a captain that treats them well. The rest of the voyage is uneventful. Upon arrival, they find their camp in need of a face lift and quickly getting busy setting things back up again.

Captain Seavey and Archie leave the crew to begin the hunt without them while the two of them return to the town of Leland on the mainland for another load of ice. Dee has very little to say. By now all the guys know the routine and have teamed up back around Lake Tamarack. Dee's shoulder is healing pretty well and he finds he can begin to put a bit more stress on it, but he still prefers the solitude of the hunting spot he's chosen for himself. He has set his ticking clock and metal pail combination along his favorite game trail and is making himself comfortable when something catches his attention that should not be happening—he hears shooting way off in the southern part of the island. This is a circumstance that Dee definitely believes is worth investigating.

The island is some seven miles long and at its widest maybe four miles. The shooting is probably close to three or four miles from their camp. There is a lifesaving station on the island, but it's way over on the east side. (Captain Seavey has intentionally positioned himself and the men on the west side, not wanting to have any engagement with officials of any sorts.) The rest of the crew is positioned around the Lake Tamarack area. It's swampy and full of cedar and not wanting to take the time to fetch one of them, he opts to investigate alone. There is a trail running along the beach that will take him nearly to the end of the island. The shooting is now from the Lake Tamarack area as well as the southern region. Dee is sure the lake shooting is the crew from the *Wanderer*, but is totally mystified by the southern shots.

The shooting noise grows more clear and distinct as he draws closer to its source. There are only a few residents on the island. The number of shots and how they seem to overlap indicate there are several people doing the shooting. What he sees next sets him back on his heels. There in the distance is a four-masted ship anchored some 200 feet off shore. It appears that there are maybe a dozen men shooting at some objects floating around the ship as in target shooting. He's close enough to hear their loud shouts echoing across the water, but remains in the underbrush unseen.

"What the hell are these idiots up to?" asks Dee out loud as though by doing so an answer will materialize. It only takes a closer look—a hanging banner suddenly unfurls in a gust of wind with the distinct inscription BOOTH FISHERIES answers this question.

"My God, the Booth people have re-surfaced," exclaims Dee to himself. Making his way back to camp, his thoughts are swirling with how he believes Seavey is going to react to this news.

"The captain sure as hell ain't gonna go for this bull crap."

The sharp cacophonous crack of rifle shots follows him all the way back up the trail. It's obvious to him that these guys are not much more than a bunch of city slicker thugs hired by Booth to encroach on their hunting grounds. By the time he arrives back at camp, the boys are beginning to hang their morning kill on the buck poles. As usual they have managed to harvest enough to fill the *Wanderer's* cargo hold.

"Where you been Dee? We was getting concerned after we heard all that shootin' in your direction. Then when you didn't show up right away, we figured you might ah got mixed up in sumpin'," says Willis overtly concerned.

"It's that goddam bunch from Booth that was doggin' us all the way from Chicago," says Dee swatting at a deer fly buzzing around his head. "They ain't nothin more than a bunch ah Zig's city slickin' goons."

With nothing else to do but wait for Captain Seavey, Dee leads them to where he caught sight of the ship. It remains anchored in the same spot, but the shooting has ceased. On closer inspection, they detect a dingy tied up on the beach.

"The bastards have come ashore," says Dee with a distinct tone of distrust in his voice.

"How many of 'em do you think there are?" asks Willis. Being second mate, he's been left in charge and feels he should be doing something, he's just not sure what.

"I counted at least a dozen that was shootin', but they wasn't actin' like they was crew. They was all dressed up with fancy suspenders and fedoras—you know like them city slickin' gangster types," reports Dee more specifically.

Willis ponders this for a moment. "I'll bet Zig hired a bunch of sharp shooters to do his huntin' after Cap'n told him ta get lost." He pauses for a moment with a worried look then adds, "Cap'n sure as hell ain't gonna go for this jack."

In the late afternoon, the *Wanderer* returns with its belly full of ice. Little by little Captain Seavey is whittling his supply of liquor down. In this instance it was booze for ice. On the Great Lakes, alcohol trades better than money with many vendors.

After anchoring in the deeper water, Captain Seavey and Archie ferry themselves to shore only to be met with a distressed-looking crew. Within minutes Willis brings them up to speed with the day's happenings.

"What do you think they're up to Cap'n?" asks Willis, looking for verification of what he already suspects. As was earlier predicted, Captain Seavey goes into a fury.

"If this bunch of pretty boys think they can horn in on our operation, they better be ready for a fight. I'll kick their asses up around their necks and you boys can take turns kickin' their damned heads off."

The crew always looks forward to their Captain's straight forward leadership resolutions. Even though they're pretty much predictable, it nevertheless takes the anxiety out of things, putting them all on the same page.

Dee, together with Captain Seavey, know this island like the backs of their hands. In a quieter and more reflective moment, Seavey, directing his comments at the crew, says "I'm pretty certain this bunch ain't nothin more than a caboodle of morons with guns. This sure don't mean we can dismiss 'em. But what it does mean is that for now, we're gonna sit by and not do a damn thing until they show their hand. At that point if they get in our way all bets are off for this lot."

Letting this imperative sink in, he's done with being reflective, returning to the task at hand.

"Okay boys, let's get this venison cooled down for now. We'll work on the rest of it later," roars Seavey over any other questions. It's apparent that he's not taking this surprise threat lightly, but getting the meat on ice is imperative. The type of venison going for the big bucks is the aged carcass that has been hanging in forty degree temperatures until it takes on a greenish hue. Taking care now assures the meat can develop this property during the voyage to the Chicago market. With this task readily accomplished, he has a moment to eyeball the Booth ship, who he is sure has also been watching the *Wanderer*. Rubbing his hand across the stubble growing over his chin, he works out a plan. Gathering the crew together, he's ready to announce a solution.

"I'm sure this moron, Zig, will try something stupid. I'm just not certain when or where. In order to cover all our bases, we're going to split up. Willis, you, Ob, and Jack stay in camp tonight. Set up a watch like we do on board and keep your eyes peeled. It's hard to tell what these weasels are up to, but I know damn well I don't want to be taken by surprise. The rest of us will stay on board and do the same."

The mosquitoes begin coming out to hunt their prey. This compels the party to break up with those remaining on shore getting inside and the others making their way to the ship. Captain Seavey steps into the darkness and a shot suddenly rings out. The slug whizzes by only inches from his head. It is every man is for himself and everyone dives flat to the ground. Willis immediately doused the lantern and, along with everyone else, is quietly lying as still as death. A half a dozen shots ring out whizzing over their heads. The terror continues for several more bursts. For the moment they are defenseless. Their rifles are in the cabin and out of reach. From the sound of splintering wood, much of the attention given by these assailants is to the cabin as volley after volley rips through the walls. The darkness readily reveals the locations of the attackers by the bright bursts of fire from each rifle barrel. Captain Seavey has long since drawn his pistols and fires back at each one of these fiery positions. After hearing a scream from one of the assassins, the firing ceases. The sound of breaking underbrush announces a hasty retreat of these would be assailants. It's obvious one of the combatants has been struck.

The whole crew remains still for several more minutes listening for any sound of a returning assault. In a low, but audible voice, Captain Seavey finally breaks the silence. "Anyone hit?"

Each crew member, even though some voices are shaky, announces their safe condition. Again, in the same low voice, he orders, "Everyone back to the ship!" Stumbling through the dark down to the shore, they all manage to get aboard the jon boat. As quietly as possible, they make their way to the safety of the *Wanderer*. Once aboard Captain Seavey prepares for a hasty retreat.

"Weigh anchor and set the sails!"

Within minutes they are putting distance between themselves and the island along with its imminent danger. Seavey is far from willing to surrender to this assault and orders a temporary retreat toward the far north end of the island to await daylight. Upon arrival, first mate Archie sets the anchor and forms the watch rotation for the rest of the night. Meanwhile, the remainder of the crew retires to their bunks hoping to get some rest after all the uproar.

Captain Seavey has also retired to his quarters. Pulling a jug of moonshine from under his bunk, he pours out a large glass. Sitting on the edge of his bed, he stares wide-eyed at nothing in particular as he drinks and reviews the evening's happenings. The whiskey, along with the steady, gentle rocking of the boat, the absence of mosquitoes and rifle shots soon soothes his raw nerves enough to allow him to fall into a slumber.

Without warning or having given an invitation, he once again finds himself being confronted by his adversarial phantom Indian women, Abequa. He feels the usual coldness and chilling dread upwelling in his whole body. He knows what is coming and he can't wake himself up to avoid her charges against him.

"You do remember when you selfishly sold all you owned and abandoned your young wife and daughter to chase a pipe dream of riches in the gold fields? You do remember when you came back that instead of making it up to them by supporting them, you then abandoned them for this ridiculous pirate life that satisfies some sick need you seem to have for the absurd? God has no room for the likes of you. Why would He ever consider rewarding you for your repulsiveness? You are lost and you will suffer in hell in a way much worse than your family has suffered trying to survive without your support."

Her diatribe of charges against him hits the same way on every one of her visits. He has no defense. When she slips away, she always leaves him heartsick, guilty and forsaken. It's the very thing this demon knows will destroy him. In the morning, he awakens with the reality of this mental imagery unwilling to demonstrate any restraint. Abequa's entire purpose is to accuse him, forming his guilt into insufferable and diabolical hauntings that hang over him like a dark cloud. His first thought is that he must find a priest. He has confessed his sins many times to many different priests, always receiving the same penance.

"Reunite yourself with your family in whatever way is possible."

Arriving on deck and refusing Ginny's offer of breakfast, he orders Archie to set sail to Leland, which is at least a couple hours away. Most of the crew has seen their captain like this many times in the past. They know when he appears like this to follow orders and don't press for any explanation. As soon as they are within sight of the harbor, Captain Seavey takes the wheel. He settles on a spot where he seems to have anchored at some time in the past. With only a curt, "I'll be back before noon," he orders the dingy lowered and leaves for shore alone. Once on shore, he walks directly to the livery stable and rents a horse. Within minutes, he is on his way to the church of St. Mary Of The Lake. A half hour later he arrives. After letting Father Martin's housekeeper know he's there, he goes directly to the confessional.

Father Martin is no stranger to Captain Seavey. He's very aware of Seavey's activities and his past life as well. Like every other priest along the Michigan and Wisconsin coastline, they have all become acquainted with the demons living in this man. His confessions always remain the same in how he has abandoned his family. The penance he's asked to perform remains the same. He receives the promise of absolution upon his amends to his family. His intentions are honest in that he has a strong desire to fulfill his penance. With a renewed sense of fulfilling this commitment—but just not today—he always feels much better when he leaves the confessional.

The promise to arrive back on board before noon is kept. As usual, the problem of the hour takes precedence. He orders the crew to quickly set the sails and return to the island. Once again, he has successfully avoided taking the next step to returning to his wife and daughter.

"We're going to find out who those pecker-woods are. I think I already know, but if the guy I hit is still layin' there and is dressed like a city slicker we'll know for sure who we're dealin' with," says Captain Seavey with his jaw set and his eye directed toward the island.

Later that afternoon they arrive within sight of the location where they had their confrontation the night before. A ship on the horizon catches Seavey's eye. Putting a telescope to his eye lays all the unanswered questions to rest. It's a four-masted schooner belonging to Booth Fisheries. It's obvious to Captain Seavey that they have taken up residence in the same camp they were driven from by gun shots the night before.

Alerting the crew, Seavey takes on a patient attitude. "We're going to stay back boys and let them think they were successful in driving us off. They'll probably be sailing out tonight for Chicago if they used our hunting spots," says Captain Seavey.

"The deer are thicker than flies in that area," chimes in Dee. His attitude is as of one who is witnessing his house being burglarized in broad daylight and helpless to prevent it.

"Don't worry too much my friend. They are about to receive the scourge of Captain Seavey. But this time they will be the ones terrorized."

Next, he has them prepare the ship for combat. All the rifles, boxes of ammunition, a dozen two pound cannon balls for the swiveling bow cannon, and all the oil burning lanterns are brought up on deck. Assessing the present position of the sun against the distance between himself and the Booth ship, he judges precisely how much time he has before dark to provoke the Booth ship to pursue him. Bringing his ship within 200 yards of their anchored ship, they can easily see crew members scurrying around the deck armed with rifles. Knowing they are out of range for any killing shots, Captain Seavey orders the crew to send a volley of rifle shots their way. Within seconds they are returning fire. With that maneuver completed, Captain Seavey feigns a retreat. As predicted, the Booth ship prepares its sails to give chase. Both Seavey and Zig are well aware that the *Wanderer* is no match against the Booth schooner which with its four masts is much faster. Seavey's crew is also aware of this and is perplexed at their captain's order to retreat knowing that in a matter of time they will be overtaken. The sun is beginning to sink below the lake level slowly pulling the darkness in behind it.

"Get those lanterns lit boys and hang 'em where they can be seen. I don't want these pecker-woods to have to strain their eyes to find us," roars Seavey. It's obvious he's enjoying this adventure. The rest of the crew is not having as good a time as their captain. They're left wondering what he could possibly have in mind with this dangerous ploy. It's obvious to them that pissing off a foe much bigger and stronger is clearly risky.

The Booth ship is rapidly closing the distance between them, thus heightening the anxiety of the entire *Wanderer's* crew. Captain Seavey's attention is clearly fixed on the positions of the two ships.

Abruptly, he redirects his attention for just a moment to first mate Archie. "Prepare the cannon!"

Quickly turning to second mate Willis, he orders, "Willis, take the wheel and bring her broadside to their port side. The rest of you get below."

In one sweeping motion, and before the Booth ship can react, Willis has turned the smaller ship to their port side. Captain Seavey, in the meantime has taken over the cannon, hurling another order to Archie. "Be prepared to reload."

With that, he directs the cannon muzzle directly to the Booth ship's port side water line. BOOM! The report of the cannon is distinct and terrifying to those on the receiving end. The Booth ship rocks from the cannon ball finding its mark. A roar immediately rises from Captain Seavey back to Archie.

"Reload!"

In less than thirty seconds, Captain Seavey is relighting the fuse. BOOM! Once again this monster belches its contents directly into its target blowing yet another hole in the belly of this giant challenger. Each of the holes in the side of the Booth ship is quickly sinking below the water line. There is no question the ship is definitely in distress.

"Reload!!" comes yet another roaring imperative from this former prey now turned predator. BOOM! Another cannon ball rips into the bow. Clearly the ship is lost. Quickly finding they're forced to abandon ship, the crew runs about frantically trying to lower their life boats. Soon water is replacing the air in the ship's lower deck as a mixture of air and water begins to spew out of every crevice creating a geyser like spectacle. Captain Seavey gives the sinking vessel one last look as the glistening moonlight reflecting off the water changes shape. It appears to be bouncing as fast as it can away from the disturbance causing it.

Satisfied that this threat is undone, Captain Seavey gives the order to set sails to the south.

10 MARY SEAVEY

"The years have passed on and left their trace," wrote the Quaker poet in the "Indian Summer Of The Heart." This leads us to Mary Plumly. She was only fourteen years old when a tall dashing young man with an eastern accent and a flair for excitement proposed marriage to her. He worked for the Bureau of Indian Affairs, he was ambitious and he held the promise of becoming a solid husband. She readily accepted, becoming Mrs. Daniel Seavey. Within a couple years, she gave him a daughter. Then, of course, all things soon changed.

Many years have passed now. She is thirty two and he thirty eight. He has been absent from the family for nearly ten of those years. Lured by the prospect of riches, he left the first time for the Klondike gold fields only to return broke and destitute. Her hopes were that he would resume a normal married life. These hopes were soon dashed. Instead, much as his father had done before, he abandons his family once again—this time for the lure of the sea. With some help from her family and hiring herself out as a domestic servant to a wealthy Jewish family in Milwaukee, she has managed over the years to raise her daughter alone.

That is until now. Their daughter, Josephine, known as "Josey," has besieged her mother to help her find her absent father. As a very young girl, she adored him and has never understood why he left. Now she is in her late teens and determined to have her questions surrounding his disappearance answered. In some ways, she glamorizes their past relationship, but on the other hand, as with many abandoned children, she is fearful that in some way, she may have been to blame for him leaving. She has secretly held this torment inside all these years.

"I want to see him Mamma. Either you go with me or I go alone. I know you know where he is."

Mary has also held a mixture of love and hate, balled up with resentment for her estranged husband. She can readily identify with her daughter's frustration. This may be just the excuse she needs to confront him one more time. Hopefully, both of them will then be able to put to rest any romanticized notions of him re-entering their lives. On many fronts, both of them feel they have been victimized by this offending husband and father, and in their eyes this puts him in a very poor light. Their impressions of him have been created by hurts which neither of them deserved. Neither is sure what they hope to accomplish with such a showdown, nonetheless, both are determined to have a face-off while faint hopes continue to lead them. After all, here is a man who boasts there isn't a human alive who can whip him in a fight, and has been known to endure the rigors of these battles for hours, but who lacks the durability to be a husband and a father.

Standing on deck of the car ferry *Ann Arbor #1* carrying them from Milwaukee to Frankfort, Mary has her arms resting on the side rails with her eyes gazing at the water. She finds herself helplessly mesmerized watching the bow of the boat slicing its way through the soft surface of the lake, carrying her ever closer to her destination. Since she has no activity in which to escape, she finds herself with no other choice than to entertain her recollections. There is nothing before her in any direction except breaking waves lapping against the horizon. In many ways over the past ten years the world seems old and worn, but today it looks brand new.

Soon the distant jutting of the tan colored, high-bluffed dunes of Frankfort come into view. At first glance, they give the impression of some odd aberration floating on the lake's surface. The closer they get, the more singular the beauty of nature's carving becomes. The majesty of these crown jewels has nourished the inhabitants of these Great Lakes for thousands of years. It comes to Mary that this is the most freeing exuberance she has felt in a long, long time.

The Frankfort harbor is separated by a north-south breakwater that endures the buffeting seas to produce a calm channel of entry. The 250-foot car ferry propels itself forward seemingly mindless of the conditions as it enters this windless waterway.

The captains are usually good about taking passengers on board, but then everyone is left to fend for themselves. Mother and daughter soon find themselves standing alone with bags in hand on the docking apron of this behemoth. The thirty-man crew hustles around ignoring them as they go about their seemingly endless duties. Making their way through this mayhem with bags in tow, they begin to shuffle their way to the only hotel on their side of the bay, the American House Hotel. Fussing with a small picnic basket, the two of them quietly eat the remainder of a bread and cheese lunch they had brought with them. Worn out after a day on the water, they are content to discuss nothing. Exhausted, they are pleased just to get into bed expecting they will have more to talk about after they are rested.

The clanging of cleaning buckets in the hallway by the housekeeping crew announces the arrival of morning. The two of them find their way into the hotel dining room for breakfast. Being a teenager, Josey is more inclined to view this as an adventure while her mother remains much more pensive. Mary is hoping this does not turn out to be some kind of wild goose chase. Turning to one of the boys cleaning tables, she emboldens herself to ask, "Do you know if there is boat captain here named Seavey?"

"You talkin' about Cap'n Seavey?" answers the boy. Without waiting for her to reply, he points out the window toward the bay just as the *Wanderer* is making its way into the harbor. Mary cautiously swings her head around as though she expects he will be standing directly behind her. Instead, an old recollection has involuntarily made its way to the forefront of her thoughts. For a moment the familiarity of this ship makes time stand still. She recalls the many times she waited in the harbor and how excited she became when she finally saw his masts coming through the channel. She watches as he makes his signature turn to face his ship toward the opening leading to the lake. Her head feels faint and her hands feel numb as the intimacy of this scenario continues to capture her. Managing to sit down for a moment, she regains her presence of mind. Before the boy can leave, she makes one more request. "Are you able to get a message to your Captain Seavey?"

Without hesitation the boy answers, "Hell yes...excuse me ma'am. I mean heck yes. My brother Doe worked for him til he got married."

"Your brother is Doe Pierce?"

"Yup that's my brother and I'm Frank Pierce," answers the young man, "but he always calls me 'The Kid'."

Finding her composure once again, she asks the boy, "What would you prefer I call you—Frank or Kid?"

"Frank I guess. My brother's the only one that calls me Kid."

"Okay Frank how would you like to earn a dime?" Mary propositions.

"Hell....aah heck yes ma'am. What do you want me to do?"

Quickly dashing off a note, she folds it, places it in an envelope, and hands it to him along with ten cents.

"By the way Frank, you said your brother Doe used to work for Captain Seavey, where is Doe now?"

Pointing through another window, he replies, "He lives right there behind the bar."

As she looks across the street, she notices Frank taking advantage of her attention being in another direction as he and Josey catch the other's eye.

Quickly getting things back in order Mary asks, "How long before you can get this done Frank?"

"I get off for lunch at 11:00, I can do it then," he assures her.

Realizing they have some time to kill, Mary looks toward Doe's house. She sits contemplating what to do. She and Doe are close to the same age and had a good rapport back in the day. Finally making a decision, and being sure to take Josephine along, she makes her way across the street to Doe's house. Her knock on the door is soon answered by a lady that Mary has never seen before. It's apparent that she is pregnant. Mary introduces herself and Josey and asks if Doe is home.

"Yes, he is. Let me get him," says Daisy, offering them chairs. Coming in from a garden project in the back yard, Doe is pleasantly surprised to see Mary sitting in his living room.

"Good grief girl is that you?" he besieges her, grabbing her hand in his, and all the while staring into what at one time been a familiar face. "It's been all of ten years." Turning toward Josephine he continues, "Don't tell me this is little Josey!"

Josephine is taken back some as she recalls this kindly man whom she referred to as "Uncle Doe" when she was six.

"Yes Uncle Doe, I'm Josey," she admits while extending her own hand to him.

Taking her hand in his, he can't help but marvel. "Well haven't you turned out to be a pretty one!"

After introducing Daisy, Daisy takes charge. "Please stay for lunch. I have plenty of sliced ham and we'd love to have you stay." Mary takes a moment to look out the window. She can see who is coming and going from the hotel.

"That's very kind of you. Tell me what I can do to help."

"You do nothing. This will only take me a minute."

Mary is left now with Doe. He has some idea why she is here in Frankfort, but is reluctant to come out and ask. Nonetheless, he proffers what would seem a sensible question under the circumstances, "What in tarnation brings you to Frankfort?"

Not wanting to sound as though she has anything to do with this journey, she points toward Josephine.

"Josey's been wanting to see her father for some time. It seemed like a good time to do it."

Meanwhile across the bay, Frank has presented the closed envelope to Captain Seavey. "Thank you Frankie," he says handing him another dime. Opening it, he immediately recognizes the hand writing as that of his alienated wife.

To Captain Silvers,

Your daughter has been adamant to see you. If you can find time we are at the American House in So. Frankfort.

Mary Silvers"

(From happier days the references to the surname of "Silvers" comes as a private joke between the two of them, comparing him with the famous pirate Captain John Silvers and her as the pirate's wife. She has preferred to keep it.)

He stands dumbfounded for at least a full minute with the letter still in his hand. A sickening feeling provided by his Catholic guilt rolls over him like a Great Lake sou'wester. *"Maybe my penance is coming to me,"* he imagines. Folding the note, he sticks it in his inside coat pocket next to the yellowed and worn divorce decree and makes his way to McDart's ferry. It's a launch provided to carry passengers across the Betsie Bay from Frankfort to South Frankfort and vice versa. With his mind full of Abequa's forebodings, he resigns himself to make the trip. He's blind as to what may lay ahead. *"What can of worms am I opening?"* is his singular thought as he disembarks the ferry and makes his way toward this unsettling rendezvous. He's not propelled by any one thing he can readily point to other than Abequa, but he knows to run away would be even more problematic.

Josey is not mentally in tune with the conversation going on between the adults. She is off in another world. Her sentiments have lionized her devotion toward her father. After all, she has developed many of his features and has been told repeatedly by her mother, "You act just like your father." This was intended to be a criticism that her psyche has now turned into something she's grown proud to demonstrate. She has developed a make-believe relationship, a friendship that can never end providing the reality of him entering her life never occurs. But now, she is willing to risk gray clouds forming over her sunshine. *"What if he really did leave because of me?"*

Trying as hard as she can, she cannot bring his image to mind. She can only create a narrow, marginal concept of him, intermingled with a feeling of him touching her hand, her face, her hair. Much of what she had taken for granted as a child is seemingly lost. This is the very thing she hopes to re-establish between them. All this changes in a flash as she catches sight of the very, very familiar form of a man slowly and purposefully making his way toward the hotel. She begins to rise slowly, not saying a word, eyes fixed on the window, heart pounding, mouth too dry to form words even if she wanted to. She begins to pick up speed as she makes her way toward the door. Mary is slow to notice her daughter's uncharacteristic behavior until she sees her bolt out to the street. "*This can only mean one thing!*"

Ignoring everything else, Mary's head snaps toward the window. Her eyes fully expect to see what had so dramatically changed her daughter's comportment. THERE HE STANDS! He's staring at the front of the hotel as one would if he were looking to make repairs, but on this summer noon it can only be in hopes of repairing the broken heart of his daughter. Mary, is unable to move beyond the porch. She stays back with her hand over her mouth covering a gasp. Josey, walking much slower, is now within fifteen feet of her father. She can only stand still and stare as he hesitantly looks back with a very uncomfortable and very puzzled expression. It's clear he doesn't recognize his progeny.

Hesitating for a moment, she moves a couple of steps forward. He is now beginning to realize that her intentions are directed at him.

"I'm supposed to meet some people here today. Do you work here?"

"No, but maybe I can help. Exactly who is it you're looking for?" she asks, realizing he has no idea who she is.

"A lady with a little girl," he manages to spit out.

"How old is this little girl?" she asks

Begging the question, he stalls his speech. It's obvious he's playing for time. "I'm really not sure but..."

"Would she be seventeen?" quizzes Josey. Her attitude is turning from elation to frustration at her father's seeming obliviousness.

"No, no she's much younger...like little, you know...little," he says holding his hand at waist height.

Josey feels victimized again at the callowness of this grown man. The tears begin to well up in her eyes as her disappointment surfaces.

"I'm seventeen, Daddy," she blurts out, "and you don't even know who I am!"

He stands doe-eyed staring at this young women. Abequa flashes into his mind with her convicting gaze. Words are not coming to this normally outspoken man of the sea. He is struck weak and helpless before the judgment of this nearly grown progeny. It isn't so much her words that convict him, it is the years he's missed being in her life. He begins to tremble with the full force of her words striking him like a surgeon's knife, only this time there is no anesthesia. Stumbling for words that aren't there, he attempts to begin with a nervous laugh and a lot of unnecessary blinking.

"Well haven't you grown up to be quite the young lady?"

This is the best he can bumble out from his nearly paralyzed mouth. Continuing to stand there with hat in hand, he's not sure what his next move should be. What remembrance is familiar is how she would hound him until he would pick her up and bump her head on the ceiling. "Bump me Daddy, bump me," she would shout. Believing he has, at last found some common ground, a little grin begins to form on Seavey's face.

"Want me to bump your head?"

Having taken on much of her father's looks and mannerisms, she also begins to form the same knowing grin. They continue to gaze at one another for only a moment. A common bond gluing a seemingly dormant accord between this father and daughter is proving to have endured the ten years of bad weather separating them.

"Ya, I do," she says laughing and crying at the same time. Their spirits have found one another as they break through with a renewed affection in an embrace.

Mary has stood by watching this developing kinship stagger its way to this disturbing closing. In one way she is happy for her daughter, but a bigger part of her would like to have seen some revenge taken. *"After all, shouldn't she require some form of reparation? He left her with no explanation, no goodbye and she let him off with a hug,"* is her thought.

Now Seavey's attention has turned. He is consciously looking around for something else.

"Where's your mother?" he quips in an attempt to not sound anxious. Just as he says these words, he feels a jolt go throughout his entire body. There across the street stands his abandoned wife, deserted and cast aside for the sake of his selfish, but, nonetheless, overpowering desire to be free. Motionless, he returns her gaze. He feels all the guilt and remorse that Abequa has made his own. Her light colored bustled dress gives her a young carefree appearance, but her expression reveals a much more labored aspect. She has lost her young girl delicacy and has grown into a mature woman of beauty. It's the beauty that comes with having been victorious over hardships. This kind of beauty is translated into a strength that's seen in things as simple as how a woman stands. Their eyes meet. Hers seem to exert a forcefulness he doesn't recall she had.

He is once again overcome with an overwhelming urge to run. His penance has found him this time, and as usual, he resists its sanctions. But for the moment, he's trapped between reconciliation with his daughter and his yet unreconciled wife. She waits, boldly not shifting her accusing gaze. He's on the hook and he knows it. Taking his daughter by the hand, more as a hopeful ally, he makes his way to this yet stalwart looking opponent. It's apparent that she is making no attempt at all to meet him on any other terms than her own. Doe and Daisy stand by, not sure where this liaison is going to land.

Seavey has been convicted by his guilt and shame to not even attempt to act as though he were nothing more than a carefree pirate, swashbuckling his way through life. He presents himself to her, still with hat in hand, as a vassal. Secretly, he's hoping she will see him as a poor victim of his own passion, unable to change, only in need of her understanding. Unfortunately for him, she has never once considered letting his selfish ways go unnoticed, nor does she wish to be portrayed as the poor abandoned wife. Furnished with an ample supply of honest dignity, she boldly stands in front of him. Not knowing what to talk about, he merely hopes to find a bit of common ground.

"She's grown up quite a bit Mary," he stammers.

Mary remains silent for a moment, measuring her words. Her first reaction is to return his comment with, *"Yes Seav, she certainly has—unlike her father."* With a second thought, rightly determining this as too belligerent for a first meeting, she manages to hold her tongue and politely reply, "Yes, she certainly has." Mary knows there is plenty to talk about. She finds keeping her comments polite and innocuous is difficult at best, but at least for the moment viable.

Both Seavey and Mary are downplaying their need to react toward the other for the sake of Josephine. Seavey would like nothing more than to get on his ship and sail into the sunset. On the other hand, Mary has ten years of stored up resentments she would like to unload and sink his ship. Instead, they use the postponement to attempt to scrutinize the other without being obvious.

Seavey notices how much more of a woman she has become. After all, she was only fourteen years old when he married her. He had begun to have intercourse with her before marriage and when he confessed his sin to the priest, he then withheld absolution until Seavey agreed to marry her. They were married within the week. One thing is clear to Seavey is that he has never learned to live with his regrets. It's obvious his past is shaping his present as he wrestles with guilt, shame, and self-condemnation.

"So what are you doing nowdays?" is the best that he can come up with for conversation. The absurdity of the question strikes a laughable chord in Mary.

"What kind of details do you want to hear Seav—maybe like how your daughter is in the best school or how we vacation abroad or maybe how we've been a part of the inner Milwaukee social circle?"

Her own hurts begin to surface as she stands face to face with this physical giant, who is no more than a dwarf in her eyes.

"If you really want to know..." looking him square in the eye, she concludes that it's a useless endeavor and lets the words drift off.

"Just forget it Seav, and don't worry yourself about what we've been doing."

The sarcasm is dripping, even from her body language, as she turns sobbing and walks back across the street. Daisy has curiously stood by suspecting things may not go well for this reunion. She readily puts a loving arm around this plainly distraught new found friend. She is a ready ally, as she hasn't wasted any love on Captain Seavey herself. She's seen him as a competitor for her husband's considerations and has a ready supply of animosity to add to anyone's list.

"Come in dear and I'll make you some tea," says Daisy continuing to console her.

Meantime, Josey is left alone standing in the street with this awkward giant. She has heard her mother's lamenting over her father's absence since he left. For whatever strange reasons, many young girls in this position begin to lionize their fathers, creating a hero who could save them if it were not for an antagonistic mother. She stands readily awaiting the attention she is sure she will get when her mother is out of the picture.

He finally pulls himself together enough to make a suggestion.

"How'd you like to come on board and meet the crew?"

A big smile makes its way across her face at the thought of this adventure. She is profoundly happy and sure she is picking up where they left off ten years ago.

The afternoon wears on. Josey couldn't be happier reacquainting herself with her father. Mary, in the meantime, has accepted an invitation from Daisy for her and Josey to move into a spare bedroom for the duration of their stay.

11 Kaz Jenc

Mary and Josey have stayed with Doe and Daisy for a week. Mary has kept her distance from her estranged husband choosing to keep things tolerable for the sake of their daughter. Thankfully for Josey, she is leaving with a renewed sense of belonging. Her father did not disappoint her even once. Without admitting it, Mary rather envies her daughter for her renewed rapport with her estranged father.

But time moves on and the chessboard of people in Seavey's life are all moving back into their respective places. His wife and daughter are well on their way back to Milwaukee and he has gotten word that a Pollack from Manistee is making a lot of noises indicating that, "There ain't a man alive that can beat me in a fist fight and that includes the likes of Dan Seavey."

"Wadda ya make of this hunyuk Dee? Ya think I outta go down there and tune him up?" asks Seavey over a glass of whiskey.

"I don't know Cap'n, he's younger than you and been fightin' more regular. Time might be on his side," answers Dee giving it not more than a moment of thought. Listening, Seavey takes another slow sip as though deep in thought. With Seavey a challenge of this sort cannot go unanswered, despite Dee's reservations. "What say we stop by where this pecker-wood hangs around and check him out?"

They haven't had any action since they sank the Booth ship and this is exactly the type of things that gets this crew fired up. "There ain't nothin' in the world like a damn good fight," says Ob. He acts as Seavey's second when it comes to fighting. This is the kind of stuff that excites these men as much as being a pirate.

Unlike Olympic types of athletic competitions that are determined by conditioning, these contests are driven by who can drink the most and still stay standing, or whose mouthy bravado can intimidate his opponent the most effectively. Size, such as Captain Seavey's, can be a compelling deterrent. Nevertheless, the ability to imagine that one can piss against the wind and not get wet will more than likely drive a competitive spirit further than size alone.

This Pollack from Manistee is just such a fellow. Unlike a lot of testosterone driven males, his sizzle has some steak under it. As far as Dee has been led to understand, he's twenty-six years old, smaller in stature, but quick as greased lightning. His name is Kaz Jenc. To date, he hasn't lost a fight.

"He ain't lost a fight because he ain't fought me yet," surmises Seavey, taking another sip from his glass. Without another thought he says, "Yup, I think that's what I wanna do—pay Mr. Manistee Hun-yuck a visit. Set sail lads, we're goin' for a bit o wayfaring." Within the hour, the ship is sailing out of the harbor heading south for the twenty mile journey down the coast to Manistee.

Ginny doesn't even pretend to make sense of her male counterparts. She busies herself with making a lunch which brings to light the awareness that once these boys start drinking, a consideration for food will be the last item on their minds. She takes the last of the chilled venison left after their supply was sold on the Chicago market and makes Captain Seavey's favorite stew. Watching and listening to the men chatter while serving lunch, she is particularly aware of Dee's overwhelming enthusiasm for this latest escapade.

Dee, in turn walks a fine line in his attempts to kindle the same sort of exuberance toward his activities with Ginny as he does for the types of schemes spawned by Captain Seavey. She is the first to point out his obvious shortcomings, but at the same time, she has to admit she is more often than not overtaken with some of their pirate antics, taking some vicarious pleasure in these wild capers. After all, as they each agree, it keeps boredom from invading the mundaneness of ordinary sailing. At least this is what she's come to expect.

The port of entry into the city of Manistee is the Manistee River. Timber is a big part of the economy in this bustling region. For the most part, it remains a Polish community supported by sawmills. Seavey has found it to be a ready and willing partner in whatever endeavors he wishes to share with them—especially his moonshine whiskey business.

Captain Seavey, with his cap one hand and a cigar in the other makes his way to the front door of Polooka's tavern. Pete "Polooka" Casperoski is behind the bar where he's been since his father had him washing beer glasses when he was no more than ten years old. He's a first generation immigrant from Poland. His father always said he was made in Poland even though he was born here two months after they arrived.

"Seavey, I know why you're here and I'm not so sure I'm gonna like it," says the dismayed bar owner. Seavey breaks out into a broad smile.

"Wadda ya mean Polooka? I'm only here for a glass of your watered down beer," says Seavey. Polooka gives him that look that says he didn't just fall off a turnip truck.

"Don't give me that bullshit Seavey. I've heard all about Kaz's challenge."

"I don't know what you're talking about," lies Seavey, coyly shoving his cigar between his teeth.

Polooka coolly considers Seavey's attempt to downplay his purpose for being here. He has a begrudging respect for this big sea captain for more reasons than one. The most recent being his stock of untaxed liquor from Seavey's seemingly never-ending supply. But he also knows that if this ruckus starts in his bar it will mean broken furniture and at least a day closed for repairs. Since Kaz Jenc made the challenge from Polooka's there is no doubt in his mind that his tavern is going to be the chosen location. On the other hand, Polooka is well acquainted with these testosterone driven males of his day. He's well aware that once a challenge is issued, no matter how surreptitiously it may have been presented, there can only be one end—a fight to the finish with only one opponent left standing.

Word soon gets around town that Seavey's schooner is tied up at Polooka's landing. It doesn't take long before a crowd begins to form in the bar. Seavey's crew is quietly taking bets. The odds seem to be favoring the home town boy; after all he's younger and certainly much more verbose about his triumphs. It's readily apparent that he's captured the support of the twenty-something crowd. On the other hand, a few of the old-timers are far from ruling Captain Seavey out despite the ten or so years difference in their respective ages. It would be rare to find any one of these middle-aged men who would bet against Seavey.

By evening, Polooka's has become a smoke-filled bustling enterprise of mustached beer drinking boosters. His patrons are primarily men who are more concerned with the potency of a drink than its color or taste. The building was originally designed as a warehouse to vend fruit and vegetable produce, but as the number of orchards began to grow in the area, the owners outgrew the building and moved on. Polooka's father bought the building and turned it into a tavern catering to the ever growing influx of Polish immigrants. It still maintains its original warehouse atmosphere. The bar is centered on the back wall with three sides. This design allows for maximum table space. There is no doubt that Polooka's is holding the distinction of sponsoring the main feature in town. A few drinks help pick the betting up along with some added bluster. This braggadocio never fails to spew from minds that have been overcome with the effects of unfettered alcohol consumption.

"Kaz's mouth has a way of overpowering his ass," is the assessment of one whose scars indicate he's been in more than his share of scraps.

"Well, we'll see if your old fart can get his fat ass off his bar stool without hitting his head on the floor," says a kid barely old enough to wipe his own ass.

"Don't worry about it sonny, all you're gonna see is two hits—Kaz and the ground," says another.

For over an hour Captain Seavey, along with Ob, has been seated at a back corner table nursing a glass of whiskey. Neither is saying much, but appear to be deep in thought.

"Wadda ya think Cap'n, time to get the party rollin'?" questions Ob. He accompanies this question with a knowing little grin. Captain Seavey returns a little nod. Within minutes they return to the ship to make some last minute preparations. With little to no conversation, they begin a routine they have carried out many times before. It begins with Seavey layering heavy clothing on his upper body, two woolen sweaters, topped with his signature vest and coat.

By the time they return, the tables and chairs have been cleared back against the wall. The noise level is above anything that this place has undergone for some time. The target of the shouting soon becomes apparent as Kaz, along with his entourage, make their way through the back door. It's a cacophony of shrill whistling accompanied with a chant, "KAZ, KAZ, KAZ," not showing any indications of getting much quieter.

He isn't a particularly large man when compared with Captain Seavey.

He's at least a hair over six foot, maybe topping out at 225 pounds. He has a dense black mustache, but even with this attempt at looking older, he nonetheless conveys a bravado that only the young find appealing. The crowd takes turns slapping him on the back as he follows his second to a table in the opposite corner from Seavey's.

Ob takes his time crossing over to meet with Kaz's second to lay out the terms of engagement. It's agreed that the first man to remain down beyond a ten count will be declared the loser. Otherwise, it's to be a bare-knuckled free for all with no holds barred. They both agree to have Emil Hoffnagle, a German from Arcadia, to be the impartial third man on the floor. Emil is a man in his sixties and has been a part of these male hijinks for generations. He's trusted by all involved to have his word be final when it comes to counting a man out.

Kaz has stripped down to reveal a well-muscled chest and arms. This tactic is designed to intimidate his opponent as well as assure his fans of his prowess. The small bead of nervous sweat forming on his brow indicates things are not so calm on the inside. Nonetheless, the increasing flow of adulation continues to bolster his ego. The odds are five to one in favor of Kaz Jenc, the hometown boy.

Emil arises from somewhere in the crowd, walks to the center of the room, and strikes a bell he furnishes for just this kind of occasion.

"Listen up boys. These two men are going to duke it out till one of 'em can't get up or answer the bell. It's been agreed to have five minute rounds with a minute rest in between. I won't stand for any assistance from any of you for either fighter during a round. From here on, they're on their own. It's a winner take all from bets. May the best man win."

There are at least a hundred people packed into the tavern. The common denominator linking them all together is their taste for liquor and the desire to see blood.

Both men are on their feet when the bell goes off. For the first time in the lives of these two men, they meet. With fists poised for action, they circle one another. Suddenly, with cat like speed, Kaz throws the first punch. As it connects to the jaw of Captain Seavey, the crowd lets out a whoop. Emboldened by the approval of the herd and the seeming ease with which he managed this maneuver, he throws another punch, then another. So far they're all unanswered. The first round finally ends with Seavey never throwing a punch. The crowd cheers as the rippling, sweaty, beefed up shoulders, chest and abs of their champion glisten in the lights. Without bothering to sit down, he raises his arms in a victory salute with the purpose of inciting them to bet even more on his certainty to walk all over this obvious "has been" opponent.

The second round begins with Kaz being much less cautious than he was in the first round. Captain Seavey is still in a defensive mode with hands up safeguarding his head. This leaves his torso wide open and un-protected. Seeing this as an advantage, Kaz lets loose with a barrage of punches bombarding Seavey's body with blow after blow. The round ends as the first round with Seavey never throwing a punch and Kaz having let loose with at least fifty.

The hometown crowd is ecstatic as they continue to place their bets in opposition to this apparent washed up, aging warrior. The odds have jumped ten to one with one round left before all bets have to be in. There is a sudden push to make an even more determined gamble on Kaz as the money flows from one hand to another. After all, why wouldn't they bet this way? Seavey has shown nothing more than a pathetic demonstration of some former skills.

"Yer washed up Seavey, might as well quit while ya still got one live braincell left," comes a catcall from some unidentified voice in the crowd. Undaunted, Seavey answers the bell once again re-entering the fray for another round. Being fully dressed in a boxing match further intensifies the crowd's condescending opinion of his abilities. At this time, Kaz smells victory and is determined to lay his opponent on the planks. He releases a flurry of punches striking everything that is not protected. Without a doubt, Seavey looks the fool, his coat fluttering with every landed blow. Again, the round ends with Kaz definitely the winner. He has thrown everything he has in the hopes of putting Seavey away. His arms are dangling at his sides, exhausted and drained. The look of frustration at his still standing opponent is obvious as he makes a feeble attempt to raise his spent arms in his now signature victory salute.

It's fully expected that Captain Seavey will never last another round with the beating he's taken thus far. All eyes are on their champion as his corner people prepare him to take out this ridiculous, farcical, washed up old pugilist once and for all. But with no one noticing, Seavey prepares to return to the floor coatless, vestless, shirtless, and sweaterless. All of these layers were strategically worn for the purpose of absorbing the barrage of punches Seavey knew this young buck would want to demonstrate against him in the early rounds. He obliged him. By giving his over-inflated ego an opportunity to show his fans what he was capable of doing, Kaz has produced exactly the tenderized, bone-wearied opponent Seavey expected. Kaz has punched himself out and they both know it.

The bell announces another round. Both prepare to re-enter the circle. Without a cue from any outside force, there is a perplexed silence among the revelers. With all bets in, there is a definite change taking place. From out of the Captain Seavey's corner comes a bare-torsoed, six foot six, three-hundred pound thundering giant. It soon becomes obvious that a game changer has taken place. Backing up cautiously, Kaz has also become aware that something different is beginning.

"Where ya goin' young fella? We're just gettin' started," says Seavey with an unmistakable grin of deceit spreading over his leathery face. With that said, he throws his first punch of the fight. It lands with a resounding crack as it meets the flesh and bone of this opponent's face. Feeling the full effects of this blow, Kaz can't help but try and retreat to clear his head. Seavey doesn't give him the opportunity. Unfortunately for Kaz, his arms are spent and he fails to force them into a defensive mode, much less an offensive position.

Crack, crack continues the flat sound of Seavey's knuckles on Kaz's skull. Kaz has no choice other than to run around the circle lined by his fans and attempt to stay away from what has become his worst nightmare. The booing at the sight of their retreating blue ribbon contender intensifies. The attitudes are definitely changing. The crowd has no idea what has taken place here, except they are becoming less than enamored with the antics of their local boy. His supporters are no longer showing their backing. It becomes more and more a confused, hapless feeling to watch as round after round Seavey, seemingly, toys with their champion. To rub the beating in a little deeper, Seavey has given up sitting in his corner between rounds in favor of sitting at the bar for a shot of whiskey.

They have been fighting for over an hour. Kaz's face is taking on the appearance of the quintessential battered opponent. His left eye is swollen shut while the right has a steady flow of blood from an open gash in the eye lid. His lips present the quality of ground beef as well as a broken front tooth leaving a gap allowing the blood to stream from his mouth, down his chin and chest.

With the resounding clang from the time keeper's bell announcing another round, Seavey has already decided this is going to be their last. Entering the fighting circle, both opponents square off. In spite of his battered appearance, Kaz's arms seem to have begun a recovery. He makes a valiant lunge at Seavey, connecting with a right hook that stuns him for a moment. The crowd goes wild at his hopeful attempt to redeem himself. But unfortunately, he's still unable to put combinations together. His arms have become useless appendages. Kaz has nothing left of any significance to follow through to hurt Seavey. Seavey, in turn is calculating how much his opponent has recovered and is reconsidering his intention to end this fight with this round.

With a penetrating left punch just below Kaz's sternum, Seavey effectively arches him forward just enough to engage his right hand in a round house upper cut. This last blow drops Kaz like a pole-axed steer. Emil is there immediately with the count. ONE, his hand rises with him bellowing out each number, TWO, THREE, FOUR. Kaz is a bloodied mass piled in a heap at Seavey's feet. He tries rolling over for no apparent reason other than he feels he should be doing something. FIVE, SIX. Now he's attempting to stand only to stagger two steps and collapse to the floor again. SEVEN, EIGHT, NINE, TEN. With a wave of his arms, he counts him out. His next move is to raise the arm of Captain Seavey, declaring him, "THE WINNER!"

Meantime Kaz's second is the only one to pay any attention to this fallen scrapper. The rest of his erstwhile fans throw their hands up in disgust muttering how much they bet and lost.

Within a half hour, the only ones still sitting in Polooka's are Captain Seavey and his ever faithful crew. Archie has dutifully taken care of the bets. After everything is said and done, they have netted $350.00. Seavey has made certain that Ginny gets a night off as he orders steak dinners for the whole crew.

Captain Seavey finds himself looking around the table. He takes a deep breath while gazing into each of their faces. His emotions have made their way to the very surface of his person. He can't help but feel at home with these simple people. A sense of warmness makes its way in. In a deep appreciation for these everyday, familiar acquaintances, he takes another rare moment to gratefully thank God. Currently it's the closest thing to a family he has. He has found these members of the great unwashed to be a faithful, understanding, strong, hard working people.

Even Polooka couldn't be happier as this crazy event has proven to be one of the best business days he has ever experienced, along with a minimal amount of breakage.

12 TUG'S REVENGE

It's quite dark when the crew, along with their newly crowned pugilist champion returns to the ship. Duke has been the lone watchdog left on board. If he could talk, he'd be at a loss for words as his tongue is all over Captain Seavey, licking his swollen eyes. With no idea what time it is, the next morning arrives on its own schedule. Captain Seavey is sitting on deck shoeless and nursing a mug of Ginny's coffee. The sun is saying it's about ten o'clock in the morning.

Glancing down the wharf, he spots a familiar looking person making his way in his direction. What he sees is a short, stocky man with a full black beard. He quickly recognizes him as an old friend and crew mate by the name of Todd "Tug" Argue. The last Seavey knew of Tug, he had become half owner in a schooner named the *Nellie Johnson,* a ship they had both crewed on years before.

"Tug, you old reprobate, what the hell brings you into these waters?" says Captain Seavey pulling on a boot.

Extending his hand, Tug pauses for a moment giving Seavey a chance to pull on his other boot.

"I was in the neighborhood and thought I'd stop by," he says vigorously shaking Seavey's hand.

Knowing Tug as he does, Seavey is suspicious that this isn't merely a social call, but at least for the moment, he's willing to give him the benefit of the doubt.

Tug attempts to make some small talk regarding last evening's big fight.

"Ya done damn good against that kid Seav. I wanna thank you. I made three bucks bettin' on your ass," says Tug laughing, still shaking Seavey's hand.

"Before you shake my god-damn arm off, what in the devil do you want out of me? Cause I know damn well you ain't stoppin by ta barrow ah cup ah sugar," slightly protests Captain Seavey pulling his hand loose.

Recognizing the ridiculousness of his behavior, Tug tries once again to present himself in a better light.

"You're right, Seav. I sure as hell ain't stoppin' by fer no damn cup ah sugar." Still not quite ready to make his case, Tug walks silently across the deck. Seavey can tell he's not coming clean about his visit and decides to chide him about it. "Come on Tug what's on yer mind? Neither one of us got all day ya know."

Turning around Tug walks back across the deck. "I don't know quite how to say this, cause I know there's a lotta talk about you bein' a pirate an all. I ain't ever pirated, so I ain't sure how all this pirate talk goes. I guess what I want to know is how do I get started doin' some of that stuff?"

Seavey broke into a grin. "The last I knew, you was a family man, Tug. What you wantin' ta know about piratin' for?"

He pauses for a moment mulling over his answer.

"You heard I bought into the *Nellie Johnson* from our ole Cap'n R.J. McCormick didn' ya?" Not waiting for Seavey to answer, he continues, "I owe the bank a payment and I ain't got the money. They're threatenin' ta foreclose against what I owe 'em and leave me sittin' with my dick in my hand." Pausing again, Tug continues on, "McCormick's okay with that

132 THE SCOURGE OF CAPTAIN SEAVEY

cuz he's in cahoots with the bank's president. It seems he's offered him a better deal if I default. He's got a son that fancies himself a shipper and needs a schooner. I'm hopin' I could get you to help me out."

Without a doubt, Tug's found himself in a pickle. Captain Seavey worked for McCormick before he acquired the *Wanderer*. He remembers how McCormick tried to rope him into a similar kind of arrangement and took him the same way when he couldn't make his payments. Seavey had, much like Tug, made a substantial number of his payments, he, nonetheless, opted to cut his losses and part company with McCormick.

"Well what do ya know? Ole R.J. is still up to his old tricks," muses Seavey as he thinks back to those days when he was a younger man trying to make his mark in a man's world, only to have his efforts thwarted by the likes of this old weasel. Now it's Seavey's turn to cross the deck as he thoughtfully chews over this remembrance. He was of the opinion that he had sufficiently buried it, but like a bad penny, memories like this find a way to keep reappearing. Lighting a new cigar, he deliberately makes his way back. When he asks Willis to bring them a couple of chairs, Ginny takes this as a cue and comes up with another cup and a coffee pot looking at both of them with interest.

The whole crew recognizes, without hearing any of the dialog between their captain and this stranger, that something's going on. They find Tug to be an interesting looking fellow. He's full-bearded, about the same age as Captain Seavey. There is an honest intensity about him that makes Seavey want to consider helping him.

Tug has a family and when McCormick made the proposal to him to buy a share in the ship, he saw it as an opportunity to move forward and raise their standard of living. Tug has never liked R. J. very well, but holds somewhat of a grudging respect for him as his employer. "After all, in days like these, when you're born on the wrong side of the tracks, a man is fortunate to have a job no matter how meager," says Tug. It's simply taken for granted that working for anyone will have its challenges. However, he never imagined that McCormick would purposely ruin him for a better money offer.

Seavey has always had a dislike for bullies and has no problem seeking reprisal. In this case, he feels that any retribution for Tug will also satisfy his repressed resentment. It's true that Seavey has a soft spot in his heart for those of God's children that are weaker and are taken advantage of, particularly by those in positions of power. To him weaker doesn't mean weak-minded, rather it refers to those whose resources are no match against a greedy foe who has more available wealth with which to destroy their opponent. Money can be a great protector or an evil foe. It all depends on the hands that hold it.

First mate Archie is summoned by Captain Seavey to join them. Introductions are exchanged and Archie is given a brief history of what is going on. Along with everyone else in the shipping business, he has also heard of Captain McCormick. It seems his reputation precedes him. On the one hand it could be argued that Seavey and McCormick are one of a kind—they both steal. On the other hand, their victims are very different. Seavey doesn't seem to mind having a reputation that accuses him of stealing, what he objects to is being referred to as a thief. To many it's a difference where there isn't any. Unlike Seavey, McCormick limits his theft to a weaker underdog, whereas Seavey usually aims at the wealthier upper crust. (It also helps to alleviate his conscience if his victims are proud and haughty.) In this case, McCormick, along with his banking buddy, fit Seavey's criteria for them to become the victims themselves.

The three of them spend the rest of the morning haggling over details. Is this task beyond their scope? Captain Seavey hardly thinks so. The information they need is gradually being sorted through. When it's noon,

Ginny has prepared a lunch allowing them to continue their pow-wow until late in the afternoon. At this time, Captain Seavey has passed the jug enough to call the confab to a close. They have produced a workable plan and all that remains is finding the right time to implement it. They spend the rest of the afternoon reminiscing over familiar stories they have all heard with each filling in details the others didn't know.

It's agreed that Tug will stay aboard the *Wanderer* until they arrive at the port at Montague on the Michigan side. According to Tug, the *Nellie Johnson* is moored there waiting on a load of cedar logs to be taken to market in Chicago. The next afternoon, in spite of threatening weather, the *Wanderer* has made her way to the harbor at Montague. The plan is to have Tug slip off the ship without being seen in the company of Captain Seavey.

"You go on ahead and wait at Mrs. Avery's boarding house. I'll let you know when we're going ahead with 'Plan A'," says Seavey with the confidence of a man who has already determined the future success of this escapade.

The Avery boarding house is on Ferry Street, across from the bank. Mrs. Avery is a widowed woman who, when her husband passed, rather than becoming destitute, turned their home into a boarding house. Tug has slipped a rifle under his ankle-length rain coat making it undetectable. As he hurriedly makes his way down through the business district to Avery's, he notes how much the weather has worsened since leaving Manistee. With the building in sight, he is struck by how the weathered siding is taking on a darker hue as the rain continues to beat against it. By the time he bursts through the door, his rain gear is dripping wet. The lobby is far from spacious. He takes only a few steps to a chest high counter that serves as a divider to divide the Avery living area from the public. The wooden floor is struggling to soak up the drippings that are noticeably beginning to puddle around him. Without drawing particular attention to his request, Tug makes sure he is given a room that overlooks the street. This is all part of "Plan A."

Mrs. Avery is happy to oblige him as she leads him to his room. As she opens the door, a clap of thunder greets them along with a flash of lightening illuminating an otherwise dimly lit room. It startles both of them with its closeness and seeming ferocity.

The room is perfect. After lighting enough of a fire in the small parlor stove to take the chill off, Tug is thankful to strip off his heavy canvas rain gear. He sets himself in a chair facing the window overlooking the section of Main Street that involves his part in "Plan A." Even though it's still only midday, the thunder clouds have nearly darkened the village as if it were night. The storm is blowing in from across the lake and is intensifying. Tug continues his watch as the hell of the gale, refusing to be underrated, continues its fury. It's soon late in the afternoon, nearing closing time for most businesses. He's paying particular attention to the comings and goings at the bank. One by one the employees exit the building leaving only the bank's president, Mr. Ferry, to lock the safe and secure the doors. The sky is black with the rain blasting sideways creating more of a sheet of water than a downpour. The thunder and lightening are keeping everyone off the streets—everyone not involved with "Plan A" that is. With the next flash of lightening, something catches the eye of this purveyor of information as he places a kerosene lamp in the window. In the next few seconds, a twinkling of light from the other end of the street blinks back. This signals the pieces of "Plan A" are in place and everything is ready to move forward.

What comes into sight in the next few minutes appears to be a group of about five men pulling a mail cart. It's impossible for any straying eyes to discern what it may be carrying as it's tented over with a canvas tarp. With rifle in hand, in a now darkened window, Tug continues his vigil. It's his job to discourage any unwanted onlookers with a well-placed shot in their vicinity. Despite Mother Nature's pounding deluge, these men have a definite purpose. Swiftly and purposely, this small contingent pulls the cart to the backside of the bank building. The thunder and lightening are relentless in their punishment on these buccaneers. Suddenly there is a thundering burst slightly different and out of sync with the prevailing thunder, but hardly enough to be differentiated by the common ear. The mail cart is unveiled long enough to exhibit its cargo—the swivel cannon has been taken from the bow of the *Wanderer* and placed on the cart. The cannon is positioned at the back side of the bank long enough to blow out the steel door securing the rear entrance. The next step is to get the cannon inside the bank and blow the safe. With two well-placed shots, the bank's safe is compromised. Within fifteen minutes, the crew has successfully emptied the vault of all its currencies. After signaling Tug of their success, they are all on their way back to the *Wanderer*.

In the meantime, Captain Seavey is not being idle. While the crew is carrying through with "Plan A," he is on board the *Nellie Johnson* schmoozing his former employer Captain R.J. McCormick and implementing "Plan B." It would be a more difficult ordeal if McCormick was easy to like, but he's not. Seavey has begun by putting to good use the remembrance of how much R.J. enjoys drinking other people's liquor. Accordingly, he has brought a jug of his own to share during his visit with Captain McCormick and the crew on the *Nellie Johnson*.

A blast of thunder announces Captain Seavey's arrival. The ship is securely tied to the pier. It's a four-masted ship and large enough to buffer most storms rather handily. Stepping on board with jug in hand, along with his false front of congeniality, Seavey announces his arrival. Although many years have passed since a certain Captain McCormick swindled him out of a share of the *Nellie Johnson*, there still remains a kind of nervous excitement about this meeting.

The ship is being jostled about enough to warrant only a quick exchange of greetings. The rain that has been threatening is just beginning. The crew is busy battening the hatches and securing the load of cedar logs lashed to the deck. With a motion of his hand, McCormick directs Seavey down below. Seavey has not been back on this ship since he was a much younger man.

With McCormick opening the door to his quarters, a flood of memories comes pouring forward. The bunk is still in the same spot, as is the desk littered with navigational maps. These have remained the same as Seavey remembers them. What strikes him in particular, is how McCormick directs him toward the same chair he sat in with the same polite bidding he had employed those many years ago when he successfully convinced him as a young man to invest in the *Nellie Johnson*. It brings to mind a resentment he hasn't dealt with until now.

"What's bringin' ya aboard the *Nellie Johnson*, Seavey," asks McCormick with a keen eye on Seavey's hand carrying the jug.

Attempting to meet this question with an amicable disposition, Captain Seavey smiles his broadest smile. "I saw yer ship in port and said to myself, 'I ain't seen my my old boss in years. I need to stop by and have a drink with im.' So here I am jug in hand."

Uncorking the clay jug, he passes it to McCormick whose eyes haven't left it since Seavey came on board. More than happy to see the jug coming his way, McCormick takes a long draw. Wiping his wet, satiated lips with his sleeve, he hands it back to Seavey who can't resist taking at least a small drink.

Up above, the storm continues to intensify, down below it's another story. After a few more pulls on the jug, Seavey suggests they get the crew together for a poker game. McCormick is well into his cups at this point. Agreeing, he leads the way down the ship's alley to the crew quarters. The alley way is fine for a man of average height, but a man of Seavey's magnitude is forced to stoop. Entering the already cramped crew quarters, Seavey's size alone has the immediate attention of every crew member.

"Boys I want you to meet Captain Dan Seavey," says McCormick.

Somewhat conspicuously, all of them are attempting to act as though they have never heard the name before. However, his reputation around the Great Lakes is known far and wide. It's not likely that somehow it missed these seamen. Nonetheless, within a few minutes Seavey is introducing himself in a more profound manner as his jug is being generously sampled by each crew member.

In short order, a barrel is rolled out to serve as a card table. A half dozen willing players soon surround it, prepared to fill the half dozen down turned wooden pails serving as makeshift seats. The game begins with the jug being passed without restraint. Time passes with the storm rolling overhead. The cabin is filled with cigar smoke and the boisterous voices of inebriated men. The game is getting serious as man after man drops out having lost to either Captain McCormick or to Captain Seavey. Soon the game is between only the two of these sea Titans.

The whiskey has definitely had its way with McCormick. Seavey on the other hand has been seen to tip the jug as often, but has feigned taking a drink. He's as sober as a judge. McCormick's drunken bravado is making its way into his betting. He's playing with reckless abandon, but nonetheless, still managing to hold his own. McCormick has won the last two hands and feels he's on a roll. Seavey, on the other hand has been waiting for this development—a combination of McCormick's drunken state to begin to give him the courage he needs in order to feel his recklessness as a form of invincibility. Seavey has the next deal. The hands are dealt. Both men peek at their cards. McCormick can't believe the hand he's been dealt. He has three kings and two tens. It's a full house and by far the best hand shown in the game. As the betting begins, McCormick is so sure of this hand, he raises at every opportunity. At this time, Captain Seavey gives what he hopes to be a final wager.

"What say, McCormick, we make this last bet a bit more interesting—your ship against mine—winner take all."

McCormick had not expected this wager. Peeking at his cards again, he can't imagine losing. It takes him only a moment to feel the contentment he'd experience in having bragging rights for how he beat the "great Captain Seavey" out of his ship. With barely a second thought, McCormick boldly declares, "You got yerself a deal." From here on, it will be a matter of conjecture for future generations. Both men lay out their cards. As McCormick sees Seavey's hand, his wide, sure grin quickly turns to a look of dismayed shock. There next to his hand of three kings and two tens is a hand of three aces and two jacks. Without a doubt Seavey has won the round. McCormick's first reaction is to sit and stare in disbelief. He can't believe Seavey won this hand. His next actions are to be his last for a while. He jumps up from his stool, overturning the table while lunging at Seavey, shouting, "You cheatin' bastard get off my ship!" With one swift right fist, Seavey lays McCormick out cold.

Turning to the shocked crew, Seavey bellows out in his most intimidating roar, "You men witnessed this. I won this ship fair and square. You all have a choice. You can stay on and work under my command or you can get the hell off my ship now!"

They all stand with their mouths agape. Seavey gives them the kind of stare that tells them they don't have much time to consider this offer. One by one they commit themselves.

140 THE SCOURGE OF CAPTAIN SEAVEY

"Aye, aye captain, I'll stay on."

"Good. Now, let's get this ship underway," he says with a definite air of authority.

The crew all jump to their feet. Reopening the hatches, they discover an old mate named Tug sitting on deck. As with most storms over the Great Lakes, they come on fast and furious and blow themselves out in good order. The next order of business for the crew is to watch their new captain throw their old captain overboard. The cold water revives him enough to watch the *Nellie Johnson* sailing out of the harbor with someone else at the helm.

Tug has managed to stay clear of any suspicion as to his part in this little fiasco. Now that both "Plan A and B" are complete, he is given back enough money to pay off his debt plus a substantial bonus to cover the aggravation these people put him through.

The *Wanderer* is up river far enough to be out of the way, but on watch for the satisfying conclusion to "Plan B." First mate Archie Kerby gives the high sign as the *Nellie Johnson* sails by and turns south at the mouth of the harbor. Its deck is loaded with cedar logs to be sold in Chicago. Archie, along with the rest of the *Wanderer's* crew, sail out behind them turning north toward Frankfort. In Captain Seavey's absence, Archie has been put in charge of the ship along with $12,000 taken in the bank heist.

13 A MILWAUKEE VISIT

Captain McCormick manages to swim to a dock with a ladder. After struggling to safety, he collapses again, but this time it's due to the alcohol rather than the punch to the jaw. It's near dawn before he comes to enough to find himself in strange surroundings. The local police found him soaked to the bone and passed out on the wharf. Dutifully, they hauled him off to jail. Stumbling to his feet, he is met with a wall of steel bars separating himself from everything other than the bunk in the six by nine foot cell he's confined to.

He immediately begins a shouting tirade against everything and everybody that God and man has ever put in charge of law enforcement. There is no one present to listen to him. All available law enforcement personnel in the area have been called in to help with an investigation of a bank heist that took place overnight. It's evening before the chief of police makes his way back to his jail. By this time, McCormick is fully sober and in no mood to hear that he can't see the judge until the next morning. His mouth begins his tirade all over again.

"That big son-of-bitch stole my ship and you lazy ass cops are lettin' him get away with it."

The chief is in no mood to listen to the blathering of how this sea captain was taken advantage of while drunk. "I'm tired and in no mood to listen to your drunken ranting. I'm going to tell you this only one time, if you don't shut your mouth, I'm going to forget you're here for a couple more days," says the chief.

McCormick can hardly contain his frustration. He feels his ship has been hi-jacked by a "card cheatin' thug." What increases his level of frustration is that he's being confined when he could be alerting the proper authorities that have jurisdiction in these matters.

In the meantime, Captain Seavey and his newly acquired ship are well on their way to Chicago. He's ordered the crew to rig the ship for maximum speed.

While rummaging through McCormick's paper work, Seavey discovers a contract between a Raymond Simon and R.J. McCormick. For the agreed sum of $500, Simon is to receive the cargo of cedar logs. It's not a familiar name to Seavey, so obviously it's a broker that he's never done

142   THE SCOURGE OF CAPTAIN SEAVEY

business with. That means it's going to be tricky to explain how he is in charge of the exchange of logs for money. Nonetheless, the rebuilding of the city after the great fire in 1877 is still underway and the hunger for building materials is insatiable. Despite the number of enemies he's managed to acquire over the span of his career, with the Booth company being one of the more recent, he's sure he can find a buyer among his own contacts.

Opting to keep the *Nellie Johnson* out of the main channel until he can figure out how he's going to free himself of this predicament, Seavey anchors off at the mouth of the river. The idea is to stay out sight of the harbor master, or for that matter, any of McCormick's associates. He orders the jon boat to be lowered and with Tug aboard, the two of them row ashore to survey the situation. Since Tug is much more familiar with McCormick's cronies, Seavey has to rely on him to keep him clear of any potential trouble. After hiring a buckboard to make the trip up river, they stop at a local watering hole to catch up on any available local news. The place is abuzz with the *Nellie Johnson*. The bartender is excited enough to pass on the information that he's heard.

"It's reported that a telegraph has been dispatched to the harbor master by a certain Captain McCormick, master of the *Nellie Johnson*. It states his ship has been hi-jacked with all its cargo and to be on the look out for it. He's also posted a $300 reward for the return of his ship and for information leading to the arrest of a certain Captain Daniel Seavey," says the barkeeper.

This is not the kind of news Seavey is hoping to hear. By keeping McCormick's crew, he has guaranteed himself witnesses to corroborate that he won the *Nellie Johnson* in a legitimate, fair and square poker game. In spite of all this support, he'd just as soon avoid any confrontations with the law regardless of how legitimate his claim may be.

In view of this news, they cut short their trip and make a beeline back to the anchored ship. "I believe we best set sail and get out of these waters for the time being," contemplates Seavey.

The crew listens with a sympathetic ear. Even though they have a claim to some of the money this timber can bring, they're more inclined to cut their losses and take what they can get. "I know all of us would like to get a bigger payday, but as far as I'm concerned, the sooner we get the weight off this ship the easier it'll be to get the hell out of here, and that includes dumping it all overboard if we have to."

Captain Seavey knows the crew is accurate in saying that they need to get the added weight of the timber off the ship. All of them have the uncanny intuition that this caper is far from being over. That being the case, and not wanting to be slowed with any unnecessary cargo, it's agreed by all that the sooner it's gone the better. On the other hand, Seavey has not become the legend he is because of knee-jerk decisions. His plan is to not miss a payday if it can be avoided.

Not certain if a sighting of the *Nellie Johnson* has been verified, Captain Seavey makes a decision to sail up the western coast toward Milwaukee. He has done business with a lumber broker there in the past. "I think we can unload this pile of sticks with a German guy up in Evanston."

In discussing this option with the crew, he airs a complaint he has with this plan. "I've given this guy business from time to time, but he's damn tight with his money. He doesn't want to pay a penny more than he can get away with. The trouble is, he's aware that when I do business with him, it's because something is causing me to avoid the Chicago markets."

Not to belabor his former point about dumping the load, the crew resigns themselves to Captain Seavey's lead. By midnight, under the cloak of a dark, cloud-covered night, the deal is being made with the Evanston German. As Seavey had predicted, this late night timber dealer is intuitive enough to suspect something is up and is giving him a discount price.

144 THE SCOURGE OF CAPTAIN SEAVEY

With no other bargaining chips, he is compelled to accept the terms. By 2:00am the *Nellie Johnson's* deck is clear. The German has his timber and Captain Seavey has $400, one hundred less than he could have gotten in the Chicago market.

The plan is to stay out of the southern part of the lake where the chances of having to deal with the federal marshals are highest. These revenuers have recently upgraded their pursuit ship from a sailing ship to a steel-hulled, steam-driven propeller ship capable of doing eighteen knots named the *Tuscarora*. So far, they have exclusive bragging rights to being the fastest ship on the Great Lakes.

Since the crew is more familiar with the *Nellie Johnson* than Seavey, he is depending on them to get more out of her rigging than he is able to at this point. Soon they are rigged with sails set to get the most out of the prevailing SW winds.

With the ship in good hands and on course toward the north, Seavey takes advantage of the lull to retire to his cabin for a few draws on his whiskey jug and a bit of well earned rest. Within a few minutes of laying his head on his pillow, he drifts into a slumber. The quietness of this rest is short-lived and rudely interrupted with the unsolicited presence of his nighttime nemesis, Abequa.

"So Captain you've managed to put yourself in jeopardy yet again for another stupid reason. And now after your wife and daughter took a week out of their lives to visit you, you're going to blow right by Milwaukee, disregarding that you know exactly where you can find them. You are truly a despicable person. I also want to let you know that despite your mother's passing, she is aware of how you disregard the well-being of her grandchild. My hope is that you grow old alone and unloved as you have left them unloved."

As has become the routine with these nether world visits, he awakens in a frightening panic, unrefreshed, depressed and unable to make a clear rational decision. Looking at the clock, he realizes that he has been sleeping for less than a minute. He feels his hands shaking uncontrollably, so much so that it is nearly impossible to put himself back into his coat. With a dazed look he stumbles to the deck.

Without explanation, he relieves the helmsman of his watch. Taking the wheel in hand, he orders the rigging reset, and with a few determined turns on the wheel, redirects the ship toward the west. In a matter of a couple hours, he spots a familiar light house marking a shallow point. Taking precautions, he maneuvers this unfamiliar vessel closer to shore until coming across a buoy light he knows will take him into a cove on the outskirts of Milwaukee. Hopefully this will be enough to conceal the *Nellie Johnson* from nosy strangers. After making his way into this small harbor, he anchors in deeper water, and follows up with orders to place some oil lamps around the deck to prevent a way-fare collision. With all this taken care of, he returns to his quarters. Still unable to sleep, and with no other choices, he waits for dawn.

Somewhere on shore a rooster crows. The sun is barely peeking over the lake's naked horizon announcing a new day. The ship's cook is in his galley putting together side pork and hot cakes. The coffee is hot and strong.

Since all on board are aware of how quickly word can spread throughout these waters concerning the alleged theft of the *Nellie Johnson*, the challenge this morning for Seavey is to announce to the crew that he is going to take time to tend to what he is referring to as "a private affair," and ask them to stand by in the midst of the risk. Captain Seavey is going through the same delirium that he has been visited with so many times before. A quick look at his face reveals the same near blank stare of hopelessness. It's a plight that he's never grown accustomed to. From time to time the crew on the *Wanderer* could expect this kind of disturbed behavior from their Master, but the *Nellie Johnson's* crew has never experienced this with anyone they have ever crewed for in the past.

He orders a jon boat to be lowered. Without a word of why or where he is going or for how long, he silently rows himself ashore. Once there, he encounters a row of farm buildings with a pasture bordering the harbor. Beaching his boat, he makes his way past a herd of milk cows contentedly chewing their cuds with nothing more than a curious gaze in his direction. Rather than attack, they are satisfied to let this interloper pass. Entering through an unlocked gate, he finds himself not twenty feet from a young man maneuvering a horse toward a wagon. They startle each other with their unexpected presence. For the moment, they are content to examine the other without speaking. Breaking the silence, the young man tenuously picks up an ax handle laying in the wagon.

"Sompin' I can do for you mister?" he asks. It's clear that he means to use the tool as a weapon if he gets the wrong answer. Captain Seavey realizing where this can quickly lead doesn't hesitate to point a finger out toward the harbor at the anchored *Nellie Johnson*. As if this weren't enough, knowing he's a wanted man, giving his name could end in a worse disaster.

"My name is Dan. That, sir, is my ship. I need to get to an address on this side of Milwaukee and am hopin' I can hire you to take me."

From what can only be described as an awkward look, it's obvious the young man is processing the veracity of this statement. For reasons known only to himself, he relaxes his attitude.

"I gotta go that way this morning myself. Give me a hand with this damn horse and I'll take you to where you need to go. But I want you to know, iffin' you do anything to change my mind, I'll beat ya into next week with this ax handle."

Grateful that things have become less hostile, Captain Seavey gladly holds the reins while the young man continues attempting to harness the reluctant horse to the wagon. Grateful that things are going as smoothly between them as they seem to be, Seavey can only hope they will continue. The young man's age is somewhere in the vicinity of early twenty something. Without a lot of fanfare, the two of them are finally on their way. With his eyes glued to the path and with the horse's strong desire to stray, the young man at last introduces himself.

"My name is Ivan—Ivan Kidder. Sorry about talkin' tough to ya Dan, but around these parts a man's gotta stay on top of things or he'll end up wishin' he had. By the way, where ya goin' anyway?"

"You can drop me off on Hickory Street or anywhere close to it," says Seavey.

"That sounds good 'cause I'm going in that area myself," replies Ivan. Little more is said. For what it could be worth, Seavey is finding something appealing about this young man's grit. Within a few minutes, Ivan is questioning Captain Seavey about the address.

"What's the address yer goin' to?"

"1544 North Hickory."

Ivan's head snaps in the direction of his passenger, almost twisting it off his shoulders.

"That's where I'm going! How in the hell do you know these people?" At this information it's impossible for this young man to be anything other than shocked.

"If you're referring to 'these people' as the people who live there, they're my wife and daughter," says Seavey with a superior air.

"Oh my god! You're Josey's dad—you're Captain Seavey, the pirate, ain't you?" Not waiting for an answer and in his sudden exuberance, he can only think to say, "Well I'll be go to hell! I've heard enough about you to write a book!"

Still not sure where this is going, Seavey measures his thoughts so as to hopefully match his words, but by the time his words formed there is a noticeable disdain to them.

"Who told you a pile of crap like that, and how the hell do you know my family?" roars Seavey now looking directly at this seeming obtruder. Before Ivan can answer, they round the corner and are directly in front of the house in time to see Josey, all smiles, come off the porch toward them. It's certain she's not expecting to see what she sees before her. She stops dead in her tracks. Her smile instantly disappears leaving a lone look of bewilderment. Simultaneously, Seavey and Ivan focus their attention on this statuesque young woman—one as a father, the other as a suitor and together exclaim, "Hi baby!" Both men look to the other as they would an intruder, Josey remains just as perplexed.

Ignoring Ivan for the moment, her attention is solely on her father. "Daddy how did you get here?"

A smile has returned to Seavey. "Oh I was in the neighborhood and thought I'd stop by."

Hoping to untangle this web of mystery, her head directly turns back to Ivan hoping for a more clear explanation. "He showed up in my front yard this morning. His ship's out behind my place anchored in the harbor," says Ivan, rather matter of factly.

Left just as confused and shaking her head, Josey greets her father with an uncertain, maybe even a somewhat suspicious hug and is nonetheless, still left completely in the dark. After all, this is not a common neighborly visit over a cup of tea for either of them.

Turning back to Ivan, Josey somewhat clumsily also hugs him. It's apparent this whole encounter is leaving each of them with a slew of unanswered questions. Over tea during the next hour, and along with Mary, they each have cleared up most of the mysteries surrounding this less than normal rendezvous.

In the preceding days, it seems that the word concerning Captain Seavey's incident with McCormick has captured the imaginations of the bigger Chicago and New York news reporters. These recent news stories describing Seavey as a pirate, in turn, have caught the attention of his wife and daughter, along with Ivan, who Josey now describes as her "fiance".

The two young people soon make their way back out the door. It seems they have a meeting with Father Delaney for prenuptial arrangements. This occasion leaves the estranged mother and father alone for the first time in many years. Mary has not been feeling well for some time. It seems she's contracted what she describes as a summer cold. She's lost a lot of weight and is coughing a lot. Nevertheless, she believes she's getting better. Today is her first day out of bed in a week.

It's been such a long separation for the two of them that sitting at the same table has no frame of reference for either of them. They find that they are nowhere near what can be described as husband and wife. They have been apart longer than they were together. A more accurate description characterizes them as two strangers whose ships passed at some point long enough to make a dent in each others lives.

Even though all of this has been readily acknowledged by both of them, they however, seem to be reluctant to pluck out that small glimmer of hope that still binds the two of them together. They discover even now under these uncomfortable circumstances that there still remains an unusual need to remain in the other's presence. It's as though the book revealing their lives together is still open and waiting for a new entry. What both are readily aware of is how loud the ticking of the kitchen clock is pronouncing the uneasy silence between them. Mary is the first to acknowledge the clock's intrusion by taking note that it is near lunch time.

"Seav, would you care to stay for lunch?"

Glancing at the same clock, then double checking it against his own vest pocket watch gives him enough time to process this foreign, but yet somewhat familiar sounding request.

"Ya know Mary, I think I got a bit a time for some of your cookin'."

The miracle within this exchange is that it's being done without any malice exhibited for the other. Maybe what's happening is that both of them have discovered that loving their daughter together as her parents is stronger than hating each other. Whatever the cause, they spend the next hour exploring the options that this new behavior is opening.

"I don't know what all this newspaper stuff is going to bring my way, but when things get cleared up, I'd like to come back and visit the both of you," says Seavey in a well-defined, decided voice.

Mary can tell by his mannerisms that this is a man, who though he is still running, it may now be more out of momentum than desire.

"Yes I'd like that," and hesitating for a moment, she adds, "I know for sure that Josey would love it."

She finds she is using a civil tone of voice for the first time in years with this derelict husband and father.

With lunch behind them, having made peace as best as possible and knowing that he can't dawdle too long, Captain Seavey opts to cut his visit short. The certainty of the peril that he and his crew are in makes getting back to his waiting vessel an emergent priority. For the first time in many years, he doesn't regret the time he has taken to reach out to Mary and his daughter. Something in his inner person gets the feeling that Abequa will also be pleased.

Hiring a wagon to return him to Ivan's farm and his waiting jon boat, he makes his way back on board to be met by a more than unhappy crew. By this time, the afternoon is waning. They are noticeably agitated. They have the feeling that by remaining in these waters they are nothing more than sitting ducks to any nosy opportunist. Recognizing their need for immediate leadership, Captain Seavey orders a rigging set to get them out of the harbor and back onto the Great Lake. This order can't come soon enough. Within minutes this well-oiled crew is on their way. Seavey has his eye to the glass as they break out of the harbor. Much to the relief of himself and the rest of the crew, there doesn't appear to be any immediate danger looming on any horizon.

14 THE *TUSCARORA*

Although things may appear to be at a stand still with Captain Seavey and his "band of merry men" sailing the *Nellie Johnson*, all is not quiet on the western shore. Captain McCormick, during a short period of near sobriety, has finally convinced the government authorities that his boat did not disappear with his permission.

"With this many days passing before these authorities can get off their ass is sure as hell giving Seavey a damn sure advantage. He could have that boat sold to the man in the moon and be back home already," laments McCormick. This is said while in the only condition he runs to in handling any crisis—drunk.

Moreover, back in the Windy City the federal government has added the *Tuscarora*, a 178-foot steel hulled, steam-powered, propeller-driven cutter to their arsenal. It is commanded by Captain Preston Uberroth. A week after this incident is reported, the *Tuscarora* steams out of Chicago in pursuit of the ever elusive Captain Dan Seavey. Aboard is U.S. Deputy Marshal Tom Currier with an arrest warrant carrying Seavey's name. Both of these men have a well developed regard for the law, but not nearly as developed as their egos.

"If this son-of-bitch thinks he can pull these stunts on my watch, he's got another think coming," states Currier bluntly. He's a lanky man in his mid-forties, well mustached in the distinct tradition of other lawmen. This recent outburst is a rare glimpse into the magnitude of this man's ego regarding a scofflaw, the likes of one Captain Dan Seavey. In his own mind, chasing Seavey down using all the technologies available assures him that this pirate can run but can't hide. He has begun by telephoning every life saving station and light house up the eastern side of the lake to be on the lookout for this pirate.

All of this widespread probing has caught the attention of the newspapers. The story is way too irresistible for the news vultures to pass up. Like so many of America's colorful scofflaws, Captain Seavey has become the focal point of many of their stories. To say the least, the public is eating it up, especially now that they have been included as part of the investigating team. Reports are beginning to stream in sighting him at both ends of the Great Lake at the same time. No report is too insignificant not to be sensationalized in a headline.

"It's all bull-shit. This pecker-wood is making a fool of us," says Currier.

Captain Uberroth is also beginning to show his frustration in running after this illusory prize. To capture such a notorious pirate as Captain Seavey will certainly be a feather in, what so far is proving to be, an empty hat.

"How in hell am I supposed to run this ship? All I'm doing is refueling and chasing after a ghost?"

After a series of failed endeavors and harking back on his training as an investigator, Deputy Currier begins to calm down. Rethinking his plan, he begins to exercise a new found patience. Often what starts as routine quickly changes to more than expected. It's evident to these high energy lawmen that this is proving to be one of those cases.

While they are refueling on the eastern shore of the Great Lake in Manistee, Michigan, what appears to be a standard report from the Frankfort Life Saving station turns into what could be a big break. The report states that the *Nellie Johnson* is definitely in the area. According to the telegram, the allegedly stolen ship is being stowed away up the Betsie River on the South Frankfort side of the Betsie Bay. The report also states that Captain Seavey has been seen in town buying supplies. This is the kind of report that makes a man like Currier wish he could walk on water.

"Captain, I need you to get this next thirty miles behind us. With a little luck, we can cut that pecker-wood off before he decides to leave," directs Currier. On the outside, it's obvious that he's trying his best to remain calm and professional. On the inside, it's another story. About to explode with anticipation, he stations himself at the front of the ship as though this perch will insure he'll arrive sooner.

Captain Uberroth does not need a second directive. Over the next few minutes, he wastes no time sending a half dozen commands to the first mate, which include the words "full speed ahead." The men passing coal receive the order and fire the boilers to a level never before reached. The result is by the time the ship is halfway to Frankfort the heat on the smoke stack is burning the paint away leaving it a scorched black-brown color. Less than two hours have passed since the ship began this action. They are within sight of the Frankfort light house and decisions have to be made.

Without a moment's hesitation, Deputy Currier offers his point-blank recommendation. "I think we should charge into the harbor, corner him, and take him by surprise."

Captain Uberroth, on the other hand is not so sure this is a good idea. "I've never been in that harbor with this ship. I'm not willing to take the chance of grounding her. I'm going up the coast at a point where I've got charts and I'm sure of the water. From there we'll have no problem keeping an eye on who's coming and going."

With his anxiety level at a fever pitch and the veins bulging in his neck, this is not what Deputy Currier is ready to hear. "I don't want to hear what you can't do, I want that son-of-bitch in irons today," he bellows.

Uberroth is not intimidated for a moment by Currier's overdeveloped sense of power. "You may be in charge of this investigation, but I want to remind you who's in charge of this vessel. I'm only going to tell you this one more time, I'm not taking this ship into waters that I'm not familiar with, and that's final!"

Currier's frustration is far from eased with the realization that Uberroth has the upper hand. All he can do is watch the mouth of the harbor get smaller behind the ship as it powers undeterred a couple nautical miles north to Point Betsie.

To imagine that a ship of this magnitude is going to merely slip into these waters un-noticed is unimaginable. Within minutes of passing the mouth of the harbor a crew from the Life Saving Station, while practicing a drill, spots the *Tuscarora*. They can only envy its crew. It's truly a ship of beauty and grace as it glides effortlessly through the choppy seas. In spite of their being under strict orders to keep the information of the where-abouts of this ship to themselves, the crew is more inclined to be behind their generous benefactor, Captain Seavey the alleged pirate.

It doesn't take long before this information has reached the ears of Seavey's first mate Archie who happens to be hanging around Peasoup's tavern in South Frankfort. Making his way up river to where both the *Wanderer* and the *Nellie Johnson* are moored side by side, he finds Captain Seavey taking a much needed nap as he has only arrived early this morning.

Unable to contain himself, he rushes into Seavey's cabin shouting. "Cap'n, our fears are comin' ta haunt us. Those revenuers have found us out. Word has it that they've anchored off this side of Point Betsie."

Adjusting to being awakened out of a dead sleep, and particularly to this kind of news, quickly gains Seavey's attention. The full details of the account remain somewhat sketchy, but alarming enough to elicit a very concerned response. After a few minutes of evaluating their options, Seavey makes his decision.

"We ain't gonna sit here like sittin' ducks and let these revenuers have their way without a fight."

Archie is all ears. "What ya got in mind Capn'?" asks Archie, trying to remain calm.

"Get this ship rigged and ready to sail," says Seavey speaking of the *Wanderer*. Turning to the first mate on the *Nellie Johnson*, he gives the same order. "Get the ship ready to follow the *Wanderer*."

Seavey's next move is to assemble the two crews on the deck of the *Wanderer*. A plan of action is quickly put together. The fiat is to have the *Wanderer* become the decoy. Taking the first mate from the *Nellie Johnson* aside, he lays out his plan.

"After the *Tuscarora* takes the bait and begins to pursue the *Wanderer*, slip out of the harbor and return this ship to McCormick. Be sure to tell him that I expect him to take damn good care of my vessel and assure him that when he wants to play another hand of poker, I'll give him a chance to win it back."

The first mate breaks out into a wide grin.

"I'll do that for certain Cap'n. I also want to thank you for a hell of an adventure and the extra payday."

With this last piece of business between themselves concluded, they shake hands and part ways, each to fulfill a new and different destiny.

As agreed upon, the *Wanderer* waits until an hour before dark and breaks through the channel and into the lake. What Captain Seavey had predicted begins to take place. With a huge plume of smoke rising above the horizon, the *Tuscarora* roars to life. They have had a crew member stationed in the crow's nest all afternoon watching for just such a move on the part of Seavey. Seeing the *Wanderer* break through the harbor under full sail is just what Captain Uberroth had expected Seavey to do.

"Perfect!" he screeches tossing his telescope aside. He bellows to the first mate to weigh anchor and orders the engine crew to fire the ship's boilers to be hot enough for a full pursuit.

A couple of nautical miles away, Captain Seavey, keeping a keen eye toward the pursuing gun boat, prepares for his next step in the action. He's well aware that on a straight course this steel-hulled, steam-driven, government ship is more than capable of overtaking him. He is also well aware of the advantage his smaller craft has in being able to tack from side to side. The *Tuscarora*, being a much longer vessel, needs more time and distance to attempt to follow the same course. On the other hand, if Uberroth decides to maintain his course and misjudges this pugnacious captain's next tacking maneuver, their worst fear will be realized—with darkness closing in, they will be left too far behind and the *Wanderer* will make a successful escape.

It soon becomes apparent that darkness is definitely going to be a game changer. Uberroth has not succeeded in overtaking Seavey. This is a horrible frustration for both Uberroth and Currier.

Currier's mouth is more than prepared to attack Captain Uberroth. "I told you this was gonna happen. We should have gone right into that harbor after him. If you'da listened ta me, we'd have that bastard in chains about now."

Uberroth is in no mood to put up with any of Currier's guff. Pointing toward himself he says, "If you ain't smart enough not to piss this alligator off before you get through the swamp, then the only person gonna be in chains will be your sorry ass sinkin' to the bottom of this lake. If you're smart, you'll go to your quarters and shut your goddam mouth!"

Currier, suspecting that with all of Uberroth's crew being in league with their captain, a report stating that he had fallen overboard is unlikely to be questioned. As much as his personality is opposed to "giving in," his second thought tells him that he may be skating on thin ice. With that, he lets out a defiant little, "Harrumph," and storms back to his quarters.

Meantime, over on the *Wanderer,* Captain Seavey is taking advantage of the moonless night. With his ship being cloaked in darkness, he decides to risk navigating without running lights. The *Tuscarora,* on the other hand, is lit up like a Christmas tree. Because of this fact, Captain Seavey knows exactly where his nemesis is positioned. Circling unseen back around and behind the *Tuscarora,* he watches as that vessel continues its path in the belief that his intent is to cross the sixty mile trek to the Wisconsin side.

The arrival of morning does little to alleviate Deputy Currier's frustrations. His missed opportunity to have Seavey by the short hairs still has him disjointed. Not having complete control over exercising the warrant he has against Seavey is almost more than he can endure. Remembering his near tragic discourse with Captain Uberroth the day before, he's careful to measure his words.

"No sign of him this morning?" questions Currier.

Captain Uberroth's eye is stuck to his telescope scanning the horizon for the elusive *Wanderer.* Reluctant to get back into a confrontation with a United States Deputy Marshall, Uberroth lowers his glass. He is also careful to answer as civilly as he can. "No, but I believe he may be trying to make us think he's heading for Wisconsin. With the wind coming out of the west, he and I both know he wouldn't stand a chance of outrunning us if that is still his plan."

Not completely understanding this "sea talk," Currier asks again, "Does that mean you know where he is or you don't know where he is?"

"It means I know where he's not," returns Uberroth. "Our best bet will be to steam down the eastern coast and start this process all over again."

Still smarting from Seavey's successful outmaneuvering tactics, both Currier and Uberroth realize the necessity to calm down.

Eyeballing each other for the next move, Currier is the first to speak. "I realize that I got a bit over-excited yesterday. With a calmer head this morning I want to apologize."

Uberroth also is in a more reasonable temperament. "I'll accept yours if you'll accept mine." With a big grin, he adds, "I want you to know I probably would have pulled you up before you drowned."

Both shake hands and begin the day with what they hope will be a co-operative working arrangement.

The day is also breaking for Captain Seavey and the *Wanderer's* crew. They have successfully outsmarted the *Tuscarora*, but Seavey is also smart enough to realize this is only a small battle in an ongoing war. Seavey remembers well when he was on their side of the law and how there is a sense of personal pride in not letting a perpetrator outfox you. He can't help but know he has definitely crossed the line now and is making this a very personal vendetta for all involved.

Captain Seavey discusses plans with first mate Archie Kerby. "I know these Revenuers ain't about to go home with their tail between their legs. They got it in for me good now. But I ain't runnin' like a baby girl either."

Archie knows well that he and the crew would probably be exempt from any prosecution as they are required to follow their captain's orders or risk being charged with mutiny.

"I don't suspect I've ever seen ya do such a thing Cap'n." He pauses for the moment then adds with a most sincere voice, "You can depend on me and the crew to do our best to back ya up."

"Yer a good man Archie," says Captain Seavey. They spend the next fifteen minutes devouring one of Ginny's breakfasts of pancakes, eggs, and side pork. They were all in agreement that sooner or later there would be a serious confrontation with the *Tuscarora*. The plan, for the time being, is that if they are cornered and have to go down, they will go down with their heads held high.

Archie suggests they would have a better chance by going back to Frankfort to wait since they are more familiar with the Lake's shifting personality around that area than anywhere else. As a matter of fact, Captain Seavey is plotting a maneuver in his own head that he is sure will be the demise of the *Tuscarora*.

Meanwhile, back on the *Tuscarora* other plans are being mapped out. Currier, while he is sitting in on Uberroth's discussion with his first mate, is doing the best he can to understand where all the navigational talk may be leading. Uberroth is convinced, with the wind conditions as they are, that Seavey has no other option than to remain along the eastern shoreline. His plan is to steam back as well as renew his telephone contacts with the various Life Saving Stations along the coast. He sets his course to Ludington, Michigan and an hour later is navigating this very impressive ship into the Ludington harbor. It is definitely a head turner. A ship of this magnitude with all the latest technologies is the envy of every seafarer that lays eyes on her. Word has gotten around as to why a vessel of this importance has decided to harbor in their community. The town has come to a standstill as the gawkers assemble along the docks.

"Ole Seavey may have met his match with this baby," says one man.

Another agrees. "This is the fastest son-of-bitch that's ever weighed anchor on this lake or any other. I think ole Seavey may be meetin' his Waterloo."

Another who claims to have crewed with Captain Seavey at one time is not so quick to count him out. Pointing toward the *Tuscarora*, he makes his point. "This here ship may be a lotta things, but goin' head ta head with Seavey may be more than her captain has reckoned on."

While all this hullabaloo over his ship is going on, Uberroth is busy having his coal supply topped off and making his telephone calls. On returning to his ship, he has an extra bounce in his step. Speaking directly to Deputy Currier, with a large grin, he makes a rather succinct announcement. "Our pal Seavey has been spotted back at the Frankfort harbor. With a little luck we can cook his goose right in his own pot."

The excitement around this latest news invigorates the entire crew. Getting underway is almost a labor of love—or at least as close to a labor of love as this type of work will permit. Within the hour they have finished with the coal delivery and are breaking out of the harbor into open waters.

Uberroth shouts orders to his engine room. "Full steam ahead!"

This tough crew down below the deck knows exactly what that means. This ship was built with the idea that there are no rivals. Its design is meant to make known to every captain on the Great Lakes that it will run you down if needs be. It's more often referred to as a gun boat. It's purposely designed with several cannons as well as a swiveling Gatling gun mounted to the decking. The idea is not merely to match any firepower directed at them, but to meet it with a superior and overwhelming show of force. A well-placed cannon ball at the water line of an opposing vessel is guaranteed to send it directly to Davey Jones's Locker.

Back in Frankfort, Seavey is more than certain that this is merely the beginning of a show down with this ship load of Revenuers. For Seavey, a challenge of this sort cannot go unanswered despite his reservations. He is preparing his defense. He has sent Jack up the three hundred foot dunes that run along the shoreline with a set of signal flags and a telescope. He has a two-fold job: one is to signal when he sees the Revenuer's ship and two is to turn up the exact position of a rocky sandbar that's plagued the hulls of ships that were not aware of its location. What makes this particular reef so dangerous is that it's a good half mile out in the lake marked only by a buoy that's rarely monitored. Jack makes good on directing the *Wanderer* safely to the reef. Captain Seavey hooks a line on the several buoys and drags them to a new location. No sooner is that task accomplished than Jack sends a signal that he has sighted the *Tuscarora*.

"The game is on," announces an excited Captain Seavey. With this information, he re-rigs the sails preparing for what he expects to be a high seas chase.

With the *Tuscarora* now only a half mile off his bow, Seavey positions himself in such a way that it will give Uberroth the impression he is making a run for it. His next move is to order the ship to turn hard to the port side. Watching the *Tuscarora* react brings a smile to Seavey's face. They are predictably falling into his trap. The *Tuscarora* is on a full throttle straight line heading directly toward the *Wanderer*. There is no doubt in either of their minds that the big government steam ship will quickly overtake Captain Seavey's much smaller wind-driven vessel.

Now within shouting distance, Captain Uberroth is on his megaphone. "Drop your sails and set your anchor in the name of the United States Federal Government," he orders in his most official voice. At the same moment, as though to put a period at the end of this imperative, a cannon ball whizzes past the *Wanderer's* bow.

Instead of capitulating, Captain Seavey orders a hard turn to the starboard side. His eye immediately turns back toward the *Tuscarora*. Being a bigger ship, it cannot respond to these quick turns. What happens next is a textbook Seavey maneuver. The *Tuscarora* continues on course and at full throttle slams head long into the unmarked reef. The sound of the smashing hull resounds throughout the ship's entire infrastructure as it plows its way deeper into this submerged stone and sand reef. Every person on board is caught unawares and thrown forward. After picking himself up from the deck of the wheel house, Uberroth can feel the blood streaming down his face. It turns out that his head went through one of the wheel house windows. A glass shard sticks rather ostentatiously from the wound. By the time Uberroth, Currier, and the crew recover and tend to their wounded, including Uberroth himself, Seavey is sailing out of sight in the opposite direction.

The rest of the *Tuscarora* crew is busy assessing the damage. It's soon apparent with the tell-tale sandy-colored water encircling the ship that the vessel isn't going anywhere soon. From first inspection, it doesn't appear to have sprung any obvious leaks, but it is firmly resting on the sand bar some five feet below the water line. Over the next hour, Captain Uberroth attempts to free his ship to no avail. It's jammed tight. Finally, he succumbs to the obvious. Speaking to his first mate, he orders him to release a jon boat and send a commission with the assignment to send a tugboat to pull them off this sandbar.

As for Currier, it's all he can do to remain amicable. He's becoming fully aware that they are not dealing with a common criminal in the sense that Seavey would be a routine arrest. Rather than show his frustration yet again, he opts to stay out of all the craziness and returns to his cabin.

On the other hand with luck on his side, Captain Seavey sails on down the coast. With a little more luck, he'll soon be berthed in a little known cove that he has used at different times when things got too hot. It's much too small to be charted on any nautical maps and much too shallow for a ship the size of the *Tuscarora* to navigate. Nonetheless, it's a secure enough cove to protect against a storm brewing over the lake. The sun is well-hidden behind a bank of swirling clouds and the seas are beginning to roll. The upside to all of this is that the *Wanderer's* crew is accustomed to these rapid changes on this lake they call home. A happy ending for them is to celebrate any event that allows them the freedom to live their chosen lifestyle one more day.

Safely out of reach of the Federal ship and well protected from the impending gale, Captain Seavey breaks out a jug of moonshine whiskey to mark the occasion. Passing it from man to man soon loosens the pent up nerves this last episode has produced. Along with loosening nerves, it leads to loosening tongues. Soon the crew are slapping one another on the back and laughing about how they put one over on this seemingly unconquerable Federal ship.

"When that big tub hit the sand bar, all I remember seeing is their captain's head come crashing out that wheel house window, cap and all," says Ob holding his sides, hardly able to control his laughter. The rest of the crew join in bursting at the seams to recount their own renditions. Parading the absurdity of the *Tuscarora* in their failure to capture them is the only spoils won—but it's enough for these pirates of simple tastes.

With the storm brewing topside, there is little left for these buccaneers to do. Soon the whiskey is having its way with man after man buckling under its dominance. Seavey has found his way back to his own quarters, collapsing, clothing and all on his bunk. With a little more luck, he'll sleep this off by the time the storm subsides.

He would readily admit what happens next has little to do with good luck. His sleep is interrupted by a very familiar presence. It's Abequa. She is showing no mercy once again.

"Well Captain, you no sooner get back on track and before the day is over, you fall right back into your old ways. How long do you think your long suffering wife and daughter are going to remain impressed with your false promises?"

Pausing long enough to watch him begin to fall into despair, content where this is leading him, she continues, "This is exactly the reason there is no place in heaven for self-absorbed liars like you. You only had one penance you were asked to do and you cast it aside as you always do. Even if God is a God of mercy, He's more than the likes of your ilk can hope for."

The kind of depression that Abequa is able to initiate in him overwhelms him like a huge blanket of loneliness and lostness in which he can't find his way out.

"I-I-I'm doing the best I can. I didn't get this way overnight you know. It's going to take me awhile to figure this all out," he stammers with what he hopes to be the right amount of sincerity to appease this phantom tormenter.

Abequa breaks into hysterical laughter at his lame attempt to gain her sympathy. Just as suddenly her face twists into a belittling, scornful look. "You didn't get this way overnight is a truth larger than you are capable of admitting. You've been this way your entire life. You're nothing more or less than a self-serving lost sinner on his way to a well-deserved hell."

Watching him sink deeper into the loneliness those guilty of this sin find themselves trapped beneath, gives her great delight. Feeling quite sure she has him defeated, emboldens her enough to add an imperative she is sure he can, with his own strength, never achieve. "This defect could be overcome when you put as much value on caring for your family as you do yourself!! But then, you and I both know it's way too late for you."

Abequa is perfectly capable of convicting him and then leaving him hopeless. Hearing her say these words of condemnation has the same effect that it always does. Upon awakening, his depression has him at the brink of suicide. It's been reported by some that dogs seem to possess a sense of these spirits. Duke is no exception. He looks forlorn under the table, hoping for some comfort from his master. It's obvious the poor creature has also undergone some form of trauma. Unfortunately, Seavey has nothing to give this trusting pet as Duke is trapped under her spell as well.

Archie has known him long enough to realize when he takes on this demeanor that it's best to let his captain work through this depression the way he always does. With as few words as possible, this compassionate first mate finds that as usual, Seavey wants the jon boat dispatched with only himself as its passenger.

Assuring him that they will be here for him when he returns, Seavey can only muster a slight nod of approval. Rowing to shore, he secures the small boat and begins his quest for a Catholic church. At this point, he would gladly crawl on his knees to a confessional if only to hear the priest absolve him. Making his way into the small village of Onekama, he inquires of the first person he encounters as to where he can find a priest.

"I ain't much of a church goin' man, but I'm sure there's one at that little church right there," says the stranger pointing to the smallest little chapel Seavey has ever seen. Looking at the placard across the front it denotes it as a chapel dedicated as Chapel of St John By The Lake. Silently, without as much as a thank-you and still staring straight ahead, Seavey begins his trek to the chapel door. There he is met by a kindly looking, older priest in need of a haircut and his ear hair trimmed. He's dressed in a long cassock that leaves only a pair of worn sandals visible.

"You takin' confessions today Father?" he asks with his usual sense of urgency.

The old priest is taken by surprise. It's been years since anyone has sought him out with anything near that kind of request and particularly with this type of urgency. Giving him only a brief once over, he quickly answers as though this opportunity could slip through his fingers. "Yes son, I think I can do that."

Looking around for the confessional in this tiny structure, all Seavey sees is an altar with a crucifix gracing the corpus of a dying Christ and a statue off to the side of a risen Christ. The old priest motions him to take a seat in one of the half dozen pews. Without a lot of fanfare, the old priest takes a seat in front of Seavey, turning half way around to face him.

A bit confused Seavey asks, "Is this where we're gonna do this?"

With a knowing little grin the old priest answers, "This looks to be about as good a place as any."

At once Seavey senses something comfortable about this kindly looking old cleric. For some strange and unknown explanation, Seavey feels protected in this environment. Stranger yet, within these surroundings hardly large enough to hold a dozen parishioners, he feels incredibly free from those uncertainties that are beginning to haunt him.

"Well, let's just hear how bad you are," says the old priest with a snarky little grin.

"I've been a lousy husband and even a worse father," says Seavey.

Keeping a keen eye open for any facial changes, he notes the lack of any antagonistic reaction. This lack of a negative judgment encourages him to continue to lay out more and more of his sins.

"It sounds to me like you have joined some pretty good company. St. Paul, one of the greatest sinners to walk the earth killed Christians before God knocked him to the ground. He received God's forgiveness for each of those hateful moments. I believe with all my heart that his promise to forgive men like Paul is also large enough to handle your transgressions."

The next thing Captain Seavey realizes is that an hour has passed. This is as long a confession as he has ever made. In a very convincing way, this old priest has pried his way below almost everything Seavey has ever dealt with in his other confessions. He's going straight through the feelings and intellect, through his hopelessness and despair, directly to Captain Seavey's soul. By this time Seavey finds himself revealing to this wise old confessor things about himself that he never felt he could with his previous confessors. He always found the guilt to be more than he could bear to speak aloud. But now his guard has been neutralized to the point that he has thrown himself down the gauntlet of powerlessness to risk revealing his dealings with Abequa. Even though this confessor is willing to hear about this underworld villain, it turns out to be a frightening moment for Seavey. He begins to questions his own wisdom in provoking her. *"After all, one should not kiss this devil good morning till he meets her,"* is his sudden thought.

When Seavey attempts to pull back on this subject, to his surprise, the old priest is not only listening but engaging him to tell more of this seeming under world oppressor. After listening to Seavey's fearful depiction, the old priest weighs in on his theological options. "Do you believe in the saving contribution God supplied for us in Christ?"

Seavey had gone through confirmation classes when he was a young man. He understands in a very simple straightforward way what this old priest may be asking.

"I don't know how much I know about all that, but I don't disbelieve either," says Seavey displaying a much humbler mode. He is becoming more and more aware of his own powerlessness as the old priest presses forward. This is definitely an area he feels very uncomfortable revealing.

The old priest listens to Seavey's struggle with his muddled theology. With a very serious gaze, he looks into the eyes of this reprobate sitting before him. Then in a positive, clear voice he begins to speak.

"The biggest fear the Abequas of this world have is the light of God's promises to be with you, forgive you, protect you, and save you from their devilish apparitions in spite of your many sins. You must remember that these apparitions are part of the diabolical underworld. Their sole purpose is to destroy you."

The old priest stops long enough to let Seavey digest what he's telling him. When he's satisfied that his point is being understood, he begins again.

"It's Satan's job to accuse you. He has no power when you embrace the truths of the God who created you to share eternity with Him. When you embrace the truth of His Christ's victory over your sins, God no longer remembers them, leaving you completely forgiven. If you will embrace this simple truth, they have to leave."

Each time the old priest speaks, Seavey feels a peace, a serenity that he has never experienced in previous confessions. He's not sure he understands everything that's being said, but he can warm his hands on the love produced through this encounter and that seems to be enough for now.

When this confession is finished, the old priest by virtue of his office as a called ordained priest freely absolves him of his failures and charges him to go forward trusting God to give him the will and the strength to do the next right thing.

"I think you know what to do next. Stop beating yourself up. You've been forgiven. Start acting like it. Go, begin today by showing your wife and daughter what you are becoming."

It's obvious by the relaxed demeanor Seavey has taken on that much of what this old priest has shared with him today is changing his heart.

"What happens if I fail again?"

"Well, I believe our Heavenly Father knows we can never achieve as much righteous as we think we can achieve. Like any good father, He'll be there to dust you off again."

Thanking the old priest for his time, he slips his usual contribution into the poor box and makes his way out of the chapel into the light of a new day. Glancing back at the placard, he notices the word "Episcopal" written where he usually sees the word "Catholic." Not sure what that means, he's sure of one thing, *This is the best damn confession I've ever made.* There seems to be an extra snap to his gait as he makes his way back to his waiting ship. The crew is showing their usual strained patience with their captain's idiosyncrasies. Nonetheless, they welcome him aboard and are ready to move on to the next adventure.

15 A CHANGED MAN

Meanwhile, checking back with the troubles visiting Uberroth and Currier, their forbearance has nearly run dry. The tugboat designed as the work horse of the sea and the only boat capable of freeing the *Tuscarora* has to wait out the storm. This leaves Captain Uberroth to watch his ship begin to suffer stresses that may not have taken place had the tug responded sooner. Some of the rivets have strained causing the vessel to begin to take on water. Much to the dismay of Deputy Currier, Uberroth has decided to abandon the chase.

"The structural compromises to the ship's hull are putting us in grave danger. If I risk putting her at more than half speed, she could pop more rivets. If that happens all the pumps in the world aren't going to keep her afloat. We're going to have to get back to the Chicago ship yard and get her patched."

As long as the craft remains afloat, to men like Currier this is an unnecessary delay.

"Uberroth do you realize this means you're giving that pecker-wood a free rein to roam these waters unmolested?" protests Currier.

Attempting to downplay his failed role in this whole debacle, Captain Uberroth makes his stand. "That may be the case, but my first concern is your welfare, the crew's welfare and the preservation of this vessel. If you want to abscond with a dingy and roam the waters hunting down your pirate, be my guest. The rest of us, while we still have a ship under us, are heading for Chicago."

None of this verbiage helps much to ease the tensions between these two. Adding to their misfortunes are the bruising and soreness to nearly every inch of their bodies caused by the ship's crashing into the reef. These hurts are not readily going away. Even more than either is willing to admit, it's their bruised egos, festering below the surface that are presenting them the most problems.

To make matters even harder to deal with is another unexpected scene. As the crippled *Tuscarora* begins its journey back to the shipyard in Chicago, Captain Seavey makes what can only be viewed by this defeated Government crew as a victory lap around them before freely sailing off unmolested. (Jack had remained faithful to his calling as the ship's lone signalman from his perch atop the high bluff. It was his flag message concerning the *Tuscarora's* fate that enabled the *Wanderer* to boldly flaunt that lap around this nearly disabled Revenuer vessel). Silently watching this display of arrogance only serves to fuel both Uberroth and Currier in their resolve to bring this menace to justice. Just below an audible level, both vow to themselves to be back.

On the *Wanderer*, it's definitely a celebration. After returning to the Frankfort port for supplies and to reunite with Jack, they set sail again.

After Captain Seavey's last confession, he feels an overwhelming need to render a gift back to all the people he has offended. He has in mind to start where it all began.

"Archie! Set her on a course to Milwaukee!" roars Seavey in his boldest voice, patting the ship's rail and pointing toward the south. How, after years and scores of confessions, this obscure elderly cleric has been able to finally reach into the soul of this aging reprobate remains a mystery. But whatever the reason, the result is that in typical Seavey fashion, he is on a fast track to Milwaukee and his long suffering Mary.

Years back when this fiasco first began, it was a matter of obligation to obey her husband's wishes that she remained at home with their daughter. Soon it turned into an obligation with the fear that she couldn't depend on him for a livelihood. It's a cowardly thing to leave a young wife to fend for herself. It slowly became apparent to her that she was much more married to Seavey than he was to her. Her parents did what they could, but without the pity of strangers, she would not have made it. Many times, she felt she had more in common with the dead than with the living. In the early years, she served as a domestic to a wealthy Jewish family in Milwaukee who gave her and her daughter a place to live and a small pittance in exchange for her service as a domestic servant and nanny to their three children.

Employing some inexplicable rationale, she would never condemn Seavey. Rather, she lived on the hopes he'd soon return and rescue them. As the time slipped into years with no word from him, her heart wilted and she lost all faith in him. If he had returned early on, she feels she could have loved him in a healthy way. That feeling has now changed and love without nurture becomes a hurtful resentment. Unfortunately love does not seem to readily grow in this environment, hate has much more success.

Her health has begun to deteriorate. She has developed a persistent cough that plagues her more often than it should. Nonetheless, she is preparing for her daughter's wedding and struggling with an even stronger sense of abandonment once again. When asked why she hasn't married again, she dares not linger long on that thought. That would involve an effort that she has not found the strength to undertake. To hold the resentment and the hatred she has toward him takes no effort at all. It seems to be enough.

Back on the *Wanderer*, Captain Seavey has retired to his cabin. As a result of the spiritual awakening brought on by the old priest, he's decided to take up prayer again. It feels much more comfortable than other times he's attempted it. He finds himself becoming re-acquainted with an old friend his mother had taught him about as a young boy; a God who loves.

Digging around in an old trunk that hadn't been opened in years, he's come across the rosary his mother gave him when he made his Confirmation. He fingers the smooth beads remembering how bored he would get saying a rosary with his mother; it seemed to take forever. These feelings linger as he continues to analyze the number of beads. For the moment, he doesn't feel he's up to tackling this big a project. He finally settles on reciting the creed and praying the "Our Father." All in all, the whole affair takes less than a minute, but what a minute. The power of these words lingers in his thoughts much longer.

The crew fully expects that when he emerges from his cabin he will be roaring drunk, but is surprised at his mild-mannered disposition. Archie, in particular, has noticed a marked change in his captain since Onekema.

"Cap'n I've known ya longer than anybody on this here ship and not to be gettin' in ta your personal stuff, but what the hell has come over ya?" Not waiting for an answer, Archie adds, "Don't get me wrong whatever it is ain't bad a-tal, but the crew is used to you roarin' around here a lot more."

Captain Seavey sits quietly as he listens to his first mate. It's obvious that he's struggling with the "what and how" to express what he wants to say. He is still uncomfortable with his feelings, even though he finds himself drawn to this new spirituality. "I ain't sure myself what's happenin' ta me. I just know that ever since I saw that priest down there in Onekema, I been lookin' at things differently," says Seavey in a hushed tone. His eyes dart from one thing to another as he tries to find the words to continue.

"I just know for now I gotta get right with Mary." Pausing again, he drops his head and with his thoughts seemingly whirling around searching for a direction, he adds, "After that for all I know, hell may be out for breakfast." Now with his head back up and looking Archie straight in the eye, he says, "That's the best I can do for now." With that said, he leaves Archie and walks across the deck to attend to something that caught his eye.

Far from being what anyone would describe as chaste, Archie has always had a special admiration for Mary. As much as he is committed to his captain, privately he's always thought she got the short end of life being married to him. On the other hand, in opposition to his own feelings, he has a great deal of admiration for Seavey's resolve to reunite with Mary. To him it seems like the right thing to do.

The voyage is blessed with decent weather. It's a couple of travel days before they arrive at Milwaukee. Not wishing to repeat the same experience with Ivan, Captain Seavey makes a decision to berth the ship in the public ship yard. This also allows the men a pass to the local gin mills to let off a little steam.

Pulling Archie aside and out of earshot of the rest of the crew, he says, "I'm not sure how this is all going to work out. I may be back tonight or tomorrow. Keep an eye on things."

"You know you can count on me Cap'n. Take your time and we'll see you when you get back," says Archie with a smart salute. Seavey salutes back, but more as a gesture of confidence in his first mate. In all the years Archie has been first mate, he's never doubted his abilities to manage the ship and the crew in his absence.

Whistling for Duke, he says, "C'mon old fella, yer goin' with me." Then grabbing a small overnight grip, he makes his way to the nearest barbershop for a haircut, a shave and a bath. The barbershop is typical of most. The barber is a mustached gentleman, well-curled and trimmed. His well-oiled dark hair, slicked tight to his head, gives him the appearance of a Mississippi paddle boat gambler. His accent is definitely German.

"You vant whole verks Herr Capeetan?" he asks with what can only be described as a patronizing smile.

When looking at Seavey's appearance, for anyone to imagine he could get by with anything less would be delusional. After all, he spends nearly 100% of his life, awake and sleeping, in the company of men. This time his hope is to spend some time with an ex-wife he has all but ignored for ten or so years. It may be a simple thing, but when one considers that he has had no regard for her all this time, this simple beginning of cleaning himself up is a good start.

Within the hour, he has a haircut, a shave, a bath and a visit to a haberdasher. At last, he's on his way to walk in unannounced on a woman who will have every right to throw him out on his ear. The closer he finds himself to the residence, the more like a stranger he senses himself to be. What he sees as he rounds the corner is a small buggy with a horse tethered to a post in front of the house. Not sure what this may indicate, he cautiously makes his way to the door. Rather uncertain what to do next, he softly knocks on the door. Hearing footsteps coming toward the door, a wave of apprehension overtakes him. He is relieved as the door swings open and he is greeted by his daughter, Josey. As much as his face reflects the relief that she isn't a male suitor, her face nonetheless reflects the strained look of one who is undergoing a great difficulty.

"Daddy?" she blurts out, hardly recognizing him all cleaned up with a new suit. She practically throws herself into his arms. The next person he encounters is a well-dressed man carrying a small valise. He makes a point to address Josey. "Your mother is a very sick women. She is going to need complete bed rest for a long time," says this stranger. He speaks with the conviction of one who has dealt with these kinds of circumstances in the past.

Finding a moment to digest some of what is being said, Seavey asks, "What the hell is going on here?"

Getting hold of herself, Josey realizes some form of introductions are in line. "Daddy this is Dr. Thacker. He's been treating mother."

The two of them shake hands. Captain Seavey is still in the dark. Taking the lead once again, Dr. Thacker begins, "I presume you're Mrs. Seavey's husband?"

"Yes I am…sort of," says Seavey with the same perplexed look.

"Well, your wife is a very sick lady. She has a critical case of consumption. To be honest, there isn't a lot that can be done. She's going to need around the clock care. I also suggest you pray." With that said, he leaves telling Josey to call on him if he's needed again.

Mary's house has always been dim, but now it seems to have taken on an almost silent darkness. For a moment, which by its foreign nature seems to be much longer, Seavey is trying to process what he has just heard. *"Oh Jesus don't let her die now. Please not yet."*

It's the most honest, heartfelt prayer of his life. It contains a mixture of reasons, one is a selfish reason, the other not. He needs her alive to fulfill the penance to reunite with her if she'll have him. The other is truly unselfish in that it contains his desire to make her life as fulfilled as he can.

Josey is also dour with this turn of events. Taking her father's hand, she leads him to a small bedroom. The curtains are tightly closed, forcing a darkness across the frail body laying on the bed. He can see that her eyes are closed. The dimness of the room gives her skin the gray appearance of death. Taking care not to wake her, Seavey draws a chair to the side of her bed and puts her hand in his. The hand is lifeless, but for the moment this intimacy, as delicate as it is, is enough. When they first met, she was just blooming into a young woman. There was a frailty about her then. When she and Josey made the trek to Frankfort to hunt him down, the first thing he noticed was the strength she had developed, beyond any he had ever imagined her to acquire. But now she seems to be back to the place where he left her when he abandoned his position as a husband and father.

Without notice a faint voice rose up seemingly from out of the pillow her head is lying on. "Is that you Seav?" The voice is weak, but determined.

The question causes his heart to skip a beat. He finds himself squeezing her hand as he bends over her. "Yes Mary it's me," he manages to say before his eyes begin to fill with tears, "and I'm here to help you get well."

She manages to squeeze his hand enough to acknowledge that she approves and falls back into a silence. Wiping his eyes with a corner of her bedding, he sits back down and lets out a long sigh. It's of the kind that's long overdue. It's the sort of sigh acknowledging that an old wrong is beginning to be made right. In spite of their long estrangement, he finds a strange sense of new hope. Instead of seeing the two of them as a beaten down people, his mind's eye gives him a vision of what their life could hold with both of them becoming more whole than they have ever been. Even on the darkest day there is sunlight on the other side of the dark clouds. He is determined to keep this vision alive as a promise of better days to come.

By the time the day begins to wane, he has spoon fed her a chicken broth that he personally prepared. He also has put together a mustard plaster to be applied to her chest in the hopes of relieving her cough. By night fall, he has made a bed on a couch outside her room. It's much too short for his height, but it's adequate in that it won't allow him enough comfort to sleep through what could be Mary's need. Duke has also found an empty spot on Mary's bed. She seems to welcome his occasional hand licking. He in turn seems to sense her condition, snuggling closer to her.

A few days pass. To say they went by quickly would be an overstatement. Sick people can give the impression they are dying, just lingering, just biding their time till death finally has its way, or suddenly one day they begin to show signs of rallying. This morning is one of the latter. Mary begins to show signs of returning from the brink of her grave. She asks for something more substantial than the chicken soup she's lived on for the past several days. Seavey and Josey couldn't be more accommodating.

By the end of the week, Mary is sitting up and taking care of her own bathing and eating. Her strength is far from 100%, but she is beginning to smile again. Seavey has every intention of staying. This decision necessitates that he return to the *Wanderer* and give them sailing orders.

Archie is more than just a little happy to see him. The crew is being their usual impatient selves. If they aren't raising havoc with the local constabulary, they're bickering among themselves about the absence of their captain. Luckily, on Captain Seavey's return none of them are in the local hoosegow and are more than ready to sail. Pulling Archie aside, he gives him a thumbnail account of the past several days.

"You want me to believe that you can become a landlubber?" questions Archie after listening to Seavey's account.

"Naw Archie, you don't have to worry about that, it's just that Mary needs me right now."

Archie has been a bachelor his entire adult life, but he has always had a soft spot in his heart for Mary. He loves Captain Seavey like a brother, but his unfaithfulness to her has always bugged him. Not willing to dwell on the subject any longer, he decides to change the topic.

"What do you want me and the crew to do in the meantime?"

"Take the *Wanderer* and head to Frankfort. I'll telegraph old man Crane and tell him we'll take a load of his shingles to Chicago."

"That sounds like a good option, but you let the crew know."

"I can do that right now." says Captain Seavey. With that said, he explains to the crew that he is going to be absent for awhile. Assured that everything pertaining to the well being of crew and ship is settled, he returns to attend to Mary. Admittedly, when he left, she was preparing herself for him to remain absent once again and is pleasantly surprised when he returns.

Seavey is far from feeling he is washed clean in Mary's eyes, but it's his remote hope that she will tolerate him long enough for him to convince her of his apparent transformation. At least for the present, she will take all the help she can get. For now, she has him busy making repairs around her home that require the hand of a man. He's content to see her begin to thrive and willingly continues to perform any domestic assistance that will make her life less stressed. Little by little, she takes on more. After the end of the second week, Mary has made a strong comeback.

There is a fine line between being the kind of woman who gets things done and one accused of being bossy. Mary has learned out of need to walk that fine line. She doesn't flat out begin to make demands on his time, rather she begins in a quiet and unobtrusive way to question his time line. "Seav, do you have a moment to...", or "Seav, can I trouble you to..." or "Seav, would you mind..." She gives the impression that she is considerate and is always careful to thank her benefactor.

By the third week, Mary is back in full force helping Josey plan her upcoming wedding. Seavey's thoroughly appreciated for all the support and work he's freely bringing to the table, but is yet a ways from being trusted enough to be invited back into Mary's bedroom. Consequently, he contents himself to be bunking in a spare bedroom at the home of his future son-in-law, Ivan. The only thing he is happy about with this whole set up is that he's gotten to know this young man much better and found him to be nothing like himself at the same age. Unlike himself, this young man is putting all his efforts forward to secure a stable future for his daughter and their progeny. This insight alone is worth all the inconvenience of traipsing from one house to the other.

Josey's big day has finally arrived. The bride is radiantly beautiful. Her wedding dress has been designed by one of Milwaukee's better seamstresses. Mary is also beautifully appareled in a bustled gown perfectly fit for the mother of the bride. Seavey is in awe of the beauty of these two women. One with the freshness of youth, the other with a much more mature beauty.

"Seav you need to run down and get a shoeshine. You can't go with shoes scuffed that badly," complains Mary as she hustles from one unfinished detail to another.

Seavey glances at his shoes and makes an executive decision. "They look okay to me."

Soon off on another project, Mary quickly forgets anything to do with Seavey's dull shoes.

By 2:00 o'clock on this Saturday afternoon all have gathered at the church. A small bouquet of summer flowers are hung on each pew. Young people, friends of the bride and groom have selectively chosen their seating arrangements. The females, by how well they're positioned to view the bride's gown, the males by how quickly they can negotiate an escape when the ceremony ends. Father Delaney, vested with the proper seasonal vestments, has taken his appointed spot in the center of the Chancel. The maid of honor, Ivan, and the best man await the grand entrance of the bride. On cue, the bride confidently makes her way down the aisle, arm in arm, with her father. Mary's beaming smile is all the approval that Seavey needs to realize that he has finally begun to step up in standing in Mary's eyes.

A reception is held in the parish hall with a group of elderly church ladies doing the cooking and serving. Soon it's the end of a beautiful occasion and the beginning of two relationships that have the promise of growing over time; that of a daughter and new husband and that of an estranged mother and father. The bride and groom are soon departing. Mary's eyes fill with tears as the reality of this occasion slams its way into her world. Turning to Seavey, she places her arm through his and silently begins the trek back to her empty home. The reality of it hits her as she opens the door to what had been the home of a mother and daughter entangled in the day to day occurrences of life. Now this has all come to an end. The need to feed and nurture a progeny has taken a new and unknown twist. This thought has succeeded in working its way into Mary's psyche. It predictably brings about something, which is a common closure for mothers in these situations—she breaks into more tears.

Captain Seavey has risen to the top of many decidedly impossible tasks in his career, but there has never been an occasion where he felt as helpless as he does at this very moment. It would be a lie if he refused to admit his first thought is to get back to his ship, to a world that he knows. But his second thought is to sit quietly until something comes to him that will be of some greater use. *"This is the kind of stuff you ran from, now sit here and figure it out."* A middle-aged man attempting for the first time to try his hand at adulthood is a humbling experience. Nonetheless, all good things have a humble beginning. It often begins with a revisit to things learned at the knee of a kindly mother, grandmother, or father.

Suddenly from one of these sources comes an age old adage *"Do unto others as you would have them do unto you!"* Simple and often recited until it has become trite, but powerful when the vastness of its healing power is demonstrated. Suddenly from one of these absent loved ones, their spirit speaks very loudly, *"Get off your ass and console your wife!"* Without hesitation, he lifts himself out of his chair. Going over to his inconsolable wife, he puts his arms around her, drawing her close. He can feel a collapse of her strength as she succumbs to the strength in his arms. Soon the tears have finished. Her nose has finally emptied out what one could believe is every last drop of moisture in her head.

"I knew this day was coming. It doesn't matter how I prepared, now I know there is no way to prepare oneself," laments Mary, blowing her nose yet again. Seavey rightly decides that since he knows nothing of these domestic stresses, it is best if he just listens.

16 A MAJOR PROPOSITION

The days turn into weeks. Over the last couple months, Archie has arrived and left again several times as Seavey finds reasons to remain in Milwaukee. Today his captain is again sending him on another voyage. Archie doesn't mind keeping himself and the crew busy. What puzzles him is the effect this latest "Come to Jesus meeting" has had on his captain. He has managed to hang with Seavey through a lot of close calls, but this latest change has him at a loss as to where their future together is going.

Seavey has to a large extent, established himself as a bulwark against Mary's empty nest syndrome. Nevertheless, he's finding that he can't stay here under these sedentary conditions forever. The pull of the sea is agonizingly torturous and interferes with almost every husbandly, domesticated effort he is undertaking. It's beginning to reoccur to him why he made that fateful decision some ten years ago to leave. He's semi-confident at this point that it may be a good time to bring the subject into their new accord. In the last few weeks, she's invited him back into her bedroom and he does not want to jeopardize this new found trust with the threat to fall back into his old ways. On the other hand, it's a subject he can't ignore.

It's a nice early fall day. They're sitting on the porch enjoying the weather along with each other's company when Seavey decides to take the chance.

"Archie and the crew are going to be making their way back here in the next few days. They're anxious to get back to Frankfort. I'm wondering how you'd feel about the two of us accompanying them and spending some time there this fall?" He is trying to bring the matter to a point of discussion without creating a hostile environment.

It's apparent to Mary that he's visibly nervous about bringing this matter up knowing how she has felt in the past about his seafaring escapades. With little thought, she says, "You know Seav, I thought about that. When Josey and I came to visit, I thought then that getting out of the city to a friendly place like that would be a nice change."

For a second Seavey sits dumbfounded. The full force of Mary's words soon sinks into his mind. He never expected it would be this easy.

"Woman, you will never cease to amaze me. Let's get to packin'." It's all the words Seavey can think to pull together for the moment.

When Archie and the crew arrive, Captain Seavey has arranged for the entire gang to man wagons loaded with every type of household good anyone could ever imagine.

"It's a damn good thing we ain't got nothin' in the hold Cap'n or we'd play hell getting all this stuff on board," says Archie.

Ginny is particularly interested in getting to know Mary. The thought of having another female on board is delightful. Mary is also somewhat taken by the sauciness this woman uses to keep her rightful place with all of these men.

"If it weren't for me, these guys would have all been sold for pigs. They get to stinkin' worse than heathens. And I don't feed 'em lessen they take a dip in the lake, clothes and all. A person with a bad nose can smell 'em even in a strong wind," says Ginny with the confidence of a woman who takes very little unnecessary crap from any man.

The two of them are seated in a spot where in spite of their seeming interest in getting to know one another and not wanting to appear meddlesome are, nevertheless, positioned in such a way to oversee the work being performed by the men. Duke is the only one disinterested.

Ginny has always had a soft spot for the old sea dog. Having been separated from his benefactor for several days, he's content to place his head in her lap and let her massage his floppy ears. Mary, on the other hand, has a keen eye on how this bunch of heathens are handling her furniture.

Unable to stand it another minute, she's out of her seat. "Don't stack that chair against that dresser, you'll scratch them both." With that she's hastily hoisting her skirt and climbing to the top of the wagon along side of Ob. This gesture has brought all work to a halt. Not sure what move to make next and out of a fear of this woman's impending wrath, they all stand like errant children. The last thing these men could ever be accused of would be having knowledge of how to pack female possessions.

"Where in the name of all that's holy did you men learn how to pack?" asks Mary, trying to control her temperament as each of these male malefactors are ready to blame anyone but themselves for any incorrect stacking. Ob is the first to begin to undo what has been placed in the wagon. Mary places a firm hand on his arm.

"Don't pull everything out Ob. We only need to be a little more careful with these pieces. Many of them were given to me by my grandmother."

It's obvious by their frustrated looks that not one of these men recognizes doing anything wrong. When it comes to filling a cargo hold, they pack it as tight as they can. They're quickly becoming aware that packing a cargo hold and packing Mary's things have nothing in common.

Seavey, as a husband and at the same time captain of his vessel has weaseled out of any involvement in this operation. He's opted to remain on the sidelines pretending to be busy with other matters and let Mary and the crew work this packing matter out among themselves. After all of Mary's demands are met, and things finally get packed to her satisfaction, Seavey steps back in, to get things under way. This is all a brand new experience for him. Always having complete command over his ship and now bringing an ex-wife aboard, who expects special treatment, is for the first time in his swashbuckling career placing a bit of pressure as to where his boundaries begin and end.

The trip to Frankfort, and hopefully a new beginning for these two, is underway. The weather on the lake is breezy. Short of being referred to as cold for this time of year, it's at least cool. The chores about the ship flow with the constant changing wind conditions. Rigging is forever being monitored and adjusted. Mary has, by past experience, found that by staying top side she can prevent seasickness. This, by far the cooler spot on the ship, has resulted in her bundling herself into a long woolen coat hoping to block the wind. Captain Seavey has purposely placed himself at the helm. He has wanted to be here more than he has wanted food. After his long absence, he is thoroughly engrossed in how much he has missed his vessel. He's reacquainting himself with every little tug and pull the ship exhibits. Now with one arm on the wheel and the other around Mary, he can't imagine heaven being much better.

She, in turn, realizes that this ship is without a doubt her strongest competition and pushes in closer. Nonetheless, this may also be the best she can hope for. She has to admit that this is the happiest she's been in years. Wiping her eyes for the moment, she slowly tries to recapture her emotions. Her thoughts seem to be flying around with the wind. For the first time in her marriage, she feels she is not alone in this relationship. She is discovering that they have come a long way over the last few months in healing the wounds of the past.

Without an explanation due anyone, or a regard for what the rest of the crew may think, she finds herself wanting to kiss her husband. He is suddenly caught off guard as she grabs his lapels and pulls his lips to hers. For Seavey to say that this wonderful scheme of hers isn't welcome would be an understatement. The crew, on the other hand has never seen their captain become so giddy. He's acting as though they are the only two on this vessel. Not one of the crew members can explain his markedly bizarre behavior. There isn't one of them sure how this strange transformation is going to eventually affect the nature of their lives aboard ship. Up until now his behavior has been at least somewhat predictable. But now, in light of this new development, it could be a game changer. They are sure to keep a wary eye on how all of this is going to play itself forward.

"It's good to have you out here, Mary," says Seavey, as he obliges her kiss with one of his own.

"I know, Seav. I think I always wanted these moments with you but didn't know how to go about doin' it. I never thought you wanted me."

Her words hit him like small bullets as he becomes aware once again of his rude departure a decade before. "I know somethin' got ahold of me, Mary. I can't tell you exactly what it might of been, but it was mighty powerful. I can't tell you that I ain't got a bit of it still, but it don't feel as potent."

"I hope not, Seav, I surely don't want to go through losin' you all over again." After another hour or so at the wheel, Captain Seavey is ready to turn the watch over to Ob. He and Mary make their way to his cabin for a little nap. Mary has a little knowing smirk that holds a mixture of mischief as well as condescension.

"Seav, you honestly don't have a clue what day this is do you?"

"It's Sunday."

"Ya okay so it's Sunday, but what month and day?"

Seavey looks at her with a suspicious eye. He's been back with her long enough to know when she's up to something roundabout.

"It's October, toward the end of the month."

"It's the 26th and it's our anniversary you shit-head?"

Left dumbfounded, he's at a loss for words.

Breaking into a grin, she points to a wall hanging. "Well I'll have to admit, I wasn't aware of it either until I saw your calendar dangling there, but I wouldn't trade a million bucks for that dumb look on your face."

Realizing that she had purposely set him up for this, he also breaks into a grin. "I got a damn good idea to spank your ass good and hard for that shenanigan."

"You do that and I'll get the sheriff on ya," she says.

Still laughing (more of a laugh of relief) he says, "Yea, you go ahead and do that cuz if I told him what you just pulled on me, he'd hold ya down til I finished."

Still carrying on like newlyweds, they remain in their bunk, spending the next hour rewarding each other for finding new treasures within the other.

The voyage to Frankfort remains uneventful as far as the weather is concerned. Mary enjoys watching the hardwood trees along the coast as they begin to change color from their welcomed deep greens back in May to the deep yellow, red, and orange of October. It's a time for things of spring and summer to reach maturation and carefully surrender all they produced to the cleansing power of winter. These things in turn will be broken down into their smallest atoms and avail themselves for next spring's new life.

The familiar lighthouse at the mouth of the Betsie River is a welcome sight. It may be noted that the life of a sailor is one of continual contradictions: first he can't wait to be on board, sailing out into the open seas, and then he can't wait to get into port and get off "the old tub." The members of this crew are no different. They are looking forward to the coming off season as the gales of November are all too familiar. The lake is always like a wild beast lying in wait for those with ill-conceived notions of subjugating her. Only the foolhardy are foolish enough to risk a Great Lakes voyage outside the safety of a harbor for the next five months.

While still in Milwaukee, Captain Seavey had telegraphed ahead to Doe and Daisy asking them to be on the look out for winter lodging for himself and Mary. They are not the only people on the look out. Bill Wilson, the Harbor Master at the Frankfort Life Saving Station has been asked by the Federal Government to be on the look out for Captain Seavey.

After tying his ship to a public dock, Seavey's first undertaking is to look up Doe and get the low down on the local gossip. He finds him at Crane's shingle mill.

"You probably showed up at the right time. There's been a Revenuer snoopin' around here askin' questions regarding your where-a-bouts since you hung 'em up on the sandbar."

"They still hangin' around?" asks Seavey.

"Nah, he strutted around town actin' like he was real important, but nobody knew enough ta give 'im much to investigate," returns Doe. "Besides they had ta get back ta Chicago before their damn ship sank."

"What about that Bill Wilson fella?" asks Seavey, with a bit more concern.

"Oh he's a weasel. Chances are he's already telegraphed Chicago to let 'em know yer back in town."

The look on Seavey's face indicates he's contemplating his next move. Doe catches the clook and tries to head off any serious concern.

"All the reports from the guys at the Life Saving Station state you brought home some major damage to their ship. They all figure it'll take until spring before we have ta worry about 'em showing up again."

As usual in the life of Captain Seavey, he determines to adapt to the present situation and regroup when danger presents itself at some later date. In the meantime, he's determined to live life one day at a time.

"By the way Doe, how'd ya do about gettin' a nest for me and Mary?" asks Seavey now on a lighter note.

"Well, if you don't mind doin' some work here at the mill, ole man Crane's got a company house fer rent. Go talk ta him, he's in the office right now," says Doe.

Thanking him, Seavey heads for the office. He's met there by a familiar face. After all, he has been contracting his ship to carry Mr. Crane's shingles to the rebuilding of Chicago after the great fire for years. Crane, an early immigrant from Scotland, has always had a fascination with the stories he's heard about the exploits of Captain Seavey. He, along with everyone else has a difficult time separating fact from fiction. He's kept up as well as anyone on the stories circulating concerning Seavey's daring heist of the *Nellie Johnson*.

"Seavey, you old sea dog, come in and a have a seat." It's clear to Seavey that this is not the normal business relationship that he's fostered with Laurence Crane. It's true they share a similar background and both carry the same eastern accent, but he is being much more patronizing than he's ever experienced with him in the past.

Thanking him, Seavey takes a seat. Crane offers him a cigar. Captain Seavey obliges him and lights it from a box of matches placed on Crane's desk for this very purpose. He's becoming more apprehensive by the minute as to what Crane has on his mind.

Crane is still sporting a wide smile as he places himself back behind his desk. With both elbows upright, resting on the desk top with the fingers of both hands interlocked, he leans forward. "Captain you've created quite a legend around yourself in these parts."

Quite surprised at how this meeting is beginning and not sure where this conversation may be leading, or why it's coming up in the first place, Seavey takes the cautious road. "I ain't sure I know what your talkin' about."

Maintaining his stare straight at Seavey, Crane continues, "I heard about your fight down in Manistee." Crane stops short of disclosing why this should interest him.

Seavey takes a long slow drag on his cigar, answering Crane's stare with one of his own. He slowly releases its fumes, adding to the blue haze already hanging in Crane's office. He uses the time to imagine where this grinning Scotsman may be going with all this. All the time Crane continues to look straight at Seavey. It's as though he expects him to give him a long elaborate blow by blow description of the fight.

Seavey isn't buying into it and gives him a rather curt reply. "So?"

"Well, 'so,' you beat that guy's ass within an inch of his life."

Crane is now getting demonstratively excited. He's out of his chair and begins to pace around the as yet mystified Captain Seavey.

"You beat the best they had and what did you make?" Without waiting for an answer, Crane attempts to answer the question himself. "What maybe a couple hundred bucks?" Still occupying the floor he begins to elaborate on another scheme of his own. "That's chicken feed compared to what you could make with the proper management."

By now Seavey is getting a bit more curious about what Crane may be leading into with all of his exuberance.

Crane continues. "I know with the proper hype we could have the fight of the century right here in Frankfort. I've got a lot of contacts down state that make their living promoting prizefights. With the right fighter win or lose I could make you a minimum of $2500. More than likely with these people I know, it could easily be double that."

Crane has managed to arrive at a point where he has now captured Seavey's complete attention. "You honestly believe we can make that kind of money out of these chaw spittin' yokels here in Frankfort?" Seavey finally begins to ask questions.

"Hell no! With these high rollers in the prizefight business that I know, they will supply enough in side bets for us to clean up. As far as the initial offering, I'll put up the initial purse to get their attention."

In the past five minutes Seavey has gone from the hope that Crane could supply him with a modest house to rent, to Crane offering him enough money to buy two of them.

"Am I hearing you straight? Did you just offer me $5000 to win a prize fight?"

"You heard me right Captain, and at least $2500 if you lose."

Seavey remains sitting. In all truthfulness, he's stunned. In an attempt to process all that's been said in the past few minutes, he mildly puffs on his cigar. Finally responding in a less than convinced voice, he says, "Where the hell you plan on holding an event like that up here in the boondocks?"

"You let me worry about that. Right now all I need from you is a signed agreement to hold up your end of the bargain, to agree to show up and fight. What's more I'll throw in a rent free house of your choice."

Captain Seavey has had a business relationship with Crane for years. He's watched him build a lumber business from a small one man operation to one of the largest shingle mills in the world. Anyone that has ever had business dealings with the likes of Laurence Crane knows the bare knuckle tenacity this backwoods business tycoon brings to the table. Seavey has continually held his own success to a formula that always places him one step ahead of his opposition. In this instance, he is fully aware that he has met his match in Laurence Crane.

"I'll tell you what Crane, you draw up your agreement and if I like it, I'll sign it," said Seavey still deep in thought. They shake hands and agree to meet for lunch the next day and go over the paper work.

For obvious reasons, Seavey remains stunned as he returns to his ship. A ripple of fear goes through him. Not certain how he's going to approach Mary with this, he avoids the subject for the time being. *After all, I'm not really certain I'm going through with this project just yet,"* he muses to himself. He does what he has always done when he's confronted with a dilemma; he draws his trusted confidant, Archie, aside along with a jug. In the past, he and Archie have spent hours going over various projects and this one is no exception.

Archie learned long ago that his usefulness in these discussions was not to try and change his captain's mind but rather to point out ways to make the undertaking work better to his advantage. After explaining to Archie the whole of Crane's offer, Archie more or less agrees with Seavey (as he always does) to make the deal if the agreement looks okay. This is all Seavey needs. Now he feels free to begin to visualize himself caught up in this fiasco.

It's been brought to his attention by more than his immediate family that he has not been a very good husband or father. In light of this, he wants to be up front and bring Mary on board with this "Crane proposal." In doing so, he realizes what part of this proposal he needs to lead with. Looking like a Cheshire cat he takes her aside.

"Mary I've got some good news." He quickly measures her demeanor for a reaction. Satisfied he's standing on good ground, he announces in his most enthusiastic voice, "I talked with Mr. Crane today and he said that if I agree to work for him this winter, he'll include rent for whatever house you choose as part of my pay."

No other news could have lighted her face as quickly or brighter than her husband's announcement. "Oh Seav, you're such a sweetheart! I already know what house I want."

"Really? Already!"

"Since Doe and Daisy have a little one coming soon, they are vacating the house they're in now and moving into a house owned by a journalist named John S. Perry. Daisy says they will have room enough there for her father to come live with them, since her mother passed away this past summer. I've loved that house ever since Josey and I stayed with them back in June."

"Perfect! I'll let Crane know tomorrow," says Seavey.

"Is that when you start work Seav?" asks Mary.

"Not exactly, but we're working on that now."

Not sure when the right time to tell her about the fight may be, he senses this is probably not the time. Instead, he suggests they take a look at the house and talk to Daisy about when they will be able to make it available.

By the time they make their way to the house, Doe has finished work and is home to greet them. Before Seavey can get him aside, he blurts out, "Hey Cap'n I heard about your deal with Crane. It's all over the mill."

Seavey's head snaps toward Doe to shut him up, but it's way too late. Mary also notices how Seavey reacted to Doe's announcement. Now her head snaps in the direction of her husband. He's doing all he can to force a grin, but Mary's stare is becoming uncomfortably intense, and he's having difficulty making it work. Looking at both of them, Doe has just caught on to what can of worms he may be opening, but it's way too late.

With both hands on her hips, Mary has the feeling something is going on without her being aware. Using her most unamused facial expression, she returns both of their guilty looks with one that tells everything.

"Just exactly what is going on that I need to know? — and don't tell me *nothing*," she says. Doe realizes there is no putting the worms back into the can, the cat is out of the bag, the beans are spilled. Regardless of what metaphor one will choose, they all come down to Doe opening his mouth before he should have.

With facial gestures alone, she excuses Doe and turns her attention toward Seavey. "Okay Seav, spit it out, what the hell is going on?"

"Nothing that I wasn't going to tell you."

"Well then why haven't you?"

"Because I'm not real clear on all the details myself."

"I'm beginning to get dizzy from this circle your twirlin'. Just get to the point," says Mary. It's becoming clear her level of agitation is rising.

"When I went into Crane's office to see about a job for the winter and some housing, he offered me a different proposition." Still trying to spin an acceptable way of telling her that Crane has proposed a course for him to have his brains knocked out, he stalls long enough for Mary to begin to come unglued.

"Damn it Seav get to the point!!"

"Okay, okay, Crane offered me some big money and a house. In return I'm to fight in a prize fight he wants to promote."

Mary stands staring at Seavey as though he had just told here he was planning on wrapping himself in chains and throwing himself into the lake.

"What in the name of God are you thinking? You aren't twenty years old. You have to be out of your mind." For the moment it's all she can think up to say.

Doe feels he owes his former captain some support.

"In all honesty, Mary, I've seen him fight. If there is anyone you should be worried about it's the guy they throw in the ring with him."

Turning to Seavey again. Her words are coming fast and furious.

"You brought me all the way up here to have me worry about this stupid stuff? I can't believe I fell for your nonsense again."

Seavey is stung by her rebuke. "Don't talk like that Mary. I brought you here because I want a better life for us," he replies. A weakness is clearly heard in his voice.

"Don't give me that B.S. Seav. You don't have a clue what I need or want. You don't even know me, so how can you know what a better life for me means?"

"Don't say that Mary. I know you want a house of our own. This gives me a chance to do that for you."

A long silence follows. Seavey, desperate to get this behind them finally forms a thought. "I know I disappoint you. You've given it your all in trying to change me. I'm probably not, by a long shot the person you want me to be, but I don't think I'm the person I used to be. I know at the moment you feel your moon is upside down, but I also know this opportunity will give us at least a leg up on getting something we both want."

At this point Mary isn't sure what she's most angry about. She's sure she's angry about Seavey attempting to keep her in the dark about something he's planning to do without including her. The very thought of this makes her boil.

"Okay Seav, as far as I'm concerned, if you want to get your damnable brains beat in don't expect I'm going to fan you and feed you eggnog—just don't keep things from me!"

Seavey wisely listens to her without comment. He has always admired her outspoken tenacity when she's dealing with others, but when it's directed toward him, it's different.

17 THE MITCH LOVE FIASCO

As with most of life's circumstances, people quickly adapt in one way or another. Winter is crowding its way forward. The geese are honking their way south. The *Wanderer* is berthed for the winter. Seavey has signed all the papers Crane has managed to put in front of him. The Pierce's have moved to the Perry house, and he and Mary are settling into a domestic arrangement new to both of them.

In a restless world, love is often ended before it's begun. At this juncture both Seavey and Mary are aware of the long sabbatical between the two of them sharing the same space. They soon find that if this arrangement is to last, they both need outside lives apart, but not exclusive of each other.

Mary has joined the altar society at St Ann Catholic Church. Seavey, on the other hand, has returned to one of his old ways. He, along with his old hunting and fishing buddy, Dee, has set up a seine net operation at the mouth of the Betsie River. Their main objective is to supply enough fish to fulfill the community's insatiable appetite for the smoked variety. Since the unexplained disappearance of the game warden, the only problem with his and Dee's fishing venture is that there are others who feel they also have a right to fish illegally.

He and Dee have no problem with that providing they find their own location (which basically translates into "find yourself another Great Lake, this one's taken"). The other concern is those who, as a result, feel they can help themselves to Seavey's netted fish.

Captain Seavey has a reputation for carrying a couple of handguns. He makes no bones about being able to supply himself with whatever form of firepower a situation may demand— be it a pistol, shotgun or long rifle. Lest anyone doubt his marksmanship, he will personally demonstrate it for you with a few well placed holes through your hat.

To date, he and Dee have boldly brought their fish smoking operation from the fish camp further up the river to a shack they put together along the shoreline. From here they can keep an eye on their nets. This is primarily Duke's job. He's more than capable at sounding an alarm. To further insure a poacher-free day, Seavey has run a secret line from the seine net to a dinner bell. Anyone attempting to pull a net, also unknowingly, pulls the cord that rings the bell sounding the alarm. The next thing this "would be" poacher hears is the crack of a rifle. He should consider himself fortunate that he was still lucky enough to hear the shot. By now he's convinced more than likely he won't hear the next shot and can't drop the net quick enough. It doesn't take much imagination to understand who controls the smoked fish market in these parts. In spite of not having a game warden to point out rules, the idea that there are no rules among poachers is ludicrous.

Meanwhile Crane is moving forward with his quest to bring what he is describing as the "fight of the century" to the north country. He's got a stack of newspapers from every major city in Michigan, Wisconsin, Ohio, Indiana, and Illinois to research all the major fighters from these regions. He's sure he's found the right fighter to pit against Seavey. He happens to be from downstate in the Detroit area. His name is Mitch Love, or as the Detroit papers call him, "Big Mitch Love, The Problem." It further states that for the right money, he'll fight your fighter anytime, anyplace, giving a contact agent by the name of Sam Bergman, along with a telephone listing.

Crane has one of the few phones with a private line in this area. Not trusting any of his office personnel to keep their mouths closed regarding what he may be doing until a time of his choosing, he closes the door and makes the call. The call takes a few minutes to connect through all the long distance lines. Suddenly there's a female voice on the other end.

"Bergman Promotions, Shirley speaking."

"Hello, is Mr. Bergman available?" shouts Crane into the mouth piece.

"Whom may I say is calling?"

"Tell him it's Laurence Crane from Crane Lumber Company in Frankfort, Michigan."

"One moment please."

In a moment there is a male voice on the other end of the line.

"This is Sam Bergman, what can I do for you Mr. Crane?"

"I hear you got a fighter down there named Mitch Love that's pretty damn good. I got one up here that I believe can give him a pretty good fight. Think you might be interested?" asks Crane.

"What kind of money we talkin' about here?" returns Bergman.

"$5000 for the winner and $2500 for the loser?"

"You boys got that kind of money up there in the boondocks?" laughs Bergman sarcastically.

"Don't worry about the money Mr. Bergman. We got enough to go around."

"I do worry about the money, since that's my job."

"If it will put your mind at ease, I'll put $7500 into an escrow account with terms agreed upon by all parties," says a confident Crane.

"That will be a damned good start. Also what is the seating capacity of your arena?" Bergman continues to question.

Crane comes back with, "Let me ask you Mr. Bergman, how many do you think your boy can draw?"

"With the right publicity I believe we could draw 500?"

"With merely word of mouth, we'll have our town double that number. With the right kind of publicity we can easily see that number exceed 1200," says Crane. He's giving the impression that he has been down this road many times.

"You have a facility that can accommodate that many fans?" asks Bergman, a disbelieving tone clear in his voice.

"Yes sir," says Crane. "We have the Betsie Bay arena. We can accommodate that many and many more." There is a confidence in his voice that convinces Bergman this can become a done deal very quickly.

"When exactly, do you want to hold this event?" questions Bergman.

"I believe we can have everything in place here after the first of the year, say on the first Saturday in February."

"On our calendar, that date is open. You get your paper work to us and we'll do the same, and I believe we can work out a deal."

The middle of December brings thick, dark clouds rolling in from off the lake. These are becoming the norm as the days grow shorter. One bright spot is becoming the focal point for the dreariness—the upcoming fight. Placards featuring "Roaring Dan Seavey," as he is becoming known, vs. "Big Mike Love, The Problem" are appearing throughout the region.

As excited as Mary is to be working with the ladies at St. Ann preparing for the Christmas season, the buzz among the town's males (usually after a few drinks) is to come off as an expert on the manly art of pugilism. All the towns in the region have men hanging around in taverns clamoring over the upcoming hullabaloo coming to Frankfort. As is predictable with men, when the opportunity arises to inform another with his high level of expertise in a sporting event, bragging rights take center stage. This is especially true when the event is of the magnitude that this one is quickly becoming.

Crane is assembling wooden bleachers to sell off as prestige seats to anyone willing to pay the price. The desire to be counted in the midst of these big spenders, and to be seated among what will be regarded as "big city high-rollers," has an unexplained obsessive pull to it. To all women this phenomenon of masculine honor remains a mystery, but to a male, from infancy to his last gasp, it remains a driving force. As much as it costs, and as wasteful as each man knows it to be, he is, nonetheless, driven by hormones deep inside his male psyche telling him it's well worth the cost.

The training controls for Seavey are carefully laid out by Crane. He has researched each of these regimens and found them to be verified by the best trainers in the country. Seavey's contract demands strict adherence to these controls and he is now in a full training mode. The first and foremost demand is that he soaks in a salt water bath for several hours a day. The strategy behind this procedure is that it will toughen the skin and allow him to withstand heavy blows. The next requirement is that he eats only red meat and drink at least three quarts of mineral water a day, freshly drawn from the flowing well in Frankfort. He also is to abstain from all alcoholic beverages except mulled red wine and under no circumstances is he to engage in sexual activity. As far as the last two go, it would be easier to demand that the Pope become a Methodist. He more or less interprets this to mean that these are at the very least not to be done in public.

Captain Seavey is well acquainted with the notorious attention he has basked in most of his adult life. He is a natural self-promoter and is particularly prone to well cut suits, wearing them well. His massive size exaggerates a well-defined personality that he has fine tuned throughout his life. Very few, including politicians, educators, entertainers, and artists can claim the attention Captain Seavey is culling. This is all due to the American paradox of its inhabitants desiring fair and equitable laws and at the same time a fascination with scofflaws that are capable of disregarding those laws providing they do it with an entertaining and artistic flair. All in all, he is easily packaged and sold as a celebrity.

The usual negative editorials from women's groups are expounding on the evils of pugilism, describing the art as an enterprise of uncivilized brutality. It nonetheless serves as more free publicity in spite of their negative connotations.

As Christmas and the new year, each with their individual significance arrives and passes, the preparations for the "fight of the century" intensify. The Frontenac Hotel boasts enough rooms for the many expected "down staters." Among the city people arriving early are news reporters as well as pulp fiction writers, all looking for a scoop. Crane has entertained most of them, always conscious of controlling what will be written.

A few always manage to slip by and seek out Captain Seavey personally. On this particular occasion a man identifying himself as Norval Nucum has successfully sought out Seavey as he is soaking in his tub of salt brine. His tub is located in one of Crane's outbuildings. Up until now, he has not been disturbed by outsiders. Extending his hand to the somewhat startled Seavey, Nucum says, "My name is Norval Nucum, I'm from Chicago. I represent a group of businessmen also from Chicago. They've sent me here to offer you a proposal we hope you'll give some serious consideration."

Still somewhat taken back at this outsider's tenacity in hunting him down, Seavey ignores the extended hand.

"I have a room at the Frontenac. I'd like to have you meet me there so I can explain my proposal in a clearer way."

It's obvious to a seasoned con man like Seavey that this guy is representing a part of Chicago's underworld that have in various ways tried unsuccessfully to horn in on his initiatives. Growing more suspicious as this unwelcome intruder presses him to listen to his, as yet, unspoken proposal.

"Whatever you got to propose can be done right here in the next minute because after that I'm going to throw your skinny ass in this tub. The only difference is I'll be coming out and you won't, so make it fast!"

Nucum is more accustomed to discussing business matters on his own turf and becomes visibly disturbed.

"That dumb look you're giving me right now has taken ten seconds of your minute, so you better think about using the few you have left a little wiser," says an even more agitated Seavey.

Realizing how thin his ice is at the moment, he begins. "Captain we all know that most of the money that's made on these events is through betting. The people I represent are big betters. They are ready to offer you $10,000 if you will guarantee that you will not do enough to win this fight, otherwise, they will not be able to guarantee the safety of you or your family."

Seavey has dealt with these mobsters on many occasions and expects nothing more or less from them. With a look that very few men still living have ever witnessed, he begins. "You take this message back to your boss.

You tell him he can take his money and buy himself a nice cemetery plot because if anything happens to any member of my family, I'll personally rip out his guts while he's still alive—do you understand me?"

Without waiting for an answer, he now extends his own hand, but not for the purpose of shaking Nucum's. Rather he grasps him by his lapels and in one powerful move hurtles him, clothing and all, into the tub of brine. As he comes up for air, he toys with his struggling, thrashing body by dunking him long enough to make him believe that he isn't going to come back up. The last Seavey can see of him is his wet body stiffly walking through the freezing air in an attempt to make it back to his hotel room while he's still alive.

The temperature is doing exactly what it has done for centuries in these parts—plummeting. This is precisely what Crane has been counting on. With just days before the big event, he is answering the mystery of where this huge Betsie Bay Arena is located, which he has billed on all the placards. All of the bleachers he's had built have been stored along the shore line. Now with teams of huge draft horses, he commences to have them dragged out on the ten-inch thick ice. They're soon placed in a circle with what is quickly shaping up to be boxing a ring in the center. This is developing into what is now being called the Huge Betsie Bay Outdoor Arena. Other phenomenon also begin to appear as the final day approaches. Small outhouses are strategically placed around the perimeter. An enclosed wagon, to be used as a food and beer concession stand, is also in place, along with steel warming barrels filled with wood and coal placed uniformly around the whole circumference. The temperature has been predictably in the mid-20 degrees range. With this much fire, Crane hopes to keep the air temperature from going any lower.

Sam Bergman arrives by rail adding to the several hundred others who have already made their way to this northern outpost. Crane has arranged to have a buggy pick him and his entourage up at the station and take them to the hotel. Giving him time to settle in, he's reserved a private dining room for the two of them to go over the terms for the following day.

Meeting now for the first time, Bergman can't restrain himself. "I saw your goddam Betsie Bay Arena on my way over here. Why the hell didn't you tell me the son-of-bitch is outside?"

Crane is being as gracious a host as he can be. With a mischievous smirk he says, "Cause you never asked the question."

From the look on Bergman's face, it's certain he's not finding it humorous. "Well I'll tell you right now, if I didn't have so goddam much invested in this, we'd be on our way back to civilization."

The dinner and meeting are soon over and all the rules that can be agreed upon are given to the referee. Once the fight begins, it becomes his realm. His word becomes the last word.

The custom is to not have the fighters meet until the moment the fight begins. This precludes any notions that they have any clandestine agreement concerning the fight between themselves, or in some cases some fighters begin the fight early. This tradition of meeting first in the ring is being adhered to for this bout. Today, these two heavyweights are going to also adhere to wearing padded gloves. This will hopefully eliminate turning the bout into a wrestling match and allow for a longer fight, permitting each fighter to punch more often. The rounds are agreed to be timed at three minutes with a minute rest in between. The fight will continue until one man either throws in the towel or goes down so hard that he can no longer stand. A fighter may drop to one knee at any time to stop the action. He may do this if he is hurt or needs an extra rest. In doing so, he will forfeit a point for each instance. The third man in the ring is the referee, named Charlie Luxford and said to be quite a fighter in his own right.

Each fighter has been kept on opposite sides of the bay until now. It's one o'clock on a Saturday afternoon in February. The sky is a clear blue for the present, but there are some ominous clouds hanging out over the lake. With a little luck they'll stay out there for a few more hours. The signal is given to bring the fighters in. They emerge from separate buildings provided by Crane for each fighter to prepare himself. Seavey has been housed on the South Frankfort side of the bay and Mitch Love on the Frankfort side.

Captain Seavey is by far the favorite among the local population. However, Love has certainly caught the attention of the locals. They're accustomed to seeing Seavey, and although he remains their man, all heads are turned toward this other equally strange physical phenomenon. Those who have had the luxury to follow Mitch Love's long career have watched him crush every opponent he has encountered. They in turn, are more prone to put their money on a sure bet.

Unlike many of Seavey's former opponents, which have been young bucks hoping to put a feather in their cap by taking out an aging legend, the man making his way across the ice is most likely of the same age as Seavey. He's shorter, but probably the same weight. He wears a pair of knee length knickers with wool stockings and an ankle length coat made from the fur of gray wolves. His head is covered in a fur hat contributed by the same animal. His face is smoothly shaven, as is his head, but *smooth* ends with the appearance of the coldest, meanest eyes, and eyebrows that at one time may have been much thicker, but have now been replaced by scar tissue. His face also bears the crushed cartilage of a nose that has undergone many hard blows. His ears are thickly cauliflowered and his neck is as large as the average man's thigh. His girth is nearly as round as he is tall. His gait, in spite of his size, is light and sure, giving the impression of a man prepared to do battle.

Seavey makes his way across the frozen waters with his corner man,

204 THE SCOURGE OF CAPTAIN SEAVEY

Dee. Clinched firmly between his teeth is the stub of a cigar. He's wearing his captain's cap and a long naval bridge coat. He gives the appearance of being studiously tasteful and vaguely the outdoors type. His six foot six inch stature places him nearly a full head above his opponent. His demeanor is austere and unforgiving. He's definitely not the individual an opponent would readily choose to do battle with. The out-of-towners are just as curious about this local legend whose exploits have managed to capture the attention of the national press. He's been described as a pirate, a whiskey drinking, skirt chasing scoundrel, and a type of Robin Hood who takes from the rich and gives to the poor. But for this event, he's regarded as a worthy pugilist that the locals can feel confident to place a bet on to win.

As the crowd is given the opportunity to look the contestants over, the betting is getting fierce. Because of Love's long winning career, the big money is being placed in favor of him winning. The big city bookies are having a field day with the odds favoring Love, while the locals are still betting on their man, Seavey. Doe is handling most of the betting for his cousin, Laurence Crane, as well as for Seavey himself. The big money odds favor Love. In the event that Seavey can manage a win it will be huge.

The ring itself has been shoveled free of snow and a layer of pot ash laid down to prevent slipping. Cigar smoke and whiskey breath permeate the air surrounding the ring. With the sun shining in a cloudless sky, temperatures have risen to a point or two above freezing, making for an ideal outdoor event.

The time has come for the bout to begin. Each man is led to his designated corner. As Love sheds his heavy fur coat, what is revealed is a bare-waisted man with a massive chest and arms that resemble pistons. He circles the ring flexing his muscles displaying to the crowd his pronounced prowess. He has the look of a man who believes his past wins will predict his future and he will win as surely as he always has. With this demonstration over, he wisely opts to slip on a cotton pull-over to prevent his muscles cramping from the effects of the cool air.

Seavey enters the ring as he has in the past. He's professionally dressed in a suit coat, vest and as usual hidden beneath these are special cotton pads surrounding his upper body to absorb the body shots he's sure to receive. His fanfare consists of lifting his gloved hand to salute the crowd, a returning roar follows. The local crowd is especially vociferous causing the referee to wave his arms in hopes of getting the bout started. With the crowd finally calming down enough, he recites the rules both parties agreed upon to govern the fight.

A ship's bell has been provided to signal the beginning and end of each round. The referee brings both fighters to the center of the ring and with a wave of his arm he begins the contest. Love predictably takes a lunging shot at Seavey's jaw in an attempt to control this fight from the beginning. Seavey is able to block much of its force, but is nonetheless, getting an estimate as to how hard his opponent can strike. The round goes much as Seavey's early rounds usually do with him receiving most of the blows as he calculates his opponent's strengths and weaknesses. This, of course, always influences the early betting against him. It's true this tactic makes his supporters nervous as he takes blow after blow with no answer of his own. If the past means anything in this fight—and it's always a big "if" that he'll discover his opponent's weakness in time—he'll begin to turn things around.

In the meantime, he appears to be taking a beating his supporters feel he needn't take. By the end of the fourth round, the big city betters are increasing the odds for Love to win in the next round. They can't understand how Seavey made it throughout the early rounds. The betting now appears to be more furious than the fight itself.

Love is proving to be a hard hitter, but is somewhat limited in reaching Seavey's jaw because of his shorter stature. Seavey, on the other hand, has discovered a vulnerable opening for him to begin to take advantage. By the end of the fifth round, he is ready to begin his strategy. Going into the sixth, he marks a change by slipping out of his coat and sporting just his vest. This is mostly a signal to himself that he believes he has his opponent figured out and is going to begin an offense.

The round begins with Love believing he is going to pick up where he left off. Seavey on the other hand has changed his strategy. He places a well developed overhand right that catches Love on the left side of his head, throwing him off balance. Although it staggers him, it's more out of surprise than being hurt. An impromptu roar emits from the home crowd as men jump to their feet. Some are aware of Seavey's habit of being a slow starter. Love isn't about to let a crowd reaction like Seavey received go unanswered.

He throws a body shot that would have broken Seavey's ribs, if he hadn't padded them so well. The fact of the matter is because Seavey is so much taller, the ready target directly in front of Love is Seavey's midsection. He's hammered on him unmercifully. Seavey's lack of reaction to these punches which have been so powerfully delivered is a mystery. Love has in previous fights already forced his opponent to drop to one knee just hoping to get his breath back. His failure to give major damage to Seavey in these early rounds when he's strongest is frustrating Love. It's beginning to show now in these later rounds when Seavey is beginning to come on strong. Love's reaction time is also suffering as Seavey continues to slip in a powerful overhand right to a spot on his head that is beginning to daze him. To add to their frustration, a snow squall has blown in off the lake pelting them with twenty mile an hour winds. The worst part is this has further hindered Love's ability to see these punches coming.

By the time the fifteenth round is finished, Love's left eye is closed. Seavey is continuing to pummel that side of Love's face with impunity.

Love has not been able to develop an effective defense against Seavey slipping this punch in time after time. Love's ineffectiveness in being able to produce an adequate defense has put him behind in these later rounds. He's spending all his efforts attempting to avoid that damaging overhand right. Now that he can no longer see out of that eye, he is more at the mercy of his opponent than he has been in his entire career.

Seavey, like all predators, smells weakness in this antagonist. Much to the chagrin of his handlers, Love is spending much of these rounds trying to avoid Seavey's hammering. By the end of the twentieth round, it's evident that things have reached a point of no return for the Love camp. Both Love's eyes are now closed disabling him from answering the bell for the twenty-first round. Suddenly a towel is tossed into the center of the ring landing at the feet of a waiting Captain Seavey. A wild whoop goes up from the home crowd. There can be no doubt to a passerby who won this contest. Nothing can stop the stampede of supporters as they charge the ring. In seconds the crowd has this 300lb. giant on their shoulders carrying him in a victory lap around the ring.

In the meantime, Doc Jamison has ordered a stretcher to carry the defeated Mitch Love to his office. Love's face is swollen so severely that there is little resemblance to the undefeated boxer who so confidently entered the ring a couple hours earlier. The only person, other than Doc, to accompany the battered pugilist is his corner man.

As for Bergman and the rest of the high-rollers, they have suffered a tremendous financial setback. The odds in the first few rounds had risen to as high as eight to one, favoring Mitch Love. Having to pay out is a brand new experience for this troupe and pay out they do. The lines are long and to insure payment Crane has entrusted Doe along with a dozen other mill workers to oversee and correct any improper payouts. These big time bookies have found themselves in a pickle. There is no escape. They are locked in a small town with only one way out and that's by rail which won't be available until late the next day. Forced to pay up, one can only imagine how badly they feel the sting of this twenty round defeat.

Meantime the Seavey camp could not be more elated. Mary had avoided the fight, but even from her home, she could hear the roar of the home town crowd. Restless and not being able to endure the suspense any longer, she makes her way to her husband's dressing room. Not sure what she may encounter, she pauses before going in. Cautiously, she opens the door. What presents itself is a man sitting in front of a large glass of whiskey, still alive and still in possession of his wits. The smiles on everyone's faces tell the whole story.

Mary is not smiling as she bursts into tears. The tension of the past few months is finally able to release itself as she falls into Seavey's arms in uncontrollable sobs. With bruised hands, he wipes the tears from her face. Reaching down into his pants pocket, he pulls out a thick roll of bills and hands it to her. "Here's your house, babe."

Now that the money is all in, Crane and Doe have satisfied their concern about the city slicker possibly attempting to dodge any unpaid gambling debts. Bergman has been paid the loser's purse of $2,500.

There is no question as to who the winners are in this venture as they gleefully sort through a table covered with greenbacks. With his "Grand Champion" title of sorts and the $5,000 winner's purse plus another $10,000, Seavey is satisfied he did what he needed to do. With his arm around Mary, he happily makes his way along Frankfort Avenue to their home.

18 ROOT BEER SHIPMATES

Mary has certainly found living with Seavey to be challenging. It's not as though this is something new to her.

"After all, didn't I choose to come back here with him and try and make a go of it?" she muses to herself. She busies herself for the rest of the winter making their new home an inviting place in which to live. He has also found all this togetherness to be stretching his forbearance. He has spent much of his life answering to neither man nor beast, living his life in accordance to a code of behavior, whether good or bad—whichever he finds convenient. Much of this has changed since he has re-established a relationship with Mary. What he is discovering is that, despite this re-kindled love affair, he is beginning to yearn for spring when he can get back on the Big Lake and get his sea legs back. He has made up his mind that, for the sake of Mary, he is going to give up his pirating and become a legitimate shipper.

It's the middle of March. The ice on the lake is beginning to break up blowing in huge three foot thick pack ice and jamming the harbor mouth. Seavey is at his ship every day making preparations for the shipping season. There is a flurry of orders coming to Crane Lumber Company from Chicago to Buffalo and including every port in between. Crane has indicated that he is going to need every available shipping vessel he can contract to insure he gets his product to buyers. Seavey is preparing for a lucrative season working with Crane.

On this particular day in March, Captain Seavey is entertaining a couple of ten year old boys. They were hanging around the harbor chattering young boy talk about what they were viewing. He hears them and invites them aboard for tour of his ship. They are full of questions about his ship and the life of a sailor.

"Are ya ever scared you're gonna sink in a storm?" asks a freckled face boy named Tom.

Seavey respectfully mulls on the question for a moment. "It's always good to have a healthy fear of the lake. Most of the scary stuff comes when

210   THE SCOURGE OF CAPTAIN SEAVEY

ya haven't experienced a storm. I've got a good crew who know their job and have got us safely through a lotta bad situations."

The other boy is a blond haired Swedish lad named Andy. "How fast can ya make her go?" he questions.

"As fast as the wind blows her," laughs Seavey.

The questions go on for some time. Seavey has sent Jack to the store to buy a few root beers for his guests and himself. He's returned with the goods and Seavey has invited the boys to his cabin for a drink. The three of them are getting to know each other pretty well when Tom feels comfortable enough to ask his next question.

"My Dad say you're a low down thief and a killer, but I don't believe him." Still sipping on his root beer and looking at Captain Seavey, it's somewhat implicit though not direct that he would prefer to hear a denial from Seavey himself. It's clear in Seavey's face that the question has hit him on his blind side.

"Oh I don't know about all that. A lotta people gotta lotta different ideas about what I do, but most of it's just talk," says Seavey trying his best to put a good face on the question.

They're just finishing their root beers when Tom hears a familiar voice.

"Tom? Tom, answer me. Where the hell you hidin' out?"

Tom's demeanor suddenly turns from the innocence of a curious ten year old to the ghastliness of one who is in big trouble. Hurriedly placing his empty mug on the table, he bolts to his feet.

"That's my Dad. I gotta go." With that said, he's out of the cabin, up the short flight of steps to the deck. He's met by the stern stare of his father waiting on the dock.

"What the hell do you think your doin'? I told you I didn't want you hangin' around these sorts. Get your little ass off this tub and get for home."

This is all being overheard as Captain Seavey and young Andy emerge from below. Seavey recognizes the irate father as one of his long time detractors in the community. Being an officer at the bank placed this man in a position to have heard the rumors of his possible involvement in the bank robbery down the coast as well as pirating the *Nellie Johnson*.

Tom is on a full rush to obey his father. After all, he's been caught red-handed in the presence of the very scoundrel his father had told him to avoid. No sooner had he hit the dock, than his father grabbed him by the nape of his neck with one hand and pulled his belt off with the other hand and commenced to give Tom a good thrashing. In the next moment, this father feels a firm grip on the nape of his own neck. In less time than he can say "Jack Robins," he finds himself bent over with a stinging sensation on his own buttocks. It seems Captain Seavey has had enough of this loose-lipped disparager and is treating the situation head on in typical Seavey fashion. With his own belt doubled in half, he is repeatedly giving this businessman a taste of his own medicine. Finished with his mission, Seavey holds the man by his lapels with his huge hands and with his stern face staring down into the pudgy face of the terrified banker, he quietly says, "Don't treat my shipmates that way." The man is near tears as he is shoved off to reconsider his attitude.

19 HEAVE TO!

Winter has become an old man, long of tooth. The ice has all but left the harbor. Captain Seavey has reorganized his crew, restocked his ship's larder and has a load of lumber on board designated for a market in Chicago. The ship is fit and the first voyage is close at hand. The entire crew is experiencing the growing excitement that always precedes it. The weekend is over. Seavey has spent much more time going to Sunday Mass and much less time chasing down confessionals. This coming year promises prosperity. He's updated much of his rigging and is anxious to put them to the test. Since he and Mary have set up housekeeping, he is considering putting his pirating days behind him. He and Mary have talked with the priest about getting remarried. The priest informed him that in the eyes of the church, they are still married.

Monday is a good day to begin a work week. It's barely daybreak. The wind is coming out of the east as it usually does in Michigan this time of the year. Archie has assumed his position as first mate and is busy setting sails to get them out of the harbor. Captain Seavey is at the wheel for the first time since last fall. There is a bit of nervous jitters that always accompany the first voyage. The bay is filled with dozens of schooners all in various stages of readiness. The trick is always to find and hold a position through the channel leading out into the Big Lake. The wind changes quickly on this inland lake. An inexperienced man at the wheel could easily spell disaster with these unforeseen changes. More than once, a bad wind change has forced a vessel into a break wall or rammed it into another ship. Captain Seavey puts a great emphasis on caution and patience as he weaves his way through this mayhem.

In a short time, he has maneuvered through this challenge and is roaring orders to his first mate. Archie is already prepared, ordering the mainsails hoisted. The east wind snaps the sail full in a second putting a stress on the mast poles they haven't felt in months. The stress soon gives way to the ship coming up to speed.

Second mate Jack is the first to sound the alarm to an old concern becoming a new concern. He's working with the telescope to stay abreast of other ships in their locality as to their course and what sails they may be utilizing.

"Cap'n I think we may be in for some trouble," he says, handing Seavey the telescope. Seavey puts his eye to the glass bringing into view a scene he had hoped would be behind them. "DAMN!" is all he can say handing the glass back to Jack. "Keep an eye on them, Jack. Let me know the minute they do anything."

"Aye, Aye Cap'n," says Jack, as he readjusts the glass to view the 168 foot propeller driven revenue gun ship with the big black letters spelling the name *Tuscarora* written across her bow. There is no question as to their mission. Seavey expected to see them again, but he was depending on the men at the life saving station to give him a little warning.

Captain Preston Uberroth has retained command of the *Tuscarora* in spite of the damage caused to her under his authority. Deputy Marshal Tom Currier is in possession of a reissued arrest warrant naming a Captain Daniel Seavey, charged with piracy. Both men are facing this undertaking with renewed resolve. Since they shared the failure to bring Seavey in, they are acutely sensitive to the tricks of which this crafty sea captain is capable. Their reputations took a shellacking among their peers over their botched operation. Leaving that aside, their superiors were not so easily humored. To a large degree, both their careers are on the line. With so much at stake, they are more than a little determined to bring this affair to its rightful conclusion.

Both Uberroth and Currier are in the wheelhouse of the *Tuscarora*. Captain Uberroth is manning the wheel while Deputy Marshall Currier has his eye glued to a telescope monitoring every maneuver the *Wanderer* makes. The big cutter spent some covert time hiding out down the coast in Manistee. From here Currier sent an agent to Frankfort to observe and give an account of Seavey's activities. When the agent reported that Seavey was loading his ship, they correctly surmised he would be heading out as soon as he could.

"Bring the engines up to maximum capacity," commands Uberroth to the engine room.

THE SCOURGE OF CAPTAIN SEAVEY

Meanwhile back on the *Wanderer* second mate Jack is also observing every movement of the *Tuscarora*.

"Their pourin' the coal to her Cap'n. They're sure as hell determined to overtake us."

Captain Seavey is clearly at the worst disadvantage he has ever experienced in his long career on the Great Lakes. What brings it home is the *Tuscarora* has come within shouting distance. Captain Uberroth is shouting through a large hand held megaphone.

"Ahoy *Wanderer*. Drop your sails and prepare to be boarded. This order comes by authority of the Federal government."

Currier is following the ruckus with his telescope with the anticipation of a pit bull. He can smell victory. He feels assured that he at last has his prey within his clutches. This man is truly a menace in Currier's opinion and now he has a government issued warrant to back him up. But what he sees next is not to his liking. Instead of complying with Uberroth's order to surrender, the *Wanderer* begins to tack off in another direction. The recalcitrant captain is seemingly pulling a similar ploy as he did last fall. Currier is beside himself as he sees the ship slipping out his grasp once again. This man needs to be arrested, something has to be done. Deputy Currier has a job to do and he's ready to do that job even if it isn't entirely square-toed.

"Uberroth, if you let that son-of-bitch get away again I'm going to personally throw your ass overboard. I'm ordering you to sink his goddam ship!"

Uberroth is too busy trying to stay on Seavey's wake to pay much attention to what Currier is prattling about. Calling his first mate, Captain Uberroth lowers his voice and speaks some words in his ear no one else can hear. The first mate salutes and immediately leaves his station in the wheel house to a position out on the deck.

From Uberroth's perspective, he agrees that the *Wanderer* is attempting to employ the same strategy as she had before: to lure the *Tuscarora* into waters that will allow the *Wanderer* with a shallower draft to pass through without danger, but will ground the much larger ship. Uberroth is on to Seavey and is more than a little determined to stop him before he can maneuver both ships into this navigational paradigm. Watching Seavey tack to his port side provides just the break Uberroth has been watching for. With a single hand signal the whole *Tuscarora* shakes with the BOOM of a percussion gun.

It's enough to startle everyone on board the *Wanderer* as a shell blazes across her bow. Captain Seavey is clearly shaken. He neither expected this nor is he prepared for this kind of awakening this morning. The crew also suddenly finds their thoughts in turmoil. They're certainly taken by surprise, which is quickly turning into terror as they are gripped by the truth of their powerlessness against such firepower. They have never fully experienced this sort of overwhelming impotency at the hands of any challenger. They find themselves beginning to panic as the reality of their situation makes its way more and more outside of their experience.

Archie, along with the rest of the crew, looks to the reaction of Captain Seavey. Seavey is fully aware that this isn't a situation that can be neutralized by anything other than an unconditional surrender. A decision needs to be made quickly. That decision is squarely in his lap. *"It's my ass they're after. I can't needlessly place my crew in this kind of danger,"* is Seavey's immediate thought. His next thought results in action.

"Lower all canvas! Prepare to heave to!"

For a moment Archie is dumbstruck. It's a startling command. His mind races. This command has never been given. As long as he has been on the *Wanderer*, under Captain Seavey's command, he has never found himself in such a helpless situation. What started out as an eventful day full of new promises has without warning turned into a show stopper. Archie's words echo his captain's imperative, but his mind going in another direction. To fight or flee, he can handle, but not surrender. Nonetheless, it's not his choice. The rest of the crew is also going through the motions of their captain's directive. They are all coming to terms with the limited number of available options—something their captain recognized moments earlier.

"Drop the anchor!" roars Captain Seavey. His voice is clear and matter of fact. With this done, he makes one more pronouncement.

"All hands on deck and prepare to be boarded."

Uberroth and Currier are silent as the *Tuscarora's* crew goes about the fairly routine activity of securing the *Wanderer*. With a boarding plank in place, they both stand and wait. Deputy Marshall Currier is the first to introduce himself followed with the following address.

"I request that Daniel Seavey step forward and board the *Tuscarora*."

The *Wanderer's* crew is silent and immobile as they watch two armed lawmen board their ship. This is truly a first. Hearing these words and seeing their captain in this new setting is unsettling to say the least. In all previous situations, he would champion them through to a satisfactory victory. This time all seems hopeless.

Captain Seavey turns to his first mate. "Take care of her Archie, I'll be back," he says, handing him a hastily penciled slip of folded paper. Without further ado, he makes his way across the boarding plank. No sooner do his feet touch the deck of the *Tuscarora* than he is seized by a team of armed lawmen and put in chains. He's immediately brought before Captain Uberroth and Deputy Currier as the charges are read to him by Currier. He is then led to a steel door leading down to the brig where he is to be housed for the remainder of the trip to Chicago.

20 PETER PAPPAS

Slowly collecting their emotions, the rest of the crew look helplessly on as their trusted captain disappears from sight. Being first mate, Archie takes immediate command of the ship.

"Heave up the sails boys. Looks as though we're on our way to Chicago," he orders. There is an apparent anxiousness in his voice.

For the next twenty-four hours they dog the *Tuscarora*.

Once in Chicago, they are left to their own devices as the *Tuscarora* is berthed at a Federal dock off limits to the public. The *Wanderer* has other business to tend to. Finding their market for the shipload of Crane's lumber is quickly taken care of. As soon as Archie is able to break free, he heads to a livery and hires a carriage to take him to an address downtown. The trip into the city is definitely distancing him from an environment in which he feels comfortable. The cab eventually stops in front of an ominous looking building. It absolutely cinches the fact for him that he is completely out of his element. The big letters read MERCHANTS LOAN BUILDING.

Even though the sun has made its way through the clouds, his day is the cloudiest in recent memory. After paying the cab fare, he stands for a moment to collect his racing thoughts. Archie has done a few projects as first mate alone, but nothing as big as this assignment. Able to get his emotions under control, he makes his way into the building to find himself in a lobby peering at a panel listing the occupants. Looking once again at the name and address on the slip of paper Captain Seavey handed him some twenty-four hours before, he runs his finger down the panel of names until he comes to the name, PETER W. PAPPAS ATTORNEY AT LAW rm. 1206. With a deep sigh, he begins his stair climb to the twelfth floor. Arriving exhausted, he wonders why anyone would want to walk up these steps to work every day.

Room 1206 appears on a sign extending out of a doorway down the hall. Cautiously, slowly, he opens the door revealing a waiting room with a pretty female receptionist behind a desk peering over a pair of pinch nose reading glasses. Looking up from her work, she breaks into a warm smile. With a very refined voice, she politely asks, "Hello sir. Is there some way I may assist you?"

Other than her melodic voice it seems to be a very quiet office. The light is soft and inviting. Archie quietly closes the door behind himself and with hat in hand makes his way to the receptionist's desk.

"My name is Archie Kerby. I'm first mate on a schooner docked in the harbor. My captain has been arrested and has asked me to contact Mr. Pappas for legal representation."

Still smiling the receptionist asks the next question. "What is the name of your captain?"

"Captain Dan Seavey, Madam," he replies.

Writing this information on a note pad, she continues her questioning. "What's the nature of these charges?"

Still standing rather stoically, and without hesitation he answers directly. "Piracy."

She in turn, stops writing for a moment with a stunned look. "Did I hear you correctly, Sir? Did you say 'piracy'?"

"Yes Ma'am," he says with the same matter of fact dead pan look he came in with.

She finishes her note writing and excuses herself. "Please Mr. Kerby have a seat and I'll be back directly." With that, she exits the room leaving Archie to find a chair. He is no sooner prepared to take a seat when the pretty receptionist returns.

"Mr. Pappas will see you now, sir." She motions him to a private room inviting him once again to have a seat.

"Mr. Pappas will be in directly. May I get you a cup of coffee or a cup of tea?"

"Tea will be fine, Madam."

Archie is still standing measuring his options to sit down, when attorney Peter Pappas enters through a private entrance. Extending his hand, he introduces himself and again encourages Archie to sit.

"Please Mr. Kerby have a seat and tell me about my old hunting buddy, Captain Seavey. Tell me what sort of mischief he's gotten himself into now."

As long as Archie has been in the employ of Captain Seavey, it always baffles him how broad Seavey's alliances have extended beyond the *Wanderer*. This is definitely an uptown lawyer.

"Well sir, they say he's a pirate," says Archie in his usual pointed manner.

"Does he have a wooden leg and a parrot nowdays?" asks Pappas somewhat humorously.

Archie looks at him rather oddly, not quite sure how to take his captain's choice for council. "No sir I don't believe he does." It's the only thing he can think of to say at the moment. Generally speaking, Archie is usually not given to a lot of humor when he's in his own element and certainly not under these stressful circumstances.

Pappas is beginning to catch on to Archie's discomfort. Not wanting to belabor him, he opts to get to the meat of this case.

"Suppose you start in the beginning and describe to me what you believe brought about these charges."

Archie spends the next hour going through all the details of their connection to the *Nellie Johnson*. Pappas is writing furiously, stopping him from time to time to question a point not made clear. Finally satisfied that he has enough, he arises from his desk and walks to a window overlooking the Federal building down the street. It's a rather cozy little alcove with an overstuffed leather chair and a foot stool. It's the kind of place one would sit with a drink and contemplate.

Turning to Archie, he quickly asks, "You see that building right there

220 THE SCOURGE OF CAPTAIN SEAVEY

Mr. Kerby? That's the building you and I are going to descend on this afternoon. But right now we're going to lunch. Care to join me?"

The way it's just been asked, it sounds more as an imperative than a request. "Yes sir, I could use a little nourishment right about now."

So far the only conclusion Archie can come to is that this is exactly the type of renegade personality Seavey would be drawn to for legal council.

As the two of them make their way down the hall, Archie notices they walk past the stairway. It prompts him to point out an obvious oversight. "Mr. Pappas, we missed the stairs."

Pappas looks at him oddly. "Hell, no. That's too much like work. I take the elevator."

Pappas leads him into a very small room and the door closes behind them. There is black man sitting on a small stool. "What floor Mr. Pappas?"

"Ground, Sidney."

The strange little room suddenly begins to move. Not waiting for this experience to play itself out, Archie grips a hand rail inside the room.

"What in the hell is this contraption anyhow?"

Pappas looks at Archie, gripping the rail with both hands, when it dawns on him this hayseed has never been on an elevator.

"Lad, loosen your grip, you're only on an elevator."

Far from being comforted by this explanation, Archie continues this seeming misadventure with both hands wrapped around the hand rail until the room comes to a jolting halt and the door suddenly slides open. Laughing a little, Pappas leads the way out of the car and to the street.

"Follow me Mr. Kerby and don't step in any horse shit." That said, Pappas begins a little jaunt across the street to a small building that appears to be a stable, but there is something different about it. It is much cleaner looking without the usual scattered hay and horse manure lying about.

In one hand Pappas has a key to unlock a large padlock. In another motion, he slides the large door aside revealing a contraption Archie had only heard about, but has never seen close up.

"How do ya like this little kitten," asks Pappas stroking its shiny black paint, with the same endless smile he has had since Archie first laid eyes on him. With another hand gesture, he motions Archie to hop in and have a seat.

Archie can only stand and look at this strange looking carriage. "What the hell—don't tell me this here is one of those newfangled mechanical devices that don't need a horse ta pull her."

That's what she is," says Pappas as he sticks a crank arm in her front end and gives it a quick turn. The roar of the engine causes Archie to grip whatever is available to hang onto. Pappas flips him a pair of goggles to wear as he slips a dust coat over his suit and dons a hat and a pair of goggles for himself.

"Off we go to scare horses and old ladies," laughs Pappas as he puts the thing in gear causing it to jerk forward through the open doors and onto the street. "There are nearly as many of these German-made Benz automobiles as there are horses in Chicago nowdays," reports Pappas sounding quite knowledgeable.

After they have eaten a quick lunch at a street vender, Pappas decides it's time to make a call on the Federal building.

"Okay my friend, let's go see what kind of mischief our friend has created."

Pappas has no problem honking his horn at anything or anybody perceived to be an obstacle as he weaves his way toward his destination. Archie is hanging on for dear life. What he fears is that with Pappas's seemingly reckless maneuvers, this ride could quickly turn into a life threatening journey. The traffic is denser than anything he has ever experienced in his entire life. There are horns honking at horses and pedestrians. Not to mention other horses and pedestrians in the way of other horses and pedestrians. Everyone is in a hurry, yet no one seems to be reaching a destination.

At last the ride comes to a conclusion. Archie finds himself standing in front of another ominous looking building. Holding back just enough to allow Pappas to take the lead, he follows him to what he now has come to understand is an elevator. It makes a belching noise as its doors open to receive the next load of passengers. Again, Pappas leads the way with Archie more than willing to be a follower. He spends the next minute gazing about the wobbling car without the slightest idea as to how this contraption works.

At last they have worked their way through the maze of hallways to arrive at a complex of offices represented as the Federal Marshall's office. In a flurry of legal talk, Pappas is quickly registered as Seavey's attorney. The frenzy of everyone in this office seems to match the frenzy of everyone all through the city. Finding himself in an element that may as well have placed him on the moon, Archie takes a seat. He is content to wait, granting Pappas all the time he needs to work his way through all the legal mumbo jumbo.

A couple hours pass and Archie feels is the sensation of being shaken awaken. He had fallen asleep in the waiting room. Looking up from his chair, there is a familiar shape filling the space above him.

"Cap'n! Damn good ta see ya," says Archie wiping the drool from the corners of his mouth.

"Damn good to see you too Archie," says Captain Seavey no worse for the wear.

Pappas is finishing with some administrative work at a counter designed for just the kind of paperwork he's shuffling through. Young men, who take their positions as law clerks more seriously than the lawyers they're working for, remain unsmilingly stoic as they continue to shove forward reams of paper to be signed. Methodically, Pappas finishes his task to the satisfaction of these sycophants, and joins his client.

Brushing aside a lock of hair that's managed to make its way out of an otherwise well-coiffed mane, Pappas with a more than his usual haggard look, exclaims "Let's get out of here and get a drink."

Anxious to learn what has happened in the past two days, Archie waits until they leave the building and are settled into a local watering hole. "Catch me up Cap'n. I'm dyin' to find out how you got sprung so quick," says Archie.

Captain Seavey lets out a sigh from his massive chest. From the size of the aspiration, it more than likely has been harboring itself in there since his arrest. Instead of replying directly to Archie's question, he turns to Pappas. Pappas, in turn, is keeping in mind the time already spent with Archie. This makes him less than anxious to walk him through such complex legal maneuvering.

"Let's just say that your captain is free on a bond that assures the court he will not move the *Wanderer* from its mooring, since they have legally seized the vessel and regard the ship as security."

"What the hell's he sayin', Cap'n?" questions Archie.

Captain Seavey can tell by the anxiety in Archie's face that this news is not sitting well. "He's saying that the ship is now under the supervision of a Federal court and we can't move it or sell it without permission. In other words they own it until I go to trial."

"That's partly true," says Pappas with a knowing little smirk. "I'm hoping we can avoid a trial and get this thing killed in a grand jury."

"Do you really believe that can happen?" questions Seavey.

"For all the talk about piracy, after I read the actual charges I believe with a little work among people I know, we can get these amended to mutiny and sedition on high seas. If the government prosecutors are willing to go along with this, I think with a little more effort, and with what you have told me about Captain McCormick's little scam of offering partnerships for a fee, it can be a potential game changer. Also, we'll send out subpoenas to all of those who were privy to that 'famous' poker game. That will go a long way to verifying your claim of winning McCormick's *Nellie Johnson*.

With a look that says he's past all this talk, Pappas prepares his pen and tablet for more note taking. "Tell me again about your connection with the Bureau of Indian Affairs?" further questions Pappas flipping his tablet to a new page.

Captain Seavey went into details about how he had come out of the U.S. Navy and landed a job as Deputy Indian Agent and how many years he had worked for them with no black marks against his service record.

Pappas is writing notes and riffling pages like a man on a mission. "Keep in mind all you're telling me because we are definitely going to bring your law enforcement record into this. Oh and just in passing, if your chief accuser, one Captain McCormick, can't be found, this greatly reduces the chances of this jury discovering enough evidence to warrant a trial."

There is a long silence as Pappas lets these words sink in. It takes a minute before Archie looks at Seavey who is already looking directly at him. It becomes quickly obvious that an unspoken thought of a similar nature is passing between the three of them. That thought comes to the same conclusion, McCormick is going to be the lynch pin in this case. Everything hinges on this single witness since he is the one who originally brought the charges against Captain Seavey.

With everything that needs to be discussed on the table, at least for the present, Pappas in his usual irrational exuberance slaps his knees and in one fluid movement rises and closes his brief case. "Well boys, I believe we've accomplished what we set out to do today. I know what I have to do now. I'm sure you also have some things to discuss so, I'll find you at the *Wanderer* when we have something new to hash over." With that said, he's out the door. A minute later all that can be heard from him is his horn as he bulls his way through the crowded streets back to his office.

Seavey is quiet for the moment. With all that's taken place in the past few days, he welcomes a moment to gather his thoughts as he slowly takes a drink from his glass. As usual this liquid friend is giving him a sense of warmness that only whiskey can. Closing his eyes for a moment, he savors its sweetness letting it slide down the back of his tongue. This breather is short lived as Archie breaks the lull.

"So what do ya think Cap'n?"

With his eyes still closed and letting the whiskey make its way to its final destination, Seavey reluctantly opens his eyes to a world he wishes would go away. His breathing is slow, but not labored. "In all honesty Archie, the last thing I want to do at this moment is to think. I just want to get home."

To Captain Seavey "getting home" means getting him back to the *Wanderer* which has been his home for most of his adult life.

Archie has been around his captain for many years and knows that when he talks like this, it's time to be quiet and let him work through his demons at his own pace, in his own way. Without another word spoken, they hire a cab to take them back to the ship. On arrival, Seavey continues to ignore all friendly gestures from his crew and heads directly to his cabin. His thoughts are wild, madly bouncing off the walls of his mind.

Entering his quarters, the first thing he sees is his old friend patiently, quietly resting at the foot of his bed. His finger finds the clay ring at the top and uncorking its opening, he tosses the cork aside and lifts the jug to a shoulder, placing its opening right at the level of his waiting mouth. Its warming effect is instantaneous. Over the next two days he takes no food, satisfied with a whiskey-soaked brain that neither cares nor wants anything more than to be annihilated.

At the end of the second day, Archie's experience with Seavey is to bring the binge to an end. It's time to enter his cabin and see what damage his boss has done to himself. Reluctantly he pushes the door open. The floor is littered with empty whiskey jugs, overturned chairs, and scattered clothing. The next thing he notices is that the bunk is empty. With no more than a simple glance around the cramped quarters, he spots the giant sprawled across the back section. He's half naked with his hands folded across a bare chest. The smell of the cabin is enough to cause him to retch. Holding his handkerchief over his mouth and nose, Archie gently kicks the ribs of this seemingly lifeless corpse, producing a snort of sorts.

"You still livin' Cap'n?" poses Archie, while thinking, "*If I had a nickel for the number of times I've gone through this process, I'd have enough to buy my own ship.*"

Jack is peering through the cabin door, curious as to how he is going to be needed to get their captain back on his feet.

"Come here Jack and gimme a hand," says Archie letting out a long sigh that says this routine is not going to be pleasant. Between the two of them, one on each side of this 300 pound, 6 foot 6 inch giant, they manage to seat him on his bunk. His hair is disheveled, his eyes are nothing more than swollen slits, and his breath could deter a pole cat. Instead of any thanks, all they get is a groan that seems to come from some deep primordial region. Even poor old Duke is satisfied to sit and watch as they struggle to bring this amorphous shape into some semblance of humanity. He's always much more forgiving than his human counterparts as he licks the side of his master's grizzled face.

Ginny also appears at the door. She's been concerned with his refusal to eat. She has gone through just enough of these binges to see a routine taking shape. She's not sure just what her role should be, but as a matter of course begins to clean up the mess.

Ob is next to show up along with a bucket of fresh water. He pours some in a pitcher hoping Captain Seavey will opt to drink, the rest he pours in the wash basin. Soaking a wet towel in the water, Ob wrings out the excess and places it over Captain Seavey's head. Some of the water trickles down his bare back and chest causing him to shiver involuntarily.

Seavey's eyes are beginning to open, indicating he's possibly exiting from the land of the dead and rejoining the living.

"How ya feelin' Cap'n?" asks Archie. The concern in his voice can't be missed.

"Like a whale turd," says Seavey reaching for the water pitcher. Shaking uncontrollably, he attempts to press it to his lips. It drops to the floor shattering, addind glass and water to an already trash-littered room.

"Let's get you up on deck where you can get some fresh air and clear your head," says Archie.

"My head is pounding, get me my bromides," says Seavey, holding his head with both hands.

Within a minute, Ginny has retrieved another glass of water from the galley. In the meantime, Archie is digging around in Seavey's bureau drawers. Non-filed lading papers dominate every available cranny. At last, he comes across the elusive compound. Quickly mixing the water with the bromides creates the expected fizzy explosion. Unhesitating, Seavey grapples with the glass using both hands as a drowning man would a life-line. Still shaking, he manages to gulp down its contents with it freely streaming down both sides of his stubbled chin.

When a man reduces himself to requiring only his paltry needs, he really has more in common with the animal kingdom than he does with humans. To look at this man today, after two days of trying to kill his anxieties with alcohol and compare him with the faultless confidence he portrayed as they were leaving the Frankfort harbor a half a week ago, one would have to say that this is not the same man. Nonetheless, it's time to face reality.

The only way to get this drastic situation under control is to employ a drastic solution. Archie's patience as a nursemaid lasts only long enough to get Seavey up on the deck. Once here, there is no break as nausea overtakes Seavey. It's all he can do to make his way to the side of the ship. Bending over the rail as far as he can without falling overboard, he succumbs to his nausea. Retching with nothing more to retch, he finds himself in the throws of the dry heaves.

This is the occasion Archie has been watching for. In an instant, he has a rope looped around his captain. In another instant, he has grabbed him by the ankles and tipped him headlong into the water below. The splash is distinct, followed by a lot of arm flailing, gasping, and coughing.

"HELP! AACCHH! AACCHH! HELP!" These pleas carry the distinct pronouncements of a man who realizes his situation is desperate.

Archie has the other end of the rope stretched out enough to insure Captain Seavey remains buoyant. Under the notion that for his condition, the cold water will either cure him or kill him, Archie lets him flounder for several minutes.

"Okay, Okay get me out of this cursed water," roars Seavey in a much more trenchant and sober tone.

Following a familiar routine, Willis now throws a rope ladder over the side. Archie, along with the other crew members, put enough tension on the line connected to their captain to further aid his impaired ability to scale this simple ladder—hopefully without a repeat diving demonstration. Eventually, and not without a struggle, they manage to get him back on the schooner. He's still in one piece, a lot more sober, and most certainly smells much better.

"Who in the hell came up with this bright idea?" roars Seavey, dripping water. He's got a terrible tongue and temper when he's coming off a binge. Ginny supplies him with a warm blanket and a hot cup of tea. She's dealt with obstinate men her entire life and isn't about to let one more drunk bully her. With just a look, she's able to turn the tables.

"You say another word Cap'n and I'll personally throw your sorry ass back in the drink."

Captain Seavey is in no position to alienate a willing nursemaid. For a man in a near mortified state, a sense of clarity has staggered its way to the forefront of his thinking. Even in his cadaverous condition, this second thought comes rather quickly.

Suddenly all that he has hoped for in life has dropped to eye level. Strange as it may seem for a man in his middle-age, he takes notices of a personal phenomenon for the first time. It's something he has never been aware of before. He has always, to a large degree, patronized his crew. He now comes face to face with these same people in new light. This crew has not just depended on him for a livelihood, but is now willing to stick by him through this horrendous legal ordeal. He's discovered a life changing moment in this singular revelation; that he can't do without the support of all those surrounding him. The discovery isn't so much a discovery as much as it is a rediscovery of those things his mother had taught him as a child. In this instant, and in spite of his poor condition, he has a moment of truth, *"A man is truly rich who has friends as faithful as this crew."*

It's a foggy day externally, but when a man like Seavey can see through the fog of his own thoughts and see something clear it's a miracle indeed. The rest of the day is spent on deck in a hammock that's been attached by ropes between mast posts. Without a lot of fanfare, Willis and Jack have made an honest attempt to clean his quarters. Ginny is doing her best to bring the kind of nourishment that will nurse him back to health. He's pretty much over the nauseous stage and into the shaking phase. Again, Ginny has put together a tonic consisting of a-bit-of-the-hair-of-the-dog-that-bit-him, mixed with an ample amount of honey and warm water. She refers to it as a "whiskey sling."

By the end of the day, Seavey has recovered to the point where his demons of guilt and remorse are finding fertile ground in his thoughts. These are such that they are attacking him where they know him to be the most vulnerable. They are bringing back to mind his broken promises. Especially those he has made to Mary to end his pirate career, his addiction problem to hard liquor—particularly when things in his life run amok. Even without the aid of Abequa, she has left enough of an impression on his life to make her mark even when he's awake.

After consuming every drop of Ginny's special tonic, he finds himself succumbing to the need for sleep. With no defenses left, he suddenly finds himself being sucked into a hateful place he had assumed he was rid of. There she is, exactly in the thoughts she had left him with many times before. It's Abequa. She's in her usual reprehending, reproaching, disparaging mode.

"You're still the mongrel you've always been. Why don't you just say to hell with this phony deception you're trying to pull off with the 'good husband' crap? You think that you can live up to that kind of life? Obviously it's a fallacy. You've set your course. You're on your way to hell, so why don't you just accept it and get on with it?"

Captain Seavey would normally fall into a deep despair at this point, but something has changed within him since his visit with that old Episcopalian priest. He doesn't remember all the words that were exchanged that day, but he remembers how the old man led him back to the simple childlike faith he had experienced as a young man. Without warning, and without an explanation, he suddenly feels an unexpected warmth that he remembers having as a youngster when he and his mother would pray a rosary. It's a peace that can't be duplicated outside of some kind of spiritual awakening. It's followed by a sense of strength that he has never experienced in his many exchanges with Abequa. Some words he remembers from some bygone gospel lesson of Christ being tempted also begin to weave their way into his unconscious mind. Suddenly, without a thought, he roars, "Get behind me Satan!"

He is mindful of something entirely different about this venture. There is a new sense of purpose, as though God is pushing him. What he is aware of more than ever is that when his resolve is to keep a strong grip on his Catholic faith, Abequa's hold on him is diminished. Today this results in her promptly drifting off into the nether world that holds her. It's as though today, when his faith perseveres, she meets a wall of resistance that is greater than she is. It now becomes a cue for her to pull up stakes and wait for better days.

"Wake up Cap'n!" pleads Archie. "Yer havin' a bad dream!"

Somewhat aware of Archie's hand on his shoulder, Captain Seavey is still held between the land of the living and the dead.

As Seavey's wits begin to come around, he discovers he's gathered quite a crowd. Evidently Archie's hullabaloo has alerted the entire crew.

"You was hullucinatin' Cap'n. When I couldn't get you awake, and the way you was hollerin', I figured you was goin' crazy," says Archie obviously panic-stricken.

The nausea and the pounding in his head are easing. He is torn between his need to relieve his bladder and the fear of moving. His bladder wins out as he gingerly makes his way to the ship's head.

While he's gone, Archie summons the crew for a quick conference. He quickly explains what concerns attorney Peter Pappas had left himself and Captain Seavey with concerning the *Nellie Johnson's* Captain McCormick.

"We can't risk having him show up and muck up the testimony of the rest of us. We have no other choice than to pay him a visit."

"Count me in," pipes up Ob. "I've never liked a guy who welches on a bet."

Agreeing with Ob, one by one the rest of the crew asks to be dealt in.

"Okay, listen up," says Archie. "Our captain isn't going to be in any shape to be up and around much this evening, so we'll work on a plan tonight."

True to his prediction, by evening Captain Seavey has retired to his cabin. This leaves Archie and the rest of the crew to devise a plan to insure the grand jury has no other choice than to cut Captain Seavey and the *Wanderer* loose.

Pappas and the Federal prosecutor have agreed on a court date for the prosecutor to present the alleged charges against Seavey. The day arrives. After listening to the prosecutor's evidence, the judge, in turn, doubts the allegations are sufficiently provable, whereupon the prosecutor asks for a grand jury. This is exactly what Pappas has been waiting to hear. The grand jury is summoned to hear the case and immediately begins issuing subpoenas.

By the next morning, a plan is in action. After a telegram has been sent and an answer received, Archie and Ob are on their way to the train station. The information in the telegram leads them to procure train tickets to a destination in northern Michigan. Before noon, they have arrived at their destination. They head directly to the harbor.

The telegram was sent to an old friend in Montague, Michigan. Todd "Tug" Argue has in the past few weeks managed to satisfy his creditors with full payment of his debt. Despite their surprise at his deference to his obligation, they remain clueless to his involvement in the bank robbery.

Upon their arrival in town, a meeting is arranged with Tug at the Golden Eight Ball pool hall. Tug is sitting at as private a table as one can find in a place like this. A large sign over a door reads "NO SPITTING ON THE FLOOR," another reads "NO FIGHTING ALLOWED," which someone had penciled in the addendum "do it quietly." The place has a half dozen pool tables of various sizes. The smell is synonymous with all pool halls: stale tobacco smoke, stale beer, and male testosterone.

Since the *Nellie Johnson* has found her way back to Captain McCormick, Tug has reasserted his legal partnership in the schooner and is holding McCormick true to their agreement. For the most part, since McCormick is seldom sober enough to assume the business end of the enterprise, Tug has taken on much of the day to day operations.

Tug is sipping on a draft beer, his first of the day, casually watching a couple of loafers shoot a game of eight ball. Seeing Archie and Ob come through the door, he motions them to his secluded corner. He's looking much more relaxed than at their last meeting. Standing up, he shakes hands with each of them and motions for them to pull up chairs.

"Yer lookin' damn good Tug," says Archie, as he and Ob seat themselves at the table.

"Yeh, thanks Archie. You boys ain't lookin' too worse fer wear yerself," declares Tug with a bit of a chuckle.

It doesn't take long before they bring Tug up to speed involving Captain Seavey and the revenuers.

"I'm willin' ta help you boys out anyway I can. I hope you both know that," says Tug, in a more serious voice than usual.

"Good," says Archie. "We was hopin' we could depend on ya."

"Whatta ya figurin' on gettin' done?" questions Tug.

Ob and Archie look at one another momentarily assuring each other that they're both still on the same page.

"We need you ta make sure ole McCormick don't show up for that grand jury hearin'," says Ob.

Tug purses his lips together with the simple denotation, "Hummm. So that's what that court guy was doin'."

"Doin' what?" questions Archie.

"Oh this official-lookin' guy from the court come by and give McCormick some papers."

"More than likely they was the court papers ta testify as ta how Captain Seavey stole his ship," replies Archie, with the resoluteness of one who knows what he's talking about.

"Wadda ya think Tug? This somthin' we can get done?" questions Ob. Waiting for a reaction, he sits unblinking with his eyes remaining fixed on Tug.

Tug can feel the tension in the air. Measuring the type of response he perceives they are expecting, he pauses for a second. "Depends on what you want done," is followed by a nervous chuckle.

In spite of earlier statements he's made, making it sound like he would have preferred McCormick dead, they can tell he's hoping he isn't going to be asked to kill him.

"Whatever you can come up with short of murder," says Archie with the same imposing voice he's been using throughout this meeting.

Tug continues to roll his boot on a cigar butt laying at his foot, mulling over the possibilities he reasons will satisfy their request.

"You all know he's killin' himself with the whiskey, but unfortunately, it's going slower than what we need at the moment. Be that as it may, I believe this could be the answer to our problem," says Tug contemplatively.

Both Archie and Ob sit quietly chewing over what Tug may be leading up to.

Seeing he has an attentive audience a little smirk begins to make its way across Tug's face. "How about this scheme? You present McCormick with a case of his favorite whiskey as an olive branch from Seavey. Even if he won't accept it as such, I'll guarantee you he'll keep it. That should be enough to assure everyone he ain't goin' anywhere till that case is empty."

Archie and Ob both look at each other and then together at Tug. Smiles are quickly spreading across all three of their faces.

"I think this idea hits the jackpot, Tug. Let's light this candle," exclaims Archie, rising to his feet as a gesture to get started with the plan.

Arriving at the *Nellie Johnson* within the hour with a full case of Helmet whiskey, they find Captain McCormick holed up in his quarters. By all accounts this is where he spends much of his time nowadays.

Because of the ship's design all the amenities are a little larger than the *Wanderer*. This is evident in the size of his cabin. It's pine-paneled with its own private head and sink. This area is also equipped with a hanging wall mirror placed alongside a hook supplied for a shaving mug. The stove is a deluxe model designed for cooking as well as heating. The seating consists of built in benches around the perimeter of the room with a table secured to the floor planking.

McCormick greets them indifferently. He's not sure of the implications of this seeming invasion of his quarters means, especially with his partner collaborating with outsiders.

Tug on the other hand greets his mentor with deference, "R.J., I got a couple surprise visitors this morning. You remember Captain Seavey's first mate, Archie Kerby?" Not waiting for an answer, he immediately launches into his pretext for the invasion.

"Captain Seavey has sent this small delegation as a 'peace pipe' offering to show you he wishes to bury the hatchet, but with a single distinction, instead of an offering of tobacco, they are offering a case of Helmet."

McCormick watches with renewed interest as Ob plops the case of whiskey on a fold-out table. The chimes that only colliding, full bottles of whiskey can produce is more than enough to center McCormick's attention. His sudden change in attitude is evident as a spark of joy makes its way through his bloodshot, watering eyes. While pulling one of these full, shining bottles from its sheath-like slot in the box, a look of satisfaction comes across his pale, damp face. It's the kind of look that only a man on his way to his grave can produce as he imagines he's found a painless way of hurrying the process.

The excitement that this conciliating gift brings has started a coughing jag with McCormick. The best he can do is to circle his fingers into the OK configuration and wave them out.

Once on deck, they shake hands. They're satisfied they've done what they can, short of outright homicide, to help their cause. Promising to keep in touch, they make their way back to the train station for a late night train ride back to Chicago.

21 THE GRAND JURY

The newspapers are having a field day with this case. It only took one cub reporter at what should have been considered a routine, low profile bond hearing to break the story. The idea that the Great Lakes have produced its own brand of pirate is unique. Day-after-day front page reports have captured the imagination of millions of readers around the country. This is the stuff that reporters can expect will stimulate the fancy of work-a-day folks. The public can't seem to get enough of it as they race to the news stands to get the next update. These are the kind of events newsmen live and die for.

It's widely accepted in the legal community that grand juries are not much more than a group of citizens appointed to decide whether a prosecutor has enough legal evidence to go to court. They're certainly not skilled in the finer points of law, therefore they are more often than not at the mercy of the prosecutor's bias. In this case, the Federal government has placed a Federal Attorney to prosecute the case. Despite that, the jury foreman is a retired banker and fellow City Club member with Pappas. Pappas senses a bit more bias could unwittingly come his way, if for no other reason than they have to live in the same community after all this is long in the past.

The Federal Attorney in this case is a man named Fillmore Benson. His family had at one time been the premier law firm in the region, but that's been at least a generation ago. There is no hiding the fact that Benson has gained this appointment through old ties and old money. A case could also be made that he owed his position to men like Pappas who in this age are well connected within the Chicago legal community.

Benson is an enigmatic lawyer. He prefers a more professional style of clothing as opposed to the more trendy styles of the day. Today he is decked out in a dark Callahan frock coat with a black and white silk vest, complete with a silver fob and pocket watch. To the common man on the street, he portrays the quintessential self-made attorney. To men like Pappas who have risen to the top of their game by a healthy display of wit and charm, this man is a piker. Most in the Chicago legal field are fully aware that he has worked through the system by family position. A man of this sort can hardly be manipulated by money, but fawning over his self-ascribed achievements plays him like a violin. Without a direct postulation, it's inferred that he should get this case over with in a hurry. In other words, if he wishes to remain part of the Chicago upper crust legal community, he'll play the tune exactly as Pappas has written it for him.

The location chosen for the hearing is a downtown hotel of no particular significance other than being centrally located. The hearing itself is taking place in a small second floor ball room. The hotel has furnished the space with a solid oak conference table capable of seating sixteen jurors. A seventeenth chair is provided for the witness and placed in the center, in full view of his interrogators.

Captain Daniel Seavey is the first to occupy this seat. Benson quickly sails through the preliminaries of introducing Seavey to the jury and the charges brought against him. He next allows Seavey to explain to the jury his side of these charges.

"I worked on the *Nellie Johnson* as first mate back in aught three. My ship was up for repairs at the time. McCormick offered me a share in ownership of the *Nellie Johnson* in lieu of wages. I agreed to give it some thought. By the end of the season, the work on my ship was completed. The repair bill was greater than I had expected. The next discussion I had with McCormick was to explain to him my situation and that I preferred to have my wages. He balked indicating I had made a deal to buy a share in the *Nellie Johnson*."

"Do you have a written contract Captain Seavey stating the conditions of that agreement?" asks Benson.

"No sir, I don't. It were all done with a drink and a handshake."

"Can you explain to the jury how this relates to you taking the *Nellie Johnson* without Captain McCormick's permission?" further presses Benson.

"It coulda had sompin' ta do with it. It were the reason I put him up ta wagerin' his boat agin' mine. I knew my hand had him beat. I planned on gettin' my pound of satisfaction out of the old reprobate one way or ta other," states Seavey, rather bluntly.

"Thank you Captain Seavey, that will be all for now," says Benson as he busily scribbles on his notepad.

Deputy Marshall Tom Currier is the second to testify. Benson has allowed him to be interrogated by any juror that wishes to submit a question. Currier then ushers them through the labyrinth of legal mumbo jumbo, explaining on what basis these charges were leveled and the process of issuing the warrant for Seavey's arrest. He explains how he became involved, the troubles Seavey caused them in their effort to serve the warrant, and finally Seavey's subsequent arrest.

Captain Preston Uberroth is called as the next witness. He presents himself in full uniform, identifying himself as the captain of the U.S. Navy gunboat, the *Tuscarora*. He is also able to give valuable ground laying testimony. Much of it overlaps Currier's evidence in that it corroborates the struggle Seavey put them through to arrest him.

The next to be called is Captain R.J. McCormick, the captain of the schooner, the *Nellie Johnson*. He's been put up in a nearby hotel at the expense of the Federal Government in the hopes they can monitor his drinking behavior long enough to insure a coherent testimony. But as is usually the case with those trying to curb the behavior of a practicing dipsomaniac, they quickly become disillusioned with their lack of success.

What they are hoping to accomplish this early Tuesday morning is to pick McCormick up at his hotel early enough to delay his daily drinking spree—at least until after he gives his testimony. Nonetheless, before they even manage to get him into the car, the smell of whiskey permeates the air. With the contents of what appears to be an endless supply of hidden flasks—and all the while he is being chauffeured to the Grand Jury hearing—he continues to fortify himself with hard drinking.

There is no lack of yellow journalists hanging around outside the Grand Jury room hoping to jump on any scrap of rumored testimony that may enhance the burgeoning notoriety of this so called "Pirate of the Great Lakes." These journalists aren't exactly certain who is who in these proceedings, nor are they known for their careful analysis of context. Rather, they're more often ready to blur hearsay into a fact in order to embellish a story. After all, what's more important to insure a good reader review— fact or fiction?

Seeing this stumbling, drunken sea captain being escorted by Federal Deputies really piques their interest. The deputies are having a full time job trying to get McCormick past the horde of reporters. McCormick, on the other hand, is being boisterous and condescending to all those he comes in contact with. His rantings do not go unnoticed.

"Get me in that goddam courtroom. I'll tell 'em where the bear shit in the briar patch."

The deputies are quick to react as he continues to rant.

"If that goddam son-of-bitch thinks he can get away with stealin' me ship he's got another think comin'."

Upon entering the hearing room, McCormick manages to stumble to the appointed chair, where he is duly sworn in. The alcohol has taken over his tongue and his words become more and more slurred as the questioning steps up.

Benson has gotten by all of the preliminary questions as to who owned the *Nellie Johnson* before it had been allegedly pirated by Captain Seavey. McCormick begins to ramble almost to the point of incoherence as the alcohol settles in.

For the duration of his questioning, Benson centers on McCormick's vulnerabilities. "Captain McCormick can you tell the jury what may have led up to Captain Seavey allegedly pirating your ship?"

"Ya, I can tell you I never should have trusted the bastard on board, but he sailed for me at one time and I thought he was jus' comin' on board for a drink fer old time's sake."

"You're telling the jury that Captain Seavey worked for you at one time"?

"Yer damn tootin' he sailed on the *Nellie Johnson,* but he weren't no captain. He was a rigger. That's all he shoulda stayed, too. If it were up ta me ta day, I'd have the son-of-bitch key-hulled and then hung."

Benson pauses for a moment as he makes a few notes. Stonily studying McCormick, without deviating, he walks to where he is standing directly in front of him. Looking him directly in the eye he proffers his next question.

"Captain McCormick would you consider yourself a man of your word?"

"Damn right I do. Iffin a man ain't got nothin' else, he's always got his word." His words are more slurred and his eyelids are beginning to droop. He wipes his sleeve across his wet eyes as they begin to give in more to the alcohol than to his interrogator.

"There has been some question as to whether you owed Captain Seavey an old monetary debt. Could you enlighten us?"

"I don't know nothin' about no money he says I owe 'im. That's a bunch of malarkey."

"He also states you suggested giving him a share in the *Nellie Johnson* in lieu of his wages."

The jury room becomes very quiet as they await McCormick's answer.

"That's a lie only a crazy man could come up with," slurs McCormick.

"Tell me Captain, did you engage in a game of poker with Seavey that same night?"

"Well I can't rightly say."

Benson is becoming more direct with his questioning. "Why is that Captain McCormick?"

"Because I don't remember."

Not lightening up a bit, he hits him with a more direct question. "Is the reason you don't remember because you were in an alcoholic black out?"

"Well hells bells! Ain't you the smart one. I spose now yer gonna try an tell me it's all my fault the bastard got me drunk an stole my ship?"

242 THE SCOURGE OF CAPTAIN SEAVEY

Benson is undaunted. "There are probably going to be some witnesses that will testify that you wagered your ship in a poker hand with Seavey and lost. What will you say to that since you have described yourself as a man of his word?"

It's clear that this line of questioning is not sitting well with McCormick.

"I'll say this, there ain't a man alive who could have beat my poker hand without cheatin'. He ain't got no rights ta my schooner. Alls he ever did was work on her an 'at was damn little at that. The son-of-a-bitch is a pirate and needs ta be hung," rants McCormick pounding his fist with flying spittle accompanying each word.

Stepping back away from the witness, Benson slips on his pinch nose spectacles. He returns to his desk and spends the next few minutes making a more notes. By the time he's ready to resume his questioning, he finds McCormick slumped and snoring in his chair. He's dead to the world. It's obvious the alcohol won. Turning to the jury he gives a simple grin.

"I guess my questioning is over." With that, he motions to the deputy in charge to take over the situation.

The press is all over the situation as two deputies emerge from the jury room, one carrying him under the arms and the other has his feet. It's all the men can do to get this inebriate back to his hotel and poured into his bed.

As the day continues to grind on, so does the parade of witnesses, all of which are crew members from either ship and who, more importantly, were privy to the goings on June 11, 1908. Little more is brought forward than had already been testified to. Each of these is charged to keep quiet about what is going on and their testimony, particularly to the press. That is always the intention of the jury, but in all honesty not much is hidden from a tenacious newsman.

By the end of the day it's been pretty much determined that there had been some kind of oral contract between several of the parties and Captain McCormick concerning a shared ownership in the *Nellie Johnson*. It has also been determined that more than likely there had been a poker game that resulted in McCormick wagering his ship. Since the legality of these contracts is questionable and there is no provision in law to collect on a gambling debt, Benson is left to craft an alternative charge that will eliminate the felony charge of piracy, which has a death by hanging clause connected to it, for one reducing it to a misdemeanor of taking a ship Seavey had previously worked on without permission.

They all adjourned to the Federal court building where this recommendation was brought before Federal Judge Beauregard Beauchamp. He is also part of the same legal community as Pappas and Benson. Considering all the convoluted testimony and the unreliable testimony of a drunken plaintiff, the judge decides to drop the felony charge of piracy and accepts the lesser charge as a quick settlement for this tangled case.

Within hours Seavey is charged with the misdemeanor. He happily pays the small fine and is subsequently relieved of all further piracy charges. Pappas isn't finished with Seavey quite yet. Asking the judge for a few minutes of his time, the judge agrees. Both enter his chambers. It's the better part of an hour before the doors open and Captain Seavey is asked to join them.

Seavey is justifiably nervous over this odd turn in events. After all, he had just gone before Judge Beauchamp and been exonerated and now he's asked to meet with him once again. The only thing that is running through his mind is that Beauchamp is going to change his mind and recharge him with something worse. Directed to a chair, he nervously sits down.

The décor is exactly what he would have expected had he never entered the room. It's dark stained wainscoting with white plastered walls. There is no shortage of portraits of former judges along with a portrait of President Teddy Roosevelt. The latter is hung in a spot reserved for someone held in high regard.

What he finds peculiar is the change in Beauchamp's demeanor from the formality in the courtroom to this informal meeting in his chambers. He can't seem to be gracious enough. He's a rather portly gentleman, preferring a short suit coat to the longer versions displayed by the peacocks serving as attorneys in his courtroom. The first thing he does is offer Seavey a cigar and a drink of Bourbon from a decanter resting on a sideboard. He graciously accepts both.

Beauchamp arranges himself behind his massive maple bird's eye wooden desk. His chair is an opulent, overstuffed Morris Mission chair made from the same type tree. His elbows rest on the desk top with his fingers interlocked, suggesting a pensive pose. He has a particular kind of smile that could be interpreted as analytical or maybe curious. He doesn't waste any time getting right to the point.

"Tell me, Captain Seavey, about your days in the Bureau of Indian Affairs. I understand you were a deputy marshal. Is that so?"

Not at all sure what he should or should not be saying, he looks to Pappas for some guidance. Smiling positively, Pappas gives him a reassuring nod.

"Yes sir, I went to work for them after I came out of the Navy," says Seavey with a bit more confidence.

"What exactly were your responsibilities?" further questions Judge Beauchamp.

"There was, and for that matter still is, a lotta bootleggin' goin' on. I was also dealin' with a lot of smugglers goin' into Indian lands stealin' everything they could get their hands on. Indian artifacts from burial grounds and shootin and trappin' game was the big things," says Seavey with a serious tone.

"Did you like that kind of work?" asks Beauchamp, still prying into this point.

"Ya, I liked it," replies Seavey without a thought.

"What made you quit?"

"It didn't pay much and I had an opportunity ta buy a freight haulin' schooner cheap, so I resigned."

"How would you like to reconsider a similar opportunity?" Beauchamp's smile has been replaced with a serious gaze.

Seavey sits a little dumbfounded as he tries to process all this. Before he can speak Beauchamp speaks again.

"I'm aware of an opening for a Federal job as a Deputy Marshal for fighting piracy on the Great Lakes. If you agree, I'm pretty sure I can convince the powers that be that we need a man like you on our side."

Still not sure what all this can mean, Seavey finally speaks. "Well, your Honor you're catchin' me on my blindside. I don't know what ta say right off, but you give me a night ta consider it, I'll let you know tomorrow."

Checking his calender, Beauchamp says, "How about tomorrow morning at 11 o'clock?"

"That's fine sir, and thank-you," says Seavey, trying his best not to sound obsequious.

Beauchamp's smile is back as he rises from behind his desk and extends his hand to Seavey.

Within a few minutes Pappas and Captain Seavey are outside and out of earshot of any reporters. Pappas has his Benz parked nearby and is prepared to take Seavey back to his ship. Seavey is quiet for most of the walk to the waiting auto. He finally breaks into conversation.

"What the hell did you have ta say ta convince this Federal Judge, who just an hour before was contemplatin' hangin' me for a Federal offense, ta offer me a job in the Federal Government?"

"I suggested to him how much wiser it would be for the Revenuers to have you on their side of the law as opposed to being on the other side. After all it takes a pirate to catch a pirate," laughs Pappas. "It didn't take him long to see the wisdom in that proposal."

"That may be, but I still gotta give this some thought," says Seavey.

Knowing Seavey the way he does, Pappas laughingly says, "Oh I'm sure you'll figure a way to get the best out of both careers."

By the time Seavey has made his way back to the *Wanderer* the news of his release has reached the crew. They're elated and expect they will be soon sailing and things will return to normal. Upon hearing the news, Ginny has prepared one of Seavey's favorite meals of pancakes, maple syrup, and an ample portion of smoked and salted side pork. She holds on to the traditional concept that good food brings out the best in people. She plays a big part in the day to day contentment of the crew.

It's June and sunny. The lake is kicking up a few whitecaps from a south-west breeze. It's certainly inviting to good sailing. In lieu of this, Captain Seavey calls a meeting on deck of the entire crew. Each of them is silent as this is somewhat unprecedented.

Even on a small craft there is a maritime decorum so Archie and Jack take their places as first and second mate alongside Captain Seavey. The rest of the crew sit on anything scattered about the deck that will hold them. Seavey purposely knocks his pipe on the heel of his boot, letting the burnt ash swirl across the planks. This gesture along with clearing his throat is what he needs to signal that he has something to say.

"I've been given an offer to contemplate. The Federal Judge who was sittin' on the bench durin' my case has asked me to consider becomin' a Federal Marshal." The whole ship seems to have gone quiet. All that can be heard is the side of the ship bumping gently against the wharf.

Archie is the first to speak. "You gonna take 'em up on 'er Cap'n?" he asks. Presently all heads turn toward Captain Seavey.

"Donno yet. If I do, what you boys think about me askin' ta have you as my crew?"

One by one they look at one another hoping someone will break out with the right answer. Finally Archie tosses his cap down in the center of the deck.

"Count me in Cap'n."

This is all it takes for the rest of the crew to follow suit. The rest of the day is spent celebrating not only the return of Captain Seavey, but also the possibility of the end of one era and the birth of a new epoch.

As a man of his word and armed with a pledge of support from his crew, Seavey arrives at Beauchamp's office at 11 am as agreed. He's put on a freshly pressed suit stylized with his signature vest. The tension that had built up since his arrest has clearly left his face. Beauchamp stands in his doorway motioning him into his chambers once again. He exhibits a confident flair as he strolls past the office staff and takes the same seat he had been offered the previous day.

Judge Beauchamp takes his place behind his desk. He peers over the top of his pinch nose spectacles once again. His left arm is casually bent at the elbow, resting fully under his chest on the desk's top. His right hand is lightly bouncing a silver colored star encircled in a band of the same colored metal on the desk's surface. It has the insignia "U.S. Marshal" stamped into the metal.

Captain Seavey in turn, casually crosses one leg over the other. He is ready to let Judge Beauchamp begin the talking.

"Well lad, did you give my offer some head work overnight?" The bouncing badge has been reduced to a staccato sound as it's barely hitting the desk top. The Judge shows a bit of impatience as he awaits Seavey's decision.

"That I did indeed, sir."

"And my friend at what conclusion did you arrive?" asks Beauchamp. It's clear by the tone of his voice that he wants to get this meeting concluded.

Seavey hesitates a moment to frame his answer.

"If I can employ my own ship, choose my own crew and the Feds pay 'em wages, along with all supplies, you got a deal."

A large grin makes its way across Beauchamp's face. "You got yourself a new job, Captain."

At that moment he calls in a couple of his office staff with the necessary paperwork. When that is completed, they remain as witnesses as Federal Judge Beauregard Beauchamp swears Captain Daniel Seavey in as a United States Marshal. His authority covers all Federal lands with the distinct duties to include curbing piracy, illegal venison, smuggling, and bootlegging on the Great Lakes. Handshakes follow and some general kibitzing over the new job as Beauchamp pins the badge to Seavey's vest.

With all of the necessary preliminaries in place, Seavey makes his way out the front of the building only to be met by Deputy Marshal Currier making his way up the steps. Spotting the badge on Seavey's chest creates a startled delay in his foot work nearly causing him to trip. Seavey, aware of the effect this turn of events is having, gives Currier a mock salute with his left hand and keeps on going, leaving the disgruntled deputy struggling to recover and completely dumbfounded.

When Seavey arrives back at the *Wanderer*, the crew makes it obvious they are more than ready to change ports. Even Duke, as old and fat as he is, is leaping around like a pup.

"Okay boys, we got us a new job. Let's get back to Frankfort, I got some unfinished business there."

With a whoop from the crew, sails are rigged and within the hour they are well on their way out of Chicago and under full sails to the north.

22 MARSHAL DAN SEAVEY

Within a few days, they enter the familiar Frankfort harbor. Seavey can't help but look to the north coast line. It was there, just a few weeks ago on that fateful morning, the *Tuscarora* had been lurking, waiting to pounce on his small ship.

Now that the fear of a prison sentence is behind him, his fear associated with that incident is quickly being replaced with resentment and anger. It's funneling down to one man he knows was in cahoots with Currier. That man is harbor master Bill Wilson. Passing by the Life Saving Station only serves to rekindle his rancor. Not quite sure how he's going to exact his revenge, he gives a friendly wave toward Wilson who is standing with mouth agape.

Wilson doesn't have to wait for a rare report from some yellow journalist, he has access to a telegraph as well as a telephone and is well aware of the decisions that came about in Chicago. In spite of this seemingly friendly wave, he sees a potential problem looming on the horizon. He's well aware of Seavey's temperament and has his own ideas of Seavey's involvement in the disappearance of Game Warden Morris. The sobering reality surrounding this fear is the realization that he may be the next person in Seavey's sights.

Mary Seavey continues to cling to the old-fashioned notion that all's well that ends well. In particular, she has been updated by a friendly seaman at the Life Saving Station receiving the telegraphic messages. He continuously updated her as to the grand jury proceedings. She and Seavey had moved into a real house before all this stuff with the revenuers began. It's the first home she has ever felt is hers. Nearly every day Seavey was held, someone would ask her, "What you plan on doin' if things don't work out?" Knowing her husband the way she does, she never worried that things wouldn't work out to his advantage.

"He could fall into a barrel of horse-shit and come out smelling like roses," she said lightheartedly about her difficult husband.

On this day, she happens to be visiting Doe and Daisy when she spots Seavey's ship coming into the harbor. It's not without fanfare. Archie stands jubilantly in the bow sounding a conk-shell horn to announce the triumphant homecoming of the *Wanderer*. Captain Seavey is a little more subdued while proudly standing on the pilot deck sporting his new suit and with the U.S. Marshal badge glistening on his chest. His thoughts are wandering. Ever since his episode with the old rector in that small chapel, he has fought an inner battle. *"The things I wish I wouldn't do I end up doing and the things I wish I wouldn't do, I do anyway. What's to become of me?"*

The crew, anxious to be back in their home port, dock the ship on a pier designated as Crane Lumber Company in anticipation of getting back to work. Meanwhile, all of this noisy hullabaloo has attracted the attention of Crane. He is curiously peering out his office door, coat wide open with his fingers resting in his small vest pockets, watching as Seavey disembarks.

"Gettin ta be quite the celebrity, ain't ya Seavey?" says a grinning Crane.

Seavey ponders the question for a moment. "Not by choice that's fer damn sure!" says a more serious Seavey.

"Maybe not by choice, but then you ain't doin' much ta stop it," replies Crane still maintaining a curious grin.

It's becoming painfully obvious to Seavey that this observation by Crane is in line with his very thoughts just a moment ago. With an effort to divert himself, he fumbles around in an inside breast pocket. Pulling out an envelope, he hands it to Crane.

"Here, Mr. Crane, is payment collected on that load of lumber I delivered between my Chicago episodes."

From twenty feet away, Crane makes his way toward the envelope held in Seavey's hand. It also gives him a moment to review his options.

"Thank you. I never doubted your integrity. I knew you'd make good on it one way or another. Come on in the office and I'll give you your payment."

Together they make their way back across the pier to Crane's office. While Crane has his secretary draw up the needed payment, he addresses Seavey once again. "Before you leave today, I'd like to assure you that I still appreciate you hauling my lumber and I can certainly use your ship."

This is the kind of assurance Seavey needs to hear. That despite his legacy of not being trustworthy in many people's eyes, he nonetheless still has the trust of men like Crane.

"I certainly appreciate your offer Mr. Crane. This 'Marshal' business is flexible enough to allow me to do that."

Pointing at Seavey's star pinned to his vest gives Crane pause.

"I have no clue how you manage to pull yourself out of these quagmires Seavey, but I gotta hand it to you, you're a regular 'Harry Keller.' How in the hell did you manage this?"

"It's a long story sir." With a long deep sigh, he adds, "It's a very, very long story that I don't care to go through again."

"I guess I can understand that," says Crane remembering some of his own spotted business legacy.

Fully paid and secure in his home port, Seavey shakes hands with Crane, with the understanding that they will continue to do business with each other. Stepping out of Crane's office, Seavey is suddenly met by a beautiful female coming out of the fray of dock workers. Her eyes meet his at the same moment. Looking off to the west, the sun is sizzling its way into the lake.

"Hello Captain Seavey, you must be famished. How'd you like some supper?"

"Thank you madam, that's a right kindly offer." With that, she tightens her arm in his as they amble off to the Seavey household.

"I told you I'd be back," he says, pulling her in even closer.

"I never doubted you," she says, tightening her grip a bit more and laying her head against his huge arm.

23 CHANGING OF A HARBOR GUARD

Neither Captain Seavey nor Mary are seen by anyone for a couple days as they spend the time reacquainting themselves with each other. But like all temporal things, one soon moves to something else. This morning that something else is for newly appointed Federal Marshal Seavey to have a "come to Jesus meeting" with Harbor Master Bill Wilson. Making his way to the Life Saving Station that also houses the Harbor Master, he is met by a rather sheepish Wilson. Wilson is well aware that Seavey knows the role he played in his arrest, but he never expected things could, or would, turn on him as they have. He fully expected by this time Seavey would have been convicted of piracy and sentenced to the gallows. Instead, he is confronted by a United States Marshal bearing the same name and a hound, named Duke, wearing a hand-sewn vest bearing the insignia "Deputy Duke."

"Good morning, Captain, or should I say 'Marshal'?" He knows Seavey well enough to realize that he is skating on very thin ice. For certain there is going to be some form of retribution, he's just not sure how it's going to come at him.

"For this visit you can refer to me as Federal Marshal Seavey," says

Seavey pausing long enough for Wilson to digest this change of events. There is something compelling about the earnestness with which Seavey is attacking this situation. Satisfied that he's making an impact, Seavey continues, "It's come to my attention in the past few days that there may be some accounting discrepancies involving your position here as harbor master. As you should be aware, these are Federal waters you care for here and it just so happens you're in my jurisdiction."

Wilson face turns as gray as hawk bait. The color has left completely. His look alone tells the story. At this point, he's not sure where he stands legally, but either way, he sees trouble on the horizon.

Seavey has had enough people on the ropes to know when he's delivering a knockout punch. The last thing Wilson wants is an audit—especially driven by a nemesis such as Seavey. His breathing has seemingly ceased for the moment. A sheen of perspiration suddenly appears on his forehead, indicating he's taking the full thrust of this impending indictment to heart. For the entire time that he's been harbor master, he has taken full advantage of opportunities to further his own economic condition. It's been done through a series of agreements with locals to give telephone and telegraph privileges for a price. This concession along with bribes from shippers and skippers for turning his head on questionable practices have in a clandestine way made their way into his pocket without authorization.

After the initial shock from this sudden turn of events, Wilson's mind turns in a direction he's not sure is in his best interest. Seavey's full six foot six inches is more than cutting off the sun in Wilson's life. It also destroys any thought of physically intimidating him in any way.

"Should I turn this around?" he thinks to himself. *"I could ask him if he wants a piece of the action. After all Seavey is no damn saint. But then I really don't know how pissed he is at me for me turning him in. The deck is stacked against me if I stay. Maybe I should just cut my losses and get the hell out while I still can."*

Seavey has not taken his eyes off Wilson. He knows Wilson's choices are boiling down to fighting him on these charges or quitting and getting out of town as fast as he can.

Wilson swallows hard, pausing as he sizes up his shrinking options. "What would you say if I just quit and left town?"

Hardly have the words dropped from his lips before Seavey sinks the final harpoon.

"You've got twenty-four hours!"

The color is starting to come back around Wilson's gills. It emboldens him to extend his hand toward Seavey to shake on the agreement. Seavey looks at the lone hand, waiting. Ignoring it, he turns and begins to walk away.

After taking a couple steps, he turns back toward Wilson, raising his own hand with a finger summarily pointing directly back at Wilson. "Twenty-four hours, Wilson! Twenty-four hours!"

If this were not enough, Duke has been sniffing around Wilson's shoe. Finding something interesting, he has raised his leg and let loose with a stream of warm water that instantly soaks not only Wilson's shoe, but the lower half of his pant leg.

"Damn yer hide dog!" he bellows, kicking Duke and causing the old hound to yelp.

This catches Seavey's attention in time to see poor ole Duke flying through the air. Without a word, he takes a couple huge strides back toward Wilson. Still without a single pronouncement, he grabs him by his lapels lifting him off the ground, high enough to leave him with nothing but air between himself and the ground. With a couple more deliberate strides, Seavey has relocated him at the edge of the break wall, where there remains nothing between Wilson and the water, but more of the same air. SPLASH! He has deep-sixed this agglomeration of gasping humanity, dumping him feet first in the drink. All that's left of Wilson is a wet mass of forsaken humanity, helplessly gasping and bobbing around at the mercy of anyone willing to give him a hand.

In deference to their good relationship with Captain Seavey, the Life Saving crew ignore his victim, allowing him to thrash around for a minute before they throw him a line and hoist him up to safety.

The next morning Wilson boards an early passenger train leaving for Ohio. Both Doe and Seavey watch as the train rattles past them. All that can be seen is the top of Wilson's head sitting alone on his way out of their lives. Doe shares the same disdain for Wilson as Seavey. Seavey readily concedes that he had little legal authority over Wilson, but in relating the previous day's circumstances to Doe, he can't help but recount the shocked look on Wilson's face as he threatened to expose him.

"You sure as hell stuck it to that pecker-wood. He ain't been nothin' but a pain in the ass since he was appointed ta the job," says Doe still laughing over Seavey's account of the event.

Seavey is listening to and watching Doe's reaction with a bit more than passing interest. He suddenly changes his demeanor to a more serious tone before breaking into a broadening grin.

"Doe, how'd you like to take ole Wilson's job?"

This question catches Doe off guard, but at the same time it's not one that he will put off. "How the hell you gonna make that happen Cap'n?"

"Oh I think we can make it happen today," states Captain Seavey rather confidently. With that said, he gives Doe a slight slap on the back and motions him to follow. Within a couple minutes, Seavey is knocking on the door of a man named Dudley Pennbrook. He's a bachelor serving as village president and has the authority to appoint Doe, if he sees fit.

Dud is beholden to Captain Seavey on several different levels. More than likely the one standing most recent in Dud's mind is how on several occasions when Seavey brought Squeaky Schwartz a fresh batch of Chicago's soiled doves, he introduced a pretty young one to this lecherous old bachelor for an hour. Not wanting to upset this arrangement, Dud is more than receptive to listening to Seavey.

After no more than a fifteen minute update on the sudden departure of Bill Wilson, Dud signs Doe on as the interim Harbor Master with the assurance that when he brings it before the council he'll have their approval. Handshakes are crossed between them and the deal is sealed.

Once back on the street Doe feels a surge of gratitude for having a man like Captain/United States Marshal Dan Seavey leading his team.

"Cap'n, I don't have a clue how in the Good Lord's name you get all this stuff done."

"Let's not get the Good Lord's name behind this yet. I'm still workin' on that part," says Seavey with a half a grin.

Both are assured they have produced the beginning of something new. Soon they find themselves enjoying a lunch with Daisy and Mary at the American House restaurant. For the moment all four are contentedly catching up on events leading up to this pleasant reunion.

24 BUTCH

As things go, the world seemingly finds a way to encroach on pleasantries. Soon after things have begun to settle, Marshal Seavey receives a telegram from a source in Michigan's Upper Peninsula—Naubinway to be exact. It seems there is a gang of bootleggers that are raising havoc selling whiskey to the local Indians. Never shrinking from a challenge Marshal Seavey organizes his posse, conveniently made up of his regular crew, readies the *Wanderer* for battle, and embarks through the Straits of Makinac to the eastern side of the Great Lakes into Lake Huron.

It's a calm, quiet August morning when he arrives. The streets are dusty and strewn with horse manure. The distinct screech of a cicada is heard announcing to its listeners that summer is winding down. The name "Naubinway" is an Ojibway Indian word for "place of the echoes." It's a lumbering town and as raw as any frontier town could imagine. The local constable is a man named Earl. If he has a last name, no one deems it important enough to remember. When the law is needed or a grave dug or a roof needs its cedar shakes patched, Earl is the man who is summoned. Most issues he can readily handle, but in this case things have gotten out of hand.

Seavey has brought along Archie as his deputy, armed with a rifle. Seavey has a pair of pistols holstered. Both men are adequately identified by the badges pinned to their chests. The two of them make their way to a local watering hole, a place named Snuffy's. It was stated in the telegram that Earl could be found here most of the time. Being that Naubinway is no more than a few streets scattered around a bunch of clapboard businesses, it doesn't take them long to find the address. It's a small tavern with the familiar smells of cigar smoke, spilled beer, sweat and pickled eggs.

Earl proves to be a middle-aged man with stooped shoulders, either from choosing the wrong parents or from spending a life time at hard labor. Either way, shaking hands with Seavey brings a kind of knowing smile to Earl's face, confident that in this case he made the right decision. What Earl may have given up in stature, he's made up for in tenacity. It doesn't take him long to explain his dilemma.

"The problem I got is that the guy runnin' the bootleggin' gig is my sister's boy. He could be standin' over a body with a smokin' gun and she'd swear to God he didn't have a thing to do with it. He ain't nothin' more than a bully and a thief, but my sister would never let me live if I did anything to harm her precious baby."

Quietly listening, Seavey can sympathize with this lawman's quandary. "What do you expect from me?" asks Seavey.

"Well, I'm thinkin' if you haul his ass in, she'll let me off the hook," says Earl. There is no mistaking the worry in his voice.

"Tell me some about his operation," says Seavey with a bit of reservation in his own voice. The last thing he wants is someone's mother gunning for him.

"He's sellin' to the goddam Indians. I got enough trouble with the goddam white drunks in town without havin' a bunch of drunk Indians raisin hell!" laments Earl. He's nearly shouting now.

"To tell you the honest to God truth, I'm as scared of him as I am my sister. He made it clear that there ain't no lawman, man enough to bring him in and he ain't makin' no distinction about it bein' family," continues Earl. It's clear this whole debacle with his nephew has him by the short hairs.

This latest proclamation suddenly has more of Seavey's attention than all of the rest of Earl's vexations about his sister. "What do you suppose he means by that?" says a much more interested Seavey.

"It means, he says when it comes to a fist fight, there ain't no lawman able to take him—at least not around here," says Earl, qualifying his earlier statement as he looks at the size of Seavey.

Archie is sitting quiet. He knows his boss well enough to know they won't be leaving here without their man.

"Tell me about where his still may be," questions Seavey a bit further.

Earl's frustration has become more and more animated as he pours out his anger at his own inability to take care of this problem without outside help. "This damn reprobate has gotten so damned bold, he don't even try to hide it anymore. He just laughs at me. He's got a couple of goons that hang around like lap dogs waitin' on him hand and foot."

"Tell me somethin' Earl, you up ta lookin' him up this afternoon?" asks Seavey much more concisely.

"I ain't crazy about it, but I'm the feller that called you fellers inta my hornets' nest. The best I can do is ta show ya around."

"By the way," asks Seavey, pausing for a minute, "what's this peckerwood's name?"

"Otis Redman Jr., but he just goes by 'Butch'."

"OTIS REDMAN!" shouts out Seavey. "Is his old man the Otis Redman from Escanaba?"

"Ya, as much as I hate to remember him as my erstwhile brother-in-law. He married my sister long enough to reproduce a clone of himself, except this one is bigger, but just as stupid," says Earl with a clear tone of finality.

For the first time since he arrived here things are making sense. Seavey is getting a clearer picture of what is awaiting him. His mind drifts back to that miserable weasel of a man who caused him all the problems a year or so ago. Otis was the pathetic coward who set fire to their sawmill, giving him the burn scars on his arms as a reminder. Now he's being confronted again, only this time as a U.S. Marshal, by the spawn of the same offender.

"Okay Earl, you just cleared things up for me. I gotta pretty good idea what kind of dink we're dealing with."

Looking a bit puzzled, Earl asks the obvious question, "You know his bunch?"

"I know 'em good enough to know his old man had an asshole transplant that rejected his body."

This visual analogy brings the first hint of a smile to Earl's face in some time. "Marshal, you just nailed that one. Yes sir, you just nailed that one," says Earl with an ever widening grin. "And my nephew is just like him. They remind me of ah couple ah baby birds—all mouth and ass."

With this interval of well needed comic relief behind them, what lies ahead is anything but. The kind of men they are dealing with is too often more visceral than thoughtful. They can prove to be dangerous since no one can, with any assurance, predict their next move. For the most part, the only thing certain about their kind is that they will do something stupid. For men like Seavey, the best that can be done to avoid getting hurt is to take advantage of them making a bad decision.

"What say we get this show on the road?" says an anxious Seavey, now that he is aware of who he's dealing with.

"Tell me what you want to do," says Earl.

"First off we need to do a little surveillance. We need to take a look at their modus operandi, especially when it comes to what kind of set up he's got and how many men he has and how well they are armed," says Seavey.

Earl is taking this all in with a steady nod indicating he's on board with everything Seavey is asking for.

"I can cut right to the chase and show you everything you need to know. Butchie boy is still living at my sister's. He's got a set up down by the creek. It's hidden from my sister, but everybody else is aware of it."

Seavey is attentive, taking in all that Earl is explaining with a look that indicates he's ready to hear all the information Earl is able to offer.

"Can we get a look without bein' seen?" asks Seavey, indicating that he's ready to make a move.

"We sure as hell can. I been doin' it for months." With that said, Earl downs the rest of his beer and slams the empty glass on the bar. "Let's go!" he adds, kicking his chair back with the deliberation of a man on a mission.

Marshal Seavey and Deputy Kerby are equally anxious, chugging the remainder of their drinks, as they follow suit.

Once outside, Earl explains they will have to travel on foot in order to remain as obscure as possible. They soon find themselves on a dusty road that is more of a logging trail than an official road. It winds through a twisting maze of wooded terrain. It's not long before they hear voices ahead. Earl quickly crouches, placing his finger to his lips.

"Shhh," he says. With his other hand, he motions them off the trail. With the voices getting clearer, he leads them to a brushy knoll. From the crest, they are able to peek over the crown undetected. Before them appears a simple set up for distilling whiskey. It has a mash pot, a cooker, a condensing coil, and a collector capable of holding large quantities of distillate. Being only some thirty yards from the two noisy men, they are able to hear every word of their discussion.

"Butch is gonna be happy with this batch," says one of the men. He's an older man, maybe in his sixties, thin built, toothless, and with a somewhat grizzled appearance.

"Ya, this batch is good enough to sell ta them city folks, never mind them Injins."

"Maybe, but you know Butch, he's gonna wanna keep them Injins from goin' over ta Engadine fer their whiskey. He'll sell to 'em—good whiskey or bad whiskey—makes no never-mind," says a younger man with a distinct limp.

Remaining out of sight and as quiet as only the sound of their breathing allows, the three lawmen are content to watch a while longer. They are soon rewarded with the appearance of a larger man driving a buckboard wagon drawn by a single black and white speckled mare.

Noticeably agitated and trying his best not to disclose their location, in a whispered tone Earl gasps out, "That's the 'meat-head' right there!"

Climbing down from the wagon is a large young man with a shock of unkempt hair and a stub of a cigar between his teeth. He immediately begins shouting orders.

"Lets get these squeezins loaded. I got people waitin' in line with cash."

With very few words, the three of them load the wagon. Within fifteen minutes Butch is on his way, leaving the other two men with orders to start another batch.

Waiting until the wagon can no longer be seen or heard, Seavey has devised a plan. "Follow me boys, we're goin' on a visitin' journey."

With that, he's up on his feet with both pistols drawn, making his way down to the distillery. Earl is decidedly staying behind, not wanting to be a visible part of this. Archie, on the other hand, is right on Seavey's heels. From the surprised looks on the faces of these two bootleggers carelessly going about their task, it's obvious they have been caught with their pants down. The last thing in the world they expected was to have outside law-men interfering with their activities, especially not one as intimidating as Marshal Seavey.

"Either one of you donkeys decide you can out run a bullet have at it!" roars out Seavey.

Both men fall back with hands in the air at the sight of this onrush of lawmen with guns drawn, their badges flashing in the sunlight. Archie quickly disarms them. A couple of pistols are all that's found.

With another swift movement, Marshal Seavey grabs a nearby ax and with a few well directed blows leaves this still a useless pile of metal.

Making it as straightforward as he can, with a look that can't be mistaken for a bluff, Seavey puts a finger on both their chests, roaring in a tone that can wake the dead. "You tell your boss that there's a lawman available who is goin' ta kick his ass up around his head and then kick his damn fool head off." This message is accompanied with a look that can't be mistaken as idle bluster. To make his point as succinctly as possible, he adds a swift kick in both their behinds sending them on their way.

With Butch absent and both these men vanishing into the woods, Earl comes out of hiding.

"I think you made your message pretty damn clear Seavey, but I know that nephew of mine ain't goin' ta take this lightly. He just may be dumb enough ta come lookin' fer ya," says Earl.

"That's exactly what I'm hopin' he's dumb enough ta do," says Seavey.

Having accomplished all they can for the time being, they make their way back to Snuffy's tavern to await the outcome. With a lot of ceremony, Snuffy has added a high-back piano to his establishment in hopes of capturing a more cultured clientele. A local aficionado is belting out an old French tune he remembers from his mother's teaching. He hardly makes it to the end before the bulk of a man comes storming through the tavern door. It's most definitely Butch and he's accompanied by his two lackeys. There is little doubt as to his mission. The way he has swung the door nearly off its hinges and the fire in his eyes screams he is seeking retribution whereever he can find it.

In a matter of seconds, he believes he has found his target. Heading straight to Seavey's table, he crashes his fist on the table hard enough to make the glasses of beer jump. "You the lawman that thinks his balls are big enough to tear up my still?"

Marshal Seavey very slowly, but with determination arises from his chair.

"I believe you just spilled my beer young man," says Seavey, in a calm, passive tone that will, unmistakably, quickly turn aggressive with the slightest provocation.

Realizing that this lawman is not going to be intimidated readily, he ramps up his bluster. "You take them damn pistols off and I'll show you how I'm gonna take care ah your problem," says Butch with the bluster most under challenged and untamed bullies communicate.

Very slowly, with the same passive determination and with a firm gaze on Butch, Seavey un-holsters his two pistols and carefully lays them on the table.

This is already further than any man in the region has gone to stand against Butch's bravado. It takes him aback for a moment. He begins to blink, pausing as his brain struggles with how to advance to his next—as of today—untested step of action.

Meanwhile, the piano player has stopped playing. He's had enough experiences in places such as this that when things start to heat up, he knows it's best to quit playing and stay out of the way. Snuffy is already coming out from behind the bar pulling tables and chairs out to the sides in hopes of keeping them out of the fray.

Pulling his coat lapel aside, Marshal Seavey exposes his badge and is the first to speak. "Otis Redman, Junior, my name is United States Marshal Daniel Seavey and as of now I'm placing you under arrest for the manufacture and distribution of illegal whiskey."

Seavey says this with the sternness of a hanging judge. Any right-minded person would have never pushed themselves into the corner that Butch is suddenly finding himself in. Unfortunately for Butch, he doesn't possess the foresight to realize that he's placing himself in a difficulty that's going to be impossible to resolve in his favor.

"Well ain't that sompin'? You in my neck of the woods and you're tellin' me where the bear shit in the briar patch? I don't see that happenin' Marshal what-ever-your-name is," says Butch, spreading his feet in a stance that indicates he isn't planning on going anywhere he doesn't choose.

He's nowhere near the height of Seavey, but probably well over three hundred pounds. His weight distribution is such that most of his weight is distributed around his waist. His double chin gives him the appearance of not having a neck. He looks as though someone plopped a head on a belly, then jammed a couple fence posts into the mess to hold it upright. The smell of whiskey is on his breath as he begins to breath heavier in anticipation of a showdown with Seavey.

Without warning, he lunges toward Seavey connecting with a hard right hook to the side of his face. There is no doubt that this blow will be answered—and answered it is with a straight right to Butch's face, breaking his nose. The blood spurts out of his face like a spigot. Wiping his arm across his face and seeing the damage on his sleeve merely serves to enrage him more. From somewhere down in the bottom of his enormous belly comes a primordial growl as he charges Seavey, slamming him to the floor. Seavey, in turn, finds himself pinned down with this giant mass smothering him. With one bold move he has both his thumbs pressing into Butch's eyes. Butch, in turn, slams his head into Seavey's skull. He accomplished a release of his eyes, but he left his face there a moment too long. The next sound is another primordial groan as Marshal Seavey has Butch's nose firmly between his teeth. They both begin to rise as Seavey's bite is rightly sending the message that if something doesn't change Butch will spend the rest of his life without a nose. With much maneuvering, Butch finally gets to his feet with Seavey still firmly attached to his nose. Butch is totally helpless with his head cocked in a sideways position. Realizing his advantage, Marshal Seavey gives his nose one last hard crunch. At the same moment, he releases him, giving him a severe blow to the back of his already traumatized head. This has the devastating effect of knocking Butch unconscious.

In the melee, they have managed to break a table and knock the piano over. Seavey is truly winded at the moment and wants to secure his prisoner. He lifts the end of the overturned piano and slides Butch's head under it.

Archie is paying particularly close attention to how this outcome is weighing on his boss.

"Somebody get this man a beer!" shouts out Archie. Archie has gotten hold of a wet towel and is busy cleaning Butch's blood off Seavey's face. Not willing to wait, Seavey has managed to get himself onto a bar stool and is forthrightly gulping down what's left of someone's pitcher of brew sitting on the bar.

Finally catching his wind, Seavey decides it's time to get his prisoner properly manacled and back to the ship. To do so, he lifts the piano off Butch's head. Butch isn't moving much less making a sound, which is fine with the Marshal.

"He ain't come to yet," notices Archie, as he grabs a pitcher of water and dumps it on Butch's head. Butch doesn't even wiggle. His face is a bloody mess. The smell of whiskey is still fresh.

"Somebody get me a hand mirror," yells Archie. One suddenly appears from some place. Placing it in front of Butch's mouth, Archie is hoping to detect some vapor. It's not happening. Next, he places his hand on Butch's heart. After a few other locations are tried, Archie makes another pronouncement.

"He's stopped breathing and I can't get a heartbeat. I think the son-of-a-bitch is dead!"

Doing their own investigations, Seavey and Earl quickly come to the same conclusion.

"What the hell am I ever going to tell my sister? I agree with most people that for his entire life he's been nothin' but a pain in everybody's ass, but nonetheless, he's all she had left," bemoans Earl, nervously running his hands back and forth across his hair.

Neither Seavey nor Archie are able to solve that for Earl. It's one of those questions that despite the amount of thought given to it will have no satisfactory answer.

Seavey sends a telegram to the Chicago headquarters with a report stating the outlaw expired while resisting arrest. By the next day, he and the crew are on their way back to Frankfort.

25 A SPIRIT OF CHANGE

As usual, the crew is happy to get back to home port. That's certainly not to say that within a short time they won't be just as anxious to get back out on the water. For the likes of this crew, it's a nice life with a nice balance.

Their new role as lawmen still has the promise of enough diversity to keep everyone interested. In reference to their newest identity, setting aside their pirate life in favor of a life as lawmen, Seavey tells them, "Maybe it ain't so much what we give up as much as what we take up that will make us rich. Anyway it sure as hell ain't gonna hurt ta give her a shot."

Captain Seavey—as the crew continues to refer to him—had decided back in Chicago to keep the *Wanderer*. His plan all along has been to balance his freight business with his government duties. With a reputation like Seavey's, it's not unusual that those who are expected to trust him hold reservations.

"I know ole' Capn' Seavey. It's gonna take more than a badge ta make that ole boy walk the straight an' narrow," says one barroom analyst.

Not to be out done, another chimes in with yet another insight. "Ya, that ole' boy can tell the truth even iffin he has ta lie ta do it."

The bad part about being a lawman with a tainted reputation is that you're hardly good enough to be accepted wholeheartedly by law abiding citizens and too good to be trusted by the scofflaws.

Nonetheless, they're all back home with time to waste until Captain Seavey comes through with a fresh undertaking.

Mary hardly misses Seavey until she sees his ship come around the bend in the bay. She has learned to be resourceful, in the event he does not return. Maybe it's because of the long years she fended for herself. Not being inclined to over analyze their relationship, she goes about her business purchasing furnishings for their home. This, along with wallpapering the house for a fresh new look, has occupied all her spare time since Seavey was called away to this Naubinway fiasco.

Now seeing his ship berthing at Crane's landing, she realizes how anxious she is to see him. Today she is especially exuberant. She has just taken delivery this very morning of a house full of furnishings from the Arcadia furniture company and is excited to have someone to share her exhilaration.

Meeting him at the dock, her exuberance can hardly be concealed. She is practically dragging him down the street. To say that Seavey is anything but pleased with the reception he's getting would be an understatement. What she has not revealed to him is the cause of her jubilation. By the time they have reached the front door, her animation can hardly be contained. Making Seavey close his eyes, she leads him through the door.

"Okay Seav, open your eyes."

With her own hand apprehensively over her mouth, she stands by waiting for his reaction. Doing as he is asked, he slowly opens his eyes. He looks about the room thoughtfully. Never in his life has he even imagined such a home. There is nothing that could compare to what Mary has put together. All he can do is stare in amazement. There are chairs, couches, tables, electric lamps, a brand new bedroom suite, carpets, pictures on the walls, an icebox in the kitchen, along with a gas stove, and frilly curtains on the windows.

"I can't believe this." These are his only words.

Mary, trying to interpret whatever reaction her husband is sending, is not sure what these words mean.

"You can't believe what?"

"This is absolutely unbelievably beautiful," he says. This affirmation is coming from the mouth of a man whose only luxuries, for the most part, are to eat and sleep at reasonable times.

A big delightful smile spreads across her face while throwing her arms around his neck and giving him the biggest kiss she can muster up.

"I was hoping you'd like it!" she shouts in her glee, "That just makes it perfect."

Walking him over to a large Wellington chair, she turns him around and gives him a little push. He plops down, sinking into its cushion. Before he can absorb this attention, she is pulling off his shoes and propping his feet up on a matching ottoman. Still possessing the same blitheness with her next move, she deposits herself on his lap.

"You've come back home and we've got new furniture. All this in the same day. Nothin' could make me any happier," says Mary.

The next morning arrives on time and it happens to be a Sunday. It's been a while since either of them have found their way to St. Ann Church and Mary has a strong desire to go.

"I think we need to go to Mass today," suggests Mary in a voice that Seavey recognizes as more of an imperative than a mere suggestion. Discovering that this sentiment also appeals to him is a surprise. Even more surprising is how the words from that old confessor in that small remote chapel are still resonating in his thoughts. For him, the focus of God has switched from justice to mercy. This revelation has proven to be a life changing thought for him. He feels that he can now approach a loving God and receive Christ's body and blood in communion. This insight has changed his whole attitude.

They choose a 10:00 o'clock Mass. Others have also chosen the same Mass. Father Daniel is busy arranging the altar, the readings, the prayer list, and the other endless details a priest meets before celebrating a Mass. On one of his perfunctory rounds, he spots Seavey with his badge pinned to his vest. This brings him out into the nave to acknowledge and congratulate him.

"Dan and Mary, I'm so happy to see you both," he says while grasping each of their hands in one of his. Then turning directly toward Seavey, he continues, "And I want to particularly congratulate you on your promotion," he says tapping Seavey's badge with his fingernail, producing a slight metallic ring.

"Thanks Father. I'm gonna try my best ta do right by it," says Seavey, a little sheepish, but at the same time sounding very deliberate. At this point, he's sure Father Daniel hasn't heard about his escapade in Naubinway ending in tragedy. As far as Seavey has come with his new found God consciousness, he can't help but feel somewhat intimidated by this clergyman. It's a feeling that comes when sinners are made to see their sins in contrast to the goodness seen in another. It's almost like the feeling Peter must have felt when Christ turned and looked at him after he had denied Him the third time.

"I do want to ask you a question Father," says Seavey, still with a hint of his previous embarrassment.

"Certainly you can," responds Father Daniel.

It's apparent Seavey is more than a little embarrassed for what he is about to reveal. "I been thinkin' I'd like to start studyin' the Bible again and I'm wonderin' if you have an extra I could borrow for a while."

He's harking back to a time when as a young man his mother had him studying with their local priest. It wasn't so much that he was ever opposed to it as much as he saw it as an obstruction to the pull of the world, which he hadn't as yet experienced. Now he's experiencing a longing to return to this misty point in his life.

The reaction of the priest brings a smile, but the reaction of Mary is one of complete surprise. He can feel her astonishment. It's the kind of look that says, *This is sure one for the books.*" She says nothing, only willing to watch what kind of recommendation is to follow.

"You are sure to have one today! And what's more, I invite you to study with me if that will help you," says Father with an added exuberance.

Seavey's uneasiness is apparent in trying his best to hold to his decision in light of Mary's reaction. Never satisfied until they have all their questions answered, she is going to want to dig into this decision beyond his ability to give her a satisfactory answer (as only wives seem to do best).

The Mass soon begins, but Mary's mind is predictably going in all directions. Is this another one of his unannounced deflections that seemingly is not going to include her? Or even if it does, what makes him think he can push his interests into her life without consulting her first? All in all, she hears very little of the homily as her mind continues to churn in loose directions.

By the time church is over, she has developed a severe resentment. Seavey can see it in her pinched face. Even her demeanor and her posture have become very rigid. By the time they reach home, Seavey figures he better fish or cut bait while he still can.

"Mary, you are actin' as though I were questionin' Father about entering the priesthood."

"Seav, I never know you're making changes in your life till you suddenly make a sharp turn. Just about the time I think I have you figured out, you change all the questions."

"I'm tryin' to bring about some changes. Think about it for a moment. It all started with you," discloses Seavey.

For the next hour, Seavey gives her a run down on Abequa. He describes all his confessions in trying to rid himself of his guilt for how he had mistreated her and Josey, how he stumbled on that old Episcopal priest who opened his eyes, how it resulted in changing his actions, and how now he needs to review everything he's held near and dear to be sure he hasn't distorted good and evil.

After pouring his heart and soul out, Mary is satisfied with his sincerity. She knows B.S. when she hears it and is not hearing it in this revelation. Still not quite sure where this transformation is going to leave her, she makes a further appeal.

"What do you expect me to do while you play priest with your life?"

Seavey is quite confident he is on the right track in assuring Mary that he does not intend to desert her and enter a monastery just because he wants to study the Bible.

"How about I make a deal with you Mary, if I don't become a better husband to you with Father's help, I'll quit the lessons?"

This last affirmation is enough to unruffle Mary's feathers. This is the assurance she is seeking to go forward with her husband's professed need to explore his own dysfunction.

26 THE CALICO JACK

Seavey is adamant about resuming his childhood passion for God's word. He made a commitment to meet regularly with Father Daniel and for the most part has honored that commitment. But to be sure, old habits, nonetheless, die hard. Seavey finds his Christian attitude is easy in theory, but at times impossible to adequately carry out in real life. Father Daniel has assured him that in spite of the struggle, the word *continue* is as important as the word *God*.

Soon he's called to go back out on the water. A young up and coming bootlegger is storming his way around on the Great Lakes. His name is Luther "Loot" Rackham. It seems Loot has gained possession of a gasoline-powered, motor-driven, forty-foot launch boldly christened the *"Calico Jack."* The story is he named it after an alleged pirate of the same name. Loot claims this pirate was his grandfather. According to reports, he's been bragging that there isn't a masted schooner that can catch him. Seavey has been called upon by his superior in Chicago to put a stop to Loot's unfettered illegal whiskey business.

Suspecting that the same high-tech tactics of telephones and telegraph that captured him will work again, he contacts all the life saving stations and harbor masters on both sides of the lake, asking them to be on the lookout for Loot and the *Calico Jack*. This tactic proves to be just as efficient *for* him as it was *against* him. By afternoon, he receives a call from an Upper Peninsula harbor master that the *Calico Jack* is sitting in port at Escanaba.

The decision is quickly made to get back on the water, but not until Ginny has approved. She is particular about her larder. She keeps most things stocked at all times just for these sail by the seat of your pants occasions, allowing for at least a week on the water without replenishing provisions. Even though Dee is her husband, he knows along with all the rest of the men, it's best to stay out of her galley. She has a place for everything and unless you want a tongue lashing it's best to let things stay that way. Taking the rest of the morning to load the ship with the needed provisions, she manages to satisfy her audit of necessary supplies.

Captain Seavey also has his own provisions. Now that he is a full fledged U.S. Marshal, he keeps his cannon visible at all times. He makes no bones about also having an arsenal of rifles (these were previously used to supply Chicago with venison). He has added an indefinite quantity of dynamite and, of course, he has his ever present signature pistols under his coat.

Soon a course is set and they are underway. The ship runs around the clock with a change of watch every four hours at night and five hours during the day. Second mate Willis Wells is on watch when Escanaba is spotted through his ever present telescope. It's just before dawn. Captain Seavey has left strict instructions to awaken him the minute this happens.

In a matter of minutes Seavey is on deck, telescope in hand.

With a satisfied smile enveloping his face, he says, "Sure enough, there she be." Of course he's speaking of the *Calico Jack* cozily harbored in plain view.

Turning to Willis, he enjoins him to anchor down the coast out of sight. It's not long before they're sturdily anchored at their previous timber cut location. The ship is bobbing a bit as the southwest breeze kicks up a few white caps. Despite the rigging tied in a fold back in the gear, the wind teases any loose piece of material as though it's preparing it to drive the ship.

Next on Seavey's agenda is to hold a crew meeting. It's obvious to Seavey that they are going to have to do a bit of detective work.

"Hear me out boys. We gotta be smart on how we deal with this. It means we gotta sneak inta town without anyone payin' us any attention," says Seavey.

Willis is the first to question this decision. "Cap'n, them folks at the Buckhorn and especially that McClain bunch are sure as hell gonna remember us."

"That's why, at least for now, you and I ain't goin' anywhere near that place," responds Captain Seavey. "What you and me gonna have ta do Willis is find a way around in the woods where we ain't bein' seen by these goons. I got a sneakin' suspicion that pecker-wood Otis Redman is gonna be a part of this fray. Meantime Archie, you and Ob go hang around the Buckhorn. Keep your eyes and ears open for any boneheads that may have information on the wherebouts of either ole Loot or Otis," orders Seavey.

Not quite finished, he next turns to Dee, Ginny, and Jack.

"You three stay with the ship and keep her ready ta light out. We may have ta leave in a hurry."

His coordinating instructions last all of five minutes. Ginny has hastily prepared and stuffed a beef sandwich into each of their pockets. The yawl is quickly dropped into the water. Captain Seavey, Willis, Archie, and Ob take their places in the small boat. Although Seavey has instructed them to keep their badges under cover until needed, each is duly deputized and armed. The wind is to their back making easy work of rowing the 200 feet to the shore.

Looking around their previous work site, they find things pretty much as they left them. The ruins of the burned out saw mill and even the rope Seavey used to tie Otis to the tree are still in place. Knowing the layout of the area is definitely a plus.

Captain Seavey remembers the trail that connects them to town. Enjoining Archie and Ob to use it to make their way to the Buckhorn tavern, he gives them final instructions. "Willis and I are going to hang back along the woods. We'll keep an eye out for the two of you. If you have some good information to pass on, come back down the trail and we'll intercept you."

Within the hour, Seavey and Willis spot Archie and Ob on the trail. Anxious to discover what they have to offer, they give a light signal whistle causing the two to stop and investigate. It only takes a second for them to see Seavey and Willis standing some twenty feet off the trail in a bushy area.

"What you boys discover?" asks an anxious Marshal Seavey.

"Loot's here alright. We run into most of his crew. They been here a few days and pretty well drunked up."

"What about Loot? Where's he at?" questions Seavey.

"From what we could gather, he's gettin' ready to haul ass out of here. You were right Cap'n, he's made a deal with Otis. They loaded most of his whiskey on the *Calico Jack* last night. All their waiting for now is for Otis to finish bottlin' the last of his batch," reports Archie.

"How many they got in the crew?" is Seavey's next question.

"From what we could gather without bein too nosey, they got about six or seven besides Loot," further reports Archie.

Giving it a couple minutes of further thought, Seavey turns to Archie and Ob, gives them a few instructions, and sends them back to the ship.

Willis is not privy to all that's being said between them as he has set himself up as lookout. Surprised to see Archie and Ob going off in another direction, he ventures to ask Captain Seavey about the new developments. Seavey ignores his inquiries by dodging the question with an imperative.

"You'll know soon enough. For now we're going to pay our old friend Otis a visit."

Careful not to be spotted before they spot someone else on the same trail, they make their way down the track to Otis's cabin. It's the same familiar cabin, except Otis has added an extra out building. It's really not much more than a lean-to, but it looks and smells like a distillery.

Remaining back in the woods, they make a wide circle around the whole complex to insure themselves of no unwanted surprises. They can hear voices coming from the cabin. Without a doubt, it's more than likely Otis and their man, Loot. The only new concern they've become aware of, other than the distillery, is they have spotted a hound dog. So far, he seems content to lay on the little covered porch in front of the cabin door. Fortunately, he hasn't spotted them yet.

"How we gonna get around without that critter puttin' up a fuss Cap'n?" questions Willis.

While he's still asking the question Seavey reaches into his pocket and pulls out the beef sandwich Ginny had placed there earlier that morning. He tears off a piece and throws it in the direction of the old hound dog. Expectantly, the hound raises his head along with his ears. So far he hasn't seen or heard enough to set off a barking alarm. Tossing him another piece, he's up on his feet and racing toward the discarded scraps.

His nose has overcome his desire to bark as he laps up another piece and looks for more from this deceptively friendly benefactor.

With his sandwich all but gone, Seavey motions Willis to give him his. By this time the hound has made his way to their wooded lair without making a sound other than the smacking of his drool-ladened jowls. Seavey pats him vigorously as he teases him with Willis's sandwich. The hound reacts predictably. All he's interested in is another sandwich. Seavey now places the sandwich on a tree limb just out of the hound's reach. Taking advantage of the dog's preoccupation with getting his mouth on the beguiling, unattainable meal, Seavey motions Willis to follow. With guns drawn, they quickly make their way across the dusty yard to the same familiar door they kicked in the previous year. Seavey makes his way to a small window, where he surreptitiously peeks through a tattered burlap curtain. Suspicions are quickly verified.

It's obvious to Seavey that the two men sitting inside are in the latter stages of inebriation. He recognizes Otis immediately. The other man is noticeably younger, fitting the description of Luther "Loot" Rackham. Satisfied his quarry is at his finger tips, Seavey makes his way back to Willis.

With the same powerful kick he had used on this same doorway before, Seavey, once again unhinges the entire door letting it fly across the cabin floor. Both men are sitting at a small table with their heads laying on the only cleared off spots its cluttered surface can offer. Neither is in any condition to be startled by much.

Loot is a man of slight proportions. He's a hard looking man with sandy colored hair, maybe all of five and a half feet tall, maybe 130 pounds. Barely managing to open one eye, it's long enough for him to study as best he can a giant of a man placing a set of manacles on his ankles and wrists. Otis isn't in any better shape. Over the years, he's become his own best customer, drinking a couple quarts of his personal concoction each day. Looking at Otis, Seavey sees the same pathetic individual he has encountered numerous times over the years, and that's not to discount the recent showdown he had with Otis's son, Butch.

Otis is drunk, but not so drunk as to not recognize Seavey. He remembers his run in with him the year before. He remembers how miserable Seavey has made him throughout his life. How he sent him to prison years ago, how he took everything he had the year before in exchange for his life, and he has recently gotten word that Seavey killed his son. The anger and hate for Seavey has been fomenting. Now that Seavey has violently intruded into his life once again, and the condition Otis is presently in, brings all his hatred to the forefront. He's watching as Seavey's back is turned, busily manacling Loot. Knowing he's in all probability next, sends him over the edge. Like a mad man, he bellows out, "Seavey you're the son-of-a-bitch that killed my boy. Now you're gonna die!" At the same time he drew a pistol from his belt and cocks the hammer back—BAAM! The gunshot startles Seavey. He whirls around in time to see Otis slide out of his chair and land dead on the floor. Whirling back around to Willis, he sees him standing dumbfounded with a still smoking pistol.

Quickly assessing what in split seconds has just transpired gives Seavey pause.

"I guess I owe ya one Willis," says Seavey with his eyes locked on the gun still clinched in Otis's dead hand.

"Don't worry yourself about it, Cap'n. I know damn well you'd do the same fer me," answers Willis with the confidence of a man who knows he has just performed a righteous act.

The old hound makes his way back into the cabin. His master is dead on the floor. To this old hound that fact takes a back seat to approaching Seavey once again with the wanton look of one who would just as soon settle for another sandwich.

Meanwhile, Archie and Ob have brought the *Wanderer* into the harbor and anchored off some 200 feet from shore. The last instructions Seavey gave Archie and Ob before they returned to the ship are now in place. Following these orders, Ginny has made herself up like she used to when she worked for Squeaky. She and Archie row to shore and head directly to the Buckhorn. Before going in, Archie has her go over what she is to do one more time.

"Don't worry Archie, this is gonna be a piece of cake," says Ginny taking some vicarious pleasure in an old art she has set aside since marrying Dee.

Once inside it doesn't take long for her to make her way to Loot's crew. They're loud, raucous and all sitting at the same group of tables. As soon as Ginny walks in the whole crew quickly makes her the center of their attention. Proving yet again, that when it comes to seducing men, women can skip the rehearsal. For a good share of her young life, she skillfully crafted her profession. Ginny knows all about men.

"Full bellies, empty balls about sum up 100 percent of the male population," she's been heard to declare.

Within fifteen minutes of entering the Buckhorn, she is whooping it up with these young tigers. Adjusting her dress to show off as much of her female equipment as she dares, she openly flirts with each of them. In another fifteen minutes, she has the whole crew heading for the *Wanderer* to continue their play. She has promised to introduce them to the rest of her troupe, which they expect to be as ready and willing to frolic as she appears to be.

In another ten minutes, she and Archie make their way back to the *Wanderer* in their yawl, followed by the *Calico Jack* crew in their yawl. Eaten up with lust, this group of alcohol drenched male hormones vigorously rows alongside Archie (hardly noticing him). They feel compelled to keep this willing female as close as possible and in plain sight. Under ordinary circumstances this group of young men would be considered as good paying tricks, but in these circumstances what awaits them is a rather rude awakening. Arriving first, Archie assists Ginny to the waiting ladder. While maneuvering her way up the ladder, Ginny further entices these young bucks by squealing as a breeze seems to have blown her dress nearly up around her waist.

Struggling to be first up the ladder while attempting to catch a glimpse of what might be awaiting underneath her dress, they almost capsize their small dingy. Waiting for Ginny to safely reach the deck, Archie turns his attention to keeping order, by allowing only one man at a time to make his way up onto the deck. Acting in a somewhat official capacity, he waits for a signal from above to send the next man up. Having flawlessly accomplished her bit of this fiasco, Ginny makes herself scarce. Watching through a cracked door, she observes each of the *Calico Jack* crew hitting the deck only to be met by Ob, Dee, and Jack with waiting manacles for each of them.

As the signal comes from the deck, it's Archie's turn. Making his way to the top of the ladder, he is encountered by a grinning crew. There before him, nearly covering the deck, are the six crew members of Loot's ship. They have a rather somber look as they discover they've been boon-swagged.

Preparing to begin the next phase of this operation, Archie once again makes his way to shore. Like clockwork, he is summarily met by Captain/Marshal Seavey and Willis with one corpse and a drunken prisoner.

The next step is to meet with the local undertaker and dispose of Otis. Promising the government would pay for any simple burial, Marshal Seavey leaves the undertaker with paperwork holding his official signature.

Now regardless of which way they turn, the job of disposing of their prisoner is directly on their horizon. It should be pretty straightforward. He needs to be shipped to Chicago for the charges to be properly attached to his crimes and then tried in a Federal court. But Seavey has had his eye on Loot's motor launch since he first caught a glimpse of it sitting in the harbor. The *Wanderer* is getting to be antiquated with a few dry rotted planks. She definitely is going to need some major repairs by next season. Captain Seavey may be conjuring up other plans for this old lady of the lakes than repairs.

Loot is taken to the *Wanderer* in chains where Seavey has him in his quarters for interrogation purposes. He's nearly sober and beginning to realize the fuller implications this detainment is going to have on his life.

Marshal Seavey begins the process by giving Loot a full dose of intimidation.

"You know you're going to be charged with anything they can throw on you and make stick. These federal prosecutors are eager for promotions and that only comes by aggressive prosecutions. You're facing a lot of prison, Loot."

Seavey watches Loot's reaction. After all he is still in his twenties and facing years in prison. Loot's demeanor tells it all. Fear and tears are beginning to well up in his eyes.

Seeing he has Loot against the ropes, Seavey throws in yet another possibility. "Chances are they'll also throw a charge of piracy on you. That alone is a hangin' charge."

Stepping back again, Seavey watches as Loot begins to shake at the prospect of hanging. Letting him stew in his own grease for a few more hours assures Seavey that he not only has Loot on the ropes, but that he has him on the ropes in a corner.

Eventually calling on Archie, Seavey orders him to bring Loot back to his quarters for another round. The few hours that Loot has been stewing alone with his thoughts has clearly tenderized him even further. Seavey is ready to capitalize on this deterioration of Loot's ego.

With an obvious voice of concern, Seavey asks, "How you doin' Loot?"

Still filled with the emotions brought on by the prospect, at the very least, of spending his youth in prison, or maybe chancing ending up on the end of a rope, he is lost for words and merely shakes his head.

Still continuing to study Loot, Seavey measures what he is about say.

"Ya know, Loot. I kinda have a soft spot for ya. You kinda remind me of myself when I was your age. I know what it's like to face a prison sentence and feel there's no way out. That's why for the past few hours I've put myself in your corner. I think I've come up with a plan that will satisfy both of us."

For the first time since Seavey handcuffed him, Loot looks him in the eye. Still not saying anything, his demeanor alone tells Seavey that he has Loot's full attention.

"Fer sure you're gonna lose your ship to the revenuers in all this hub-bub." Still looking directly at Loot, he continues, "But I kinda like you and I think I've come up with a plan that could set you free."

There is no question now that he has Loot's undivided attention.

"I have some salvage papers here stating that the *Calico Jack* has been storm damaged beyond its ability to sail. It states here that you are turning over the salvage rights to one Mary Silvers."

Archie's eyebrows go up at this proclamation. Not sure what his boss is up to, he opts, like he always does to play along with it. Mary Silvers is the name Mary Seavey had chosen when she was annoyed with Seavey's pirating antics. It was more or less a put-on, playing off the name of *Treasure Island's* Long John Silvers. As a matter of fact, she had it legally changed and has signed many legal papers using it.

Loot has no clue who Mary Silvers may be and could care less. At this point all he is aware of is that his back is against the wall. He knows very well that he's not in a bargaining position. He has gotten himself involved in an enterprise that is ending in disaster.

"Damned if I do, damned if I don't. Where do I sign?"

Other than getting a few personal items from the *Calico Jack*, Loot is done. He is well aware that he is getting a break on one hand, but it's the nature of young men like Loot to blame others for their failures. Seavey is the obvious target of Loot's resentments. If he could in any way make Seavey suffer for wrecking his life, he would. On the other hand, he realizes his own powerlessness. He's in way over his head. Wisely taking Marshal Seavey's advice to heart, he and his crew make themselves scarce before someone decides to change their mind.

Speaking to Dee, Seavey says, "Dee you're pretty damn good with motors, let's get this tub down to Frankfort where we can look her over pretty good."

"I gotta hand it to ya Cap'n, ya sure as tootin' know how to get a deal done. This here boat's gonna be a money maker," says Dee, "and it's already loaded with Otis's whiskey."

Jack is paying close attention to what's being said. He adds his own two cents worth of expertise and announces in a very authoritative voice, "I hear that if ya run out of fuel that these here motors can run on whiskey."

With Jack even entertaining such thoughts, if stares could kill, he'd be dead.

27 A DREAM COME TRUE

The two ships prepare to sail in a convoy toward Frankfort. Seavey has split the crew with himself, Dee, and Ob on the motor launch, the rest on the *Wanderer*. They're all busy prepping their individual ships. Ob is busy with a can of paint and a brush making some changes Captain Seavey has asked to be done to the *Calico Jack*. Soon their departure is underway.

The motor launch quickly proves to be a time saver, as it isn't necessary to tack against the wind like the sailing ships.

"The way this ship is set up, I believe we can carry 25% more cargo than the *Wanderer* and make at least a couple extra trips to Chicago in the same amount of time," says Dee with confidence. Captain Seavey is also visibly pleased with the design and mobility of this updated Great Lakes workhorse.

"I think we made a good trade," he adds after making a few precarious tactical maneuvers.

"I wonder if Loot still believes he made the right decision," contemplates Ob, still cleaning up his painting materials.

"Knowin' the kind of guy Loot is, he'd be cryin' a river of tears either way. At least this way he's got a life time to tell his story—however he wants to tell it," says Seavey with a little chuckle.

At work with the duties of keeping this newfangled vessel on course, the harbor at Frankfort soon looms on the horizon. The *Wanderer* remains at least an hour behind. Captain Seavey, not inclined to wait for the slower vessel is busy acquainting himself with the ship's modern gizmos. After a few false tries, he manages to struggle through implementing a message on the vessel's ship-to-shore radiotelegraph to the Life Saving Station.

MARY SILVERS

WILL BE ARRIVING WITHIN THE HOUR — HAVE A SURPRISE.

SEAV.

Doe, being the new Harbor Master is the first to be alerted of this first ever ship-to-shore telegraph message from Captain Seavey. Surprised, but then again not overly surprised at this seeming innovation. After all, anyone working with Captain Seavey is on alert for the unexpected.

Doe has taken it upon himself to personally deliver the message to Mary. She is as mystified with her husband's unusual act of sending any kind of message as is Doe. Still mystified, together they make their way to the harbor. There are several ships in various stages of entering or leaving, but no sign of the *Wanderer*.

Suddenly directly in front of them an unfamiliar vessel blasts its horn. Both are surprised to see Captain Seavey standing in the bow waving his familiar wave. He looks tall with a particularly proud grin. They are even more surprised when they read the freshly painted monicker on the bow's rail—*MARY SILVERS*.

Both Mary and Doe spot this innovative display at the same time.

"Oh dear God, what has he done now?" Mary's voice fades into nearly an inaudible mumble. She throws both her hands over her mouth as a gesture of uncertainty.

With his eyes totally fixed on Captain Seavey in possession of this new ship, Doe is unable to answer Mary's question and remains as dumbfounded as she.

"This is either awfully good or awfully bad." Such is the only thought that Mary can bring to mind as she continues to watch her husband tie up at Crane's launch. With a special spring to his step and a wide grin, Seavey hops off the vessel onto the dock. Facing the uncertainty of his wife's demeanor, he attempts to explore for her reaction.

"What do you think?" questions an obviously elated Captain Seavey. This question is on the same scale as an adolescent boy questioning others' thoughts toward his new pony.

Knowing her husband as well as she does, Mary's eyes narrow, her hands are propped on both her hips.

"Are you sure you want to hear what I think?" Answering a question with a question is Mary's way of trying to manage the outcome this question may eventually lead to.

Seavey does not look enthused with Mary's seeming displeasure. His proud smile has diminished into a frown.

"You're a tough woman, Mary Silvers." Breaking once again into his charming grin, he quickly adds, "But then you're lucky cuz I like tough women."

Her head is beginning to hurt and it's taking all of her effort to constrain herself.

"I know there's a story behind this boat and I know it's probably a good one, but I'm not sure I want to hear it," responds Mary. The constraint in her voice can't be mistaken.

Having worked for Captain Seavey for many years, Doe is just as dubious about Seavey's possible moral/legal tactics as Mary. On the other hand, he is less concerned with how this new ship came into Seavey's possession than Mary and is more than anxious to hear the story.

Putting his arm around Mary, Seavey shoots back to both of them, "Let's go have a drink and I'll tell you all about it."

An hour later, after lunch and a few drinks, Mary's concerns begin to dissipate. She feels that she may be getting her bearings. He has once again managed to convince, not only himself, but also Mary and Doe that the end justifies the means.

"After all, if we give Loot enough rope, it's just a matter of time before he hangs himself again," self-righteously philosophizing, Seavey adds, "meantime, I've eliminated his potential to be a bigger pain in my ass."

As they continue to move through the rest of the shipping season, the, "often" Marshal Seavey, and the "always" Captain Seavey, along with the crew, are in the best position they've been in for their entire careers. They are secure in the idea that they are managing quite well balancing their shipping business with their law keeping duties. As usual, they're always prejudiced in their own behalf resulting in seeming success with both.

Now days and especially during the off season, Captain Seavey is often seen carrying his Bible through the streets of Frankfort. He's diligently keeping his pledge to study with Father Daniel. He's bound and determined to convince Mary that he can study and still be the best "damn husband she's ever had." As the winter rolls on, Mary has also taken a shine to a woman's Bible study directed by Sister John Martin. Both seem to have found a comfort in this exercise at this period of their lives.

The plight of the *Wanderer* is that it's an aging ship with little value as the insurance premiums continue to rise. As luck would have it, it mysteriously catches on fire and burns to the water line. When asked how he felt about it, Captain Seavey was overheard to say, "Well a fast fire always beats slow profits."

Now what can be said against that?

HARDLY THE END